FLAMEFALL

ALSO BY ROSARIA MUNDA

Fireborne
Book One of The Aurelian Cycle Trilogy

FLAMEFALL

ROSARIA MUNDA

G. P. Putnam's Sons

G. P. PUTNAM'S SONS
An imprint of Penguin Random House LLC, New York

Copyright © 2021 by Rosaria Munda

G. P. Putnam's Sons is a registered trademark of Penguin Random House LLC.

Visit us online at penguinrandomhouse.com

Library of Congress Cataloging-in-Publication Data
Names: Munda, Rosaria, author. | Title: Flamefall / Rosaria Munda.
Description: New York: G. P. Putnam's Sons, [2021] | Series: [The Aurelian cycle; 2]
Summary: "After a brutal revolution, Callipolis is ravaged by famine and the Pythians
are ready for revenge, so it's up to Annie, Lee, and newcomer Griff to decide
what to fight for, and who to love"—Provided by publisher.
Identifiers: LCCN 2020049819 (print) | LCCN 2020049820 (ebook)
ISBN 9780525518242 (hardcover) | ISBN 9780525518259 (ebook)
Subjects: CYAC: Dragons—Fiction. | Orphans—Fiction.
Loyalty—Fiction. | Famines—Fiction. | Fantasy.
Classification: LCC PZ7.1.M825 Fl 2021 (print) | LCC PZ7.1.M825 (ebook) | DDC [Fic]—dc23
LC record available at https://lccn.loc.gov/2020049819
LC ebook record available at https://lccn.loc.gov/2020049820

Printed in Canada
ISBN 9780525518242
1 3 5 7 9 10 8 6 4 2

Design by Lindsey Andrews
Text set in Sabon LT Std

For my father and my brother,
fellow dreamers

1

NEW PYTHOS

GRIFF

Julia's missing, and I'm in a terrible mood. Not improved by the weather, which is cold and damp, but in New Pythos, it's always cold and damp. I'm gutting fish in a back room off the dragon lairs when Scully comes to find me.

"Dragonlord here to see you," the lair-master says.

That's the one way to make my day worse. Bran and Fionna, the other two squires on fish-gutting duty, exchange a look. We're up to our arms in bits of fish bone and scales; the stink of the fish oil will follow us out of the lairs, and now I'm going to miss the one perk that comes with prepping dragon feed—sneaking the remains home. I rise, wiping my hands on the work rag.

Scully hates the sound of my perfect Dragontongue, which is why I always try to use it. "Which dragonlord"—I pause just long enough for him to wonder if I'll add—"sir?"

Scully scowls. This is why he keeps putting me on fish gutting. Lip. Not to mention our clans hate each other. "The one you serve," he says in Norish.

Most days, that would be good news. Today, I just wish it were Julia.

On the balustrade outside, Delo Skyfish waits for me.

I remember as a child being struck by the Callipolan exiles, when they arrived on New Pythos: at the ghostly pallor of the Stormscourge survivors, at the warm brown skin and tight curls of the Skyfish lords. Delo Skyfish no longer looks like the ragged urchin that washed ashore ten years ago, but he's still striking, and at the sight of his fur cloak and freshly coiffed hair, I'm conscious of my own stinking state.

I bow low.

"Your presence is an unexpected honor, my lord."

Delo mutters, "As you were." I straighten; Delo is scowling at me, like he knows I'm trying to discomfort him. He's my age, taller than I, but slenderer. "The Triarchy-in-Exile wants to speak with you."

I hug my arms around my chest, shivering from the sea spray coming in off the water. We're dwarfed by the cliffs above and the citadel atop them, and by the limestone pillars of karst that jut from the sea into the sky. "Did they tell you what for?"

I use the formal *you*, and when Delo answers, he uses the informal. When we were younger, and I was still figuring out Dragontongue, he tried to get me to use the informal, too, or speak to him in Norish, which he was learning at the same time, but I refused. In trials of will with Delo, I win.

"They want to question you about Julia," he says. "She's missing."

As if I haven't noticed.

"Why would I know where Julia is?"

Delo hesitates. "Ixion—told them."

2

From the way he says it, I don't have to ask what.

The last time I saw Julia, her lips were on mine. In the dark I could feel, not see, her smile as she bunched my shirt to raise it. She always smiles, like what we're doing is a game, and it amuses her to win.

Ixion told them.

I've stopped walking, and Delo stops, too, turning back to me. His face says everything I need to know about what's about to happen in the Glass Hall. He doesn't say *I'm sorry*, and I don't say *Ixion had no right*. By now, I'm no stranger to the humiliations Ixion devises.

Like being called before the Glass Hall as Julia's peasant lover stinking of fish.

As if he'd heard me think it, Delo reaches into his satchel. "I brought you a fresh shirt."

Most of Delo's clothes are blue, the color of his House, but this shirt is plain, undyed—appropriate for a peasant. Even so, it's finer than anything I've ever owned, and I'm likely to ruin it with muck. I pull it over my head, and when I look up, Delo's watching me. He looks away, down. The shirt smells like him.

I follow Delo up the winding outer stairs, carved into the side of the cliff and looking out over the North Sea, that connect the lairs where I work to the citadel at the summit. Both were built by the ha'Aurelians in the original conquering, when they invaded Norcia with their dragons, subjugated my people, and renamed our island New Pythos. The dragons' bloodlines dried up in the cold not long after, but the lords remained.

And now, for the first time in generations, they have dragons again. Twenty-five dragons, brought as eggs by the Callipolan exiles ten years ago.

Dragons for revenge.

Dragons for the exiles' surviving sons. Dragons for the sons of the lords on whose hospitality they imposed. Titles for their children in a future, greater Callipolis.

But there weren't enough sons. The exiled Triarchy was forced to present the remaining hatchlings to others. Female dragonborn, like Julia. Bastards, who trickled in from Callipolis's vassal islands, once despised for their illegitimacy but now needed.

Dragons were still unclaimed.

So, with a fleet not yet filled, the dragonborn resorted to a measure few believed would work.

They had the remaining dragons presented to the sons and daughters of their Norcian serfs.

And the dragons Chose.

They call us *humble-riders*.

* * *

Delo and I enter the Glass Hall, and in the moment it takes to draw in a breath I'm able to observe the room. A great expanse of rippled glass windows look out over the karst pillars rising from the North Sea, and the combined dragonborn courts of my ha'Aurelian rulers and the Callipolan exiles surround us in a ring of stiff-armed chairs. In the center sits Rhadamanthus ha'Aurelian, the Greatlord of New Pythos, who also assumed the vacant title of Aurelian triarch after the Revolution. No Aurelians from Callipolis survived to contest it.

Three chairs to the edge of the ring seat the highest-ranked dragonriders of the Three Families. Ixion Stormscourge, Rhode ha'Aurelian, and—the seat is empty, waiting for him—Delo. The three Triarchs-presumptive. When Callipolis is regained, and reunited with New Pythos, they will share the triple throne.

I kneel, place my palms flat on the floor, and stare at the stone between them.

Delo says, "I present to the Glass Hall my squire, Griff Gareson of Clan Nag, humble-rider for the Pythian Fleet."

He remains by my side, leaving the waiting chair beside Ixion empty.

"Welcome, Griff." I don't have to see the man speaking to picture him: Rhadamanthus is a bear of a man, his auburn hair graying, his golden skin lined. "Ixion informs us you might have . . . privileged information about Julia."

Rhadamanthus is known in the clans for being a hard man, but I have found, compared with the whims of the Callipolan exiles and their dragons, his rule measured if harsh. I keep my eyes trained on the flagstones between my hands. "I'm afraid Lord Ixion is mistaken, Your Grace. Lady Julia has never treated me as her confidant."

Ixion snorts. Rhadamanthus's son Rhode, who does everything Ixion does, snorts, too.

Lady Electra's voice comes crisp with disdain. She is Ixion and Julia's great-aunt, a Stormscourge widow since before the Revolution, and the choice to draft Norcian dragonriders has always sat poorly with her. "I always find it unnerving when they speak Dragontongue too well."

Delo shifts weight in his boots beside me. I ask my hands, "Would my lady prefer that I speak in Norish?"

"No. Thank you. This is a waste of time, Rhadamanthus."

"I don't believe him." Ixion's voice cuts through the adults'. Cold, frayed, like the very words he says bore him even as he speaks. This many years into training with him, his voice alone has the power to make me break into a cold sweat.

I know to associate Ixion's voice with certain things: pain, fear, and humiliation.

"Rack your brains, Griff, see if she didn't let something slip while she was rutting with you—"

"Ixion," says Rhadamanthus sharply.

Rhode has caught Ixion's drift and decides to play, too. "How's Agga?" he asks. "Maybe she'd help you remember? We can have her brought in. With her brats."

I watch my fingers, splayed on the stone, curl beneath themselves. I wait for someone to say *That won't be necessary*, but no one does.

They only took on Norcian riders who have families. Ixion and Rhode figured out why early on. They learned my sister's name fast.

Delo's voice comes from close, lowered. Bracing. "Griff, think. Anything from Julia that seemed a little . . . off?"

Off. Julia's always been so unpredictable, *off* seems like a meaningless word to use about her. But then I remember something.

"She was writing a letter. Recently."

"And?"

Julia's half-dressed form, curled over her writing desk, her long hair let down for the night. I remember noticing, at the time, how her night-robe had fallen from one shoulder to reveal a sloping angle of bare, burn-scarred skin. At the sound of my tread, she jumped and turned, one arm flattening over the letter behind her. But when she saw me, it relaxed. *Oh. Only you. Come here . . .*

"She didn't want anyone to see it."

Rhadamanthus's chair creaks as he leans forward. "But you saw it? Did you see to whom it was addressed? Its contents?"

I did see it. I could see it from her bed. She left it lying unfolded atop her writing desk when she pulled me onto her mattress. Open, every word exposed to my eyes, this letter she didn't want anyone to see.

"I don't . . ."

I am gripping the stone, the explanation thick on my tongue though it has no reason to be. I wait for someone else to remember it; but, absurdly, they don't. As if I speak Dragontongue too well for them to remember to associate the laws their people enforce on mine with me. Delo, beside me, shifts, as if he understands. But Ixion beats him to it. He sounds torn between amusement and irritation.

"Griff can't read."

Lord Nestor speaks for the first time. "This is pointless, Rhadamanthus. I told you it would be a waste of time to question the boy—"

Nestor is Delo's father and our drillmaster, strict with his riders in the air and stricter on the ground. He is a sky-widower: a rider who lost his dragon. Delo says it's a loss you never recover from and the cause of his father's foul temper.

I'm pretty sure Nestor would have his temper toward *me* either way.

I force the words out through anger. "She seemed agitated. Afterward. She talked about . . . family. And loyalty."

Julia's fingers in my hair, absently pulling curls straight, our bodies wound together beneath blankets softer than any my family has ever seen. *Would you always love your sister? Even if she betrayed you? What would you do, if she betrayed you?*

The strange, unexpected dampness on my shoulder, so unusual I did not realize at once what it meant. That Julia was crying.

Rhadamanthus drums fingers on the arm of his chair. "You're suggesting she was writing Leo? The cousin who rides for the Usurper? We forbade her contacting him, after his last refusal."

Delo speaks, his voice a murmur, as if he's realizing as he speaks. "But when has Julia ever listened, when something was forbidden her?"

Silence meets his words. As if the others weigh Delo's point. And all the while I kneel in front of them, proof of it.

Ixion's cold voice trickles over me, breaking the silence.

"Didn't see fit to report any of this earlier, did you, Griff?"

I lift my head and look at him. Ixion's face is an elongated, lined version of Julia's: the same jet-black hair, the blazing eyes set in a pale face, the same thin mouth prone to laughter. But where Julia's laughter can be cruel for being uncaring, Ixion's is just cruel.

Don't say it.

But then I do.

"I did not think it my place to share the Firstrider's business with her Alternus."

For a moment the only sounds are of the gulls, whose cries come muffled through the windows, and the echoing of my own stupid, reckless words in the glass-walled room.

Ixion leaps to his feet, his mantle rippling.

"Gareson should be flogged *for his tone*."

Though I should feel fear, all I feel is fury. *Do it, Ixion. Settle it on the ground. The only place you'll ever be able to beat me.*

Beside me, Delo takes a half step forward, between Ixion and myself. Another mistake: The last thing Nestor needs is further reason to suspect that his son has grown soft toward his inferiors.

"Enough," Rhadamanthus says. "We're wasting time. We need to deploy search parties south."

* * *

I wasn't always Delo's squire. In the beginning, I was Ixion's.

Ixion was imaginative in his cruelty. *Do you want to know where I learned this?* he would ask. The answer was always the same, even when it couldn't be true: *Palace Day. From peasants like you on Palace Day.*

By the time Julia and Delo found out, and told Delo's father, the abuse had escalated to the point that injuries interfered with my riding. Nestor Skyfish doesn't care much about humbleriders' well-being, but he does care about the well-being of the fleet. I was transferred to Delo; Ixion was deemed unfit to be served by a squire.

Ixion never forgave either of us for it.

Outside the Glass Hall, Delo and I make our way to the exiles' extension of the citadel known as the Provisional Palace. Each of the Three Families has their own armory, with an interior entrance to the lairs.

"That was rash," Delo murmurs, when he sees that the Skyfish armory is deserted, and we're alone. "You shouldn't have pulled rank on him like that."

"I can't pull rank on him. I'm not ranked."

Humble-riders didn't participate in the Firstrider Tournament. Delo lifts an eyebrow. Like he knows I'm just being stupid on purpose.

"Julia isn't here to protect you," he says.

You think I don't know that?

Our gear hangs on hooks along the stone wall. I fetch Delo's armor while he shrugs on his flamesuit. His armor's been polished recently, by me; the Skyfish lilies are shining in their crest. I've served as Delo's squire for years now, but the one thing that's become less, not more, comfortable over the years is arming him. He holds his breath. I talk, a lot. "What was he like?" I ask as I work my way down his side, clasping buckles and tightening straps. "Leo? You must have known him, before."

Delo is staring fixedly at the wall, past me. "I always thought," he says, and pain enters his voice, "that Leo had a good heart. But I thought that about Ixion, too, before Palace Day."

When he's armed, I step away from him and he unfreezes. I hasten into my own flamesuit—a castoff from Delo, tight in the shoulder, long in the leg, but serviceable. Then I gather our gear before following Delo down the spiral stairs to the lairs, carved into the rock and lit by narrow windows that face out over the sea. Our dragons are stabled side by side, and Delo always makes a point—though he clucks a greeting to his skyfish, Gephyra, as he passes her—of accompanying me to Sparker first.

Sparker, like all the dragons ridden by Norcians, is chained and muzzled.

The muzzle is a safety measure. It was a precaution put in place when we sparked. I'd be flattered if it didn't make me and Sparker so miserable.

The muzzle doesn't come off, but the chain does, and Delo keeps the key.

I'm used to it—lords know I've had years to get used to it—but even so, the sight of Sparker straining against that muzzle, choking himself with the collar as he strains to reach me, never stops hurting. And as if Delo knows it, he always blocks the sight from me. Unchains Sparker with quiet cluckings to calm him. And then jumps out of the way as Sparker bounds toward me.

Sparker's a stormscourge, *my* stormscourge, black as the night, oversized and overspirited, and when I embrace him, he leans into it so hard he nearly bowls me over. His wingspan, pride of the aerial fleet, is already so large that when he twitches his wings open, they beat the stone walls on either side of us.

"Missed you, too," I murmur.

He growls, the most his muzzle permits him to do, and I hold him tighter, and wish for the thousandth time I could tear the damned thing off. They keep it loose enough in the jaws so he can eat, but not breathe fire. I reach up, rub where it chafes, and he lets out the smallest pleading grunt that makes everything inside me ache.

"I know."

I've thought, more than once, how it would have been easier for everyone—Sparker, me, and the Triarchy included—if he'd Chosen a different rider. A dragonborn rather than a Norcian. Then I would have lived the peasant life I was born to: fishing like my father on a ha'Aurelian charter, lost in an untimely storm on the North Sea. Sparker wouldn't have been muzzled or chained.

But Sparker never seems to blame me, and for all the ways it makes my daily life hell, I've never felt anything but pride at the fact that Sparker is mine, and I'm his.

Most of the dragonborn hold it against us both.

Delo is watching us, something stirring in his eyes, but when I meet them, he looks away.

I saddle Sparker in silence, take up my pike and shield, and follow Delo's lead as we launch out the lair mouth and take to the air over the crashing waves.

We turn south in search of Julia.

2

FIRSTRIDER AND ALTERNUS

LEE

It's been five hours since I killed my cousin.

In the infirmary ward, there are visitors. Crissa. Cor. Annie, briefly, her face haloed in light from the door. There are medicines for pain and medicines for sleep. And then I am alone, and I am somewhere else.

Six. Julia and I are playing in the Palace gardens. Our fathers are dragonlords; the world is before us; we are certain that, one day, we will be great like them. When we laugh, we do it until our sides hurt. When we shout, we do it for the world to hear. And when we pretend to kill, and pretend to die, it's thrilling and glorious and *fun*.

Seven. We are in my family's parlor, and I am watching blood seep across the rug. The parlor has narrowed to spaces I can look and spaces I can't. So much screaming that I've stopped hearing it. Someone says, in a language I barely know: Don't look away. Watch. Watch them get what they deserve. My last sister has stopped struggling. A knife glints, lowers. My father's pleas dissolve.

My father on his knees before Atreus, saying: *Please, my son.*

Eight. The orphanage is always cold. A red-haired girl too small to fight is fighting children twice her size. I move between them. I learn the girl's name. *Annie.*

Nine. I stand in a square and watch my father's dragon lose its head. I stand in the yard and hear Annie say it: *That dragon killed my family.*

Ten. A dragon looks me in the eye and Chooses me. Atreus looks me in the eye and sees a lowborn orphan. Annie looks me in the eye and keeps the secrets we have learned to hold between us.

Forward, forward, forward. Happiness of sorts, the kind that comes with racing toward the future, with forgetting. Until, seventeen. Wings on the horizon, my family returned from the dead, a forsaken hope risen with them. My cousin Julia, smiling across the booth of a darkened pub as she tells me I look like my mother and that she's missed me.

Annie, standing in front of a ruined home, dropping to her knees to demonstrate how a serf kneels before their lord to ask for mercy. Her fingers tracing the path of my father's dragonfire.

Julia sur Erinys, in the air. Pallor and I, against them.

Fire.

Julia's helmet at my feet on Pytho's Keep. Atreus, laying his hand on my forehead as if to absolve me of my blood, my past, my crime.

Rise, son of Callipolis.

"Lee?"

The sun has set, but even in the darkness I know the silhouette over me is Annie's. I know the touch of her hand on my face, the smell of her breath warm and close. The sounds I don't know: someone weeping. And then I swallow and the sounds stop.

Annie folds the bed linens back and curls into bed beside me.

It feels like someone else speaks with my mouth. "I came back to you."

My voice sounds foreign in my own ears, thick and strained like my tongue is drunken.

I hear her, feel her, swallow. "I know. I knew you would."

Her arms are around me, the way I used to hold her.

"Annie, the body—"

Her thumbs press under my eyes, wipe outward. "I'm going to return her."

"They said you could?"

Annie is silent for a moment. Then, with an edge of steel: "Don't worry about that."

"Didn't know you were such a . . . rule breaker."

She sniffs, something like a snort. Her lips touch my forehead. "You don't know the half of it."

There are fewer nightmares after that. The smell of her, the warmth of her, like an anchor when I start to drift too far. When I can't remember why I did what I did, when I can't trace the steps that led me to become someone who killed their kin.

Her lips on mine, tentative like she's asking me to remember something.

We're monsters. Even if they call us something different.

I taste her lips, taste her tongue, taste her mouth like I seek to drown. I did it for this. For you. Annie, warm in my arms.

Is it enough?

Can it ever be enough, worth the breach when Erinys screeched the loss of Julia—?

Predawn light cracks through the infirmary curtains when she stirs beside me.

"It's time. I should do it now. Lee—there's something. There's something I need to tell you before I go."

She extricates herself from my arms, enough that there is space between us. Helps me sit upright. Movement, even slight and careful, burns like new fire. Our hands are twisted together; her face close, her rumpled red-brown hair soft around her face, flattened on one side from the pillow.

"Atreus was there with his Guard because he—didn't intend for you to come back from Pytho's Keep."

While I'm staring at her, trying to make sense of why she would think this or what it matters or means, she starts talking again.

She starts talking about Palace Day.

She has to say it twice for me to understand her.

Atreus didn't save you on Palace Day.

"No, he did, he said—"

"What language was he speaking when he gave that soldier the order, Lee?"

She is staring at me, waiting for me to say it.

Callish. The language I barely spoke before she taught it to me.

I fight the rising panic with the part I do remember, because it was in Dragontongue.

"But before that, my father asked—he told my father—"

Annie's eyes are filling with tears. I stare back into her buckling face and intuit what she is thinking, remembering. What she can't bring herself to say.

That empty words are given to comfort dying men.

I pull my hands out of hers.

"If Atreus didn't want me to come back from the duel," I tell her, and I tell myself that this is ridiculous, that I know it's ridiculous, even as I hear my voice shake—"then why were there witnesses?"

Annie's fingers twist on her lap.

"I brought the witnesses," she whispers. "I defied orders to bring the witnesses."

For a moment, the only sound is the Palace clocktower, tolling the quarter hour.

Rise, son of Callipolis.

Annie's liquid eyes wide, watching me. Waiting.

And then there's the sound of my own breathing as I fight for air.

Annie reaches for my hands again and I snatch them back. "Lee—"

"I killed Julia for a man who wanted me dead?"

"You didn't do it for him—"

The words trip a wire that snaps, and I let out a burst of laughter that sounds nothing like myself. "Because I did it for you?"

My voice is so loud it echoes on the whitewashed walls. Annie flinches. I slow my words. "Did you know?"

Annie's voice cracks. "No! I didn't know when Atreus asked me if you would, I only realized after—"

"Atreus asked you if I would?"

Annie blanches. Freezes. Like she's taken one step too far onto ice. And then inhales a shuddering breath like she's realized she can't stop now.

"He asked me if I thought you'd do it," she whispers, "and I said you would."

"Because you knew I'd come back to you."

She recoils at the echo of her own words like a slap.

Suddenly, looking at her, what had been desire shifts.

My cousin, my kin, blood on my hands. A duel I was sent to like a sacrifice. My father, lost to me in every way possible to lose someone you love.

And now Atreus lost, too.

And all of it, all that suffering, embodied in this scrawny girl, this mess of brown hair and freckles, this *serf*—

Who has asked and asked and asked of me until she has left me with nothing and still expects me to come back to her.

"Lee—?"

Annie's withdrawing slowly, the way she'd back away from an inhaling dragon. I can feel it building, fire at the back of my throat, a pressure. The words come out stiff and halting.

"I think you should go."

As she rises, her face half-afraid, all I can feel as I see that fear is satisfaction.

"I'm going to return Julia's body," she says.

Does she expect me to thank her?

At the thought, at the bloody absurdity of it, I feel a smile spread across my face like it belongs to someone else.

She sees my smile and her face crumples. The words tumble out as they break: "I'm so sorry, Lee—"

"Get out."

ANNIE

It's been less than a day since Lee sur Pallor named me Firstrider and Fleet Commander of Callipolis. Hours since he killed his cousin and childhood friend in a duel to prove his loyalty to the regime that killed his family.

Eight years since he learned his father killed mine.

Nine years since we became friends.

Ten minutes since he withdrew his hands from mine and bared teeth at me in a way that made the hair on the back of my neck stand on end.

His body is a cage, I tell myself, and he's trapped in it.

I leave the ward with the smell of Julia's dragonfire lingering in my nostrils. I push the image of Lee's vacant smile from my vision. I push the thought of my own guilt, my responsibility, for this boy's suffering, from my head. I don't have the luxury of being distracted by guilt, or pain, or sadness.

I focus on what I can control.

I don't have permission exactly. When I asked General Holmes about returning Julia's body, he told me the matter needed to be considered carefully first.

We don't have time for that. It's the second day. And I intend to return it before a dignified return is not possible.

I'll deal with Holmes on the other side.

I will need backup to return her body. I let my mind cycle through the list of candidates as I make my way through the quiet Palace. Lee recused himself, naming me Firstrider and Fleet Commander, placing Aela and me at the forefront of a war against the dragonlords who once incinerated my home.

Lee may not have been ready to lead this war, but I am.

Returning Julia's body will not just be a favor to Lee: It will be an opportunity for New Pythos to learn my name.

Backup. It should be a skilled rider, someone from the Fourth or at least the Eighth Order, who could have my back if the mission gets hot. They should have sufficient fluency in Dragontongue to be an asset rather than a handicap. And because this is one of my first selections as permanent Firstrider, it should be a choice that broadens, rather than concentrates, the reach of my authority in the Guardian corps.

There was a time when the Cloister bustled with Guardians eating and studying and arguing in the solarium. That was before the threat from New Pythos. Now, those who aren't sleeping off a night shift are on patrol along the northern coast, and those who aren't on patrol are supervising ration distribution in the city. I suit up in a deserted armory and make my way down to the dragons' caves.

Aela is in Pallor's nest, curled at his side as if Lee's distress had leaked down, through the stones, into his dragon, and she seeks to comfort him. I cluck to her and she launches to her feet, wings snapping open, tail twitching. Pallor's nostrils flare at my intrusion. The silver of his scales glows in the darkness of the torchlight, Aela's amber tone a warm glow. I have to stand high on my toes to throw the saddle over her back and lengthen the girth another notch to fit it under her wing joints.

"You're getting too big for me."

With her and Pallor nearly full-grown, and both sparked, I wonder—as I've begun to wonder whenever I find them together like this—when she'll begin to lay. Eggs, more dragons, a future for Callipolis. Aela lets out a snort of satisfaction, smoke puffing from her nostrils, and crouches obligingly for me to hook a boot in her stirrup and swing into the saddle.

"She'll be back," I tell Pallor.

Aela's wings unfurl like sails as she kicks off. The feeling of the ground falling away fills me with a familiar relief; I've long since stopped being able to distinguish it as Aela's or my own. We glide down the cave corridor in near darkness, up through the Firemouth chasm that pierces the center of the Inner Palace, and finally burst into daylight above. The Palace, the arena, the karst of Pytho's Keep, and the city radiating from it shrink to map-size below us as we rise. An autumn breeze blows fresh on my face and I fill my lungs with it.

Minutes later, Aela lands on the opposite side of the river in the central square of Southside, where ration cards are being distributed by the city guard.

Power sur Eater and Rock sur Bast are the two Guardians on monitoring duty. It's not a popular assignment: Citizens have started noticing that rationing is unequal among class-metals, and tension riddles the square as people eye one another's wristbands. Despite the sour looks of citizens waiting in the queue, Power manages to look bored. He lounges at the booth while his dragon circles at a safe distance above, alongside Rock's. Rock looks less at ease, every muscle of his hulking body tensed. I dismount and pat Aela's flank, sending her back into the air where she joins Eater and Bast, a flash of aurelian red alongside their black, their thick stormscourge bodies and broad wings dwarfing her by comparison.

Rock squints at me. "How's . . ."

He stutters to a halt and goes a brilliant red.

Of all of us, Rock has taken the news of Lee's dragonborn identity hardest. I can't blame him: Rock and I are both high-landers and former serfs of Stormscourge House, but I had years to adjust to the idea that I was friends with the son of people who hurt my family. Rock's had little more than a week.

I try to think of an answer and feel my eyes prickle. How is Lee? So hurt he just turned on me like a feral dog.

"He's been better."

"Do you think he'd want visitors?"

Suddenly, I could hug Rock. I restrict myself to nodding. "Soon. I think he could really use that."

Rock nods, avoiding my eyes.

In normal circumstances, Rock—gentle and giant where Power is lithe, unpredictable, and cruel—would be my choice of mission partner without thought. But returning the dead cousin of your best friend to your former lords is not normal circumstances.

I turn to Power.

My backup: a native speaker of Dragontongue; a member of the Fourth Order, with skills in the air to match mine; and, most recently, singlehandedly responsible for trying to get Lee arrested and spreading rumors that cast doubt on my fitness to lead.

It's time to change that.

Power has a boot propped on one knee, as if ration supervision were a spectator sport. "Commander?"

I place a map of the North Sea and a copy of the ancient Dragontongue epic, the *Aurelian Cycle*, on the table between us.

"I'm going to pull a Book Twenty-Four."

Book Twenty-Four: where Uriel returns the body of his enemy's fallen son across enemy lines.

Rock looks bewildered, but Power only lifts an eyebrow. Guardians raised on the Janiculum know their dragonborn poetry.

"Ambitious," Power says. "Even for you."

"I'm looking for a rider to come with me."

Rock's mouth has actually slipped open. After all, he's spent the last seven years fielding the same birth-based insults from Power as I have.

Power's smile begins. "Just one?"

"Yeah. Just one. If they're good enough."

With a flick of an invisible speck from the table, Power slides to his feet. At the far end of the booth, an Iron woman receiving her ration card from the city guard begins to argue, her shrill voice rising, as she points at the Bronze family who went before her. Class-irons farther down the queue are looking over.

Not since the Famine of my childhood have I seen such wild eyes.

Iron receives less than Bronze. Bronze less than Silver. Silver less than Gold. As dictated by the state when they had to decide, with starvation inevitable, which populations were of greatest value and which would endure the greatest losses. These are the inequalities that have begun to define every second I spend on foot in the city.

Power flashes a grin at Rock as he lifts his silver-and-gold wristband to his lips to blow into its summoning whistle. "Do Callipolis proud, Richard."

Above us, Eater and Aela fold their wings into a dive.

* * *

Julia's body lies shrouded on a table in the Palace infirmary, in an unheated room chill with the autumn cold. Overcome with sudden hesitation, I pause at the threshold. Power is the one who approaches the table and with surprising care rolls back the wrappings hiding her face.

She looks like Lee. The same long pale face, the same dark hair . . .

"Where's her helmet?" I ask. "She should be wearing it."

Power looks around the room and points at the pile of discarded gear Lee returned. It's caked with soot and dragonsblood.

"We should wash it."

"Yeah. And her armor."

Power's usual hatred for the dragonborn seems stilled in the presence of the dead. The next half hour is spent in almost complete silence as we work. I wonder if he, like me, is remembering other burials. We both know how to prepare a body.

When we're done, he lifts Julia as gently into his arms as if she were sleeping, and carries her out into the courtyard off the Palace infirmary where our dragons wait. Aela greets me with a subdued nuzzle to my palm while Power secures the added load to Eater's side: Even the dragons are quiet, as if they sense the gravity of what we're about to do.

We take the dragons along the usual flight path north. When we reach the coast, we leave the patrol route behind. My knowledge of the North Sea is piecemeal, but its extensive karst outcroppings—especially as we veer east toward New Pythos— are sufficient to navigate from the maps we've studied ever since the Pythian threat reared its head.

"How much of the *Aurelian Cycle* do you have memorized?" I ask Power as the Callipolan coast shrinks behind us. Wing to wing, Aela and Eater fly about thirty feet apart. Shouting distance.

Power's patrician credentials include a childhood of Dragontongue tutors he delights in complaining about. "Too much."

"Good. Drill me."

We race across the North Sea as I shout the Dragontongue that I intend to say, and Power corrects me till I know the lines cold.

Finally, we see what we've been waiting for: a patrol pair, dragons like ours, coming toward us, their armor the gleaming white of New Pythos. A skyfish, so pale it looks more silver than blue, with long wings all the slenderer compared with the great stormscourge at its side.

The first of the Pythian fleet I've ever seen at signing distance.

I wave the parley flag and we descend for Wayfarer's Arch.

3

THE BODY

GRIFF

I've cursed most of this life on New Pythos, squiring included. But the one thing I'd never curse, would never be able to experience except with sheer mad joy, is flying.

What's it like? my sister, Agga, always asks. *Describe it to me.*

I try to put words to it. The way the North Sea becomes layers of silver, fog rolling off the waves. The way you feel the light flood your veins, like dragonfire. The way it feels to weave through the forest of karst pillars that rise from the sea around New Pythos in all their jagged splendor. The karst forest that surrounds New Pythos is called Sailor's Folly.

Sailor's Folly, dragons' delight.

The five karsts nearest New Pythos, surrounding it on all sides, are the Norcian clan-karsts. There's no joy like surfing the wind through the clan-karsts on the back of a dragon: circling the sheer walls of Turret, racing over little humpbacked Knoll, winding through Kracken's bony arms, skimming over shaggy Thornrose with her sprawling vines. Best of all is the Nag, my own clan-karst, her nose deep in the water, the standing stones of her shrine on her crown, and the arch beneath her chin just wide enough for a dragon's wingspan to pass through. These are my people's stones, and when I'm coursing between them on Sparker's back, I don't feel cursed. I feel like the luckiest Norcian in the world.

That's what I try to describe to my sister, when she asks. I try not to talk about how it feels to see the ha'Aurelian mines defiling the bases of our clan-karsts and hollowing out their insides, the little squares of barges below ferrying ore back to the main harbor. They make Norcians do the mining, for their meager trade. Since the war with Callipolis was declared, fewer traders than ever dare deal with New Pythos, but even before that it was only the boldest who dared make the passage through Sailor's Folly.

As the search party pairs fan out, heading south toward Callipolis, Gephyra nips at Sparker's side and the two dragons begin their dance. Though I ride a stormscourge, I've never regretted being transferred into the service of a skyfish. They use speed where we use force, and even if it's not the usual combination, it's long since become a rhythm we understand. Where flying with Julia has always been a battle—a thrilling battle, a contest of great wills—this is easy. This is home.

Gephyra urges Sparker faster, lower to the waves, in a race we'll never win but love to join in as we weave our way out of the pillars at the periphery of Sailor's Folly. It's dusk, and the sky is filling with light, the fog breaking into ragged clouds, the karsts lit with gold.

In the air for the first time since Julia disappeared, I feel the weight on my chest lift like it's been blown away in the sea wind.

And then I see them.

Two riders who aren't ours. An aurelian and a stormscourge, approaching. Their riders wear the red armor of the Revolutionary fleet. We slow at the sight of them.

The stormscourge is bearing a load.

A body-shaped load.

The aurelian rider waves a white flag. In the sunset, it glows orange.

Delo signals with an arm to the nearest karst, jutting from the ocean. It's Wayfarer's Arch. The dragon perch on which Julia met Leo, a month ago.

The four of us descend. All the while, I can't tear my eyes from that swathed load, strapped to the side of the stormscourge.

The two pairs dismount and approach one another, leaving our dragons on opposite ends of the platform. The Callipolans are wearing the Revolutionary crest of the dragon breathing circlets of fire. The stormscourge rider is tall, the aurelian rider shorter, slighter. When they remove their helmets, I realize the aurelian rider is a girl. A girl with cropped brown hair that glows red in the sunset and eyes that seem to bore into us. She speaks in accented, but grammatically perfect, Dragontongue.

It takes me a moment to realize she is reciting a poem.

Though her coloring is pale like a Stormscourge, she has the shrunken build, the accent, the unmistakable *look* of a peasant. But no peasant I've ever known could recite poetry in Dragontongue with such command. A chill goes down my spine.

What are you?

The words she recites, her face scrunched up in concentration:

Come, then, accept this offering, give protection for my body
And with the dragons' grace be my escort as I make my way
To the shelter of the child's ancestral home.

Her recitation means nothing for me, but when I look at Delo, I realize it does for him. Tears have begun to course down his cheeks.

"Bring her to us," he rasps.

The other Callipolan rider, with a close-shaven head and skin as brown as Delo's, has gone to his dragon and is undoing its load. And then, with slow and careful steps, he carries the swathed burden in both arms across the platform. He lays it between himself, the girl, and us.

I kneel and part the folds of the shroud. Julia's helmet obscures most of her face, but I don't need to see more to know.

Even though, since her disappearance, I've feared this is how it would end, for a moment the sight of her colorless face doesn't register. Because how could this hurricane that I've been buffeted by for as long as I can remember—this protector and superior and commander and *lover*—how could it end like this, still and small and motionless—?

More words are being exchanged between Delo and the peasant girl, but they come distant, too distant to hear, as I lower my face to Julia's and feel how it has gone cold.

ANNIE

The shorter, stocky boy, whose stormscourge is the largest I've ever seen, kneels beside Julia, presses his face to hers, and begins to weep. Something about his gait, his manner, jars me like a stone out of place.

The Skyfish is tall, slender, with finely curling dark hair. He speaks with forced calm, though his face is wet.

"Tell me what happened."

"Julia made Leo choose a side. He chose."

The Skyfish's eyes widen.

"They dueled, fairly. He asked that his cousin's body be returned to her people."

At our feet, the stormscourge rider presses lips against Julia's eyes, nose—mouth. The sound of his sorrow strums through me.

"Who are you?" the Skyfish asks.

"My name is Antigone sur Aela," I take a breath, preparing to say it for the first time, "Firstrider of the Callipolan Fleet."

The crouching boy lifts his head to stare at me.

The Skyfish doesn't blink. He answers: "I am Delo sur Gephyra, Tertius."

He bows rigidly. It's the bow I've seen patricians give each other in formal introductions: a bow between equals. And though it's been nine years since I was a dragonlord's serf, it still feels like the earth has turned upside down to watch a dragonborn bow to me. I force myself to return the politeness as Delo did it, lightly and from the neck. Not the obeisance I was taught as a child.

"You're not Tertius," the crouching boy murmurs. "You're Alternus now, my lord."

Because Julia's position has opened, and the ranking has shifted.

Delo blanches. But what I hear is the address.

Lord? What business has one of the dragonborn addressing the other as *lord*?

"Who are you?" I ask the other boy.

Delo blinks and his glance flits between us. As if it only now occurs to him that it is possible for me and the other boy to speak to each other. The other rises from where he crouches by Julia's side. Blue eyes blaze, set startlingly bright against an olive complexion, lined at the corners in a way that make his age hard to guess, although I'd imagine he is the same age as Delo—two or three years older than I.

"Griff," he says. "Griff Gareson."

No drakonym. No ranking. And when Griff bows to me, he bows low.

I look from Delo to Griff, then back again. Where Delo wears heavy armor bearing the water lilies of Skyfish house, Griff is dressed only in a flamesuit.

And I do the math we should have done at that first sighting.

There are known to be at least twenty dragons in the Pythian fleet. But of dragonborn children who survived the Revolution, who were of an age to bond with dragons, there couldn't possibly have been so many.

"My lord," Griff says, dragging his arm across his wet face. "Should I take Lady Julia on Sparker?"

"Yes. Thank you, Griff."

I hear the difference in addresses, Griff's formal *you* against Delo's informal.

And then I notice something else. Something I should have noticed from the start, but missed in the shadows of that great hulking stormscourge's horns—

It's muzzled. I feel myself sway with horror.

The Pythians have taken lowborn riders, too.

And the most unsettling thing of all, that when Griff lifts Julia's body into his arms, it's with the care and gentleness of something between a servant and something else, something more—

Power's hand grips my shoulder tightly.

"We have company," he murmurs.

On the edge of the platform, a dark form rises up. A fifth dragon: another stormscourge, slithering over the edge as if it had come upon us from below, slate gray except its crest and tail, which are tipped with silver. This one's armor emblazoned with Stormscourge heather. He takes off his helmet and for a moment my breath stills because I see Lee.

And then I shake my head, clearing it: not Lee. This boy has the same dark hair against pale skin, the same gray eyes, the same build and gait, but there is a cruel edge to the lines of his face that are absent from Lee's; and he is, like Delo, older.

There's only one person this can be. Julia's brother, Ixion.

"You should go," Delo tells us, as he turns to face the newcomer.

Griff has frozen, his arms around Julia, and under Ixion's gaze, Griff shrinks. For a moment, Ixion stares at the body in Griff's arms. His shoulders tighten. The wind blows across Wayfarer's Arch, carrying silence.

Then Ixion swings back around to face me. His lip curls as he looks me over. Like he's just spotted something so offensive it turns his stomach.

"You're that peasant bitch."

Griff flinches.

And it's that flinch, not the words themselves, that ignites something inside me. I ball my fists and lift my chin.

"Yeah," I answer, "I am."

Griff's eyes go wide as if I'd just shocked them open. I resist the urge to return his stare.

Delo takes Ixion's arm. "Antigone sur Aela will be granted safe passage back to her people in accordance with the traditions of ours."

But Ixion shrugs him off as if he hasn't heard him. He steps forward.

"Maybe Leo lets you forget. But I won't. You're a Stormscourge serf. *I own you.* And after this war I will make sure you and all your stinking kind remember it."

Aela's wings snap open behind me. I hear her growling like it comes from my own throat.

Delo moves to stand between us.

"Enough."

No. Not enough. Never enough. I feel as though the dragon were inside me, clawing its way from my gut. I feel a restraint and look down: Power has seized my arm.

"Annie," he growls. "We're outnumbered and this isn't the mission."

Ixion lifts his bugle to his lips and blows. A piercing note splits the air. Summoning other riders.

"Annie, let's go."

Aela and Eater charge to our sides and we scramble onto their backs. I'm only half on when Aela kicks off from the ground, and I clamber the rest of the way into the saddle as the ground falls away. Ixion's stormscourge leaps as if to follow us, and Power sur Eater spews fire down.

"Come on, come on, faster—"

Wayfarer's Arch falls away below us, but the stormscourge that launched after us is on our tails, and other dragons are appearing on the horizon, drawn to the sound of Ixion's bugle.

"Make for the stratus—"

We rise, weaving, urging our dragons as fast as they can go. Aela pummels the air with her wings. I abandon the reins to cling to her neck, flattening myself against her back and burying my helmet against her hot scales as the wind tears at us.

Our dragons burst together through the cloud cover. It's so dense that Power sur Eater disappears.

"Annie?"

"Here."

Lost in the white, we make our way south.

In the silence and the cloud cover, my thoughts race. The sight of that muzzled dragon, of Griff Gareson's bowing, of Ixion's sneer, *I own you*. And like deeper notes of the same melody, earlier memories play in time, a symphony of anger. *There, there, you've learned your lesson now, haven't you—?*

I've learned my lesson. How many times do I need to keep learning it?

When we finally dare to breach, Callipolis is in sight again and the Pythians are gone. The sea turns to coast and the coast turns to plains and from those plains Pytho's Keep rises, the city spread below it. I look down upon my island unseeing.

Before, I thought of this war as something to withstand. An attack Callipolis must defend against.

But that was blinkered. This isn't a war to defend against: This is a war to win.

Back in the Palace, when we've dismounted and unsaddled our dragons at the mouth of the arena entrance to the caves, Power squints at me.

"You all right?"

"No, I'm not *all right*. I'm pissed."

I've spilled over, Aela riding my emotions as she growls behind me; Power's face is suddenly glowing in the light of the fire she bellows upward. His eyes flick behind me, to her fire, then back at my face. There is something shining in his eyes as he looks at me now, like he's taking me in, a look I remember from the days—they seem long ago now—when we trained together.

As if he finds my fury beautiful.

"So, you're pissed," he says. "What are you going to do about it?"

Aela pants behind me, catching her breath as she contemplates a second burst of flame. And behind Power, Eater paws the ground as if readying for a fight: Power's pupils have dilated; he's spilled over, too, while watching me rage.

It's too strange, and I'm too angry to care.

"I'm going to get that muzzle off Griff Gareson's dragon," I tell him, "and I'm going to raze New Pythos to the ground."

Power smiles, a ragged, crooked smile that lights his face.

"Damn straight," he says.

For a second, I find myself grinning back. Grinning stupidly, furiously, wildly, and it feels good.

And then I remember who this is: Power, the boy who threatened to break my arm two weeks ago—Power, who never gives kindness without matching it with cruelty—

I step back abruptly. Power's eyes flicker as they search my face, and his fingers reach up to rub his neck.

"We should go in," I say, averting my gaze as the heat in my own face rises.

Inside the Cloister, Duck finds me, the waves of his unruly hair sticking up at odd angles, like he's been running a nervous hand through it. He holds out a memo stamped with the seal of the four-tiered city, the insignia of the Inner Palace. "Annie, they delivered this early in the morning. From the Ministry of Defense, the War Council meeting was moved up a day—you're supposed to be there—"

My stomach lurches: My first time attending the War Council as Firstrider was something I was planning to prepare for tonight. "When?"

"An hour ago."

I take off for the Inner Palace at a run.

GRIFF

Delo has no interest in joining Ixion's manhunt, and so the two of us make our way back to New Pythos, bearing the body, alone. I hold her in my arms and think how this will be her last flight. Delo lets us fly in silence, as if he wants the same privacy I do.

One last flight with Julia. One more hour to hold her.

What's come over me, that suddenly I'm counting these minutes?

By the time we land, I've composed myself. We've come to the Stormscourge balustrade instead of Skyfish. Delo rings the bell for assistance and then comes to my side, fearless of Sparker's wrath. Where his jaws have been hindered, his talons work just fine, but he never turns them on Delo.

"Griff, I'll take her now."

Servants have rounded the corner, stopping short when they see us with the body. Delo turns to them. "Tell Lady Electra that her niece has been found. Lower the banners of the Houses to half-staff. And find the Greatlord."

I'm still holding her when Delo steps closer. He touches my arm.

"You should leave before they arrive."

Because as Julia's peasant lover, I'd be the first thing the grief-struck dragonborn would catch in their crossfire. And Delo knows it.

And though I'm relieved he thought of it, and relieved to be released from duty, when I realize this means saying goodbye, I consider staying anyway.

"Griff," Delo says, like he's waking me.

I kiss her, one last time, and give her to Delo for good.

Then I leave, down the winding servants' stairs of the citadel and out the Humble Gate, through the five-pointed crossroads of Conqueror's Mound, and down the windswept hills to the village of Clan Nag. It's after dark, the narrow streets lit by nothing but stray cracks of light escaping through shutters, and glowing windows of the lesser ha'Aurelian manors towering over us on the hillside.

I touch the Nag's fading clan-sign over our lintel before letting myself in. Agga meets me at the door, her hair a dark smudge around her face, frizzy from the mist. "What happened?"

It must show in my face. She's whispering, which means Becca and Garet are in bed. Agga minds other children during the day along with her own—her lungs are too weak to work in the smelting shops with the rest of the women, or on the barges that ferry ore back and forth from the karst-mines—but it's late enough that all the other children have gone home. Granda sits by the fire, a thick blanket around his bony shoulders, asleep.

"Let's sit out back," Agga says. "Have you eaten? I saved you dinner."

The soup looks to be mostly fish-flavored water; grain imports have been down since our attack on Callipolis brought on an embargo from the Medean League. I ladle soup into a bowl,

Agga fetches a blanket to wrap around herself, and we climb over the little ones where they're curled in the back room and out onto the stoop. The sound of sleepy gulls and the distant lapping of waves below is all we can hear—until, as always, Agga begins to cough.

"How much ginger have you got left?" I ask.

"A bit. But that's all right, Lady Julia should give you more soon, shouldn't she?"

I put the soup down, wrap my arms around myself, and groan aloud.

"Did you anger her?" Agga whispers.

A rare time we fought, Julia forgot Agga's medicines for a month. Afterward, she laughed the whole thing off as a joke. I did, too, but learned the lesson. I shake my head. "Worse than that."

From the citadel, mourning bells have begun to toll. We both know the sound.

Agga lets out a low breath of understanding and wraps her arms around me. She holds me for the long minutes while they toll the requiem, and with their noise to hide it, I surrender myself to grief. In her arms I don't try to understand where it stops being about Julia and starts being about what she gave and what she took and the terror that gnaws most of all at what happens now. With Julia gone and Ixion ascendant.

"Mumma?"

The walls are thin enough that even with the door pulled to, the little ones can hear us. Agga turns at the sound of Becca's voice, folding her into her arms when she appears on the stoop beside us and kissing her on the top of her clumping hair. Becca's hair sometimes seems bigger than she is.

"You should be asleep."

"But I heard you and Griff." She reaches out, presses a small palm flat against mine in greeting. "Were you riding Sparker, Uncle?"

Whatever the dragonborn might think of me, I'm proud to say I'm a proper celebrity among the children of Clan Nag. As is Sparker, whom they call by name but have never met.

"I was."

"I wish I could fly a dragon," Becca says with a sigh.

I can feel Agga tense beside me, drawing in a breath, as if she's thinking, as I am, that she hopes no such thing ever is asked of Becca. The burns I spent a childhood coming home with were ones Agga tended. But she answers lightly. "Well, one day your lords may need it of you, and then you will. But for now, your *mother* needs you to go to bed."

Becca giggles. She allows herself to be scooped onto her feet and patted back in the door. She makes one last attempt from the doorframe.

"Tell me a story, Uncle? The one about the Nag and the Great Dragon—"

"*Bed,*" Agga and I say together.

We listen to the sound of her burrowing back into blankets beside Garet and wait, breath held, for the silence to hold. Then Agga touches my hand and speaks in a whisper that wavers.

"Tell me what happened."

She cries while I tell her. Harder than I did, and I know old memories are welling up. Of Mam's passing, which I barely remember. Of Da's, which I do, though that wasn't so much with the news as the lack of it. Of her Eamon's not returning from the mines two years ago, of the little ones hers alone to take care of. I wonder if she thinks I must be heartbroken, as she was.

I test it. *Heartbroken.*

But if this is heartbreak, then it pales in comparison to what I saw Agga go through that day.

So I add something else. Something to make her tears stop. Now my arm is the one around her, holding the blanket up to keep her warm.

"The rider," I tell her. "The one who brought the body, from Callipolis. You'd never believe it, Agga. She was Firstrider, like Julia. But she was a peasant, like us."

Agga gives a watery laugh of awed delight. "She told you?"

"She looked Ixion in the eye and told *him*."

ANNIE

Only when I enter the tower of the Inner Palace known as the Defense Wing do I realize that I don't know where the War Council meets. I pause, clutching a stitch in my side, and ask the first adult whose path I cross. He gives me a look of deep skepticism.

"Isn't it the Firstrider who attends War Council meetings?"

"I was promoted."

The man, middle-aged and graying, frowns at this news. "I'll escort you."

He leads me down a winding staircase and knocks outside a somber, oak-framed door on the lowest floor. Then, at a call from within, he opens it.

"Antigone sur Aela, Firstrider," he announces to the room.

The War Room is empty save for one person: General Holmes, seated at the far end of an oval table, sorting papers.

Holmes's uniform is a black silhouette against the red banner of the Revolutionary dragon, the circlets of the four class-metals represented as coils of dragonfire, hanging behind him. The room is windowless, built to be safe from air strikes: We're underground, level with the Firemouth, with lanterns overhead casting long shadows on the stone walls.

Holmes looks up when I enter. "Antigone. I'm sorry you missed our meeting. I was not aware your patrol schedule had changed at such short notice."

My mouth dry, a hundred excuses shuttle through my head, each worse than the last. I raise my fist to my chest in the Revolutionary salute. "The fault is mine, sir."

Holmes does not accept my apology, or acknowledge my salute, and so I remain standing, my stomach curdling. I'm making a mental note *never* to be late for this man again when Holmes's words jar me from thought.

"Master Goran and I spoke this morning. To review your performance history. He brought to my attention concerns that I was not previously aware of. You have a very long disciplinary record."

The last time I spoke to our drillmaster, I pulled rank on him in front of the entire corps. Goran's always taken the presence of females and lowborn riders in his corps as a kind of personal offense; now that I've given him a legitimate reason not to like me, I can only imagine what he'd be willing to say to my superior.

"Permission to speak frankly, sir—"

"I am aware that Goran is a bigot, if you are about to point that out. He has been dismissed."

I close my mouth.

Holmes says, "I've also received word from the infirmary that Julia Stormscourge's body was removed by two Guardians, despite my warning against rash action."

My fist against my chest, I think I feel my heart miss a beat.

"Thank you for taking that . . . initiative."

I swallow hard.

"Now *I* will speak frankly," Holmes says. "I respected the nerve you showed in defying the First Protector and ensuring the safety of Lee sur Pallor, who is—as far as I am concerned—Callipolis's true Firstrider even if he has recused himself. I am grateful to you for bringing to my attention that one of our finest military assets was in danger. But do not mistake me: I have no need for a commander of the aerial fleet who can't follow orders. I will give this warning once and never again. Do we understand each other?"

His words echo faintly against the stone walls of the empty War Room. My voice comes out faint. "Yes, sir."

"Good. Dismissed."

Fifteen minutes later, my numb steps have taken me out of the Inner Palace and back, not to the Cloister, but to the Palace infirmary.

But when I push open the door to Lee's ward, I hear another voice inside. A voice I am used to associating with good things—encouragement, and respect, and kindness.

Crissa's voice.

The other sound, the sound I didn't know to recognize before the last twenty-four hours, is of Lee breaking down.

Lee, who last looked at me with the smile of a monster, because he was in pain past reaching.

I back away from the door—from Crissa's soothing voice, from Lee's weeping—my boots soft on the infirmary tiles. I've spun and am about to leave at a run when I hear her behind me.

"Annie. Wait."

Crissa closes the door behind her. And then, before I know what she intends, she has crossed the length of the corridor and taken my hand. As always when I stand this close to her, I'm just a little struck by her beauty. She's tall—almost as tall as Lee and Cor—with golden hair that falls like a shining curtain down her back, and bright blue eyes set in a round face.

"Annie, I told him it was done. I'm done—standing between you two. I want you to know that."

That's what she thinks this is about? Romance, a choice between her and me? I let out a noise somewhere between a laugh and a sob.

This is about the fact that right now it hurts Lee to even look at me, for what I've cost him.

"You're not the thing standing between us. You've never been the thing standing between us. The thing standing between us is—*us*."

I choke on it.

She should leave me then, for scoffing at her kindness. I wait for her to. But instead, she just says, "Hey."

Before I realize what she's going to do, she's put her arms around me.

For a moment, I let her, and after everything that's happened today—Lee's stricken face and Ixion's sneer and Holmes's waiting alone in the War Room to tell me who the real Firstrider is—I think for a moment nothing has ever felt so good.

And then I remember who I am, this girl's superior now, her fleet commander.

I cannot let myself be comforted like a little girl while I weep.

I will go to the Firstrider's office and weep alone.

I step backward and drag a hand across my face. "Thank you, Crissa."

"Of course, Annie . . ."

"You should go to him. He'll—he's going to need you now."

"As a friend," Crissa emphasizes.

Whatever she wants to call it.

I smile, and nod, and leave her with Lee.

And then, in the Firstrider's office, after I've dried my tears, I do what I do best. I push aside thoughts of Lee, that awful noise he makes when he wants to stop crying but can't. I push aside thoughts of Crissa with her gentle bedside voice, comforting him.

Instead, I fix my thoughts on Ixion Stormscourge and Delo Skyfish and that muzzled dragon beside Griff Gareson.

And I begin to plan.

4

—

THE FUNERAL

GRIFF

Julia's funeral is held in Folly Shrine, the garden that sits along with the Glass Hall in the center of the citadel with a view of the sea and the karst pillars of Sailor's Folly on all sides. Norcian standing stones frame the view from the garden, each slab carved from a different clan-karst, though the ha'Aurelians subverted the stones generations ago into rose trellises and marred them with gargoyles of their dragons.

In the old days, before the conquerors built their citadel around it, this was the shrine where we crowned our high kings.

The Greatlord Rhadamanthus officiates; Ixion's storm-scourge, Niter, is present to light Julia's pyre. The sun is setting, the sky full of dying light. The dragonborn are gathered in a semicircle around the pyre: ha'Aurelians in burnished red of the rose; Stormscourge in black; Skyfish in blue; the Bastards wear the sigils of their Houses in gray; and the humble-riders are outfitted according to the rider they serve. Behind them stand the Norcian clan chieftains, appointed by the ha'Aurelians in a mockery of our old institutions. The rest of the Norcians are congregated outside the citadel on the sloping hillside of

Conqueror's Mound, to witness Julia's ashes being strewn from the parapet.

As Rhadamanthus begins to read the Rites of the Fallen Dragonlord, the sense of his words fades. Julia lies arrayed in full ceremonial armor, her black mantle spread over the pyre. The visor has been shut over her face to preserve its dignity in death. But as I look at her, I imagine the armor gone. I imagine the girl I remember who dared, when we were alone, to strip naked and laugh aloud.

The dragonlords of old used to take peasant girls into their beds, she told me. *Why shouldn't I do the same?*

That was her explanation, when it started. After the glances had begun to ricochet between us like sparks. It wasn't a question I was expected to answer. When I was summoned, I went.

But because I'm a cocky bastard, I told her I wanted things in return. Medicine that my mother died for lacking, that my sister needed. Food when food was scarce.

My requests amused her, but she granted them. Julia liked power.

It was something we had in common.

"...and that in death your spirit may unite with your dragon, that you may no longer taste the bitter loneliness of a landed spirit, may this light of your dragon-kin send you forth into the fire of the next life."

Ixion gives the murmured order to Niter, who ignites and fires at the base of the pyre. Dragonfire makes fast victims: The wood catches quickly, and the fire spreads. The wind off the sea catches the smoke and pulls it south.

Rhadamanthus lifts his arm, and the attending dragonborn rumble out the ritual question.

"But who will feast with her? For even the rider requires companionship."

I have a chalice of wine in one hand, a dagger in the other. I hold the chalice out to Ixion, who takes it without looking at me. Hoarsely, he recites: "I, your next of kin, offer this libation as the first of many feasts that you share in the next life with House Stormscourge."

He raises the cup to his lips, drinks from it, then steps forward. He empties the cup over the growing flames, which sputter but continue to rise.

The second question rumbles from the mourners. *"But who will serve her? For even the dead require due comforts."*

I step forward, so that I can feel the heat of the flames burning my face and arms. Julia's silhouetted form is barely visible in the crackling fire. When Delo asked me, before the funeral, if I'd like to perform the Offering of the Servant, he made clear that one of Julia's maids-in-waiting could do it in my stead.

"And ruin one of their pretty hands? No. It should be me."

But protecting a maid's hand wasn't the reason I wanted to do it. The real reason is—it feels right. Whatever Julia was to me or I to her, the truth of it was always this. A servant's debt. It seems the fitting way to say goodbye.

"I, as servant of your house, offer my blood in lieu of life that in the underworld you be ever served and honored."

I extend one hand, open it palm up, and raise the dagger over it. I can feel the eyes of the dragonborn on me, but the ones I'm most conscious of are Delo's, wide and brown as he watches from the Skyfish section.

Do you like it? he asked once, when Julia first began to summon me.

Course I like it. Why wouldn't I like it?

He never asked again.

The dagger slides diagonally across the soft flesh of my palm, deeply and slowly. Blood wells. I turn my hand, make a fist, and watch my blood drip into Julia's consuming, uncaring fire.

A fitting goodbye.

I step back, face burning, fist clenched to stanch the blood and ease the sting, and Rhadamanthus concludes the ritual.

"Lit with the fire of your dragon, warmed by the love of your house, kept in comfort by the care of your people, may your next life contain all the joys and none of the sorrows of your last."

The flames devour the pyre with a fury befitting Julia. I don't look away.

Later, after the sun has set and the audience dispersed, Delo finds me. A feast in Julia's honor will be held tonight in the Greatlord's Hall, where I will serve at Delo's table, but in the time between I find myself lingering in the frozen garden beneath the old standing stones, watching the final embers of the pyre die. Delo takes a seat on the stone bench beside me. I don't realize, until coolness spreads over my palm, that he has begun to dress my hand. He brought ointment and gauze to the ceremony for the purpose.

"I can do it," I tell him, reaching for the gauze.

Delo doesn't pull away. "Let me."

I sit very still, feeling the cool relief of ointment, the brush of delicate fingers as he fixes the bandage. If we were in the armory and I were tending him, this is the point where I'd start talking, but tonight, I want the silence. And perhaps because it's dark or perhaps because he's sitting so close, I let myself wonder.

When he asked me if I liked it, what had he wanted me to say? It was from then that the silences and the forced conversation grew.

What do I wish I'd said?

I can see very little of his face, but I see when his fingers flick to his eyes. Composing himself.

"Griff," he says finally, "I need to tell you this. Before—before someone else does."

He looks up, pausing in wrapping my hand, his fingers light on mine.

"Ixion has demanded to reclaim you as his squire now that he's Firstrider."

The last glowing embers of Julia's pyre have blown out. The sky is dark overhead. "I thought your father said . . ."

"My father doesn't want to get on the wrong side of the fleet's new commander. None of them do." Delo's fingers twitch, then resume binding my hand. "I'm sorry. I think Ixion's just—trying to prove a point—"

I pull my bandaged hand away and flex my fingers.

"When?" I ask.

Delo scratches at his hairline, turning his face from me. "The details haven't been decided yet. I haven't given over Sparker's key or anything—"

I run my thumb along the underside of my wrist. Burn scars have reshaped the skin over the years, but the faint impression of the earliest scars remains. A semicircle of indentations left from Niter's fangs, on Ixion's command, when we were twelve and I had outperformed him in the air.

Seven years later, will he be any less creative?

"Tonight. I'll serve him tonight, at the feast. It will be better if we don't delay."

It has always felt like borrowed time, serving Delo. *This* has always felt like borrowed time.

But still, we're sitting next to each other, our knees touching.

"I'm sorry," Delo says again.

"You should challenge him." I speak against better judgment. "Challenge him for Firstrider."

Delo lets out a laugh. "Griff," he says. "We both know that wouldn't work."

Delo has a block when it comes to Ixion. He always has.

And Ixion's good. The only one who's ever been able to beat him was Julia.

Julia and me.

Or at least, me before Sparker wore the muzzle. The thought invades, unwanted, unwelcome: *Antigone sur Aela isn't muzzled.*

But that line of thinking is dangerous, and I push the thought of the Callipolan Firstrider away.

* * *

There was one humble-rider who tried to rebel. Or at least, that was what they told us. Roxana ha'Aurelian's squire, Mabalena, was accused and found guilty of sedition six years ago. The Norcians of New Pythos gathered to watch her punishment on Conqueror's Mound. Mabalena's dragon's throat was slit, and then, as Lena writhed from pain at the loss, her family were taken one by one into the air, on dragonback, above the square, and dropped.

Years later, I still remember what it sounded like. The dull, wet thunk of each human body flattening on unforgiving stone, their screams silenced. The sounds of Mabalena's pleading—first in Dragontongue, then Norish—dissolving into incoherence. The way Roxana watched, stone-faced, Rhadamanthus's hand on her shoulder. Rhode was the one who performed the punishment.

Mabalena was dropped last, but lower, so that she alone survived. She serves in the citadel and is brought out when occasions call for a reminder. The dragonborn call her Mad Lena.

We were thirteen.

At the time, I believed it. I believed she had been planning a rebellion, and I was amazed at her courage and daring. How had she done it? I was resentful she hadn't seen fit to include me.

It took me years to realize that, at thirteen, it was unlikely she had planned anything. She was a weak rider, her dragon more of a liability than an asset. She'd be an affordable loss to the Pythian fleet, best put to use as a message to the rest of us.

The message worked, because since then, there have been no more Norcian riders accused of sedition. And then we sparked and proved everyone's fears right, and after that, the muzzle; and so even the ember of the idea died. The dragonborn are careful to remind us of what waits on the other side instead: *When we retake Callipolis, your families will be rewarded. They'll be given land of their own, freedom and riches, as payment for your service.*

I'm not sure I believe that. But I believe what I saw them do to Mabalena's family.

And that's why, when I think of Antigone sur Aela, facing Ixion down and smiling as she admitted her low birth, I know better than to follow the fantasy to its conclusion. To the buried dreams she evokes. I know what lies on the other side.

Dreams are deadliest for the dreamers.

* * *

Three banners hang in the Greatlord's Hall: to one side, the Triarchy's dragons in eternal chase, circling the black clover of exile; to the other side, the five stars of the Norcian clans; and in the center, the ha'Aurelian rose choking those five stars, the sigil of New Pythos.

Tonight, in honor of Julia, the lawful-born Callipolans join Rhadamanthus at the high table under the Pythian banner, leaving the Bastards to dine at their own lower table, and displacing the Norcian elders from Clan Thornrose usually afforded the honor. When I pass my lair-master, Scully, seated among his clan with Leary Thornrose, the supposed High King of the Norcians, they try to summon me and I bow an apology not without satisfaction.

"I'm serving at the high table tonight, sirs. Perhaps I can find another to assist you."

My failure to address Leary as *Your Highness* is not missed; the sight of their puckering faces is sweet. In the old days, the five clans chose a king ourselves, and Clan Thornrose was no greater than the other four. The ha'Aurelians offered them favored status, positions on the citadel staff and in their guard, to turn them traitors against the rest of us. Leary's face, dyed blue with woad in the sign of his clan-karst, is a ceremonial mockery of kingship that I don't let my eyes linger on.

At least none of Leary's or Scully's sons will ever serve on dragonback. Thornrose alone of the five clans does not have squires in the fleet; Rhadamanthus knew better than to give one clan that much power. And so, even if I'm never invited to sit at the high table as they often are, at least tonight I'm serving at it and they're ousted.

I'm making my way up to the dais when a dragonborn child tumbles out of his bench at the junior table and beams up at me, his black funeral vestments a jarring contrast to his gap-toothed grin.

"Griff! Master of the skies!"

"Little lordling Astyanax!"

This little lord, unlike the Thornrose traitors, is one I have a fondness for. Astyanax is the Greatlord Rhadamanthus's youngest child. He has the ha'Aurelians' bowl-cut auburn hair, their golden skin and black eyes—and by some accident he's got a better heart than Rhode's and Roxana's combined. Or maybe I'm biased because he's young, halfway between Becca's and Garet's ages. The dragonborn are like feral animals: cute before they start to bite. I ruffle Astyanax's floppy hair and catch Rhode glaring at me from the high table.

"Run along, little lordling."

Legs leaden at the prospect of waiting on Ixion, I make my way into the kitchen, where the other humble-riders gossip in Norish as they shoulder dishes and jugs of wine. When Fionna learns why I'm serving Ixion, she puts her hand over her mouth. "*Transferred?* Dragons help you."

"Thanks, Fionna."

Bran, Rhode's squire, quirks his bushy brow at Fionna. He's a head taller than me, and I'm a head taller than Fionna, so he fairly towers over her. Dishes are balanced precariously on his long arm. "Griff's just got to remember not to show off in the air this time."

Fionna giggles, the bloom of a burn scar that spreads from her ear turning as pink as the pitcher of rose wine she carries.

"And you?" I ask Fionna.

Fionna served Julia. Her teasing smile falters. "I'm with Roxana now."

Roxana ha'Aurelian hasn't had a squire since Mabalena was dropped. But Mabalena is something we don't talk about.

Bran touches Fionna on the elbow. "You'll be fine," he murmurs, and his free hand lingers there just long enough for me to notice.

He notices me noticing, and drops his hand like lightning.

Good. Because if that's happening, they'd better get better at hiding it. That's not a union the dragonborn would allow in a hundred years.

The toasts go up in Julia's name throughout the dinner, a background noise to my concentration on Ixion's meal. Dragonborn I've never spoken to, who probably only ever thought of Julia to grind their teeth about her when she was alive, speak eloquently about her *daring spirit* and *resilience* and *honor to her father's name*. As if they hadn't resented her, every step of the way, for the customs she systematically defied. It was on her insistence that females were presented to dragons at all, and after that, that they competed in the Firstrider Tournament.

The Firstrider Tournament that she won.

It was always like riding a storm, flying with Julia. Like teasing the edge. And now I'll never ride like that again.

I haven't eaten since breakfast, but the adrenaline I run on trying to remember Ixion's preferences—which I once had memorized but haven't had to think of for years—leaves no room for appetite as I attend to the bounty Ixion picks at lazily. It's only when I'm placing his main course in front of him that he notices me. His hand darts over, seizes my left wrist, and turns it over.

"Someone bandaged your hand."

I stare down at the fine-spun gauze that my family would never be able to afford, and that no court physician would ever waste on me. Delo, seated across the table, raises a cloth napkin to his lips and presses, a line forming between his eyes. He and Ixion are only a few seats down from the head of the table, where the Greatlord dines alongside his wife and the most esteemed exiles.

Ixion lifts his eyes to Delo, holding my wrist with his thumb and forefinger all the while. Fionna, refilling wine a few dragon-born down, glances in my direction with eyebrows raised.

"Delo," Ixion says. "Tell me what you think of Antigone."

Delo returns his napkin to his lap. Around them, conversations fall silent as they realize what Ixion's talking about. Nestor, Delo's father, has lowered his goblet, his head cocked as if to better catch his son's conversation.

"The Callipolan Firstrider?" Delo's voice is calm. "Not much. Our conversation was brief."

"You know she didn't earn that title. Leo handed it to her. That's what's being said. Handed the title of Firstrider over to a *peasant*."

Ixion's fingers remain looped around my wrist.

"Mmm," says Delo, spearing a bite of his seared swordfish.

"I don't know which one I'm looking forward to roasting more, that peasant-loving traitor or his serf whore."

Murmurs of agreement go up around the table. Rhode raises his goblet and the riders toast to it.

Death to the peasant-loving usurpers.

Fionna drops the pitcher. It falls to the floor and shatters, splattering wine across the flagstones. Around the table, the dragonborn who'd been ignoring us look up, remembering our presence. Even the lower tables are looking over, the Bastards and the lesser ha'Aurelians; Nolan, one of the Bastards' squires, stands with his shoulders around his ears as he watches us from the main floor. Fionna begins to bend for the floor but freezes when Ixion speaks.

"Fionna." Ixion's eyes have lit up. He drops my wrist, and I withdraw my arm, the feeling returning to it. "What do you think of the Callipolan Firstrider?"

"Nothing, my lord."

"You're sure of that? Sure you're not inspired?"

Fionna's new mistress, Roxana, is studying her squire with sudden interest. Roxana's golden face is flushed with wine and Fionna's is draining of color under the bloom of her burn scar. Delo's younger sister, Phemi, speaks from farther down. "Oh, leave her alone."

Phemi shares Delo's impatience with squire-bullying. Mostly, I think, because it bores her.

Ixion's attention travels to Phemi, and Fionna ducks down and begins scrabbling to clean up. None of the other humble-riders move to help her: Enough training kicks in in this moment to avoid any signs of solidarity.

Solidarity among the Norcian riders has always been regarded as a threat.

"Careful, Phemi," Ixion tells her. "Don't want us to think you're a peasant-lover like your brother—"

Phemi has two brothers—Delo and her twin, Ethelo—but no one has to ask which brother Ixion means. Phemi's own squire, Moira, stands frozen at her elbow, about to refill her water goblet; Phemi invites her to pour with an irritable flick of her wrist while Delo bites from his fork and begins to chew. His mouth full, he asks: "Do you want Griff's key now, or later?"

Ixion twists to face me, then looks me up and down slowly.

"Now," he decides.

Delo hooks his finger under the chain that holds Sparker's key, lifts it, and holds it out. Ixion is smiling at me, and Delo isn't looking at me at all.

Look at me, by the dragon, look at me—

But that's madness, because he shouldn't. And he doesn't. Ixion takes the chain, pulls it over his neck. Down the table, Electra, Rhadamanthus, and Nestor are no longer making any pretension of talking: They are watching the younger generation.

Ixion lifts his goblet to Rhadamanthus, smiling. To the table as a whole, he says:

"Leo was not my late sister's only correspondent. I discovered something interesting while sorting her papers."

Ixion has the gift of summoning the attention of a table. Rhadamanthus lowers his goblet.

"Julia," Ixion says, "was also writing Princess Freyda, of Bassilea. They were quite the pen pals."

This is news to everyone listening, including me. Then again, Julia did write a lot of letters. But Bassilea, a mainland empire whose coast spreads east of our shores and stretches down to the Medean Sea, is best known for keeping to itself.

"The daughter of the God-King?" Nestor barks down the table, incredulous. "What on earth would they write about?"

"Of the many topics their letters covered, one was how they were surrounded by older men dismissive of their ability to ride."

Nestor purples. Ixion smiles at him. Roxana snorts into her fist.

"Freyda claimed a dragon?" Rhadamanthus asks in surprise.

"It seems the Callipolans have inspired dragonborn ladies all across the Medean."

"That's an upset to their succession practices," Delo murmurs, dabbing his mouth with a napkin and looking up.

Ixion nods, still smiling. "I believe that a visit to Vask may be warranted. To inform the princess of the passing of her friend. And the cause of her death. It might interest her in our cause."

"We've tried to make allies of the Bassileans before," Rhadamanthus says, with a hand lifted in dismissal. "There was no interest. Particularly not after the Medean League's embargo."

"There was no interest," Ixion corrects, "from the God-King. You never tried the daughter. And, as Delo points out, her succession status seems to be . . . a variable."

Ixion tilts his glass to his lips before adding: "She is of marrying age."

Ah.

Lords help Freyda, then.

Rhadamanthus looks at Nestor. "We will review Julia's letters and consider it."

Only late, when the drinking is done and he rises to leave the hall, does Ixion remember me. He orders me to come with him, as I've been waiting for, and every nerve of my body goes on end. I've lost track of Delo as the night progressed; my attention is entirely focused on Ixion, my stomach writhing with a sick mixture of fear and loathing and anticipation. So I don't know if Delo sees us leave the hall.

Ixion's chambers are a corridor down from Julia's, disconcertingly familiar from years of visiting her at night, in the

Stormscourge wing of the Provisional Palace. Inside his chamber, Ixion slumps in a chair and I light the room. This part of our service, too, I've not done for years: Delo always dismissed me rather than have me act as his manservant. A luxury I discounted as I grew accustomed to it. As I kneel to unlace Ixion's boots one by one, the old training returns to me like muscle memory. I help Ixion out of his livery and into a sleeping smock and fix my gaze on anything else in the room but the object of my hatred: his desk, strewn with papers, beside a high bookshelf.

It seems a shame you can't read, Julia once remarked.

You could teach me.

Her answer, teasing: *But then you'd know what I was writing.*

Pain shoots through my palm. I look down.

Ixion has taken my hand. His fingers prod the bandage again, testing it. He looks up at me, searching for a reaction. I can smell the wine on his breath; I can dimly see, in the candlelight, the chain of my dragon's key beneath the smock I just pulled over his shoulders. Within reach.

With fingers clumsy from drink, Ixion removes Delo's bandage and tosses it on the floor. Then, smiling into my face all the while, he digs fingers into the cut on my hand until it reopens.

"That's better," he says. "Good night."

5

SOUTHSIDE'S DAUGHTER

ANNIE

The first meeting of the War Council that I attend alongside General Holmes and the First Protector, we discuss the aerial attack on New Pythos being planned for late fall. It must happen before the cold takes the dragons' fire, but after as many as possible of our fleet have sparked. New Pythos is naturally well fortified but not impregnable; Holmes believes a retaliatory strike is overdue.

I listen with half a mind on his words, the other half on the fact that for the first time since Lee's duel, I'm in the presence of Atreus Athanatos. I sit at the far end of a table he heads. Atreus has not looked at me once during the meeting; for the most part he listens rather than speaks as Holmes directs the agenda. The Protector's usual drab tunic, a particular contrast to the others' uniforms, would make a less imposing man fade into the background of this room. As it is, I am aware of his every movement, like a hare sensing a hawk.

A man like Atreus cannot be the sort to take thwarting lightly.

The notes I have prepared are clutched in my lap beneath the table, and by the time it's my turn to speak, I've folded and unfolded them so many times they are as soft as fabric.

"Antigone?"

"I wanted to propose an alternative strategy."

I am the most junior officer at this table by several years and the only female. Since assuming the title of Firstrider I've become more comfortable with public speaking, but that confidence seems to have fled me now. My voice sounds high in my own ears, and to my horror, it shakes slightly. I can't look at Atreus; but I also have trouble looking at any of the other senior officials currently studying me over their spectacles.

"We have reason to believe the Pythians are employing a subclass of riders. Probably from the native Norcian population of the island. They ride dragons that are muzzled."

Stirring around the table. The general's chief of staff looks up from his notes; he's the one official who's close to my age. "Why is this the first time we've heard of this?" he asks.

I look at Holmes, slightly desperate. He knows I've made contact with the Pythians, because he reamed me for it. But I can't exactly cite that unauthorized venture now. To my relief, Holmes lifts a hand at his chief of staff. "That's all right, Colonel Orthos. You have . . . eyewitness evidence . . . of such a subclass, Antigone?"

Orthos. Why is that name familiar?

To my relief, when I nod, Holmes does not inquire further. I unfold my notes but do not look at them. "I would like to seek the support of these riders. The Norcians are likely to want to buck dragonborn rule as much as Callipolan peasants did. They could make valuable allies on the inside. But not if we're bombarding their homes."

A tremor is going through my hand and I can feel heat creeping up my neck. But the collar of my uniform goes high, and in the somber lighting of the War Room it's possible they can't see it.

Holmes's chief of staff speaks again, his Palace-standard accent ringing crisply. "If it's a question of stomach . . ."

It takes me a moment to understand: He's referring to *my* stomach. As if I propose an alternative to air strikes out of squeamishness.

Two white-haired admirals glance at each other.

I clench my fists beneath the table.

What was it Cor told me, at my promotion? *If you want them to listen to you, you need their respect.*

"I've got the stomach to burn as many Pythian peasants as necessary, but I'd rather avoid it in cases where it would go against our strategic goals."

The word *peasant* has been banned since the Revolution; I throw it down like a glove, knowing I am the only person in this room to whom it refers. At the far end of the table, Atreus drums fingers lightly on the table; the chief of staff's thin lip curls, and I glare back at him.

Holmes's brows have traveled up his forehead. "I think we need to find out more before we can speak to the strategic possibilities of these . . . lowborn riders."

Reasonable enough. So I propose the first step.

"Then we should send out a scouting mission before an attack is launched. Our maps of New Pythos are decades old. I'd like to pinpoint targets and take surveys of the territory beforehand to minimize collateral damage."

"We could send out a scouting mission," the chief of staff says.

I stare at him. Unless I misheard, he just said exactly the same thing I did. Holmes nods at him.

"I think that would be a good compromise. Would that satisfy you, Antigone? Might be a good way to find out more about these—muzzled riders, too."

The members of the War Council are all waiting for my answer, the chief of staff smiling benevolently. No one else seems to have noticed what just happened; am I churlish, petty, to be so bothered? What does it matter if they didn't notice I was the one who asked for what they've decided to give me?

"I believe," says a cool voice from the end of the table, "that a scouting mission was exactly what the Firstrider had proposed."

I lift my eyes to Atreus, and find his lips curved into the smallest of smiles.

I stare back at him. Am I mistaken, or is Atreus *backing* me?

The chief of staff's sneer slides from his face, but Holmes doesn't notice. "Excellent!" he says, waving a hand. "Then we'll send a pair of skyfish as soon as the cloud coverage is favorable."

* * *

Back in the Cloister, at an all-corps meeting, I debrief the Guardians about the War Council's pivot toward offensive action and then, for the first time, I describe the muzzled dragon that Power and I encountered while returning Julia's body. The reaction among the dragonriders is visceral: I have to wait for their expressions of horror to subside, for the wooden chairs of the oration room to stop creaking as Guardians shift in their seats. The members of the War Council might not understand what a muzzle on a dragon means for the dragon or the rider, but the corps does.

We can all imagine what it would feel like.

Looking up at the concentric rows of Guardians surrounding me as I address them from the sunken rostrum, I take a moment to appreciate that with this audience, at least, my voice sounds sure. "Holmes would like to deploy a skyfish scouting mission to survey targets and further assess the situation with the muzzled riders. I'd like to unofficially extend the mission objective to outreach. Can a muzzled rider be singled out? Can a line of communication be opened?"

"How?" Lotus asks. "None of us speak Norish."

Norish, the language of the Norcian population on New Pythos, is a linguistic cousin of Callish, but far enough removed that communication would be next to impossible.

Unless your muzzled riders have been trained to speak the language of their oppressors.

"The lowborn rider we encountered spoke fluent Dragontongue."

Power sits in the back row, beside Darius. "Can confirm. He spoke it loads better than Antigone."

"Thanks, Power."

Lotus whistles. "Of course they do. I'll go."

Lotus, a poet's son born to a patrician family on the Janiculum, grew up speaking Dragontongue, just like Lee.

"Me too," Crissa says, lifting a hand. "Put my drawing skills to use for those survey maps."

Duck's hand shoots into the air. "Shouldn't I go instead of Lotus? Crissa's Dragontongue is decent, and my dragon's the only skyfish besides hers who's sparked."

"Way to rub it in," Lotus mutters.

Rock pats him on the back. "Any day now, mate."

Cor shifts in his chair. Our eyes catch. Duck's point is valid, but there is a history offsetting it: He has a history of fumbling under pressure; a history of getting injured; and more than that, I have a history of losing it when he gets injured, and so does Cor.

Duck is glaring at me, flushing; Lotus has sunk in his chair, arms folded. From the back of the room, Alexa whispers to Deirdre behind a cupped hand, and she giggles.

At this point, with fatigue the defining mood of most corps briefings, a bit of levity is a good sign. But it's harder to feel that way when you suspect it's at your expense. I feel a flash of impatience: It's one thing to have to arbitrate fairness in the squares of Callipolis where rations are being doled, but quite another with Guardians fighting over the opportunity to go risk their necks.

I open my palms on the rostrum. "For the time being, all skyfish riders will train for the possibility of being sent on the scouting mission."

My gaze lifts to the far doorway and I see the single figure who stands in it.

Lee.

I haven't visited him since that afternoon, when I went to the infirmary ward and found Crissa in my place; I told myself I was too busy. Now more than a week later, seeing him back in uniform and on his feet, I feel uncertainty flood my limbs, rooting me to the rostrum. The others, following my gaze, are looking over their shoulders. It's the first time most of them have seen him since he returned from the duel.

Before I can say anything, Rock lumbers to his feet and places a fist to his chest in the Revolutionary salute.

"Welcome back, Citizen."

Lee swallows. Then he nods, lifting his fist to return the salute.

One by one, the other Guardians follow Rock's lead. Power and Darius remain sitting, but they're among the few who do.

"Thank you," Lee murmurs, and the salutes shift to applause.

The corps surrounds him while I hand out schedules at the end of the meeting. They clap him on the shoulder, welcoming him back, embracing him. I watch him field their affection with that old admiration mingling with frustration, the bitterer for the time I've spent stumbling to fill his shoes: He always makes it look so *easy*.

It seems to take the room forever to empty, and for us to be alone.

He looks better than he did, his dark hair combed, the color returned to his pale face. Lingering bandages edge from beneath the cuffs of his uniform. I search those gray eyes for some indication of what sits behind: whether it will be the Lee I know or the Lee I saw smiling that terrible smile in the infirmary.

He squints at the ground between us. "How are you?"

The Lee I know, then. For the time being. And it's so easy to pretend certain words were never said. That's Lee's and my specialty.

"Stomping out fires," I tell him, snapping my satchel over my shoulder. "Turns out that's a large part of this job."

Lee's lip quirks. "Sorry. Should have warned you."

He wears no decoration except the wings of the Fourth Order; the Firstrider medal that he once wore on his breast is now on mine, where he pinned it after the duel. I reach into my bag and hold out the badge that's been waiting for him, of aurelian squadron leader. His old rank, that he shared with Cor and Crissa before the Firstrider Tournament.

He takes the badge, his eyes flicking, lightning fast, to the Firstrider medal on my chest.

"Thank you," he says.

We make our way out of the oration room together, then down the hall of the Cloister to the refectory, where breakfast is being served. It's late enough in autumn that fires have been lit in the stone hearths and Guardians are clustered at the ends of tables close to the warmth. Not until we join the line for porridge, and I notice Lee staring, do I remember what has changed since he was last here. A sign beside the porridge, scrawled in Rock's hand, reads:

4 scoops = Gold rations
1 scoop = Iron rations
Please serve yourself responsibly and return unwanted
portions, which will be shared with Cloister staff.

Lee's mouth has twisted into a frown. I explain, in a low voice so the two patrician Guardians in line ahead of us won't hear, "Rock and I started doing this after we realized some of the riders were throwing away uneaten food."

Rock and I lived on highland farms during the last famine in Callipolis, the one that led to the uprisings that became the Revolution. We're among the few in the Guardian corps who remember what it's like to starve.

Lee as well. His family may have been well off during the Famine, but in the years after the Revolution, he and I went hungry in that orphanage together. So I'm not surprised when his frown deepens. He watches me serve myself—a single scoop, on the principle that I should be setting the expectation for the rest of the corps, even if it leaves my stomach growling—and takes the same. He doesn't speak until we've taken seats at an empty table.

"I'd forgotten about ration stratification."

So that's what he's frowning about. Not the fact that Guardians were wasting food.

"We're enforcing it daily. You'll have a hard time forgetting about it now that you're back."

I don't realize until now how much I've missed the sight of him. Not just his face but his movements: the way he sits, the way the corded muscle of his forearm shifts as he pulls the bowl of porridge toward him, how he flicks dark hair from his eyes with absentminded precision as he stares down at the near-empty bowl. Lee makes even the act of eating porridge graceful.

And I can't quite keep my thoughts from the memory of those arms pressing my body to his, that neck under my lips—

And then he mutters, "Annie, how are we going to stop this?"

I drop my eyes from his jawline and fumble for my porridge spoon. "Stop what?"

Lee pushes the bowl away from him with sudden violence. "This. Everything Atreus is doing. People getting different amounts of food based on their metals test. When are we going to get rid of that *bastard*—"

His voice is rising; the edge of anger that fuels his words sets my nerves on end. It's so uncharacteristic of Lee that people turn. Cor is one of them, his brow lifting.

I mark the change in me from a month ago, how I hear words differently now: not what Lee's saying, but what others are hearing. This isn't a conversation that should be overheard by the corps. Not when the war threat and rationing distribution already leave morale on the brink.

"Keep your voice down. Finish your porridge. We can talk about this in the armory."

I think it will cool us both, taking the dragons out. But in the armory, stripping down as we've done for years to shimmy into our flamesuits, there is a moment when I look at him and he looks at me, and I feel that heat again on my own skin. And then I see the new burns, pale and shining, a geography of wounds still healing from the duel down his side.

I turn away to clear my head and speak with my back turned.

"Here's the thing, Lee." I fasten the breast of my flamesuit, up to the neck, and reach for my cuirass. "Atreus is a bastard but he's a neutralized threat. You've got the High Council backing you, not to mention the Janiculum, thanks to Dora Mithrides. The stratified rationing program is a mess, but I've been on Iron rations for weeks, and they're still better than Albans was on a bad day. *We can make it through this winter.* But not if the city is tearing itself apart. There are people in New Pythos waiting for us to fail. Do you know what Ixion called me, when I gave them Julia's body?"

I've turned to face him, reaching for my arm guards from my cubby. Lee is seated, working up the laces of his boots, but his expression of shock as I name Julia's brother is plain on his face when he looks up.

"He called me a peasant bitch, and he said I belonged to him."

Lee twitches, his fingers frozen on his laces.

"That's what we're up against. Not Atreus."

His jaw is clenching. I think, for a moment, that I've gotten through to him. And then he gets to his feet, turns his back to me, and says: "You've gotten really good at giving speeches in the last month."

LEE

I'd been looking forward to getting out of the infirmary ever since the burns began to heal and the walls began to press too close. The Cloister, the meals with the corps and homework at the fireside of the solarium, Pallor in the air over the arena. I pictured it the way it's always been, and I longed for it. It was what I imagined to push memories of the duel from my head.

But now, finding it exactly the way it's always been, it's infuriating.

How are they all just going on with their business, running the Protector's programs as if nothing has changed?

The person I'd missed most, for her absence as the other Guardians trickled through the ward with their halting greetings and their clumsy attempts at comfort, was Annie. But she didn't return, and I knew why she didn't. The words I said the morning after the duel are hard to remember, but I remember the blind rage, and her face by the end. I left the infirmary intending to apologize. But the more I see, the more I feel the desire fading.

Why is Annie going along with all of this? How can she defend Atreus?

Pallor, at least, I can return to without shame or anger. When I find him in his nest, he bounds toward me with such a rush of joy that it spills from him to me, and for a moment, it suffuses us.

"Missed you, Pal."

I've come with a bucket of fish from the Palace reservoir prepared by his keepers. Pallor happily roasts and guzzles them one by one as I look him over. The claw marks from the duel are healing well; the keepers have kept his silver scales shining and his talons clean.

"New tack for you."

The saddle and bridle were damaged in combat. Pallor wriggles in the stiff new leather, getting comfortable, and I find myself holding a breath as I climb onto his back. Trying not to think about what it was like to do this two weeks ago, when I was going out to face Julia.

The cave air cools my face as we take flight.

We exit the nests through the arena gate, and Pallor lands us on the stone platform of the Eyrie without my prompting. The familiar bowl of the arena walls encircles us and the karst of Pytho's Keep towers over us, glowing in the afternoon light. Dragons fill the air overhead, coasting on a brisk autumn breeze. A few yards up, Aela's amber wings glow translucent in the sunlight and Annie watches the other pairs of dragonriders spar.

The last time I saw the Firstrider's training bugle now strapped across her back, I was wearing it.

"You coming up?" Annie calls.

I take in the sight of the riders above us—sparring, drilling, preparing for war—and when I imagine joining them, something in me balks.

"In a bit."

Annie doesn't press it. In the air above us, she begins to lead drills. Pallor nudges, just a bit of pressure, so that I settle onto the stone bench beside him, and he leans into my hand until I begin to scratch the itchy spots under his horns. He is as content to sit this one out as I am.

Soon I'm so focused on relieving his every itch that I hardly notice when Cor takes the seat beside me. "Mind if I join?"

Cor doesn't try to make conversation. His visits in the infirmary were similarly brusque: never talking about the duel or asking how I was feeling with that bashful look the others had, which I was grateful for. Maurana curls beside him, smoke gray and monstrous besides Pallor's smaller silver form. The dragons study each other for a calculating, territorial moment, pupils turning to slits and horned tails swishing, before losing interest entirely. They curl up on the flagstones to soak in the late autumn sun while Cor and I lean back to observe the training overhead. Annie has the skyfish training for the scouting mission, with aurelians in pursuit for evasive drills.

"She's not bad," I finally allow. I don't intend for it to sound as grudging as it does.

Cor doesn't ask whom I mean. He's tracking someone else. "No. But you know who *is* bad?"

Duck sur Certa. Their weave is so regular that pursuers get them every time. And then they always slow.

"Why does he keep acting like there's a reset? This isn't a sporting drill."

"Right," Cor says, a line between his brows. "I'm just hoping Lotus sparks so he can go instead."

By the time Duck makes the same mistake for the third time and Annie has switched from patiently reminding him to shouting, Cor has his head in his hands and I'm mounting Pallor.

It does feel good to be in the air with a sky like this: cloudless, blue, crisp as an apple. Pallor snorts with delight, wings going taut on the breeze, and for a moment his joy trickles into me.

But then I tug my thoughts free of Pallor's. Right now especially, I need a clear head.

"Hey, Duck?"

Annie, Duck, and Crissa are coasting on the breeze, a few meters higher than the other pairs who are drilling. At the sound of my voice, they turn in the saddle. Annie, who's been shouting, falls silent and looks at me with her helmet cocked. Duck, who's already hunching, hunches further at the sight of my approach, like he knows he's about to get another earful. Certa's wings contract with channeled nerves and they bump down a few feet on the current we're all coasting.

"Yeah?" Duck says.

"You're going to have to keep weaving, even if you get hit, all right? This isn't like we do for tournaments. There aren't resets."

I know, from how Annie's eyes narrow, that this is exactly what she just told Duck. Aela tosses her head and snorts with a puff of ash. But Duck's gaze flickers over me like he's seeing something for the first time.

Yeah, that's right. I'm telling you from experience, you idiot.

"Okay," he says.

"So let's do it again, and this time, I want you to keep swerving no matter how many hits Antigone lands, all right?"

"Okay," Duck says again.

Crissa sur Phaedra coasts beside me as we watch Annie and Duck take off for another round. This time, though Certa's weave remains painfully regular, Duck's first grunt at Annie's hit is not accompanied by a decrease in velocity.

Better.

"Will you drill it with us, too?" Crissa asks.

Her helmet's on but her visor's up, and her bright blue eyes search my face. Her skyfish's narrow wings and slender tail blend, iridescent, with the autumn sky.

I felt relieved when she'd informed me, after the duel, *We're friends now.* It was the thing I knew needed to be done even as it overwhelmed me, with everything else that had happened, to attempt to say. Because whatever else I wondered after kissing Annie—after coming back to Annie, after saying things I shouldn't have to Annie—the one thing I knew was that I was not in a place to be with anyone else.

Crissa didn't need that to be explained. And when I'd apologized for doing it all in the wrong order, she only shook her head.

"I do usually prefer a conversation first. But I think a prison cell counts as mitigating circumstances. Anyway . . . I told Annie to go to you that night."

As soon as she said it, I realized it couldn't have happened otherwise. "Why?"

Crissa lifted a shoulder, a brow raising. "Honestly? I think I was just sick of you two being idiots."

I laughed, startled. Crissa laughed, too, a little self-consciously. Then she changed the subject.

The friendship remained. She had visited me almost daily in the infirmary after that, bringing books as she had when I was in the stockade, making jokes and conversation when I didn't have it in me to speak. The biggest difference—in the stockade we had held hands and kissed, and in the infirmary we never touched— didn't change the fact that Crissa's still one of the easiest people in the world to talk to.

Now, when she asks to drill with me, I realize that even the thought of practicing a combative drill is turning my stomach. But so is the thought of Crissa unprotected in enemy territory.

"Yeah. Of course."

We set at drilling distance, and then she and Phaedra take off and Pallor and I pursue.

Crissa sur Phaedra's weave is a beautiful thing. Skyfish are known for their speed, their flexibility, and Phaedra uses both to her advantage in a weave that is almost impossible to predict and nevertheless as fast as Pallor at his fastest. We're hot on their tail, firing ash that never quite lands, when Crissa sur Phaedra goes bold: diving down, as if to loop behind us. We fire; the hit grazes Crissa's side, and she lets out a grunt of pain that echoes in the empty arena.

And suddenly I'm somewhere else. Somewhere I don't want to be.

"Julia?"

A shot of ash hits me square in the chest, a kill shot. The heat brings me back to my senses as half-healed burns sear with renewed pain.

Crissa hit me head on with a shot I should have been able to dodge in my sleep.

But I didn't even see it coming.

Pallor whimpers, my pain pulsing through him, and that's how I realize we've spilled over. As I force him out of my head, I realize, with a burst of shame, what I just said.

"Lee?" Crissa says.

We're not the only ones who've paused in midair. Many of the drill partners seem to have taken the time to watch Crissa's and my pursuit; Annie, finished pursuing Duck, coasts a few yards away, her eyes narrowed and the Firstrider's bugle frozen halfway to her lips.

Great.

I rein Pallor down and return to the Eyrie.

ANNIE

It goes on like this for days. Lee refuses to participate in drill sessions, and I avoid putting him on patrols on the northern coast. The whispered rumor that lights through the corps, I know, is that he has flameshock. A word we've seen in history books about the Bassilean Wars to describe dragonlords who had difficulty, after particularly traumatic experiences in the air, with returning to battle.

I don't care what it's called. I'm worried that when the time comes to launch that attack on New Pythos, my top rider won't be ready for combat.

I see him occasionally with Crissa, more often with Cor. We are not alone together again.

Until the morning when I receive a memo from the Ministry of Propaganda, copied to the entire Guardian corps, that school morale visits promoting the metals test are to go in effect today, with an attached schedule.

I read the name listed beside my own and my stomach sinks.

Cor, hunched over one of the solarium tables, has the list in front of him, too.

"Have you seen—?"

He jerks a thumb behind him. "Dorm."

Lee is folding laundry at his bed and frowning at it like it's a problem he's solving.

"We're on morale visits again," I tell him, holding out the schedule. "Schools this time. They want you and me going to Cheapside Grammar this afternoon."

Lee doesn't take the schedule. "No," he says.

"No what?"

"No, I'm not going. I'm done being a show pony for Atreus. No more morale visits."

After a missed night of sleep taking a night patrol I didn't feel comfortable putting Lee on, I find this a bit hard to take.

"People are scared and it's our duty to reassure them. I don't care how you feel about Atreus, I need you to *do your job*."

His lip twists.

"Are we still talking about morale visits, Annie?"

So he's been hearing the whispers about flameshock, too. He turns away, yanks fresh sheets out of the laundry basket, and begins making his bed. I watch the muscles ripple down his back as he snaps sheets across the frame and imagine closing the distance. To do what—slap him?

How was it that mere weeks ago I kissed this boy like my life depended on it? Now I only want to shake him.

"This is the regime you chose," I tell him.

Lee pauses, hands planted on the bed, and looks at me. And then he snorts, like I've made a stupid joke without meaning to, and not the kind he finds funny.

"Yeah," he says, turning from me, "it is."

The desire to shake him drains. Guilt floods in its place.

"Lee—"

"I could go."

Duck stands by the door, like he isn't sure he should enter the rest of the way. "Sorry. I heard you two . . . talking."

His square jaw juts; I wonder what word he decided not to use. And I can't decide if I'm relieved he interrupted us, or furious. He reminds me: "We've done morale visits together before."

Lee begins stuffing folded shirts into a drawer. "It's some grammar school in Cheapside, Duck."

His tone is so dismissive that my eyes suddenly burn. *Some grammar school in Cheapside?* That's what he calls it? That was our school. Dirty and poor and echoing, but also the place where we took the test that changed us from slum orphans into Guardians. That school gave us everything.

Why won't he look at me?

Duck lifts his shoulders, shrugging off Lee's warning. "I'm good with kids."

LEE

The anger simmers even after she's left with Duck. At Atreus and his stupid morale visits, at Annie for taking orders from him like he still deserves to give them, at myself for making Annie blink like I'd hit her when I dismissed Cheapside Grammar.

And once the door slams and I imagine her going without me, I feel like an ass.

But if I went after her, I'm not sure whether it would be to apologize or fight some more.

I finish up the laundry, seize my book bag, and head for the Cloister library.

I'm behind in classwork since the duel, but without the duties of Firstridership, I've got time to catch up. Thanks to Annie keeping me off patrols of the north coast, and letting me skive off drills, I've got all the time in the world.

I'm still fuming when I run headfirst into Cor.

He's slipping out of the kitchen with a bag clutched in two hands, and freezes at the sight of me. "Lee?"

"What are you doing?"

Cor's face washes with emotions. Finally, his shoulders lift up between his ears and he mutters, "I was getting spare food for my sister."

I don't have to ask which sister. Cor only has one old enough to have gotten results back from the metals test, and a reading disability resulted in her getting Iron—*unskilled*. Meaning that she's allotted even fewer ration cards than Cor's parents, who are class-bronze.

"I know it's not"—Cor's voice rises—"fair, taking it from the kitchens, that's what Annie and Rock would say—"

"Annie and I used to steal from the kitchens in Albans all the time."

Cor blinks. "You didn't get in trouble?"

"Only if we got caught."

A slow grin spreads across Cor's face, and then he lets out a bark of laughter.

I can feel my face contorting, doing something it hasn't in a while, and then I realize I'm grinning, too.

I end up going down into the city with him. Not only that, we go to Cheapside. The added thrill of moonlighting in the same neighborhood where I'm supposed to be performing a morale visit only lifts my spirits more. This must be the appeal people like Power find in breaking the rules. Like you're trying a flick roll a little too close to the ground.

Cor's sister Ana has been transferred from her old textile house to bunker construction, Cor explains as we make our way across the River Fer. Blackout regulations, bunkers, cannons mounted on the Aurelian Walls—all have been a part of the city mobilizing against the threat of air strikes from New Pythos. The streets are leaf-strewn in autumn, and the propaganda posters have changed in the wake of the rationing crisis, now reading TIGHTEN YOUR BELTS FOR CALLIPOLIS and—one I find myself staring at—RATIONING MEANS FAIR SHARES FOR ALL.

Cor, noticing it as well, grimaces. "Shameless, isn't it? The ministry defines *fair* as 'each getting what they deserve.'"

It's the first time I realize that even if Annie and I aren't on the same page about rationing stratification, Cor and I might be.

Down in Cheapside, off the main square, we enter a gate marked NO TRESPASSING—MINISTRY PROPERTY and find class-iron workers carting backfill from the pit that will be turned into a bunker with bricks baked from the unearthed clay. The faces I see are drawn, cheekbones jutting, skin sallow. It's the first time it really hits me that the Iron rations I've been taking, in solidarity with Annie and those who have the stomach for it, are far more easily stretched across a day spent in study than in hard labor.

"Ana!"

Cor waves at a worker coming up the slope from the pit behind one of the carts. I've met Cor and Duck's sister a few times before but today barely recognize her, covered as she is head to toe in clay dust. She pulls the scarf down from her nose and mouth, revealing a strip of dust-free golden skin, and smiles.

"Fancy seeing you two here," she says.

Discreetly, Cor holds out the bag; Ana takes it. "Cheeses and dried sausage," he mutters in Damian, a language I have passing knowledge of from grammar school. "Can you go on break?"

Ana shakes her head. "Already took it."

"Anything I can do for you, sirs?"

The foreman approaches, visibly sweating from the prospect of a Callipolan official faced with an unexpected visit from Guardians: As Callipolis's rulers-in-training, we have an uneasy status as observers who will one day be superiors. Cor scowls as he looks the foreman over, taking in his bronze wristband and plump face.

Years of practice managing Cor kicks in on instinct. I lay a hand on his arm and smile at the foreman. "No, thanks, we're just leaving. Keep up the good work, Citizen."

Ana kisses Cor on the cheek, thanks him in their mother's tongue, and walks away with the bag tucked under her arm. The foreman bows us out of his construction site with a look of relief.

Outside, in Cheapside's central square, Cor kicks at the dirt with frustration that he doesn't bother to articulate. By any standards, Cheapside isn't the sort of place to improve a mood, but now less than ever: Many of its shopfronts have been boarded up from the crisis, the number of beggars multiplied and street vendors halved. As early as last summer, merchants stopped us with gifts of fruit as we passed, but today as we cross the square, no one, not even beggars, meets our eye.

Not that we would have anything to give them if they did; Guardians take vows of poverty.

"Cor!"

It takes me a moment to place the young woman weaving her way toward us: We know her from the Lyceum; she sat in the back of Dragontongue last term. In class, she never wore the green work scarf that binds her hair today.

"Megara!" Cor clasps her arm with a grin. "What are you doing in Cheapside?"

Megara smiles. "Slumming it," she says, with a rattle of her Gold wristband. She turns to me. "I don't know if we were ever actually introduced. My name's Megara. Megara Roper."

If I remember anything of her from class, it was that she talked as rarely as I did. Stripped of that context, Megara Roper seems to radiate energy. She has the same tan complexion and hard vowels as Cor, placing her somewhere between Highmarket and Southside, and shakes my hand with a firm grip.

"Megara and I know each other from grammar school," Cor explains.

"Went to the Choosing together, too," Megara adds. "Only ones from our year who scored high enough."

"You were passed over?" I ask.

Megara smiles, but her smile has an edge to it. Her eyes are startlingly green. "Obviously."

"My brother was a *passus*, too," I tell her, on impulse.

I've spent a lifetime not talking about family, but today I find the sudden urge to break the taboo. Like coming to Cheapside for the wrong reason, it feels reckless, and reckless feels good. Besides, lots of Callipolans have siblings who were *passi* thanks to the new regime's Guardian recruitment program. It doesn't mean the same thing it once did.

"Was he disappointed?" Megara asks.

They had to pull him away from the stormscourges he lingered in front of, he was so devastated. I nod.

Megara's strange smile flickers. "And that brother, he'd be Laertes Stormscourge?"

His name hits like a bucket of cold water.

"No need for coyness," Megara adds, gazing at me without blinking as Cor fidgets the toe of his boot in the dust of the cobblestones. "Most people know. And they know you killed kin to prove your loyalty."

I've spent years expecting knowledge of my identity to lead to a clubbing. But as I realize she's not joking, and doesn't mind that I'm a dragonlord's son or the story that goes with it, I nod slowly.

Megara arches a brow. "You're a real hero of Callipolis, if you ask me."

She marches away across the square of Cheapside, in the direction of the Cheapside dragon perch, pulling at her green scarf and freeing her long black hair.

Cor snickers. "You could *try* to look less pleased with yourself—"

I shove him, and he lets out a burst of laughter. Still, walking back to the Palace, my tread feels lightened.

ANNIE

School morale visits are performed without dragons, so Duck and I make our way on foot down to Cheapside Grammar. The school smells the way I remember, a combination of stale sweat and bleach, and the windows made from gaps in the cinder blocks seem even smaller. Nevertheless, unlike with Albans Orphanage, I have good memories of this place. School was always where I knew what to do. Where I was in control.

The headmistress's bun is as tight as I remember it, though grayer. When she asks about Lee, I stutter an answer while Duck watches, curious. This, like Holbin, is a part of my past life I've rarely discussed with him.

"You two were inseparable," the headmistress remembers.

My tongue is thick in my mouth as I nod and smile at her.

In the classroom, Duck takes a stool to the side of the room, I'm led to the front, and we're introduced as *very special visitors.*

"Dorian and Antigone—Annie—are both Guardians who ride dragons. Did you know, Annie used to go to school here?" There are gasps of excitement. "She took the metals test, just like you will, and scored so well she was chosen to become a Guardian. She's come here today to talk to us all about the metals system."

My speech has been standardized, prepared by the Ministry of Propaganda, almost identical to the spiels I remember hearing in school at this age, and I can recite it because I know it cold. But maybe there's something about reciting it here, now—in front of forty young faces, faces of children I'm sworn to protect, whom New Pythos threatens—that makes me hear it differently. I hear myself say it as I once heard it.

A miracle.

When they first told us about the metals test, I almost didn't believe them. A test that could let you be anybody? A test that could earn you a dragon? *People like us don't ride dragons,* I remember telling Lee. Back when I thought he was like us, another lowborn orphan.

But I was wrong, about Lee and about the dragons. And when my test result came, it changed my life.

Looking back, I can't remember most of it. A written portion, where they asked questions that were partly math and partly logic and sometimes straight-up moral dilemmas. A physical portion, where we competed in a gymnasium and adults watched. Because the test isn't supposed to measure pure intelligence or fitness. It's supposed to find what you're good at. What you're meant for. As reflected in the four test results: Gold, for *philosophical,* of highest value to the operations of the state; Silver, for *spirited*, the military class; Bronze, for *skilled labor*, and Iron, for *unskilled*. And, in a few very exceptional cases: *spirited* and *philosophical* together, the Guardian class. Wristbands of silver entwined with gold, which, tested blindly, even a serf's daughter like me could rise to become.

That's what we're fighting for. That's what I'm protecting.

When I'm finished, the children applaud. It's the loudest I can remember anyone applauding at a speech I've given.

In the time for questions, I call on a child whose hand stretches so far into the air her backside has left its seat.

"Do you ever fly your dragon upside down?"

The next child asks, "When you were flying in that tournament that time, and you did this"—he gestures with his hands in an impossible wiggle—"what was that?"

He stares at me, offering no further explanation, awaiting my answer.

"Er . . ."

"Questions about the *metals test*," the teacher reminds them.

The third child's forehead is shining with sweat, his face screwed up with the effort of remembering what he wants to say.

"Jeremy?"

"My dad says they're giving everyone different amounts of food based on their metals," Jeremy says, and slumps in his chair.

The teacher twirls her bronze wristband—most schoolteachers are Bronze, though there are the odd Golds in lower education as well—and glances at me, suddenly nervous.

Duck hops to his feet.

"Which breed of dragon's faster, skyfish or aurelian?" he asks the class.

"Skyfish!" the children bellow.

"Right you are! Another question for you, which is *heavier*, a stormscourge or a . . ."

He keeps going, first about domestic breeds and then foreign—*how many stormscourges would it take to bring down a goliathan?*—and by the end, the children are shouting with excitement, and cheer us out the door.

On the streets of Cheapside, Duck apologizes. "Hope you didn't mind me jumping in. I know there's that answer we're supposed to give—"

The ministry-approved answer to questions about rations is *Everyone is receiving the rations they deserve.*

"No. What you did was better."

But no sooner have we rounded the corner into the main square of Cheapside than we find a full-blown demonstration under way about exactly the same thing. A young woman with long black hair and a green scarf covering her nose and mouth is shouting from the dais at the foot of the Cheapside dragon perch, and her shouts are echoed by the surrounding crowd.

"Southside's Daughter wants full rations for all!" she cries, her fist in the air.

Full rations for all! Full rations for all!

"No longer will our sons and daughters slave for quarter rations while Gold bellies are full!"

It's not the first time I've seen a rally like this since rationing began, but it's the largest. It's also illegal: Public demonstrations that disturb the peace are outlawed by Revolutionary law.

"Fair means equal!" she cries.

The crowd takes up the chant. *Fair means equal!*

The girl who calls herself Southside's Daughter is confident, poised, feeding off the energy of her audience. Her speechmaking skills remind me of Lee's. I'm also pretty sure the wristband she's unclasped from her wrist, in violation of the wristband laws, and is waving before the crowd, is gold.

A street name, a masked face, a crowd riled: Everything about this scene looks like an explosion about to go off.

"Should we do something?"

Duck frowns. "Do what? We don't have dragons . . ."

But now some from the crowd are turning their attention to a bakery on the opposite side of the square. Its shopfront is closed, but the citizens begin hammering on the glass, the doors. *Bread for all!* Duck, whose family owns a bakery in a different neighborhood, bites his lip at the sight.

"We should alert the city guard. They'll sack that place if they aren't dispersed."

After we've alerted the nearest guardhouse, we make our way back to the Palace through Highmarket.

"Mind if I check on Mum and Dad?"

I don't question his reason. We find his family's bakery in Highmarket deserted, unharmed, closed for the afternoon. Highmarket's concentration of Bronze artisans and Gold customers from across the river leave it one of the neighborhoods least prone to unrest of those on the Lower Bank. When we duck inside to greet his family, Mrs. Sutter embraces me, leaving imprints of flour on my uniform, and Mr. Sutter congratulates me on my promotion. But when Mrs. Sutter asks if we can stay for tea, Duck shakes his head.

"Sorry, Mum—I've got to be back by sundown."

At my look of surprise, Duck pulls a letter from his pocket and passes it to me while he hugs his parents goodbye.

It's an authorization of deployment from the War Council. Crissa sur Phaedra and Dorian sur Certa are to fly out this evening.

From the date, it looks like Duck received it this morning, right before he offered to do a morale visit with me in Lee's stead.

A host of protests rise to my lips: that I requested Lotus, not Duck, as Crissa's partner; that Duck should have told me the memo came in; that we've been wasting the afternoon walking around the city and visiting his mum and dad when he should have been getting ready.

And then I realize why he must have wanted to spend today thus, and swallow.

"Give my love to Greg and Merina," Duck tells his parents. "And Ana, when you see her."

Out on the steps, I tell him: "You'll do great."

Duck smiles. "It was nice to spend the afternoon with you," he answers. "Like old times."

6

THE MELEE

GRIFF

The problem, originally, with serving Ixion was that I was a show-off. But we were kids; all of us were show-offs. Now I know better. This time, I'm not going to put a foot out of line. When training resumes after Julia's funeral, I partner with Ixion instead of Delo, and I give him everything he wants. Not easy victories, because Ixion likes a good struggle. But I let him win.

I'll give him no cause to feed my limbs to Niter. No cause to have Scully dock my pay. No cause to mention Agga's name.

Sparker hates it. I hate it. But it doesn't matter. On the whole, when training concludes, I'm congratulating myself on a day in Ixion's service well done and starting to let myself think that maybe he's outgrown the old games, too.

Until we're back in the lairs and Ixion informs me that Sparker's been moved to stable beside Niter. I notice with a strangled feeling that it's smaller than his last nest. Sparker's already the largest in the aerial fleet; the last thing he needs is more confinement. His wings brush the stone walls even fully folded.

Ixion approaches Sparker to lock the lead, and Sparker doesn't know to contain the hatred I've been stanching: He growls, hackles rising.

Ixion turns back to me.

"Griff?"

I reach up and seize Sparker by the muzzle. Suddenly I'm terrified, not for myself, but for Sparker, and will him to understand. *"Heel."*

Sparker feels my fear and thrashes.

Ixion watches with a look of idle amusement. "If you can't control your beast, Griff—"

"I've got him. Do it."

Ixion reaches up, hooks the lead through the muzzle, and pulls. The lead shortens.

Keeps shortening.

Shorter than Delo'd do it in a hundred years. So short Sparker will barely have head. I can feel Sparker's panic as he realizes and bucks in fear, but it's my words that tumble out.

"Please not that short—"

Ixion smiles. He loosens the chain, slowly. Until it's still shorter than Delo did it by a foot, but enough that Sparker's snout is no longer forced to the floor.

"That's what will happen," Ixion says, "if either of you displeases me. Are we clear?"

I nod. I'm shaking.

Of course Ixion hasn't outgrown the old games. He's just gotten smarter at finding the kind he'll get away with.

From the stall beside us, Niter growls. Sparker growls back, but when Ixion's eyes flash, Sparker falls silent. He's leaning on me so heavily I have trouble standing upright, backed as far away from Ixion as the chain will allow.

All I want to do is comfort him.

But I can't, not until I'm done with Ixion, so after Ixion clicks the lock shut on Sparker's lead, I follow him up the spiral stairs to the Stormscourge armory. Another squire, Nolan, is cleaning the armor of the Stormscourge Bastards in the corner. We avoid looking at each other.

"Before you return to the lairs," Ixion says, "I'd like you to deliver a letter."

He hands it to me, unsealed.

"We've got a ship bound for Bassilea this afternoon. Take it down to the docks and give it to the captain, tell him he is to deliver it to her personally. Oh, and seal it, would you?"

From another lord, being entrusted with a seal might be taken as an honor, but I know how Ixion intends it: one more form of humiliation. He wants me to look at what he's written, and know I can make nothing of it, before stamping his crest upon it.

Her. Freyda, the Bassilean princess. I'm probably holding the news of Julia's death in my hands.

"Yes, my lord."

When he's gone, my shoulders slump. Nolan, polishing the armor of the Bastards, looks up and grins. "Not a bite on you! Ixion's gone soft."

I groan aloud. "How do you handle three of them?"

* * *

Word from Callipolis is that our attacks on their trade routes had exactly the effects we'd hoped on their food stores—the poor souls are apparently starving. I'd feel more triumphant about that if Norcians weren't always starving. With winter around the corner, the Triarchy-in-Exile isn't in a hurry to strike again.

Rhadamanthus, a great scholar of the philosophy of his invader ancestors, drones on at length about making a people want to be conquered, which Ixion finds fascinating, but I find to be a load of dragon's dung. I'm pretty sure no one on Norcia was happy when Tarquin the Conqueror showed up and told us to start mining.

But training continues as before, and Ixion seems to fear, as I do, that Julia has left boots too big to fill. He's touchy in the air, eager to run drills without Nestor's help, and sharp with the dragonborn who question him.

Ixion has always been a better strategist on the ground, and knows it.

Which is probably why he has me checking, daily, for a letter back from Bassilea—even though it's far too soon to receive it. I'm on one of these trips down to the harbor when my path crosses, for the first time since I was transferred, with Delo.

"Griff?"

"My lord?"

He's smiling as he lowers his hood, and at his smile something stupid somersaults inside me. Only now do I realize how much I've been missing the sight of him. We're on the wind-beaten trail that carves the cliff down to the main harbor, and there's just enough room for us to stand to the side as Norcian fishermen carting the day's catch up to the citadel skirt us on their way.

"You're all right?" he asks.

It's phrased not quite right, not quite on the level of small talk, and that's how I know he's asking about Ixion. "Aye, my lord."

"And your family? Sparker?"

I haven't spoken to Delo since the funeral, and I've managed not to think about him, or at least not much. Not to make too many comparisons between life before Julia's death and after because there was no point. But at this question, the barrier breaks. Agga's ginger is nearly gone, without a hope for more. And Sparker, in that tiny stall, his lead just a little too short, feels so cramped that most days working in the lairs close to him I can feel it. My throat tightens.

"We're all making do, my lord."

Delo's no longer smiling. A line grows between his fine brows. But he doesn't seem to know what else to ask, and I don't know what to say.

"Griff . . ."

That's it. That's how this ends. Years of serving him, turned to silence and stiffness on the side of a road as we both search for a way to end this encounter.

Because what? You thought you were friends? You were his squire and now you aren't. That's all.

I bow to him, nice and deep to make the point, and keep going.

It's been almost two weeks since I've started serving Ixion when the Triarchy-in-Exile and the Greatlord announce that they will observe the aerial fleet. The Triarchy observing always makes the humble-riders nervous. Fly too well, they get ruffled; fly too poorly, they get vindictive. But it's easy to see why today, their observing makes Ixion nervous as well: This is his first performance as Firstrider. He informs me of the observation with a pale face and glittering eyes before unlocking Sparker's lead.

"Embarrass me and I'll shorten his lead for a week."

My awareness of Sparker mounts with my elevating heart; I can feel his frustration spiking. Ixion's eyes are on mine, tracking my pupils for a spillover.

"Yes, my lord."

As soon as Ixion leaves the stall, Sparker growls.

This is why I was never able to hold back. Because he does crap like this. I feel Sparker's fury catch, hot and vicious, like oil on a fire.

Threaten me all you want. But threatening Sparker crosses a line.

When we land on the highest balustrade off the citadel, leaning out over the sheer cliffs of the northern face of New Pythos, the exiled Callipolan court and the Greatlord Rhadamanthus are gathered to observe. Most of the fleet are in the air already, awaiting a signal from Nestor. The wind flattens the graying hair of the watching elders, their fur mantles wrapped tight around them, brooches and circlets shining in the silver light.

"For today, Lord Nestor?" Ixion asks, sliding from Niter's back.

"I was thinking you'd show us," Nestor says, smiling tautly.

Ixion dips his head in a jerking bow, his gray eyes taking in the other elders watching from the edge of the balustrade. Then he looks at me.

"Melee. Humble-riders versus dragonborn."

Humble-riders are outnumbered in the Pythian fleet two to one. Not to mention the small matter of the muzzles.

The only bright side is that sparked dragons are doused for training. I gave Niter the bucket this morning personally, with nearly a bite to show for it. The dousing means any burns squires get will be from ash, not sparked dragonfire. Not dangerous enough to kill or seriously injure.

They'll still hurt like hell.

Rhadamanthus's arms are folded over his mantle; Nestor wears a look of impatience. But neither offers an objection.

I bow, teeth gritted. "As you wish, my lord."

In the air, I wave Bran and Fionna to me, and the other humble-riders follow.

"Melee. Us versus them."

"You're joking. Why—"

"Ixion's idea."

"Of course it was," Fionna mutters.

"Do you want me to take him?" Bran asks me.

He doesn't have to say who. It's an offer to take burns—Ixion is notorious for landing full-heat hits, particularly against humble-riders. With my fury still raging from Ixion's threat about Sparker, I shake my head.

"I'll handle Ixion."

Fionna's eyes are round. "Griff, you know you mustn't—"

"I'll handle him."

The clouds hang low overhead, hugging the karst pillars that rise from the surf. Below us lies the main harbor, the trade ships and fishing boats bobbing between New Pythos and Sailor's Folly, the barges ferrying ore back from the karst-mines.

The dragonborn riders fan out opposite us, and the humble-riders tighten on either side of me.

"Formation?" Bran asks.

"Cyclone. Might as well drag this one out."

Bran lets out a crazed laugh. "With pleasure."

On the balustrade, Nestor's hand goes down, and as the dragonborn surround us, the humble-riders tighten. We form a cycling cone, skyfish circling one another at the highest level, stormscourge at the lowest, and aurelians counterclockwise at the middle height, our pikes pointed outward. It's the defensive formation that we've trained to use, in expanded form, against aerial attacks on New Pythos.

I circle lowest, along with the other two stormscourge squires, bare meters up from the surf, level with the masts of the trade ships docked in the harbor. The clouds hang low today, wisps of fog scudding across the sea, visibility going in and out, the nearest karsts dark pillars in the fog.

Ixion sends in the Bastards first, for contact charges.

Out of the nothingness a gray silhouette hurtles, wings folded and crest flattened. The dragon's rider, a Bastard named Edmund, closes on Bran's tail as I charge from below, rising to meet them from the opposite direction. I ram my pike into the dragon's side, and they feint away, Edmund cursing. I let out a barking laugh of triumph.

"Thanks!" Bran shouts from above, in the aurelian tier.

"On my tail next—"

"Got it."

The humble-riders are outnumbered but the Bastards can't break our wall of interweaving riders; one tier's blind spot is in another tier's sights, and only after we've begun to pick the Bastards off does Ixion send the second wave in after them.

"Fall back to long range," Ixion calls. "Triarchal dragonborn advance."

Dragon's bloody sparkfire.

Overhead, Roxana sur Rora goes for Fionna; Delo sur Gephyra takes on Nolan, their shots of doused ash landing with characteristic precision; and Ixion sur Niter begins to blanket Bran—until we slam into his dragon's side.

Long range can stuff it.

Sparker and Niter spiral out of the formation, latched on to each other, and as we spiral, we sink. The waves of the North Sea rise up to meet us; Sparker's tail lashes and saltwater spumes over us. Then he kicks off, and we roll to face Ixion.

The humble-riders' formation is disintegrating; the cold drafts of sea fog take the watching dragonborn on the citadel's balustrade in and out of focus. A Bastard swings round to join Ixion but Ixion raises his fist, his helmet never turning from me. Holding off the offer of aid so he can handle me alone.

Good.

As he sweeps forward, I begin to mimic him. He shies, I shy; he feints, I feint; every erratic movement that Ixion uses to such advantage sparring others, I mirror like smooth water. His jets of ash we dodge like so much harmless child's play. Back and forth across the tilting surface of the sea we scuff the waves, wiping seawater and fog from our visors. The towering cliff face and the citadel rise over us, and the harbor looms below us—

Show me the fear in your eyes.

That's all I want. I want that moment—that blissful moment—when Ixion realizes I'm toying with him. Toying with him in front of the entire ruling body of this hell-rock.

And then I'll let him win.

Ixion's erratic movements grow in surging desperation, and Sparker and I match them, the sheer delight of it, the power of it, like an elixir in my blood. In the spinning world of our peripheral vision I know the cyclone is finished; the other humble-riders have been eliminated; we're the only sparring pair left.

This kind of defiance has always been heady.

We're level with the docks now: the trade ships, the fishing charters, the ferries bearing ore from the karst-mines. There's a crack as Niter's tail slams against the side of a trawler; deckhands scramble for safety and puffins scatter with indignant squawks—

Ixion is faltering, pulling Niter back as he gasps. As Niter tires, they dip, a cresting wave rising up to greet them—

And in their distraction, we get inside their guard. Sparker latches talons and I shove my pike into the opening.

It clips Ixion's neck guard.

Ixion freezes. The helmet might be hiding his face, but I know the expression he wears. Realizing I have him. That if I wanted, I could ram the thing home.

All I need.

I ease off the reins, just a fraction, and Sparker feels the slump. This part is always the hardest—not my losing, but convincing Sparker to—and it's when I most rely on spillover, on willing our minds together to do something Sparker finds it against his nature to do.

Sparker unlatches his talons. I yank back the pike.

Niter turns toward us, and where Sparker should dodge, or charge, I hold us still. In that pause Niter fires.

I let the ash roll over my shield and flamesuit, so hot I'm robbed of breath.

Sparker gnashes against his muzzle, straining for the space to fire and not finding it. He slumps, growling.

As the ash clears, I look past Ixion. At a shimmer of silver in the fog, I spot the wings of two skyfish as they emerge from the cloud wisps shrouding the arms of Kraken Karst.

Skyfish that aren't ours, observing our melee and slithering away into the fog.

Callipolan spies.

I open my mouth to tell him—and Ixion speaks first.

"You will always be a piece of peasant shit."

That's when I decide not to say anything.

7

TEA WITH THE PROTECTOR

ANNIE

Classes have resumed for winter term in the Lyceum, with Guardians expected to continue coursework in a limited capacity. I'm one of the few who doesn't mind: I have a very particular class that I plan to take, and I've been waiting for it to begin. I make my way across the river to Scholars Row for the first day of term with a scarf wound tight over the neck of my mantle to keep out the biting wind. The sky is a turmoil of dark storm clouds, bleaching the main courtyard of color. With Duck and Crissa gone, I have to resist the urge to keep looking up, searching the horizon for a returning pair of skyfish.

"Antigone! I was hoping I'd see you at lunch."

Dora Mithrides stands on the steps of the Lyceum Club. Her default language is Dragontongue; it suits her imperious tone. She waves a fur-mantled arm, summoning me to her, as her carriage is wheeled over from the stables.

"Oh, I—luncheoned in the Palace."

There's no good way to explain to Dora that someone like me is not welcome in the Lyceum Club, which is officially open to all class-golds but in practice only welcoming to those of a certain kind of birth. Dora's kind.

Dora sniffs. "I hope the offerings in the Palace are less pitiful than the club's these days."

Eminently wealthy, patrician to a fault, Dora is the sort of Gold who's hardly noticed the effects of rationing except insofar as it lowers the quality of her social dining at the Lyceum Club. A venerable widow, she hails from one of the grandest estates on the Janiculum Hill and a matching financial empire. I'd have every reason to resent this woman, were she not one of the three adults who took my side against Atreus when it came time to bring Lee home from his duel.

The bells are ringing the quarter hour; I will, if this conversation continues, be late for my first class. I shift weight from one foot to the other and am about to excuse myself when Dora clasps my arm.

"I was hoping to invite you to a little get-together I'm throwing tomorrow evening," she says. "The club will host. For the Guardians of the Fourth Order, and some of my friends."

I was wondering when this would happen. The price of Dora's support of Lee, when I asked for it, was her interest. *In your future, and the boy's as well.*

Atreus's successor will be chosen by the Golds, when he decides the Guardians are ready to begin their rule. All but officially, the shortlist of candidates are the riders of the Fourth Order—Lee, Power, Cor, and I.

And all but officially, people like Dora, and her dinner parties, will guide that selection process.

"Nothing formal," Dora goes on, waving a bejeweled hand. "Just some friends from the Janiculum Council, a few from the Gold Advisory Council. Atreus will be there—thought it would be good to facilitate a rapprochement between him and the boy. This is a chance for us to get to know each other a bit more casually, so just be yourself, dear."

My face must show my skepticism at such a strategy, because Dora *hmphs*. "Do you have anything to wear?"

"My uniform?"

"I was worried you would say that. Here."

Her coachman has arrived with the carriage. She takes her purse from him and retrieves a parcel from within. "They tell me Guardians aren't allowed possessions, so consider this a loan."

The parcel, wrapped in white tissue paper and bound with twine, is soft in my hands. I tuck it in my book bag as Dora is assisted into her carriage.

"I almost forgot," Dora calls through the window as it begins to wheel away, "let's do the thing properly, shall we? Bring your dragons!"

When I arrive at class, I find it occupied by only two other people: Power sur Eater, sprawled halfway out of his desk; and a first-year Gold, who looks from one to the other of us with an expression of awe approaching terror. Our uniforms identify us as Guardians; the fact that the entire city watched Power and me compete in tournaments over the summer means that this first-year probably also knows our names. The storm-dimmed light outside filters poorly through narrow windows, leaving the room in almost total shadow.

"Fancy seeing you here, Antigone," Power says.

"What are you doing here?"

Power shrugs. He extends a hand to the first-year. "How do you do? I'm Power, this is Antigone . . ."

The first-year shakes Power's hand with a gurgling sound.

Power pushes a ragged piece of paper toward me. "You seen this?"

It's a torn flyer, depicting the four-tiered city, the emblem of the Inner Palace, and beside each tier a different length of bread: the longest baguette beside Gold, shortening for Silver and then Bronze, and the smallest loaf of all for Iron, an inverse image of the four-tiered city. FULL RATIONS FOR ALL, the text reads. CALLIPOLANS UNITE!

The chant the green-scarved girl had the Cheapsiders shouting in their square.

Beneath it, the words: A MESSAGE FROM THE PASSI.

"Where did you get this?"

Power waves a hand toward the dusty window. "They've been floating around on the street. City guard's going overtime trying to confiscate all of them, not to mention find the rogue printing press. The Passi—have you heard of them?"

"No."

But I can guess I've seen one of them: that girl in the square with her green scarf.

The Passi. An organized protest group, identifying itself. With pretension enough of grandeur to evoke, by the Dragontongue word *passus*, that they were among those found worthy on the Guardian aptitude test, and but for a dragon's passing them over, they would rule.

Trouble.

The professor enters, and I stuff the confiscated leaflet into my backpack as I rise with the other two.

"Three this year? That's got to be a record high . . ."

Professor Sidney turns out to be possibly the oldest, tallest man I've ever seen, his hair a shock of white atop his long head. He barely looks at us as he enters and begins writing on the chalkboard with his back completely turned.

"Norish," he says, "that's what we're learning here. Language of the Norcians, of what was once old Norcia and is now New Pythos. I'm Professor Sidney. If you're in the wrong room, leave now."

He speaks in Dragontongue. He has written *Norish, Sidney*, in the Dragontongue script with a shaking hand on the board. He turns around and his glare falls on me. I recognize the look of a professor being confronted with the unwelcome sight of a female student. "Tell me, do you *board* here?" he asks.

Usually, the Guardian uniform curbs this kind of blatant skepticism, but Sidney might not be able to make out my decorations in the dim light.

"No. I . . . board nearby."

Power rolls his eyes.

For a moment, Sidney only rasps. Then he tells the chalkboard, "Went over to New Pythos when I was about your age, a fledgling linguist. Not the last triarchy, the one before, under Argus the First. We had good relations with the ha'Aurelians then. The local population, on the other hand . . ." Sidney waves a shaking hand. "The Norcians are a good people, but primitive. They worship their karst, anthropomorphize them, claim there used to be a Nag and Kraken and so on who walked among them—and they're clannish. Too busy fighting among them-selves to do much else."

"Sort of like the highlands?" Power prompts, flicking me a wink.

I consider kicking the leg of Power's desk, but the first-year is staring at me. I lift an eyebrow at him and he flushes.

Sidney still faces the board, nodding at it. "Very much like the highlands. They were just sitting on all that ore until the ha'Aurelians got there and got them mining it. No native writing system, I had to transliterate it in the Callish script myself. No textbook to learn it with, so I wrote my own. That's what we'll be using here. If everyone will turn to the introduction . . ."

Power's good mood seems to grow as the class progresses and he tests the far reaches of bigoted remarks he can mine from Sidney. He leaves the room with a triumphant smirk that sobers when we're alone in the corridor. It's even darker here than it was in the classroom.

"You could tell him who you are," he points out.

We watch the first-year scurry off. Probably, to tell his friends that he's in a class with two Guardians and a professor who doesn't recognize them.

"*Or* you could stop egging him on."

"But what would be the fun in that?"

Power and I have always had different definitions of fun. But more than anything, Sidney's casual biases leave me ruminating. The Norcian underclass on New Pythos is so far from being the focus of our military strategy that even on the brink of a war, their language is still being taught by a senile scholar to a class of three. The casual dismissiveness of Sidney's waved hand to describe their culture—isn't that the same kind of disdain that led the dragonborn to underestimate their own people, the commoners who overthrew them? Power meant his reference to the highlands as a joke at my expense, but it was more apt than he knew.

I find an invitation to my own rapprochement with the First Protector waiting for me when I return to the Cloister after class. From Miranda Hane, the Minister of Propaganda: I'm invited to have tea at the Coach House tomorrow afternoon, before Dora's party.

I consider, upon first studying the invitation, simply not going. But I recognize Miranda Hane's handwriting. It was the handwriting that told me, on a note delivered before the Firstrider Tournament but read after, *Go show them what you're made of.* And she was one of the few adults whose integrity I depended on when I confronted Atreus on Pytho's Keep.

So the following afternoon, I go.

Like the Guardians, Atreus occupies what were servants' quarters in the old regime, and his residence remains an austere little building attached to the Inner Palace—the Coach House, so named because that is what it used to be. Atreus keeps a limited staff; his furnishings are sparse; the foyer that I am invited to wait in is little larger than the office I keep in the Cloister, and its only adornment is a tapestry from the Bassilean Wars. Goliathans, a continental breed of dragon that dwarf those from the island nations of the Medean, loom as large as whales against a faded, embroidered sky, sparring with our stormscourges and dodging Damian harpooniers. The Bassilean Wars were the last to spread across the whole sea and all its courts.

"Antigone? Forgive me for keeping you waiting. Do come in."

Atreus himself welcomes me into his parlor. He and Miranda have taken seats on opposite sides of a small tea set. Miranda offers an encouraging smile as I ease into one of Atreus's straight-backed upholstered chairs.

Atreus serves me tea himself; no servant is called.

"So," he says, when I have it in hand, "Book Twenty-Four."

It takes me a moment to understand: He's talking about the *Aurelian Cycle*. And my unauthorized trip to return Julia's body.

He doesn't sound displeased. His copy of the poem, familiar from when he taught classes with the Fourth Order last term, lies on the table between us. It has the ministry-standard stamp of banned material on its front. Atreus himself approved the ban of the *Aurelian Cycle*, for the sake of political stability. But that does not undo the fact that he loves the poem and knows it by heart.

"Did it work?"

I nod. "I quoted the lines about safe passage. The Pythians . . . understood. And ensured our return."

Atreus's smile contains mysteries of memory. "Brilliant."

Again, that strange warmth that came during the meeting with the War Council, unwanted: the pleasure of his approval.

This man tried to kill your friend. Twice.

"As a leader," Atreus says, "I think often about how important it is to recognize talent when I see it. To judge with an unbiased eye. After the last meeting with the War Council, I was left pondering how difficult that is. It is something Miranda and I have been discussing. How the biases of the old order have a way of carrying over, even with us. Even with the best intentions, we can sometimes . . . see talent only where we've been trained to see it. And in other cases, not notice it where we aren't used to looking for it. Even when that talent shines brightly."

As I begin to understand, I feel my face move with emotions I don't want Atreus to see.

I know what he's trying to do, as transparently as if he had announced it. Lee is lost to him; he is now in search of a new ally.

But I also know that Atreus is not a man to lie, nor are the sentiments he's expressing out of character. He seeks an ally, but the confessions he's offering are honest.

And I've had too many professors like Sidney, too many meetings like the one with Holmes, being underestimated and overlooked, not to feel his words like water on parched earth.

Lee. This man tried to kill Lee—

"For that, I would like to apologize, Antigone. You have proven yourself, repeatedly, to be everything I hoped for in a Guardian. Committed to the ideals of the Revolution. Unafraid to sacrifice for them. Unafraid, in short, to do what it takes.

"Naturally, there have been moments of misunderstanding—as there often are between revolutionaries, as Miranda and I can attest from long years working together on this vision—there will always be times of disagreement. What I admire, in how you have handled our disagreement, was your commitment to justice. Your difference in interpretation from my own only showed me that you are doing what I hoped, all along, the Guardians would do: think for themselves."

Atreus inclines his head, smiling. "I hope I can depend on you to continue to do so."

There is something violent, almost ugly, in the satisfying of a craving you've buried so deep in yourself you forgot it was there.

I had that feeling once, staring at a note scrawled by Miranda Hane in the aftermath of a match; I have it again now, as Atreus pours out affirmation I so long ago stopped expecting, I forgot I ever once hoped for it.

Talent that shines brightly.

Back in the Cloister, before preparing for Dora's party, I draw a hot bath to clear my head. My hair, burned halfway off in the Firstrider Tournament but growing out, is still short enough to towel dry. I let myself back into the girls' dorm to unwrap Dora's parcel.

The dress inside is black, silken, full-length with a wide, high neck. I pull it over my shoulders and rummage in Alexa's dresser for her smuggled mirror and study my reflection. Dora chose well: The black sets off the color of my hair, and the neckline makes me look adult.

You are everything we hoped a Guardian could be.

A knock sounds on the door.

"Come in."

It's Lee, in ceremonial uniform, alone. His chin freshly shaven, his dark hair slicked back and combed. The gold trimming of his black mantle, of the decorations on his uniform, glow in the low light like so many stars. This is the style of dress Lee has always looked most at home in. Like he could have stepped out of a tapestry of the old regime and into the new, ready to command in either one.

His eyes leave mine and travel down, slowly. And then they snap back to my face.

How does he manage to make me shiver with just a look?

And then a shiver of guilt, like cold water trickling down my spine: What would he think, to know I spent the last hour reeling from compliments given by the man who betrayed him? Is it a betrayal of Lee, to stand straighter because of things the First Protector said?

"Are you ready to go over?"

"I—yeah. One second."

I'm fumbling, elbows at my ears, to do up the last button of my dress. Lee closes the distance. His fingers take the button from mine. I stand quite still, feeling his touch light on my neck, holding my breath, remembering—

The button is fastened. His fingers trail upward and brush against the chain of my necklace.

"You still wear it?"

His voice is a murmur. I'm light-headed, from the mere brush of his fingertips.

"I always wear it."

My mother's necklace. The one he found, buried in the dirt by my home, when we went there together and I told him everything. The one he clasped around my neck when last his fingers traced the nape of my neck.

That Lee listened so well, and spoke so little, and sat so close. Ready to stand there with me through it all.

I turn to face him. His fingers are hooked under the chain of the necklace, drawing it out, laying the pendant against the silk of the dress with strange reverence. And then a flick of gray and he is looking at me. Looking at me like he sees me, the shutters opened.

"How was Cheapside Grammar?" he asks.

That was the last time we were alone, I realize. When he called our old school *some grammar school in Cheapside* with his back turned.

My throat catches. "It was all right. Mistress Dunbar's still there; she asked about you."

You two were inseparable, she said. It brought back a host of memories that are almost too painful now to think on: Lee sitting next to me in class, next to me at meals, glaring at anyone who so much as glanced in my direction like a dog with hackles raised. Lee sitting across from me, rapt, while I read the *People's Paper* to him back to back in the corner of a dusty play yard. *Inseparable.*

Lee nods, and standing so close to him I can hear him swallow. When he speaks, his voice is hoarse. "I was wondering if you wanted to ride with me, to the party. Since we're supposed to bring dragons."

I can't hide the confusion from my voice. "Ride with you?"

Lee reaches up to rub at the crease between his brows and squints at his own hand. "Sidesaddle, to protect the dress? That's . . . how my parents did it."

I can count on one hand the number of times Lee has mentioned his family to me. For so many years, his old life wasn't acknowledged. And in the last months—when it could be—there was still the shadow of who Leon was, and what he did, hanging over us both.

His parents. A mother, who wore long gowns and climbed onto the saddle beside her husband. A dragonlord and his lady.

Lee's mother and father, whom he's missed just as I've missed mine.

All of this, in a few words, like a delicate flower plucked from the earth and offered. For me to cradle in my hands or crush under my heel, as I choose.

I have to lift on tiptoes to kiss him on the cheek.

"Of course."

LEE

I debated whether to go to Dora's party from the moment I received the invitation. Debated it even as I pulled on the ceremonial uniform I haven't worn since the Lycean Ball, remembering the difference: then, a regime whose seal I was proud to bear. Whereas today—

I've half a mind, when I knock on the door to the girls' dorm, to tell Annie I won't go.

But then I see her.

I've begun to spend so much time not feeling like myself that I notice when I do. Joking with Cor about going hungry, moonlighting in Cheapside, getting called a hero by a classmate with a playful turn to her voice—those things pull me back. Humor, laughter, defiance.

But so does beauty. The cloud-filled sky from Pallor's back. The words of the *Aurelian Cycle*, pulled from the shelves of the Cloister library in the dead of night, rolling beneath my fingers like a living thing.

The sight of Annie, sheathed in black silk, her hair a wreath of brown fire.

I've spent years making myself not notice how she looks in a flamesuit—also black, also form-fitting—but this gown asks to be looked at, to show her as a woman, and for the brief glance I let myself take of her hips tapering to waist, of the nubs of her collarbones peeking beneath a high neckline. I remember the miracle of it, that this vision of a girl once stood on tiptoe to fit her lips to mine, that when she felt my hands on her waist, she only kissed me harder.

And as with the sound of Cor's laughter, as with the sight of the sky from dragonback, I feel the blackness part from my mind like a breaking cloud. So suddenly, so completely, that I can't imagine it ever having been. Atreus, Dora, this regime or that, what do they matter in the face of such beauty, of Annie's blush flooding freckled cheeks as she smiles up at me?

We're talking, words I hardly hear, as she lets me button up her dress and touch her mother's necklace. And then I say something profoundly stupid, mention parents I shouldn't, and instead of it falling apart as I half expect, Annie kisses me on the cheek with such tenderness that I think there, right there, I will melt to the ground from dizzy relief.

And then the miracle keeps going, and fifteen minutes later I'm explaining to her how to ride sidesaddle as I hold Pallor by the reins, offering laced hands to help her onto his back. Pallor is alert, his horns perked, his tail slightly lifted, but he knows Annie, who smells of Aela. In another life, my father would have taught me how to do this, but he's not here and so I have to guess.

Guess that I should let it spill over, just a little, into Pallor, the feelings of muddled happiness at the sight of Annie, the instinct that feels a little wrong but she never need know—of protectiveness, of possessiveness, at the sight of her standing at my dragon's side like this. So that he knows the loyalty he feels to me should encompass her.

"What if he throws—"

"He won't."

She looks into my eyes, and the cave's torchlight is enough for her to see the dilated pupils, to know that I can vouch for Pallor with the certainty that comes from spillover. She plants a heeled shoe into my laced fingers, the opposite foot from the one she would place into a stirrup, and I hoist her onto his saddle.

He sits still and careful, as if he were cradling a hatchling. I can hear her breathing and, with the heightened senses of the spillover, smell her. Just a faint scent of fear.

"Lee?"

For a moment I look up at them and remember my parents, and try to memorize it: Annie on Pallor's back. Black satin perched on silver scales, flaming hair in the dark, the halo of her face turned toward mine, trusting. My parents were always in high spirits on occasions when she joined him on Aletheia, but only now do I understand the tenderness of the moment. How looking up at them, together, I feel I'm looking at something perfect.

I hook a boot into the stirrup and climb onto Pallor's back behind her.

She eases against me, fitting the lines of her body into mine, and I wrap an arm around her waist under her mantle. Amid the feelings that are mine, and the feelings that are Pallor's, I murmur the reminder in her ear and my voice comes out hoarse.

"Summon Aela."

Aela comes to our wing as we glide out the Firemouth, and as we rise, Annie inhales so sharply I can feel her jutting hip bones quiver beneath my palm. A toll of the rationing that the uniform hides, and it brings a knee-jerk alarm and a host of memories of the orphanage. Where I learned to hate hunger but to hate the sight of her hunger, more. Learned that sometimes it was more important to watch someone else eat.

The best parts of myself, I found with Annie.

"You all right?"

Annie's fingers are clutching my arm so tightly I'm losing feeling in it. "I think I prefer riding my own dragon."

I laugh aloud. Annie twists in surprise. "What?"

"That's just . . . not a comparison any of the women in my family could have made."

For the second time today, talking about my family like an idiot. And for the second time today, Annie doesn't shrink from it. Her fingers trace my sleeve to my hand and squeeze it, and I tighten my grip on her too-narrow waist.

We've leveled with Pytho's Keep. The sun is setting, the stratus that mantled the sky shredding in the fiery light. The river is a ribbon of gold below, the rooftops of the Janiculum and the lower neighborhoods gleaming. The sun is low enough on the horizon that Pallor's and Aela's wings are lit from below, glowing in the dying light. Annie takes another shuddering breath and I know this gasp is not of fear but of sudden breathless delight.

Her gaze flows north, a wash of red turning violet turning deepest blue where the horizon meets the sea.

"I keep scanning for them to come back."

Crissa and Duck. But we're the only pair of dragons in sight. I can think of no answer to give that wouldn't be hollow comfort: Tonight, tomorrow morning at the outset, is their projected return. And the sleepless nights we've stared at the ceiling wondering if they won't don't bear discussing.

"Game for a dive?"

Annie nods, her grip tightening on my arm, and we lean close to Pallor's back as he folds his wings and we plummet. The Lower Bank rises up to meet us, Scholars Row with the War College on one side and the Lyceum on the other; and then we are leveling out, spiraling gently, to alight on the drive in front of the Lyceum Club, inside the university walls. This time of year, the ivy climbing the limestone has turned a fading red.

I slide off Pallor's back, help Annie down, and make arrangements with the porter with a barely suppressed sense of satisfaction because this—the carriages rolling in at dusk, the glittering gowns beneath mantles, the laughter from steaming breath—is a world I remember watching from child-height, but tonight with a dragon at my side and Annie on my arm, I understand at last the brilliance of my father's smile when the night was young.

"We're happy to install them ourselves, Bart, it's no problem," I tell the porter.

The Lyceum was built by Atreus, after the Revolution, and its stone stables were designed to house Guardians' dragons; tonight is the first time they'll be employed for the purpose. Eater and Maurana already occupy two of the largest stalls, built for stormscourges; Aela and Pallor dart into a third stall together and begin tracking circles at its far end, warming the stone with small bursts of fire, pleased by the snug darkness. Her hand on the gate, Annie pauses, studying the two of them making their nest, her face softening.

Pallor and Aela barely notice when we close and latch their stall, and as we enter the club, Annie tucks her arm into mine once more. The valet directs us to the upper level where the Fete of the Fourth Order will be held. On the landing, I glance at the tapestry decorating the landing of the second floor, and then I look again.

It once belonged to my father.

ANNIE

Still flushed from the flight, Aela and Pallor's contentment singing in my blood, it takes me a moment to realize why Lee has frozen on the landing of the Lyceum Club's second floor, feet from the party we're about to attend. The sounds of laughter and a low murmur of conversation seep from a room a little farther down the hall.

Then I look at the dimly lit tapestry on the paneled wall. It depicts the western cliffs off the Callipolan highlands, and on one of the highest ledges, a manor overlooking the sea. Lee reaches up, stretches the tips of his fingers, and touches them to the threads of the lowest weave.

"How . . ."

His eyes narrow on the small metal plaque below it.

FARHALL, DRAKARCHIC SEAT OF THE FAR HIGHLANDS
STORMSCOURGE PROVENANCE,
ON LOAN FROM THE MITHRIDES ESTATE

As I understand, I feel sick.

This is a landscape of Lee's family's manor. Lee's family's art. And now it's hanging forgotten on a landing of the Lyceum Club.

"Dora owns this?" Lee breathes.

After the Revolution, the new regime's auctions of dragonborn possessions went on for months. What wasn't sold was gifted to the faithful, and what was left entered the Revolutionary Collection. It's one thing to know that, but quite another to look up at one of these artifacts beside the boy it used to belong to and watch him blink over and over as he wills himself to understand. The fact that it's an accident that Lee is encountering this tapestry—because Dora likely lent spare decorations to the club without a second thought—only makes it worse.

"This used to hang in my father's study."

He sounds lost.

I have the sudden urge to step between him and the landscape. Pity mingles with something else, something closer to dread: We were doing so well, he was doing so well, until he found this stupid tapestry. I tell him, as softly as I dare, the thing I know he already knows.

"A lot of things probably belong to Dora now, Lee."

The latent nerves I've been feeling, at the thought of what comes next—the Golds I've never been good at impressing, the exposure I share with Lee's identity now known—falls away as I realize I'm not the one most in need of courage tonight. I might not be eager to set foot inside a room where my low birth will be held against me, but at least I don't have to look at the home they took from me on my way in the door.

We need to re-center. The tapestry isn't the point. The patricians' insensitivity isn't the point. The point isn't this corridor; the point is the room on the other side of that door and where it will lead.

I take a step sideways, so that Lee must turn his back on his family's manor to look at me.

"Lee, Dora Mithrides showed interest in . . . us, after the duel. You particularly. She spoke about our futures, which means the Protectorship. Succession. Her friends are in there; this is an informal audition."

In other words: *Stay with me.* But I can see the tension seizing his shoulders.

"And Atreus?"

"He's been invited, too."

"Annie, I'm not sure I want—"

No. This isn't something I'll hear. Nor is it something, at the end of the day, that I believe.

I think of how Atreus said it: The role of a leader is to recognize talent when you see it.

Lee's charisma, his effortless charm, the ease with which he walks into power—these things used to threaten me. But the difference between an advantage and a weakness is your dragon's relative position to the ground.

Now I'm the leader. Firstrider, commander of the aerial fleet, and Guardian of this city, sworn to guide it to justice. Lee is a rider in my corps. And just as Atreus recognized talent in me—now it's my role to recognize talent in him.

I reach up to cup his face in both my hands. Feeling the sharp chin, the high cheekbones, of a Stormscourge face.

"You want to lead this city. You've wanted to lead it ever since it was taken from you. You want Atreus replaced? Be the one who replaces him. *This is your chance.*"

Lee's lips have parted with surprise. "You want that?"

I hear what he means by that: me, all the history I bear. All the reasons I have for wanting someone, anyone, other than this dragonlord's son to lead my city.

How did Atreus say it? A leader should *judge with an unbiased eye.*

Lee's strengths don't have to threaten me anymore. They're an asset.

The realization leaves me with a rush of exhilaration like I'm on dragonback leaving the ground.

"I want that."

Lee reaches out to take both my hands in his.

"Together," he says, his voice shaking. "We do this together."

"Together," I repeat.

Once, years ago, we walked hand in hand through a door. Into a Choosing Ceremony that I did not think I wanted, into a room where Aela found me, and Pallor found Lee, and our new lives began.

Tonight, we walk hand in hand through a doorway again.

8

PUNISHMENT FORFEIT

GRIFF

The secret of the Callipolan spies eats at me: First, I wonder at myself for not sharing it. *They'll be seen by someone else.* When they aren't, I begin to wonder if I saw them at all.

But I know I did. And even if there are no laws for this, there doesn't have to be for me to know that I committed treason by omission.

That I continue to commit it by omission—

That I endanger everyone I know and love by saying nothing about Callipolan spies from the south. They're here to scout, which means they'll return to bombard, and I know where those fires will catch fastest: on Norcian homes, with our thatch roofs and wooden frames.

So why don't I speak?

Two days after the melee, Ixion receives his reply from Vask—borne to him in the first Bassilean trade ships to dock in our harbor since the Medean League embargoed. Freyda sent three galleys, stocked in grains and spices to trade for silver and tin from our mines. She also invites Ixion to visit. I help him pack, welcoming the news that I'll have a few days rid of him.

The morning Ixion departs, I'm finishing up breakfast when a knock sounds on our front door in a tone I'm unfamiliar with. Soft, uncertain, not the hammer of a friend or guard. Granda looks up from the tea he's nursing with still-fogged eyes, Garet and Becca stop their arguing to look up, and Agga straightens at once, reaching for her widow's scarf.

"I'll get it," I tell her.

At the door, in the misty morning light, stands Delo. The sight of his blue mantle on our front step, in an alleyway of lean-tos, is incongruous. He's never come to my home before. Julia has, more than once, I think for the novelty of it; Ixion as well, when we were children, to tell the other dragonborn about it later. But neither of these reasons suits Delo.

"My lord?"

Delo shifts weight. "You probably know Ixion's on a diplomatic trip to Bassilea. You're in my service while he's away."

That doesn't explain why he's standing on my stoop; the news could just as easily have been delivered when I arrived at the citadel. Delo looks past me.

"Good morning, Agga."

Agga smiles and curtsies. "Hello, Lord Delo."

And then she looks from him to me, that smile spreading, and the delight of it makes me scowl at her.

What?

Agga turns back to Delo. "Do you want to come in for tea?"

This was what she served Julia. Delo looks from her to me, and says: "Oh, it's fine, I don't want to impose—"

Julia always accepted the invitation without question; Agga's brow furrows at his hesitation. "It wouldn't impose."

I'm not so sure, but there's no way to argue with that, which Delo seems to realize as well as I. Garet and Becca watch with wide eyes from a crouch on the floor, quiet the way we've taught them to be in the presence of dragonborn company. Delo ducks under our doorframe. He bows to Granda.

"Good morning, Grandfather."

Granda creaks to his feet and bows jerkily.

"Please be seated," Delo murmurs. "Are these your children?" he asks Agga, with a smile at my crouching niece and nephew.

She nods, swelling a bit with pride as she gestures to each. "Becca, and Garet."

Delo greets them, and they chorus a greeting in return.

"I was sorry to hear of Eamon's passing," Delo tells Agga.

Agga's face flickers at his naming, and she ducks her head in another curtsy, fingers pushing stray strands under her black scarf. "You are kind to remember on it, my lord."

I offer Delo a seat at the table while Agga takes the kettle off the fire, and remain standing myself. For my family, tea means hot water; I don't think Agga even realizes that Delo is expecting something more when he lifts his mug to his lips and drinks. His brow furrows a fraction, but otherwise, he shows no sign of surprise.

"Biscuit?" Agga asks, which means bread.

"No, thank you," Delo says.

Julia always helped herself—a politeness that thrilled Agga even as it left me wondering what we would have left to eat later. But Delo is looking around the house, measuring. I can tell he's checking for something, but for what, I can't tell. His eyes focus on Agga as she covers a small cough in her sleeve. And then he speaks to me in Dragontongue.

"What were the medicines," he asks, "that Julia provided for her?"

I'd never told Delo she provided medicines, and I doubt Julia did, either; she hardly thought of them as she gave them to me, even to the point that I was forced, more than once, to remind her. If Julia noticed my shame in such moments, it only amused her.

Julia has wandered in and out of my dreams since her death: laughing, teasing, just out of reach. Other times, she's within reach, but the things she holds aren't.

Somehow, despite never being told this was the arrangement, Delo guessed.

I tell him the herbs curtly, also in Dragontongue, and Delo nods. Granda twists round to look at me, uncomprehending and startled; I've never spoken Dragontongue in front of him before. Becca suppresses a giggle at the strange sounds.

"I'll make sure you get more," Delo says.

I dip my head in a jerking bow. Delo frowns and flicks his wrist. I straighten. "Was there anything else she provided for your family?"

I note the ways he has padded this moment—in front of my family, but in a language they won't understand—so that I feel compelled to confess needs that pride would otherwise keep silent.

"Food. When she thought of it."

Delo drinks deeply from his hot water. His glance goes to the corner, where shoes are piled. He nods at the pair whose toes are entirely gone. "Whose are those?"

"Garet's."

Delo nods, his gaze turning to Garet, narrowing as he assesses his feet—as if memorizing their size. "I'll look into it."

Agga is glancing between us, an expression of uncertainty bordering fear at the Dragontongue, and Delo smiles at her to reassure her, a warmth that she responds to like sunlight. He rises and returns to Norish, accentless and crisp, handing her back his empty mug.

"Thank you for the tea, Agga. Griff, shall we?"

Agga's knowing smile follows me out of the house, like I've just accidentally let her in on a secret. Which is stupid, because it's no secret Delo's—

Delo's what?

Kind, thoughtful, and charming. Not smirking at my family's hot water for tea, like Julia did. Offering to help at no prompting on my part. And, if I'm not mistaken, a little tongue-tied himself now that we're crossing Conqueror's Mound together on our way up to the citadel. He is walking unnaturally fast, long legs taking long strides; I'm fairly trotting to keep up with him.

"My lord, if there's anything I can do to repay—"

It's like the words set off a trip wire: thoughts of Julia, a sudden lurch in my stomach, and heat in my face. *What do I get in return, Griff?*

"Absolutely not," Delo says.

A strange relief, a strange disappointment, a question I consider asking with mischief unfit for the moment: *Absolutely not what?* That odd silence that happens when I arm him has started to pulse between us, but this time Delo's the one who fills it. His voice is raised oddly; he squints up at the gate we're approaching. With a dragonlord in company, we enter through the Lord's Gate.

"I was glad to see your sister in such good health. And her children. They've grown."

I swallow that thick tongue and answer. "Little troublemakers, these days."

"Really? Worse than we were?"

At my bark of laughter, Delo cracks a rare smile.

I'm less surprised when we enter the muddy main yard and today's strange good luck runs dry.

Roxana ha'Aurelian waits for us, her long auburn hair loose and unbraided, her arms crossed over her bloodred mantle. She unfolds one of them to point at me.

"He should be dropped," she tells Delo.

I stop dead.

Surely, I think, they couldn't *know* I saw Callipolan riders and kept silent, there's no way to prove it—

Delo tilts his head. "Hello to you, too, Roxana."

Roxana beckons and I realize where she's leading us with a plummeting stomach. To the training pen at the edge of the few fields contained within citadel walls, reserved for target practice. Delo follows; with misgiving, I do, too, although I already can guess what we're about to find and have no wish to see it.

Inside the pen, a Norcian peasant is darting back and forth across the charred ground as he attempts to evade the dragon bearing down on him. The citadel guard, all men of Clan Thornrose, are stationed on the edges of the yard. They're usually happy to do the ha'Aurelians' dirty business, but today even they look a bit squeamish. Rhode stands outside the pen with an expression of detached fascination. Bran and Fionna, the two squires who serve Rhode and Roxana, stand at attention by the gate, their faces quite blank.

It's always considered a bonus when the humble-riders get to watch this kind of demonstration.

Rhode's aurelian is named Ryla. She's been doused, to prolong the process. As we approach, she grows tired of firing ash and pounces instead. The man screams as he topples. I recognize him: Seanan of Clan Kraken, a miner from Eamon's old crew whose children Agga sometimes minds during the day.

"Apparently," Rhode tells Delo, "some of the clans have been talking about Antigone."

Ryla flips Seanan over like a rag doll. Fionna's grip on the side of the fence tightens.

When we were younger, the prospect of Rhode becoming Greatlord after Rhadamanthus wasn't one I thought much about. Ixion was the cruel one; Rhode was just his idiot friend. But in recent years—in moments like this—I find the idea of a Greatlord of New Pythos with a dragon at his disposal enough to chill my blood. Rhode doesn't have to share Ixion's love of hurting people to be perfectly good at it.

We suffered enough under the ha'Aurelians when they'd run out of dragons. But with the next generation on dragonback again—

Delo says, "Your father wouldn't like this, Rhode."

"Are you planning to tell him?"

Delo is silent. Rhode continues to study Seanan, rubbing the stubble of his paltry mustache. "You know, Ixion has a point. It is satisfying."

Bran's voice bursts out from behind us.

"My lord, do you not think he's had enough—"

Rhode rounds on him with a lifted wrist and Bran's mouth closes. Fionna's hands are fists at her sides, her eyes squinting at the ground, averted from the sight of Seanan in the pen. Delo looks from the humble-riders to Ryla mauling Seanan. He takes a step closer to Rhode.

"Ixion isn't here," he says, his voice lowering as it intensifies, "and if that peasant dies, you'll have to pay his family the man-price."

Rhadamanthus is notoriously strict with Rhode's allowance.

Rhode sighs, lifts an arm. Ryla disengages her fangs from Seanan's arms with a low whine.

Bran hovers by the gate. "My lord, please—"

Rhode waves permission with an uncaring arm, and Bran bursts through the gate to go to Seanan. He skirts Ryla as she sniffs him with interest, and hoists Seanan to his feet. I study the dragon, wondering just how much trouble she'll be in the lairs later. This kind of thing riles the dragons, makes them more inclined to try something on their keepers. I've got more than a few burns from Ryla, and I don't look forward to adding more.

Rhode turns his back on the pen and his tone becomes businesslike. "This one"—he jabs a thumb at Seanan—"was overheard talking about a peasant Firstrider who's able to sing Dragontongue poetry like she's dragonborn herself. We were wondering where he might have heard about that, *Griff*?"

My name comes at the end of this, like a lash.

I told the story of Antigone exactly once, to Agga on our stoop the night Julia's body was returned. But Becca must have overheard us, and if she told the other children Agga minds, they would have repeated the story to their parents.

Fionna's head lifts at the sound of my name, her eyes widening. Delo watches Bran guiding Seanan from the pen with a frown, then turns to me. "Griff, did you talk about our rendezvous with the Callipolans . . . in town?"

Roxana scoffs. "Like he'll confess—"

"Yes. I did. My lord."

Delo sags. I can feel a buzzing in my ears. Nothing they can threaten me with frightens me as much as the possibility that if I don't confess, they'll trace their interrogation of this gossip back to Agga and the little ones. It's sheer luck that they haven't already.

"I didn't mean anything by it," I add. "Just . . . thought it was a good story."

Roxana recovers first. "Dropped," she repeats. "Worked for Mad Lena, it'll work for Griff."

"Don't be ridiculous," Delo snaps. "The Pythian fleet can't afford to *drop* Griff Gareson."

The way he says it, *Griff Gareson* sounds like an armored warship.

Rhode is studying me, that same idle curiosity. "He could take a turn in the pen."

From the way Delo frowns, I realize even he doesn't seem to be able to think of a counterargument to that.

I went in the pen once before. It's not an experience I'd like to repeat. I stare back at Rhode, willing my face blank.

And that's when the alarm bells go off.

The dragonborn jump. Bran and Fionna freeze where they stand. Seanan keeps swaying.

"That's a sighting," I realize.

The Callipolan spies. Spotted at last.

"I know what it is, Gareson," Rhode snaps.

It's the first alarm bell New Pythos has ever sounded not in drill, but as we set off at a jog into the citadel for the armories, I feel not fear but anticipation. I remember those two shimmering skyfish, darting into the cloud cover behind Kraken.

Easy pickings.

I think of the fang and talon marks that left tracks across Seanan's body, the way it will feel to have the same wounds soon enough, and some suicidal brazenness overcomes me.

"How about a wager, Lord Rhode?"

We've reached the fork in colonnades that will take Rhode and Roxana to the Aurelian armory with Bran and Fionna, Delo and I to the Skyfish. Rhode whips around, his eyes wide with surprise at my impertinence, but I'm grinning. Behind their backs, Bran rolls his eyes at Fionna.

"My punishment forfeit," I propose, "if I bring down a Callipolan rider today."

Delo lets out a wild laugh at my nerve, and even Rhode's tense face purses as if about to crack with a smile.

"I'll consider it," he says.

9

THE FÊTE OF THE FOURTH ORDER

LEE

The last time I shared the company of the patricians-turned-Golds who brought down the triarchy, they didn't know who I was. I was only that slum orphan who looked, so conveniently, like a Stormscourge, and danced exceptionally well.

Tonight at Dora's party, they know different. And thanks to a tapestry of Farhall hanging on the landing on the way in the door, I'm not about to forget who they are, either. These are the people who got rich off the Revolution, who bid on my family's things after cheering their murders.

But it's still freeing not to hide anymore.

And tonight at least, unlike the Lycean Ball when we debuted in Gold society, the Annie on my arm isn't pushing me away at mention of a Stormscourge resemblance. This one knows exactly who I am and just told me she believes I'm worthy of this city anyway.

A year ago, I wouldn't have been able to imagine it.

Whether or not I agree with her, either that I'm worthy of this city or that I even want it, is another question.

When we enter, Annie's arm tucked in mine, Dora Mithrides glides over, kisses Annie on the cheek with surprising familiarity, and then lays a cool hand, glittering with jewels, on my arm.

"Thank you so much for joining us, Leo."

She uses the name I gave up and speaks in Dragontongue. I answer in it.

"Thank you for taking such good care of my father's tapestries. Please, call me Lee."

For a moment Dora blinks slowly, like a frog eyeing a fly, while Annie's arm stiffens in mine. And then Dora smiles.

"The tapestry on the landing? I'd forgotten about that. Remind me—another night—that we have related business to discuss." She taps the glass in her hand with a ring on her finger, and the note that sings through the room silences it. A hand against my back, presenting me to the onlooking Golds, Dora lifts her voice. It carries easily in the high-ceilinged room despite the padding of regulation blackout curtains over the windows.

"Ladies and gentlemen of the Janiculum, join me in welcoming Antigone sur Aela and Lee sur Pallor to our little fête—and forgive me for accompanying their welcome with a small announcement. Those of you who know me know my impatience with gossip—"

There are peals of laughter.

"—so allow me to broach the subject that has been consuming all our curiosity. Yes, Lee sur Pallor is also Leo Stormscourge, Leon's only surviving son. Yes, that is the same Leon mentioned in Antigone sur Aela's biographical information. Yes, Leo— forgive me, *Lee*—has renounced the old order and proven it in a duel to the death with kin. I'm sure Lee and Antigone are both eager to discuss their private lives in even more intimate detail with all of you for the remainder of the evening—and do not neglect Power sur Eater and Cor sur Maurana, also present for your inspection—so allow me to hinder you no further from your prying except to lift my glass and toast these very brave young people, who have made the ideals of this Revolution their life's work."

By the time Dora's finished, Annie is blushing to the roots of her hair; across the floor, Cor sits frozen in a booth where he nurses a drink alone; and Power, surrounded by his usual gaggle of Gold girls, runs a hand over his stubbly head as he feels sudden eyes on him. Dora adds in a throaty whisper to me and Annie as the toast goes up: "You'll forgive my haste—I wanted to get that one in before the Protector arrives. Are you ready to prance?"

I was expecting to meet Dora Mithrides feeling murderous, after that tapestry. Instead her acerbic sense of humor leaves me strangely disarmed. She leads us into the nearest circle of conversation without waiting for our answer—and as she predicted, the prying starts.

They ask if I was present in the city for the Revolution, which sounds innocuous enough but really is a question about Palace Day, is asking *if I was there*. Which seems to come from a place somewhere between morbid curiosity and guilt. Annie's warm hand remains on my arm, tightening ever so slightly as I answer with a smile I've trapped on my face. I hear myself say: *I was there for the whole thing.*

They ask if Annie and I knew each other in the highlands. They ask if Annie knew who I was in the orphanage. Annie and I take turns answering like we're partners in a joint-attack drill. Annie makes jokes—*jokes*—about Albans, the smile fixed on her face matching mine:

"I did start to notice he always had me pretending to be the maidservant."

The Golds titter, titillated; I swing round to look at Annie, too startled to be embarrassed: This is one of those memories, cloudy with distance and never since referred to, so uncomfortable I'd hoped I imagined it. She holds my gaze with a blush on her cheeks and smirk on her lips.

I could kiss her in front of all these asses.

Dean Orthos, head of the Lyceum, is the first to ask directly about what transpired on Pytho's Keep. His voice is lowered, the tassels of his academic cap swinging as he leans inward. "Is it true, my dear boy, that Atreus was *not welcoming* upon your return?"

It doesn't take Annie's fingers squeezing my arm, or Dora glaring at the dean, to know the safest answer. I've gone on enough rounds with the Ministry of Propaganda to know when to keep my mouth shut. "I'm afraid I don't know what you mean."

Dean Orthos grunts, dissatisfied. Dora lets out an airy laugh and pats his arm.

"Now, now, Stephan, don't want Mitt overhearing . . ."

Mitt Hartley, chairman of the Censorship Committee, is chatting merrily away in a nearby cluster of Golds, his face ruddy with wine. At mention of him, Dean Orthos only glowers more. "No, I don't. Tell me, Lee"—he lowers his voice—"how do you feel about that man's committee?"

From the way he inflects this, it's clear he believes I should have particular feelings about it, because of my background. The Censorship Committee is a brainchild of Atreus, probably one of his least popular with the patricians. It has a habit of banning classical Dragontongue literature it finds to promote triarchist sympathies; unfortunately, most classical Dragontongue literature seems to.

I was more disposed to be forgiving toward Atreus's censorship practices before I learned he wanted me dead.

But that doesn't make me any more disposed to discussing a literary heritage with this patrician bureaucrat, as if after ten years of profiting off my family's massacre, he and I can get chummy over a shared love of Dragontongue literature. I flash a bright smile at Dean Orthos.

"I gave up my heritage on Pytho's Keep."

Dora lets out a *harrumph* of impatience. "Really, Stephan," she says. Her voice, like Orthos's, is lowered. "What would you have instead? A free press? You've seen what the lower class-metals print when given half a chance—"

It seems neither Dora nor the dean, from his conceding grunt, has any sympathy for the Passi's leaflets and its full-rations-for-all slogans. Of course, I realize with spiking anger, why should they? They might be opposed to Atreus's censorship practices, but they're very much benefiting from his rationing structure. They don't have sisters like Cor's thanking them for smuggled cheese—

Annie, who has been studying Orthos with eyes narrowed, clears her throat.

"Dean Orthos, does your son work for General Holmes?"

Orthos beams. "Why, yes! Lucian was just promoted to chief of staff—"

The bragging begins. I'm pretty sure I remember Lucian Orthos from classes audited at the War College; he was a few years up from us and a consistent ass.

But the War Council is Annie's problem now, not mine.

I make my escape. In the washroom, I splash cold water on my face. I look up, blinking droplets from my eyes, to find the man at the basin beside mine studying me in the mirror.

"Lee sur Pallor?"

I nod. The man extends a hand; I have to wipe mine on a handcloth before shaking it. "Lo Teiran," he says.

Lo Teiran. Poet laureate of Callipolis, and Lotus's father. I've seen him before, at a distance, at the Lycean Ball: He has Lotus's lanky frame and wiry hair.

"I hope you'll forgive my approaching without an introduction. I was hoping to ask—"

He starts talking about a poem he's writing. Commissioned by the Ministry of Propaganda, a Revolutionary epic in the tradition of the *Aurelian Cycle*, which *was so unfortunately banned by the current regime as I hope you'll—*

He fiddles with clover-shaped cuff links as he speaks. I'm nodding along, barely listening as I try to calculate the best way to escape the washroom that was itself supposed to be an escape when half a sentence he's saying gets through.

"—hope to interview you about *what really happened* on Palace Day—"

I'm not sure how I get from the washroom to the alcove outside where Annie's waiting. She's in conversation with Power, a mystery I have no interest in exploring. I find a glass of wine has been pushed into my hand, and down it.

"Sausage?"

I look down at the tray a server proffers, and it takes me a moment to understand what I'm looking at. In the middle of a rationing crisis, I'm being offered sausage wrapped in bacon and speared on a tiny silver fork.

ANNIE

I had not realized that this, moving through throngs of Golds at Lee's side, could feel so much like riding dragonback beside him. For the first time since he returned from the duel, I glimpse the Lee I know in the air: focused, decisive, ready for battle. To charm and laugh and shrug off moments of discomfort like a dragon snapping rainwater from its wings.

This is the Lee I remember. The one who won't let a tapestry stop him, much less a few dozen tipsy Golds.

And though this exposure, private turned public, should make me feel vulnerable—standing at his side, smiling with all my teeth—I feel only powerful. For the first time I glimpse how we could do this, not just tonight but from now on. Together, side by side, we're like a Damian warship. Buoyant, impenetrable, precise.

This is our story, and tonight we will own it.

And to my own surprise as much as anyone's, I'm making *jokes*.

I am aware of eyes on us, not just within the group where we stand, but from around the room: Everyone, every adult, is watching us from the corner of their eye. I've been smiling so much my jaw is beginning to ache. But I'm surprised by how good it feels to lift my chin and acknowledge the truth. Not just the truth of our history, but the truth of who I know Lee to be.

Like stripping naked leaves me nothing left to fear.

Lee's knuckles, whitening as they clench the stem of his wineglass, are the only indicator of strain; finally, when they are bone white, he turns to me. His smile goes limp like a puppet released from its strings.

"I need a few minutes. I'll be in the washroom."

"I'll wait."

As he walks away, a woman with peppered black hair touches my arm as if she knows me, and I turn to her with foreboding because by now I've come to dread her kind of conspiratorial smile. But what she says takes me by surprise.

"It's such a pleasure to finally meet you, darling. Parry has said such nice things."

"Parry," I repeat, racking my memory for an acquaintance of such a name, and the woman smiles, her heart-shaped face brightening as she catches sight of someone behind me. "Oh, there you are, darling. Weren't you going to introduce us?"

I turn. The woman is smiling at Power. He looks between us like a taste is curdling in his mouth.

I feel a smile—a real one—split my face for the first time tonight. "Hello, Parry."

I had known Power was adopted, but rather than any difference in visage, what strikes me is how open his mother's smile is in contrast to his, and how loving. I had somehow imagined Power's whole family must be as prickly as he is.

Power scowls.

"May I borrow her, Mother? Urgent . . . affair of state."

Mrs. Hesperides nods, her eyes twinkling, and I allow a scowling Power to lead me by the elbow to a shadowy corner. He lifts two fluted glasses of wine from a server's tray as we go.

"You know, I quite like her," I tell him, when we've claimed an alcove as our own.

Power lifts a finger in warning. I struggle not to laugh.

"Do not ever," he says, "call me Parry again."

He offers me one of the glasses of wine, his gaze flicking lightning fast down my dress, then up again, squinting in the dim light of the alcove. His eyes narrow on my smile.

"Are you enjoying being paraded around like a dragonlord's pet?"

I choke on the wine I've tilted to my lips. Lower the glass. The smile is sliding off my face.

Power stands tensed, half-smirking, but wary, like a dog that has bitten awaiting a kick.

The wine from my glass, splattered on his face. A backhand across it.

I do neither. Just look at him and wait. And as I gambled he would, Power wilts.

I feel a strange, cool triumph at the sight.

"It was a joke," he says.

"I want you to stop making it."

Power lowers his glass.

"To me, or to Rock. I want you to stop. No more serf jokes."

Power lifts his eyes to the ceiling. And then he says, like we're in some sort of negotiation: "All right. But I reserve the right with Lee."

I can't help smiling, because if this is a negotiation, then I just won. Even though this isn't an apology, it's more than I once could have imagined Power offering in a hundred years. Even if Lee doesn't make the cut.

"Why do you hate him so much?" I ask.

Power twitches, his mouth twisting on the rim of his glass. "My reasons for disliking charismatic dragonborn assholes are my own."

He waves an arm to the mingling Golds in the center of the floor, the wings of the Fourth Order glinting on the shoulder of his uniform.

"Even if I stop making serf jokes, do you think they'll stop thinking of it? Look around you, Antigone. Everyone in this room sees you, sees him, and thinks, *A Stormscourge with his serf, isn't that traditional.*"

I can hear my pulse in my ears. A familiar pounding.

I know this moment.

This is the point when I curl back into myself. When I start to look around the room and wonder what these Golds are thinking, looking at Lee and me, and instead of the jokes I dare to make, I imagine the tawdry history of feudal violence repeated that they see, and see it, too.

But then I shake my head, clearing it.

Not tonight.

Tonight I'm full of confidence, like a dragon riding a gale. I am done letting these tendrils of shame tie me to the ground. No shadow is so great that it doesn't shrink when viewed from the air.

"They can see what they want."

Power pauses, his glass to his lips. Then he lifts it. Toasting me. We drink together.

Lee rejoins us, white-faced. He doesn't seem to notice Power.

"Lotus's dad just asked to interview me about Palace Day. In the washroom."

"He—*what?*"

Power pushes a wineglass into Lee's hand. Lee takes it, unseeing, and downs it.

"Yeah, he—apparently he's writing an epic about the Revolution, it's a commission from the Ministry of Propaganda. He told me he thought my account would help paint the full picture—" Lee's speech is pressured, a note of humor bordering hysteria straining through, and he lets out a wild half laugh.

"Sausage?"

A server leans through our group, offering a plate of small foods. For a moment, I don't believe what I'm seeing: bacon, sausage.

But whether or not my eyes believe it, my body smells something good. My stomach, which has been clenched on Iron-size rations, growls audibly.

"Don't mind if I do," Power says, taking two.

Lee's and my eyes meet. Neither of us moves. The server moves on.

"You might as well," Power says, through a mouth full of sausage, "enjoy yourself. Perks of testing well."

Perks.

All at once the buoyancy I was feeling falters like a punctured wing losing altitude.

This is what it means to climb: bacon and sausage while the rest of the city is counting ration cards. And this is the appetizer, which only leaves me to wonder about the main.

How can the Golds feast at a time like this?

It's the kind of thing that makes me want to go back to the Palace and file a complaint of misconduct, except I'm pretty sure that the people to whom I would submit that report are in this room.

Power's eyes are on the far side of the room, where Cor sits ensconced alone in his shadowy booth like a fortress. "Do you think Cor's going to smuggle something home to his idiot sister?"

Lee rounds on Power, fists balling. I seize the back of his uniform. After this many years of handling boys who think they are handling Power, it feels like a reenactment. *"Not here."*

"Am I interrupting something?"

Miranda Hane, the Minister of Propaganda, has found us and is smiling with the edge of a teacher sensing trouble. She has, since tea with the Protector three hours ago, knotted her hair in an elegant bun and changed into a shimmering gown that glows on her warm brown skin. She points to Cor's booth, where he's been joined by a young woman.

"I'd like you all to have a brief group interview with one of my interns from the *Gold Gazette* before Atreus arrives. Do you mind?"

Hane's intern is around our age. She looks unsettlingly familiar, and has the same olive complexion and wavy hair as Cor, with whom she's laughing as we approach. She has not taken off her coat, as if she just came in from outside and intends to leave without delay. Its seams are frayed.

I extend a hand as I take a seat in the booth opposite her. "My name's Antigone."

The girl smiles at me and does not shake it. "Did you know, we were actually in the same Dragontongue course last term? You must not have noticed me, with all your patrician friends. I'm Megara Roper."

I can feel a blush spreading: The way Megara describes the course we shared, I sound like a classist snob. But the patrician friends I made in that class were the first I'd ever had.

"Shame that class ended so abruptly," Megara goes on. She blinks very little, and her eyes are bright green. "Wasn't it mysterious how our professor just disappeared, Antigone?"

Lee twirls the stem of his glass between thumb and forefinger.
Richard Tyndale disappeared because I reported him. The
official charge was sedition, to protect Lee, but the real reason
was that he was soliciting Lee on behalf of the triarchy.

Does Megara guess I filed that report?

"You a big fan of Dragontongue poetry?" Power asks.

Megara folds her arms. "No. Tyndale was my scholarship
advisor."

I didn't know Tyndale would be the sort to advise lowborn
students. Power clears his throat in a way that disguises a snort,
but my conscience prickles for the first time since charging
Tyndale with sedition.

"Advisor or no, he was a terrible teacher," Cor mutters.

Megara rolls round to glare at him, and he lifts his palms.
Like this is an argument they've had many times before. At my
look of confusion, she flicks a thumb between herself and Cor
and explains: "Same grammar school."

She rakes dark hair back from her face, produces a notebook,
and clears her throat. Her urban accent trims itself seamlessly
into Palace-standard.

"Shall we do it, then? I have an invitation from Minister
Hane to justify."

A server pauses at our table to offer refills of sparkling wine.
The boys take more; Megara and I decline, and our eyes meet
briefly as the server walks away.

Am I mistaking a challenge in her gaze?

"You're some of the smartest young people in the country,"
she begins, and I can't shake the impression she recites this with
a certain amount of irony, "and I'm told your training gives
you unmatched insight into the operations of our government.

Tell me a little about what you all see as Callipolis's biggest challenges at the moment."

"The rationing program," Cor says at once.

Megara's nodding as she scribbles. "What about it?"

"It's—some might say it's unfair."

Megara tips a pen in Cor's direction. "Indeed. So you would agree with the Gold Advisory Council that those who say it's unfair are a danger to civil order?"

Cor blinks. Power jumps in, knocking back another gulp of wine. "Absolutely. Those protesters—the Passi? Southside's Daughter?—they're a threat. They must be silenced."

Cor scoffs. "Threat? They want justice."

After watching Cheapsiders on the verge of breaking into a shopfront in a public square in the name of justice, I have very little patience for this interpretation. "You mean by looting bakeries? Because that's what I saw Southside's Daughter inciting in Cheapside."

Cor blinks. Megara watches our interchange with fingers tracing her chin, her eyes narrowed.

"So would you agree with Cor," she asks me, "that the Passi and Southside's Daughter are our greatest threat at the moment?"

I laugh out loud. "Our greatest threat is the one from New Pythos."

Megara's pen pauses on her notebook. I have the sense that I didn't give her the answer she wanted. "Spoken like a true fleet commander," she says, looking up. "Which happens to be a new title for you. How has that transition been?"

"Fine."

But she's looking between Lee and me now, leaning forward.

"What about you, Lee? What would you say about Annie's take on the threat from New Pythos? Is the war threat . . . difficult for you?"

Lee levels his gaze at Megara. "Why would it be difficult for me?"

Megara lets out a soft laugh. Lee lifts a shoulder, sips from his wine, and adds: "It isn't my place to judge Antigone's opinions. She's my commander."

Something warm and proud blooms in my chest. Our eyes meet and he lifts his glass, fractionally. Like he's toasting me.

We'll do this together.

I lift my glass to him in return.

Megara looks between us and then at the six inches between on the bench. She tilts her head, black hair tossing.

"But is that all she is to you?"

Lee blinks. "I'm sorry?"

"The city is dying to know. The Golds are dying to know. You may have taken vows forswearing marriage or family but that doesn't quite cover everything. Is there *more* between you? Everyone hopes there is. After all, wouldn't it be only . . . natural?"

A moment of thick silence follows her words. Cor has choked on his wine; Lee has gone quite still. Even in the candlelight, I can see him reddening. And for all I told Power, moments ago, that I didn't care, I can feel heat ignite in my face.

To my surprise, Power speaks first.

"Piss off, Roper."

Megara swings an arm out, holding Cor in as he rounds on Power, and turns her smile in a new direction. "Power sur Eater. Your reputation with women precedes you."

Power sneers. "Not with any of your friends, I can assure you. I don't bother with the dregs—"

Cor lifts an arm and points. "The First Protector's here."

Across the room, Atreus Athanatos has entered the room to a ripple of greetings and well wishes, dressed in a well cut but unadorned black tunic. Lee's eyes narrow on him like a target.

My stomach has skipped for other reasons. Not three hours ago, that man poured me tea and complimented my performance as a Guardian. And now, when his gaze travels around the room, he looks in the direction of our booth and—I'm almost certain I didn't imagine it—nods at me.

I resist the urge to nod back.

Dora announces him to the room.

"Citizens of the Lyceum," she says, "I would like to thank you all for coming to this Fête of the Fourth Order—the first of many opportunities, I hope, for us to get to know these four special young people a little better. Now that the Protector has arrived, I hoped he would start us off with a toast. Protector?"

Atreus lifts his glass. "Join me in toasting the accomplishments of our finest four Guardians—whose illustrious careers have only just begun. May their light continue to shine, long past my own, as a beacon to the people of Callipolis."

We drink.

Lee has gotten to his feet. Even in the candlelight, he looks pale.

"I'd like to propose a toast to the First Protector in return," he tells the room.

Golds turn to look at him, surprised at his nerve. Cor and Power are fixated on him; Megara Roper has slid away into the crowd; and Atreus has frozen, lips parted, like prey that spots a predator. Lee, still smiling, has a fury burning behind his eyes that sets my nerves on end.

I have a sudden vision of Lee, on a precipice about to jump. I just can't tell whether he's about to take flight or plummet.

He lifts his glass.

"To Atreus. Who spared my life as a child, because he was merciful. Who has been like a father to me, for all the years since I renounced my own. Who saw in me not a dragonlord, but another Revolution's son."

My nerves still with the same satisfaction that comes with watching Lee execute a perfect contact charge.

Back in the saddle.

We drink. Atreus's lip twisted, he bows deeply. "I thank you for these . . . gracious words, Lee."

"To Lee sur Pallor!" someone cries.

The room resounds with it, as glasses lift a third time: "To Lee sur Pallor, the Revolution's son!"

Lee's smile, full of ice, fills with triumph as he holds the First Protector's gaze and bows.

And then the sound of shattering comes from the floor below, and a scream rends the air.

10

SOUTHSIDE'S DAUGHTER

LEE

This night feels like one long waking. As if I've been asleep, not knowing it, and waking by stages. Because for all I've thought over the years of the ways patrician life is indistinguishable between this regime and the old, the reality of what that means is not driven home until the moment when a server offers me sausage wrapped in bacon during a rationing crisis.

And then, with the presence of Atreus, the man who I thought saved me but in fact betrayed me, the meaning of Annie's words becomes clear.

Be the one who replaces him.

I have spent a lifetime overgrowing thoughts of revenge, of turning away from that path because the wrongs outweighed the rights. But there is a blessed irony and satisfaction in realizing revenge is something I can feel justified in wanting after all. In realizing that this regime, which so casually sells my family's things and displays them in dusty corridors with little plaques to remember us by, deserves all the retribution I used to long for.

Never mind that Atreus betrayed me and wants me dead. His regime is failing, just as the last did. Feasting during a famine, warm inside while outside the city hungers. He deserves to fall.

And revenge doesn't need to take the form I pictured as a child. Atreus's life isn't what he values. He values power, popularity, and control.

Revenge doesn't need to begin with a knife. It can begin with a well-delivered speech.

And after that, the moment that most marks the crossing from sleep to waking—like cold water thrown, when I realize I have not so much woken from a nightmare as to one—is when I hear that scream.

Because then, memory becomes premonition.

The Golds around the room have frozen; silence has fallen. The sound of something heavy breaking on the floor below shocks the polished floorboards at our feet. Another shout, another scream.

Annie, Power, Cor, and I are on our feet.

I take two steps sideways. Crack the blackout curtain, look out onto the main courtyard of the Lyceum. In the moonlight, reflected by low clouds, I make out a trickle of figures moving across the dark lawn from the porter's lodge to the storeroom adjacent to the classroom building that has been converted, since the food shortage, into a public granary.

They're raiding it.

Which means the guardhouse at the porter's lodge has been disabled. The Lyceum walls have been breached. And—

Another scream from below, a thunk.

Directly below the window, servants begin to pour from the entrance to the club's kitchen, fleeing with screams. Objects are being thrown, bouncing and rolling, across the darkened green, with shrieks of laughter: casks of ale; sacks of flour; what looks like the carcass of a half-cooked lamb.

Our main.

The half-darkened faces of the raiders, illuminated by the torches they carry, turn and look up. At the window I'm watching through.

A torch sails through the air, toward me. Glass shatters, the curtains billow inward. Fire rolls across the floor.

Golds around me are screaming, jumping out of the torch's rolling path.

I unhook the ceremonial mantle from my shoulders and lunge. The mantle smothers the flaming torch; smoke rises from under the gilded lining of the mantle.

Through the broken window comes a Cheapside accent, playful and all too close without glass to muffle it: "We know you're in there."

Annie crouches in front of me, her hair a shock of red against the black dress.

"Lee?"

It's as if she knows the memories that are rising up to drown me.

Use them. Get out of this alive.

"We need to barricade the doors," I croak. "And get to the dragons before they separate us."

The shouts and crashes below are sufficient to keep our conversation private.

Annie's face flickers, understanding, and she rises. Her voice is level, barely raised, but clear.

"Power, bolt and barricade the entrances to the second floor. Cor, please escort the Protector to a windowless room that can be locked from the inside. Dean Orthos—is there a balcony on the second floor from which we can summon dragons?"

Orthos's academic cap has slid down one ear; he points a shaking finger. "Out back. Attached to the garden room."

"Thank you. Everyone else—stay away from the windows. Lee, with me."

I follow her out of the room, her orders echoing in my ears as I understand: Annie is placing a guard around the First Protector. Because in this analog to the riots I survived as a child, Atreus is the ruler whose people are scaling his walls in search of bread.

And now it's our job to protect him. Atreus, the man who engineered Palace Day—

The balcony outside is bare, summer furniture stacked in the corner under tarps. Our breath rises in steam; goose pimples are showing on Annie's bare arms. Another crash from the floor below, followed by a shriek of laughter. My hands clench at the sound; I force them loose.

Annie is looking at my hands, too. "Are you fit for duty?"

"I'm fine."

I'm pretty sure I don't sound fine. Annie exhales through tightened lips and seems to decide not to say whatever she is thinking. She stands still for a moment, cocking her head, before shaking it. "We're too far out of range."

She can't feel Aela. And the dragons won't be able to hear our summoning whistles. I have to take her word for it; my connection to Pallor has never been as strong as hers to Aela.

"The roof?"

Annie looks up, her lips forming a line. Then she reaches down to thumb the straps of her heeled shoes off her feet.

"Lift me."

I make a stirrup with laced fingers as I did for her with Pallor hours ago and hoist. Barefooted, she scrabbles against the slate. I climb onto the nearest stack of chairs, clench the gutter with numbing fingers, and heave. There's a precarious moment where the horizon tilts and then Annie seizes my arm, pulling my weight against the tiles.

We crawl together to the apex, and finally, from the roof of the Lyceum Club, we can see everything.

The porter's lodge is on fire, its gate loose on its hinges. The doors to the Lyceum granary have been thrown open. Figures silhouetted in the torchlight are racing out the doors with sacks of grain slung over their shoulders, making for the carts wheeling into the courtyard.

Below us, a ring of citizens armed with torches and garden tools have gathered at the front steps of the club. A young man with a scraggly red beard steps out from the ring and raises his voice, thick with a Cheapside accent.

"Ladies and gentlemen of the Lyceum, the Passi are here for your granary, and we might just help ourselves to your dinner, too!"

Annie lifts her wristband to her lips and blows through the summoning whistle. The sound is inaudible to human ears but below us, in the lairs, Aela will hear it.

I lift my own summoner to my mouth and then, as I take in the scene below, I hesitate.

The red-bearded man is brandishing a leg of mutton like a torch. "*These* are your rations? The Irons are scraping after crumbs and your people gorge themselves on racks of lamb—"

It's the same rhetoric I remember from the old protests. The protests that were dismissed; the famine that was excused or overlooked. But this time, I'm not a child misled by my father's lies. I know that what this man says is true. The Irons are hungry. We were eating sausage.

And Atreus deserves to burn.

Annie's order cuts through my racing thoughts. "Lee, summon!"

I shove my wristband to my mouth and blow into the mouthpiece.

We wait. The gates to the stone stables should burst open, any moment now—

And as we wait, the words burst from my lips.

"Annie, they've got a point—"

Annie starts to answer and then freezes, leaning forward, her eyes narrowing.

From the base of the club come the sounds of a scuffle and the slam of a door—and a figure is dragged from the building and into the crowd, which parts for him.

The figure is thrust to his knees. The red-bearded man holding him lifts his head back by the collar of his uniform, presses a butcher's cleaver to his throat, and as the light catches the figure's face, Annie inhales beside me.

Power.

Annie blows again, frantically, into her wristband.

"Where are they—"

She closes her eyes, presses her thumbs to them, and when she looks up at me, her pupils are dilated: She has found Aela, is spilled over, and speaks in a voice distant with double feeling. "They're trying to barricade the stone stables," she tells me. "Aela and Pallor are still inside—"

The thought of him near, afraid, and cut off from me makes my heart clench. "They're going to have to fire to get out."

Annie nods, rubbing at her forehead, and I know she's struggling to communicate with Aela over a connection that is little more than a twisted cable of emotions and images—

Another figure steps from the crowd to approach the kneeling Power. A young woman with a green scarf masking her nose and mouth.

"Southside's Daughter," Annie breathes beside me, her eyes narrowing in recognition.

"Who do we have here?" the green-scarved girl crows. "A Guardian, loose without his dragon?"

She pries Power's wristband from him.

Though I have little reason to think of this as anything but Power's just deserts—who not long ago pried my own wristband from me and planned his own vigilante justice out of spite—it's impossible, watching the rioters close in, not to remember.

I decided, a long time ago, that no one deserves this. Even if Power comes close.

Dora Mithrides's voice answers Southside's Daughter from the second-floor balcony.

"The Lyceum granary serves the neighborhoods of Cheapside and Southside as well as Scholars Row. If you rob it, you will only be hurting those your Passi claim to want to help. Unhand that boy."

Southside's Daughter lets out a peal of laughter.

Am I mad for thinking that laugh sounds familiar?

"*Serves* Southside and Cheapside? You only give them a fourth of what you're giving the Golds on Scholars Row. It's time for a reset."

The sense of her words is hammering on me like fat drops of rain. "Annie. She's *right*—"

Annie rounds on me. "Her people have taken a Guardian hostage and we have no reason to trust they'll do anything with that grain other than *keep it for themselves*. Wake up, Lee!"

I swallow down the protests clawing up inside.

Annie presses her fingers against her forehead, and exhales so hard I can hear it.

From below comes a sound like an explosion, and a warm glow lights the buildings.

Two aurelians erupt from the stone stables. For a moment they are silhouetted, silver and amber wings glinting ghostlike against the dark sky, before they settle on the apex of the roof at our sides. Another flare and the dark shadows of two storm-scourges burst forth after them.

Faces have turned upward, and a hush falls over the crowd at the sight of us on the roof above them. Annie leaps to her feet beside Aela. I reach out to steady myself with a hand at the ridge of Pallor's neck; he is growling, horns flattened and black eyes fixed on the crowd threatening below. Aela lets out a belch of fire that streams upward in a distress beacon for the city guard and any patrolling dragonriders.

Annie lifts her voice to address the crowd. "The guard will be here in minutes. Release Power sur Eater and back your carts away from the Lyceum granary."

Southside's Daughter's eyes crinkle into a smile above the lip of her green scarf and I feel another flutter of recognition. "Antigone sur Aela," she says. "I was wondering if you'd show your face." She nods to the red-bearded man, whose grip tightens on Power. He stares up at us, slack-jawed.

Annie turns to me.

"Secure the granary. I'll get Power."

She swings herself onto Aela, mindless of the dress that ear-lier she rode sidesaddle to protect, and the bare skin that will burn against the too-hot scales; I reach for Pallor and scramble onto his bare back, clamping my knees under his wing joints and clinging to his neck as he kicks off from the ground.

He lands us in front of the granary, between the carts and the Lyceum gate.

The granary's doors have been smashed open; the sounds of people shouting come from within; citizens streak in and out of the gates holding half-closed sacks of grain that spill as much as they contain as they hasten to load the wagons.

But when they see Pallor, they freeze. I tighten my knees on his wing joints to sit taller, summoning the orders I'm supposed to give the citizens before us. *Back away from the cart. Back away from the granary.*

But I hesitate. *And then?* If they refuse, do I give the command to fire? Blanket them in dragonfire, for attempting to steal grain?

Grain, while we dined in comfort at the Lyceum Club? What loyalty do I really have to this regime, to its barbaric rationing practices—

Pallor's wings are spread, his back arched, his fangs bared. A low whining growl comes from the back of his throat as he stares the raiders down. On the other side of the courtyard, flames light the night: Antigone sur Aela has fired. Another flare, violet-tinged, signals the fire of a stormscourge: Power reunited with Eater. Screams are erupting; the crowd around the club is scattering.

"They've got dragons, get out, get out—"

More raiders are emerging from the granary and clambering onto carts, seizing the reins, weighing the odds as Pallor and I block their way.

Pallor inhales to fire, his lungs expanding between my knees. He waits on my order—

In the flare of dragonfire from behind me, of Aela and Eater lighting the courtyard, I can make out the face of the leading driver as he stares me down. Teeth bared, exposed, nothing but flesh on bone that so easily burns.

Staring eyes and hollow cheeks, emaciation visible even in the low light.

His horses rear and charge, and rather than fire, I yank Pallor aside.

The carts begin to stream across the green, through the burning gate, and out into the city.

And then, as the last raiders scramble out of the granary, I realize what they're shouting.

"Fire on the rest! Burn what we can't take!"

"No—" I shout.

But we charge too late between them. The granary, and what's left of its stores, is in flames. Not from dragonfire: from a torch that someone flung.

Behind me, from the Lyceum Club, comes a keening, hair-raising wail.

ANNIE

In the space of the time it takes to land Aela between the front doors of the Lyceum Club and the mob gathered around Power, I don't process a single conscious thought. Aela and I operate on instinct: firing over the heads of the rioters in warning, and when

Southside's Daughter and her red-bearded accomplice do not back away from Power, we fire again. This time at feet.

There are screams. People begin to run, some with clothing on fire. Aela's flames are so bright that when they stop, the darkness of the night is blinding.

In the confusion, a stormscourge dives into the stampeding crowd and emerges clutching Power by the back of his uniform like a mother cat carrying a kitten by the scruff of its neck. Eater deposits Power beside me on the club's steps and Power doubles over with his palms on his knees, gasping. He rubs his throat where the cleaver traced a thin red line.

The city guard is pouring in the gate, the rioters screaming and running past them into the night, and on the opposite side of the square, a fire has begun to glow. I watch the chaos numbly, trying to remember what it was like before I knew how to do this. Back when I still hesitated before using dragonfire on human beings.

But I was setting Aela on unarmed villagers in collections for weeks. Armed rioters didn't take a second thought.

I lean onto my knees and dry heave.

"Where is she?" Power rasps.

I wipe my mouth. "Southside's Daughter?"

She disappeared in the chaos after the dragonfire. And without her scarf, she could be anyone in a black coat.

Power shakes his head. "Megara," he says. "Megara Roper."

It takes me a moment to remember who that is. "The *Gold Gazette* intern?"

Power straightens, his hand still holding his throat.

"Annie . . . I could have sworn I recognized Southside Daughter's voice."

We stare at each other. His eyes reflect the glowing of the fires around us, the people running, the city guard shouting. Dora's guests have begun to trickle down the front steps, clutching their coats and hats.

"You can't be— That's quite an accusation. That's absurd—"

Though not outside the bounds of possibility. She could have ducked out when Atreus arrived. She could have been the one to tip off the Passi that tonight, with festivities in the air, the Lyceum would have a slackened guard. She could have carried a green scarf in the pocket of that nondescript coat she was wearing—

Power shrugs. "Southside's Daughter flaunts a gold wristband. She's known for it."

The guests begin to trickle out of the building in little groups as the city guard secures the area, handcuffing the rioters who were captured and opening the lower rooms of the club for emergency burn treatment. The Lyceum physician has been woken and brought in to aid the wounded.

My wounded.

I sit on the front steps of the club, listening to the cries of pain from within. Making myself listen. As if, like nails dug into my skin, I'm checking that I still feel anything. Aela, who alighted on the roof of the stone stables once her fire was no longer needed, overlooks the commotion like an impassive, monstrous gargoyle as she gnaws a leg of mutton abandoned by the raiders. At some point someone—I think Dora—drapes my mantle over my shoulders with a gentle pat to my hair and returns my shoes.

Megara Roper is not among the guests I count emerging from the upper rooms.

Lee returns from the granary white-faced. Only when I take in his expression and look past him at the fire that is growing on the far side of the courtyard do I realize what's burning.

The Lyceum granary is on fire.

"Someone threw a torch as they were running," Lee says.

"You didn't stop them?"

"I couldn't," Lee says. He lifts a hand to his face. "I couldn't do it."

By the light of the blaze, we can make out a scattered detritus of oats and wheat, mixed with dirt and ash, strewn across the courtyard like dirty snow.

I get to my feet. "What do you mean, you *couldn't do it*? You said you were fit for duty!"

Lee spreads his hands. "Maybe I'm not fit for this kind of duty."

Atreus, one of the last guests to emerge from the upper rooms, stands feet away with his great black mantle thrown over his shoulders, in conversation with the captain of the guard—but he's watching us. Listening.

I seize Lee by the arm and yank him into the alleyway beside the stone stables, out of earshot of the First Protector. The guilt and horror that has been roiling in my stomach at my own actions shifts in an instant into fury.

"You're a Guardian. You don't get to choose what kind of duty you're fit for. Your duty is to *do what it takes*."

At the sound of Atreus's phrase, Lee flinches.

"They were hungry, Annie!"

There are memories in that sentence, memories that I can hear him pleading with me to remember, but I only feel more fury at such an entreaty. He wants to bring up Albans? Let him. I remember being hungry. And I remember bullies taking my food.

"Does their hunger justify stealing from a public granary, or qualify them to distribute the grain to others?"

Lee points up at Aela's spoils from tonight's raid. "Maybe more than us."

I can feel Aela's simple satisfaction humming, low and visceral, at the back of my own throat as she chews the fatty meat. She doesn't care that the Lyceum was serving mutton during a rationing crisis. And at the moment, I have to agree with her that it isn't our biggest concern. I raise a shaking hand to point at the fire bathing the courtyard in red light. "The only thing those—*people* have proved themselves capable of is threatening the life of one of my riders and setting a grain depot on fire."

Lee's black hair is silhouetted, a thin rim of gold, from the fire behind us. *"Those people?"* he repeats, echoing my tone. "Who—class-irons, peasants, the poor? Annie, do you know who you sound like?"

I know, from how he asks this, that he doesn't mean Atreus.

Behind me, Aela lifts her head and growls.

How dare he.

Lee takes a step backward from us both. But his face is twisted with fury, too, and Pallor, who has slunk down the alleyway after us, is growling. He and Aela have tensed, glaring at each other, wings and crests lifted.

"Was it easy this time?" Lee demands. "Firing on civilians? Did you have to think twice before doing it?"

"They were *armed*!" I shout.

Aela fires, a short jet into the sky. Pallor hisses, his crest flattening. Lee blinks at me.

He doesn't have to point out the difference between a kitchen cleaver and a dragon.

And I don't deny that it was easy.

But it saved Power's life and those of dozens of Golds who shouldn't be eating bacon but don't deserve to die for it.

My fists are curling at my sides. My eyes are stinging. "The point isn't how it feels. The point is that it had to happen or worse things would."

Lee shakes his head. The rage that I've seen smoldering on and off since the duel blazes in his gray eyes. So much rage that I have to resist the urge to take a step backward.

"I'm done choosing between evils. Not for this. This regime, Atreus, he doesn't deserve it."

I laugh aloud.

"The price for your clean conscience will be people starving because a granary burned."

Lee kicks at sludge under his heel and looks away, and Pallor whimpers.

"Am I interrupting a lovers' quarrel?"

I spin on my heel. Power is behind us, looking utterly delighted.

"What do you want?"

"I was just wondering," Power says, "if you'd found Megara Roper yet."

"No," I snap, too furious at the interruption to give a damn about Roper or Power's conspiracy theory.

"And what about Cor?" Power asks.

I open my mouth to snap again when I realize I haven't.

I haven't seen Cor since the fire started. Not since Southside's Daughter disappeared.

Cor, who openly hates the rationing program; and his childhood friend, who hasn't been spotted since the riot began, are gone, along with a dragon.

Suddenly Power's theory feels a lot more alarming and a lot less absurd.

I turn back to Lee, but he's already walking away.

LEE

Pallor and I are aloft, over the city, in minutes. Moonlight shimmers through the low clouds and casts the city in a pale glow: the twisting River Fer, the latticed hills of the Janiculum, Pytho's Keep rising in shadow. From on high, the blaze that the city guard struggles to put out in the Lyceum is dwarfed to the size of a hearth fire. With Pallor still unsaddled, the legs of my ceremonial uniform burning on his hot scales, and nothing keeping me from falling but my own clamped knees, it occurs to me that Pallor and I are violating every rule of basic flight safety training.

I don't care. My heart is hammering, Annie's fury echoing in my ears.

Those people.

How could this be how she sees it? Firing on commoners to protect Atreus and his coterie—

Hours ago, I was speechless with delight at the sight of Annie on Pallor's back, and now all I want to do is shake her. How can someone be so beautiful, so brilliant, and so *wrong*?

Maybe I shouldn't have let the granary burn. Maybe the Passi were too violent, needlessly violent, for their ends. But that didn't stop their words from being true. Callipolis deserves better than what Atreus and his hypocritical regime are giving it.

And I'm done defending a man who killed my family and now fails his city the same way they did.

I scan the shadowed rooftops with narrowed eyes and almost don't believe when I see it: the flutter of black, like a bat's wings, against the thatched roofs of Highmarket, slipping out of sight.

My knees tighten under Pallor's wings as we dive.

We find them in the sunken pit of a half-built bunker, fenced off to the public, manned by class-irons during the day but deserted at night. A dragon, its rider, and a young woman. The stormscourge is pitch-black in the moonlight. A green scarf encircles the woman's neck.

Pallor lands opposite them, and I confirm: She's exactly who I think she is.

"This," Southside's Daughter is telling Cor, "is not the way I was expecting our friendship to rekindle, I'll admit."

They turn at the sound of my boots crunching on gravel. Cor takes a step forward, as if to stand between the girl and my dragon.

"Lee?"

"Cor."

For a moment, it seems neither of us knows what happens next.

And then I turn to Megara Roper.

"You make a good speech."

Her teeth flash white in the darkness.

"So do you, Lee sur Pallor."

11

THE KRAKEN'S ARMS

GRIFF

My punishment forfeit if I bring a Callipolan rider down today.

The luck of the damned is a strange, fierce kind of luck. Fog rolls in layers over a darkening sky as we launch to flush the scouts; when we burst through the last layer, the sun is still setting above: stars to the east, gold to the west. Here and there around us, the tops of karst pillars poke from the stratus like islands of rock. The rest of the riders are breaking cloud cover around us; Sparker and I are at Delo sur Gephyra's wing, for the first time since Julia's passing, and I can't help thinking, *This is how it should be.*

Not a foreign rider is in sight, but my hopes are up. I know what we're looking for, and I've got a pending punishment riding on it. I'll find them.

"What *the hell* were you thinking?" Delo shouts. "You shouldn't have confessed!"

With the wind masking our voices, it's easy to have a private conversation.

"Like I said—"

"No. Who are you covering for? Agga? Your grandfather?"

Delo's neck is twisted, his face hidden by his helmet as he looks at me. I look back at him and for a half second experience anger matching that in his voice: *If it bothers you so much, why didn't you speak up?*

But that's not fair, because what choice did he have?

I dig my heel into Sparker's side, and announce, "I've got a lucky feeling about Kraken."

Kraken is the karst I saw those riders emerge from, two days ago. I know what the others don't: that whoever's been sighted has been camping out near us for days.

Delo slumps, exasperated. "Why?"

I put on my best Norish brogue and wave an arm. "Call it my mystical Norcian connection to the karst—"

"Your clan-karst is *Nag*!" Delo shouts.

But when I set off for the Kraken's arms, he follows, cursing. I can't hear most of it, but I make out *death wish* and *stubborn as a stormscourge*. I pat Sparker's flank affectionately at the remark and hug my pike tighter to my side.

"Aren't we?"

Mystical connections aside, I do have a Norcian's knowledge of the karsts, and I've had three days to imagine which crevices in Kraken I'd hide in, if I were spying on New Pythos. As we sweep back into the gloom of the fog, I lead Delo sur Gephyra toward the pillars I have in mind. We loop round my own clan's karst, the Nag, with her gracefully curved neck and all her crooked fissures; circle the Turret, with his densely wooded crown; and approach the Kraken with all her arms, thin arches of stone. Kraken's proved one of the least fruitful mines, and most of its floating docks are long abandoned, the mineshafts slowly eroding into tidal caves; puffins nest on the ancient standing stones of Kraken Shrine atop the arch of her tallest arm.

We latch on to the wall of the central arm and scuttle the dragons around its base like great crabs, talons clinging to crevices. When we round the sharpest slab, the Kraken's eroding mine entrance comes into view. Dragon scales glint in the darkness of the mine's entrance.

For a half second I think we might catch them unawares and corner them in their hideaway. But then a flare of dragonfire lights from the cave, and the two skyfish burst forth.

The Callipolan scouts.

Gephyra and Sparker kick off from the karst to split and tail. But the skyfish that Sparker's following puts us behind her quickly, no match for her speed, as her rider's golden braid streams out from under her helmet. She weaves into the Kraken's arms, and soon it's all I can do to keep sight of her as we wind in and out of the stone pillars.

On the far side of the arms, Delo sur Gephyra have better luck, gaining on their target, forcing the little skyfish to slow as they fire. The target's weave is ridiculously, absurdly regular, and Delo begins to land hits. Once, twice, I can hear the rider grunting with pain—

Ahead of me, the girl's helmet turns to the sound and then her skyfish swerves. Sacrificing their lead on us to cross the distance and close on Gephyra.

I complete the triangle, gaining.

She fires, a full-heat hit on Delo that makes Gephyra spiral off course, freeing her wingrider from Delo's advance. And then I intercept.

The golden-haired rider wheels her skyfish round with startling speed. Suddenly we're in range of their dragonfire. I grip the reins, brace for the blast, preparing to barrel through it—

And instead of firing, the rider says something.

Like she's speaking to me. But that doesn't make sense.

I take the opening and charge, ramming my pike into her side while Sparker's fangs sink into her leg and his talons into her skyfish's wing. I pierce armor. Her scream rends the fog. We slam as one against a pillar and begin to slide down it.

And then I realize what I heard her just say. Dragontongue. *Wait.*

Wait for what? What could she possibly be expecting—that we'd stop and chat mid-ambush?

But I don't have time to figure out what she wants. I don't have the luxury of waiting. Rhode's punishment, forfeit. Loyalty to prove. A family to protect.

Sparker and I tighten our hold.

We're scraping down the side of the karst, locked together, toward the crashing waves below as the dragon and rider both shriek and struggle. In the dusk light, distance is hard to measure, the arms mere silhouettes spinning around us. Flashes of light emit from Delo sur Gephyra as they fire on the other skyfish. I have a moment of giddy satisfaction: We'll bring them both down, we've got them both—

And then light, like an explosion, fills the fog and illuminates the arms.

The second skyfish has fired full-heat, within Delo sur Gephyra's range, blasting them back.

"Delo?" I hear myself shouting.

The second skyfish hurtles toward us, its fire blistering as it searches for me and Sparker.

We let go of the female rider, and a boy's voice calls in panicked Callish through the fog; she answers him, her skyfish kicking away from the karst.

They're rising, seeking the fog, the female rider's dragon struggling to beat the air with wings Sparker shredded; and for a moment I grip the saddle with both knees, frozen as I calculate: Her skyfish slowed by injury, could my stormscourge catch her?

But Sparker is panting, tired, and Delo sur Gephyra is nowhere in sight.

"Delo!" I shout again.

The Callipolan riders are about to be lost in fog—my last chance of proving loyalty and appeasing Rhode's rage—but at a sound from below, I know I'll let them go. Groaning, and then my name.

"Griff?"

Delo, in pain.

I turn my back on the vanishing Callipolans and rein Sparker down to the sound of his voice.

12

THE WAR THAT MATTERS

ANNIE

It's dawn by the time Power and I finish escorting the harrowed Janiculum residents home from the Lyceum. Most of the land-birds have already left Callipolis for the winter, but a few lonely gull cries break with the dawn as we bid the last Golds good night and the dragons have begun to yawn. We don't talk about the fact that Lee and Cor have vanished along with Megara Roper; I think, if Power mentions it again, the headache that has begun to pound between my eyes will burst.

As we kick off from the lower foothills of the Janiculum to ride a low morning breeze back to the Palace, Power lifts an arm.

"Annie . . ."

"I told you, I don't want to hear it!"

"No, look."

He points. Two dragons, approaching on the northern horizon, barely distinguishable from the gray that precedes dawn. Two skyfish.

Crissa and Duck are back.

I dismount Aela in the courtyard off the Palace infirmary where they descend. Phaedra has landed on her side, a wing angled into the air. A keeper kneels beside her, examining her while she snorts ash onto the flagstones and another keeper holds her still. The membrane of her wing is shredded; I can see the dawn light through the gashes.

Duck stands beside his skyfish, Certa, in his armor and flame-suit, helmet flung to the ground at his feet. I run to him, wrap my arms around him, and inhale.

"You're all right—"

"I'm all right."

Duck's face is dark with ash, and though the smell of dragonfire lingers, there are no signs of serious burns. The wind in the court-yard stirs, and two more dragons alight in it: a stormscourge and a white aurelian. Cor and Lee. Drawn by the sight of the returning two skyfish as I was, back from wherever they disappeared to. They dismount and approach us at a run. Cor seizes Duck after me.

"Dorian!"

"I'm fine," Duck says as Cor clasps his arms around him.

Cor and Lee are both still in ceremonial uniform. I feel the fury I've been suppressing rise again at the sight of their decorations. It's been hours, neither has been seen since the Lyceum was sacked, and here they arrive on dragonback?

"Where have you two been?"

Cor answers without meeting my eyes. "We were looking for the stolen carts."

"Really. Did Southside's Daughter help you find them?"

Cor stiffens. He lifts his hands, like he might to handle an overbearing mother. "Look, why don't you just calm down—"

"*Cor,*" says Lee.

But he isn't looking at me, either.

And neither of them denies it.

I feel a different rage heat the corners of my eyes.

Hours ago I contemplated leading Callipolis into the future alongside Lee. Now I'm wondering if he just walked away from a crime scene to help the people tearing the city apart.

The words form and rest on my tongue: *We said we would do this together.*

I let them die there.

Whatever I imagined Firstridership being, when I wanted it so badly, this is the last thing I pictured. Defending Golds at a dinner party and staring down my friends.

It's a shit job. But it's my job. And I will do it.

I turn my back on both of them, leaving Aela to snort ash behind me.

"What happened?" I ask Duck.

Pivoting. Back to the mission with New Pythos. The war that matters. The only thing left that I can think of without a nauseating mixture of rage and shame. Duck casts a bemused look between the boys and me, but when none of us explains our frosty silence, he clears his throat. A strange, bitter note enters his voice that I've never heard before. "Crissa . . . covered for me."

Then his eyes find mine, uncertain. "One of the muzzled riders got her bad."

Behind us, Phaedra lets out a wail, and I finally look at her. Not just her wing is torn: Her side is gashed, as if talons pierced and pulled along her flank. It's the first time I've ever heard a dragon cry from pain.

"Where is she?" Lee asks.

"They're—they're tending her inside."

Lee leaves us at a run.

Cor and I don't speak to each other as we follow, tracing

echoing steps down the ward to the sounds we can hear from the threshold of the infirmary.

Lee is holding Crissa still while they cut the flamesuit off her leg. The gashes that marked Phaedra's side mark hers; here, unlike with Duck, I breathe in not just dragonfire but the sharp, unmistakable smell of burned flesh. Crissa's face has turned into Lee's arm, buried against it as she cries, but even muffled, I feel a chill go down my spine at the sound. Lee's face is downturned, murmuring.

A muzzled rider did this. A rider I told her to attempt to contact.

The nurse pulls, Crissa screams, and Lee lowers his crumpling face to her hair. Cor goes to them.

"I'm sorry," I hear myself say as I back away.

I'm not sure who I'm speaking to, because none of them are listening.

13

—

ALOE AND GINGER

GRIFF

The burns, the cold wet of the winter fog, and the strain of hauling Delo to his quarters in the Provisional Palace end in a fever that takes two days to break. Sick as a drowned dragon, I lie by the fire, vomit in a pail, and sweat through the piles of blankets Agga's thrown over me. Whenever I wake, Agga forces me to drink more broth. All I can think—when I can think anything—is that for every day I miss, Scully will dock my pay. When I try to force my way out of bed, Agga pushes me back down.

"Don't you worry about that. We'll be fine. You need to rest."

Children she minds sneak over occasionally to peer at me, and in the fever they seem like tiny spirits, asking shrill and stupid questions.

"Do you really ride a dragon?"

Agga shoos them away, and I drift off again.

When the world comes into focus at last, Agga's sitting at my side with Becca, working a mortar and pestle, filling the room with the smell of mashed aloe as she tells Becca a story. Granda's out; judging by the light coming through the slats, it's past midday.

". . . and so the Nag told the Great Dragon, 'Never again shall you threaten our waters, never so long as Kraken and I oppose, and Turret stands watch—'" Agga spots me. "Oh, you're awake!"

"And then?" Becca asks, but Agga waves a hand.

"You know what next. Here, Griff. Have some tea."

I take it, expecting hot water, but when I drink, I realize it *is* tea. Agga's ginger.

"We shouldn't waste this—"

"I've plenty. Turn on your good side."

The sight of a poultice makes me come to my senses. Behind her, on the table, sits an aloe plant I've never seen before. And the glass jar that was almost out of ginger sits beside it, full again.

"Where'd we get aloe from?"

Agga looks surprised.

"Lord Delo, of course," she says.

Lord Delo. The whole thing comes back to me at once: not just the pursuit of those Callipolans but what came before it. Delo, offering to help us. Seanan, bitten and burned in the training pen. Rhode, saying *I'll consider it* when I asked for a waived punishment if I brought down a Callipolan.

And then I didn't.

I groan aloud.

"Save the aloe," I tell Agga. "Agga, I'm so sorry, I'm going in the pen again—"

Agga ignores me, pulling up my shirt and touching cool ointment to my side. I can't remember the last time I was given aloe; it's always been a luxury reserved for the dragonborn riders. "You aren't." She flashes me that same knowing smile she gave the morning Delo visited. "Delo got your punishment waived. That poor boy, has he been pining since before Julia? I had no idea."

"What? He's not *pining*—"

"Griff," says Agga, tapping my nose. "Try to be a fool about a limited number of things."

I close my mouth.

"He always was my favorite of them," Agga goes on merrily. "Kind and steadfast. Kept you out of trouble despite your best efforts—"

I yank the covers off myself. "Delo and I have a strictly professional relationship."

"And when we were younger, and you wouldn't shut up about him? *Agga, guess what me and Delo did today, Agga, you wouldn't believe what Delo said to Ixion, Agga, Delo's definitely the nicest of the lot*—"

"That was years ago!"

"Well, he brought the aloe yesterday."

I'd be more irritated if I wasn't so glad to see her old mischievous smile. Agga used to be a terrible tease, before Eamon passed. I scowl at her, which delights her even more.

"Agga, there's something else."

As Agga supplies fresh ginger to her mug, I lower my voice and tell her about Rhode's original accusation.

Agga's brows knit together as she understands.

"You think the children heard us talking about Antigone?"

Becca is pounding already-mashed aloe at the table behind us, half listening. "Everyone wants to be Antigone when we play dragonriders," she announces. "I get to be her most often, because I'm a girl."

Shrines on the karst above.

"It's no fair," Garet agrees, from under the table.

Agga closes her eyes. "I told you no more dragonriding games," she says. Her face is draining of color; the teasing smile she offered me a moment ago is sliding away.

"You told us no more dragonriding games in the *house*."

Which means they've been playing it in the street. Pretending to be Antigone sur Aela, the Callipolan Firstrider, in the street. Where any passing dragonborn might witness. Agga's face stiffens in horror, her eyes squeezed shut as she lowers her face into her hands.

Becca notices, tensing with fear at the sight of her mother's alarm. I take the seat beside Becca, pull her into my lap, and turn her away from Agga while Agga wipes her eyes. "Becca, Garet, you can't use Antigone in games anymore. Especially not in the street."

"Why?" Garet asks.

"It's not safe."

Becca's voice gets small. "All right."

She's thin, weightless as a bird, and I squeeze her until she squeals and squirms away, a chirrup of laughter escaping her. Agga watches us, blank-faced, unseeing, the look she had most often after Eamon went into that mine and didn't come out. I reach out to take her hand.

"We'll be fine."

***

A feast day is declared upon Ixion's return. He brings back gifts from the Bassilean court: whiskey for the lords, perfume for the ladies, and the promise of even more trade ships on their way from Bassilea. Even now, they wind their way through the karst of Sailor's Folly.

Freyda would like to resume our old trading partnership. And she would like to see Ixion again.

Feast days are one of the rare times when the whole island comes together, Norcians and dragonborn. The ha'Aurelian citadel sacrifices firewood for a bonfire, Norcian drums pound from the top of Conqueror's Mound, and water-infused whiskey runs free. Becca and Garet run wild underfoot with the other children from our village.

Tonight, Ixion tells us, in a speech from the plinth in the center of Conqueror's Mound in his strange, flat Norish, *is a time of celebration. Tonight we celebrate the beginnings of an alliance. Tonight we toast the Long-Awaited Return.*

Conqueror's Mound was once the moot hill, the meeting ground between the clans, and from it the five clan-karsts can be seen if you stand in place and turn: Nag, Kraken, Turret, Knoll, and Thornrose. Now a statue of Tarquin the Conqueror and his aurelian occupy the summit, and all eyes are on Ixion, standing between the stone dragon's haunches, not the karsts on the horizon. With whiskey flowing and Ixion's voice resounding, Norcians cheer the dream of the Long-Awaited Return as if it were their own.

I keep to the back of the throng, on an overturned barrel beside Bran and Fionna, drinking watered whiskey and willing myself to think nothing. Agga joins us and introduces a friend from a neighboring clan. It's the careful way she says this, coupled with her friend's unusual good grooming, that give it away. Agga's friend, Shea, is from Clan Thornrose—favored by the ha'Aurelians, hated by the rest of us. Bran does not take long to address this point.

"So how does it feel coming from a clan of traitors?"

Agga, who has no patience for what she calls *petty clan rival-ries*, heaves a sigh. Eamon was from Kraken. I'm inclined to agree with her most of the time—Bran and Fionna aren't from Nag, they're my closest friends, and it's no secret clan rivalries help the ha'Aurelians deflect from who the real enemy is—but Thornrose is its own case.

Shea is more than up to defending herself, though. She holds her own against Bran with a dead stare. "You're one to talk. At least Thornrose doesn't ride dragons for them."

"Would if they could," Bran mutters.

"I really don't see what you have to resent us for," Shea says, looking around at the three of us: all humble-riders. Most Norcian girls would be unnerved at such an audience, but this one seems keen to rise to the challenge. She has the scrubbed look of a ha'Aurelian house servant, and wears no wedding band. "You're *squires*. You'll probably rule Callipolis with them when all's said and done—"

Bran snorts into his whiskey. Fionna gives him a hard look.

"We won't be around that long," Bran tells Shea.

Fionna purses her lips at him. I tell Shea, "The families of the squires will be rewarded with land."

At the sound of the old promise recited so patly, Fionna lets out a strange, shrill giggle. Her hair is down from its usual braid, waist-length and full. She's kept up her cups with us, and it's flushed her burn scar crimson. Shea stares at her.

Bran places a hand on Fionna's shoulder; it's level with his elbow. "Fionna, not now," he murmurs in Dragontongue.

"Was there a joke?" Shea asks, also in Dragontongue, looking between us.

"Norish," asks Agga quietly. "Please."

My sister: the only one among us who hasn't been educated in the conqueror's tongue, the only one wearing a widow's scarf. Fionna twines her arm into Agga's with sisterly affection and reverts to our language. "Land to our *families*," she tells Shea. "Note the wording, because they're awfully vague about what will happen to *us*—"

As soon as Shea understands, she looks stricken.

Agga and I have never discussed this point, though I see from how her shoulders draw together that it's not a new thought for her, either.

"The High King wouldn't allow that," Shea says.

Fionna hiccups. "The High King?" she repeats, with a finger and a glare to the far side of the fire, where Leary Thornrose, supposed High King of the Norcians, mingles with his overlords and the guards his clan provides them. "You think that puppet can help us? Norcia is dead. And us with it."

Silence sits for a moment.

Bran gets to his feet with sudden violence and turns to Fionna. "Dance with me."

He sounds furious.

"They won't allow it."

"Fionna's right," I tell Bran.

"To hell with what they'll allow."

He takes Fionna's hand and yanks her into the crowd, their mismatched heights setting their dance lopsided. Agga lets out a sudden giggle, watching. "He's so tall, and she's so round," she says fondly, "like their karsts."

I laugh aloud at the picture, delighted by it: Turret and Knoll, dancing. Norcian clans uniting, the last thing the ha'Aurelians want. I should be scared for them, but all I can feel as I watch them dance is a wild, straining rage that feels a bit like joy.

I want Bran and Fionna to keep dancing until the whole bloody island sees.

Shea has turned to look at me with a similarly hopeful expression. All at once I understand why Shea of Clan Thornrose would be introducing herself into a circle of humble-riders. One of us could make a good match.

She would make a good match. Pretty, well-fed, clearly comfortable in her station. Our lords would permit the union. And Julia's not here to be jealous of it.

It's the kind of future I should aim for, the kind of happiness I'm allowed, and yet when I look at this girl—intrigued at the presence of a humble-rider as if at the presence of a lord—I feel nothing.

Agga looks between us with a question in her eyes, and then she touches my arm. "Refill my drink?"

She presses an empty cup into my hands, and I make my escape.

I'm on my way over to the barrels when I hear my name. Seanan, the man whom Rhode put in the pen, is beckoning from a group of men from clans Turret and Nag standing in the mouth of an alleyway off the Mound, already far in their cups.

"Griff here," Seanan says, throwing a stiff and bandaged arm around my shoulders, "saw her himself."

I realize what they're talking about and shrug his arm off.

Why is this entire rock determined to talk about the one subject they should shut up about?

"Was one go in the pen not enough for you," I say, "or were you hoping to get dropped, too?"

Seanan's eyes are gleaming with the purity of faith. "First punishment I ever took that meant something. Antigone's coming for us, Griff. Going to break us from the shackles of dragonborn oppression—"

"She's coming for us with Callipolan dragonfire, Seanan. Get your head out of your ass."

Even if I keep wondering whether he's right as the evidence lines up before me, unwanted: That rider saying *wait*. The way Antigone stiffened at the word *peasant*. What if Seanan and the children playing are on to something? What if Antigone's on our side?

Fool's hope, idle dreams, Mabalena. I turn on my heel to head away from them, round the corner, and walk nearly headfirst into Delo.

It's the first time I've seen him since we pursued the scouts. He's recovered well from the burns the Callipolan left on him, though his movements are stiff, arms just a little lifted from his sides, as if to keep from agitating their healing.

"What were those men shouting about?" he asks.

"Nothing. They're drunk."

"Are you drunk?" Delo asks.

"No."

It's not, strictly speaking, true: I've had my share of whiskey by now. Enough that the night has a liquid edge, and Delo, standing close, is lit by the bonfire as if through rippled glass. For a moment the vision shifts: I see Julia instead, taking step after step closer, sealing my fate.

"Are *you* drunk?" I ask.

Delo shakes his head. I can see the bonfire reflected in his eyes. And then I look up and realize where we stand. It was this particular alleyway, with these buckled roofs blotting the sky overhead, when Julia placed my hands on her waist for the first time. I hear my words slur.

"This is where Julia started it."

"I know."

I don't want to know why he knows that.

Or maybe Agga was right. Maybe I do.

On a wave of recklessness, I lift my tankard. "Should go back. Got a girl waiting for me. My sister's friend."

Delo blinks once. His gaze skips past me, searching the crowd. "I saw her. She's . . . pretty."

"You got a girl waiting for you, Delo?"

"Griff," says Delo, like I just asked a really stupid question.

But whatever he isn't saying only makes me more reckless. "There's always Roxana."

Delo answers without blinking. "Roxana fancies Ixion."

Or at least she fancies his title. I shrug. "Ixion's after the Bassilean princess. Seems like you have an opening."

I'm pretty sure telling a dragonlord his marriage prospects with the Greatlord's daughter ranks as one of my worst infractions in the history of my infraction-strewn service as a humble-rider for New Pythos, but Delo just looks at me.

And I can feel my heart beating.

I wait for him to take a step closer, like memory-Julia did. He doesn't.

So I do.

"You waived the punishment. Rhode dropped it."

Delo nods. I am nose to nose with him, testing it. Seeing if he'll order me to back down. I can hear his breath, feel its warmth as it hitches. He remains where he stands, gaze steady.

"Why?" I ask.

"You don't deserve it."

I should be grateful, but all I can think of is how Agga's face contorted when she realized her children's danger.

Danger for playing a child's game in the street.

Grateful? I'm not grateful. I'm full of rage. And a bit of ginger and aloe isn't enough to make me calm.

"Do the rest of us deserve it? Did Seanan deserve it? *Mabalena?*"

Delo's voice is faint. "You're different. And there's nothing I can . . ."

I remember standing paralyzed in this same place, three years ago, at Julia's approach. But this time, I'm not the one who's paralyzed. This time, I'm the one who knows what's happening. I'm in control.

Or, as much as I need to be to make the point, because I can feel Delo's closeness working on me like its own drug, and it turns out that if Julia was wine, Delo's whiskey. A proof I can't handle. The urge to touch him, those shoulders, that neck, those curls—

But anger from the depths of my being controls my movements. My face closes the distance to his, leaning so close we're both tensed with the effort not to touch. I can hear my own breath quicken.

And then a shudder as he swallows, his mouth opening as his lips turn toward mine, and I've won.

I step back.

"Bullshit," I tell him.

My body burning, hands fists at my sides, I walk away.

14

BATTLE PLANS

ANNIE

Crissa's and Duck's survey maps of New Pythos, together with
the numbers they collected on the Pythian fleet, mean we can
move forward with offensive action—and must do so quickly
if we hope to attack before the winter frost grounds the fleet.
The entire corps is activated with the exception of Crissa, who
remains in the infirmary. When I finally summon up the courage
to face her, the night before we depart, I find her sitting up in bed
but unable to leave it.

"On the bright side," Crissa says, "the dragon's bite was so
hot it cauterized itself, so there's no need for amputation."

Her light tone brooks no sympathy for the agony she must
have experienced, or the long ride home on an injured dragon.
"So you'll . . ."

Crissa guesses what I can't bring myself to ask. "Walk again?
Eventually."

As her superior, it's my job to thank Crissa for her service
and the maps she so carefully drew in exchange for a mauling.
But she's also a friend my orders got hurt. Looking at her now,
bedridden and bandaged, I can't help wondering if this is only

the beginning. It isn't helped when Crissa says, in that same light tone: "Be careful out there."

We fly out for Fort Aron the next morning.

The fort is ancient, crumbling, from the first Aurelian invasion, and looks out over the blustery cove filled with warships that will guard the coast while the aerial fleet advances into Sailor's Folly. The drafts that whistle in from the North Sea leave the dragons miserable and me shivering. I'm in the guardhouse off the ramparts, prepping gear and trying to tune out Aela's discomfort as it seeps through the stones, when Cor comes to find me. He has the group lists clutched in a hand.

"Can Duck go in Lee's group?"

I straighten from the piles of spare coolant I'm sorting. I've got Lee in reserve, leading the team of unsparked dragons covering Fort Aron. Defending is the traditional role of the Alternus, but I knew, when I assigned Lee his part and watched his face arrest, that neither of us was fooled by this reason.

It's because I don't trust him to perform.

Not after he's refused to drill. And not after that night at the Lyceum granary when he failed to follow orders. I don't know if Lee knows which side he's fighting for right now, but I'm pretty sure the side he doesn't think he's fighting for is Atreus's.

Confirmed by the fact that, when I told him he'd stay at Fort Aron, he didn't argue it. Like he's relieved I'm not going to make him choose, either.

But I'm not about to explain this reasoning to Cor, who disappeared along with Lee the night of the Passi raid. Now isn't the time to wonder about Lee's and Cor's sympathies with a radical protest group back in the city. Our eyes are facing north.

"Lee's team is composed of riders who are unsparked. Duck sur Certa has sparked."

Cor stands in front of me with his arms folded, that list tight in his fist. He's left the door behind him open, and the chill salt breeze flavors the air. The sun never seems to pierce the clouds this far north; we stand shrouded in half-light.

"Lee's sparked," Cor says.

"Lee is Alternus, he's supposed to defend—and he hasn't been seen on a drill since the duel. No one's saying Duck has *flameshock*, Cor."

This is a simplification of the call I made, looking over the list hours ago: my nerves about Duck's performance balanced with my need for a fleet of sparked riders against New Pythos.

I judged with an unbiased eye. Which meant Duck, whose spotty performance doesn't undo his ranking in the corps or his sparked dragon, will deploy like the rest.

Cor lets out a noise of indignation at the comparison. "Annie, *come on—*"

"I can't assign duties based on whom I love!"

My voice cracks. But it seems to bring Cor to his senses. He reaches up, his fingers slicing his hair. "Then can he go with you?"

It's not the request I expect from a boy who hasn't spoken to me since the Lyceum sacking.

"Please," Cor adds. "I just—I'm distracted when I'm worried about him."

Cor and I have never been close. He was always Lee's friend where Duck was mine. But it seems, in preparing for battle, even the members of the corps I'm not close to feel like family. This is a boy I've grown up with, gone home with; and even with relations frosted in an unresolved fight, he comes to me because he trusts my skill in the air and my love for his brother as sufficient to protect him.

I am strangely, painfully touched.

"Of course. He'll be my wingrider."

Cor nods, then turns on his heel, and is gone.

* * *

We prepare for a launch before dawn, timing our arrival with sunrise: maximizing, as far as they are mutually compatible, visibility and surprise. The night before, I review for the last time the attack plan in a drafty council room in which thirty Guardians have crammed in concentric rings around a single table. The sketches that Crissa made of New Pythos have been enlarged to full-scale maps tacked to the wall. We go over targets: Radamanthus's hall, the palace extension that seems to have been built for the Callipolan exiles, and the ha'Aurelian manors whose slate roofs and walled gardens distinguish them clearly from the thatch of the Norcian villages that cluster on the slopes below.

"Avoid thatch. Our targets are buildings with slate roofs only. They should be easy enough to tell apart."

Darius makes a skeptical noise. "But *most* of it's thatch," he says, in his crisp patrician Palace-standard, which seems to mean that the Norcians' vulnerability as targets makes them either good ones or unavoidable.

I point an index finger into the table. "I'm asking you to *aim*, Darius."

Alexa, another stormscourge rider, snorts into her palm. Last time Darius and I confronted each other, it was in an arena match where I defeated him in front of everyone in this room.

From the way his pale face reddens at my remark, he hasn't forgotten. He lifts his eyes to the ceiling, tosses gold hair back from his forehead, and when he realizes I'm still looking at him, he lifts his hands. "All right, I'll aim."

I proceed with the agenda: We are also to target the inordinate number of Bassilean ships that Crissa and Duck sighted in the main harbor.

"Those are trade ships," Duck objects. "Civilian vessels."

This is what I pointed out when General Holmes gave me this order, and I repeat Holmes's answer: "They're violating the embargo agreed on by the Medean League after the Pythian attack on Starved Rock. This is a proportionate response."

"The kind that starts a war," Lee says.

Another objection that Holmes rolled over.

"The God-King hasn't deployed a warship in decades. His son's sickly, and we're not even sure the king's goliathan is still airworthy."

Goliathan reproduction is closely controlled by the Bassilean monarchy, one per generation and male heir. We all know this; but it isn't quite enough to satisfy them, as it wasn't enough to satisfy me. Lee's mouth twists as he rubs at a knot in the wood of the dusty table.

"The whole point," Rock says, "is that we're not the ones who attack civilian vessels."

He's right, but thanks to this medal on my shoulder, it's my job to argue with him. I look around at the blanching faces and make the amendment I did not share with Holmes.

"Aim for the masts. Their crews should have time to abandon ship if the fires start high."

Rock mutters an expletive.

Lee's voice is quiet, studying that knot in the wood. "And the muzzled riders?"

The War Council's order in this case was clear: Crissa's injury at the hands of a muzzled rider was sufficient reason for Holmes to reject my proposed diplomatic strategy. The Norcians are to be treated as enemies alongside their lords.

And though her injury should have been enough for me, too, it isn't quite. Duck and Crissa counted seven muzzled riders, out of a fleet of twenty-three. They witnessed them forced to compete in a melee outnumbered, against their dragonborn lords.

Seven riders, I can't help thinking, could be enough to break a fleet.

I look at Duck. Duck was there when Crissa was attacked; he knows better than I what call to make.

And more than that, he's merciful to the core.

Duck frowns and scrapes at a curl at the edge of his forehead. "It's true," he says, "that one of their number attacked us and injured Crissa. But it's also true that they must be operating with some level of coercion. Those muzzles—you wouldn't believe them if you saw it."

A shudder goes through him, and the riders watching him go still at the sight.

We can all imagine it. It wouldn't be just our dragons who would feel that iron clamping down, restraining; *we* would.

Cor breaks the silence. His arms are folded. "Coerced or not, they're clearly dangerous."

Duck nods. "Of course. But"—here he lifts his eyes to mine, like he's offering me something and wants me to see it—"I'd support the Firstrider on this."

I offer him the smallest nod of thanks. "We defend ourselves. But also, where possible, show mercy."

* * *

On the ramparts of Fort Aron, in the torchlight before dawn, we do a final check of our dragons' armor and each other's flamesuits. The wind bites, and my eye is constantly on the horizon for a sign of the first break of winter storms, and the snow that will put an end to dragonfire for the season.

Duck shivers while I check his armor, standing close to Certa for warmth, her wing mantling him. But I hardly feel the cold. All I can do is count. Riders on the ramparts. Coolant shafts full. Miles to New Pythos.

Odds of return.

Medics are here, in the bay below. Cots laid out. Kits ready. Holmes informed me of all of this, to reassure me. It did the opposite.

"You all right?" Duck murmurs.

I know the clarity will come. But before the launch, without Aela's mind mingling with my own, I'm not there yet. The numbers are too loud.

"I'm all right. You?"

Duck nods. He's checking me over now, tugging on straps, testing coolant shafts with gentle pressure.

"I'm ready," he says. "I'll have your back, Annie."

Duck knows my rank, and his. He must know it's not me who's being protected. But if this is the story he's telling himself to feel courage in the face of danger, he should have it.

"And I'll have yours."

I kiss him on the cheek and as I turn away, I hear him swallow.

Aela is snorting and tossing her head, agitated by the plates of armor protecting her flanks and chest. I don't try to still her: Her enthusiasm for the fight will be mine soon enough, and I'll need it.

Instead, I triple-check us. Count the straps of Aela's armor as I tap them one by one. Run my hands over the canteens and spare coolant attached at her flank, at the valves along my flamesuit. The plates of dragon-scale armor that fold over each other as I swing my arms and kick my knees. The helmet on my head, the bootknives at my ankles, the Firstrider's bugle slung over my shoulder. Down the line, riders are climbing onto their dragons' backs, small flames lighting the ramparts as they test their fire.

I hoist myself into the saddle, strap my boots one by one into the stirrups, and murmur the order to Aela. She snorts a burst of flame, hot and true and quickly sparked.

We're as ready as we'll ever be.

I lift the bugle to my lips and sound the launch.

15

—

THE PLEA

GRIFF

New Pythos is mobilizing. After scouts return news of movement on Fort Aron, cannons go up on our ramparts, guards of halfsquadrons deploy to circle overhead, and humble-riders are stationed in shifts on the south-facing karsts to keep watch. Bran and I end up atop Turret. It's his clan-karst; he takes one look over the edge at the floating docks below, the faint echoes of the mining that carves into the heart of the limestone, and his face twists.

"She'll collapse at the rate they're going," he mutters. "Why don't they mine Thornrose for a change?"

Thornrose is the only clan-karst exempt from mining; no barges surround her chubby base, no floating docks or mine shafts drill to her center. Granda says the ha'Aurelians used to let us mine the nameless karst farther out in Sailor's Folly, but it was slower, the ferrying less reliable, the returns poorer. Once the Callipolans arrived with their dragons, it was easy enough to compel the Norcians to mine each other's clan-karsts. Turret mines Kraken, and so on.

"Nag's hollowed out too," Bran adds, as if I didn't know.

I look past Thornrose to my own clan-karst, a shadow behind the greater island of New Pythos, the shrine of standing stones sharp on her crown like ears and the switchback stairs going down her neck like a mane. The sight of the barges pulled up around her, carving out her insides, is something I try not to think on.

"I know."

Bran hands me the spyglass and leaves me with the dragons while he kicks around in the underbrush at the base of the standing stones, shooing puffins and clearing dead vines from his clan's shrine. The hammering of miners in the shafts below echo distantly on the water, mingling with the sound of carts of ore being emptied into barges that make a slow passage back to the Pythian harbor.

"Seanan's got this theory," Bran calls, and I groan, but he raises a hand, "that the scouts came round because Antigone sur Aela plans to target only dragonborn strongholds. Spare Norcians."

"Why would she care about Norcians? She's not Norcian."

"She's a peasant, isn't she? Bloody puffins."

He shoos the birds and tosses a bundle of dead vines off the edge. I pass him the spyglass, blinking my vision clear. "Seanan's theories are going to get Norcians hurt."

It turns out I'm right.

When I get off a double shift and make my way back to Clan Nag late in the evening, I find Niter, Ixion's stormscourge, lounging outside my family's front door. His folded wings spread across the alley like a deconstructed tent. The street is deserted; none of our neighbors linger outside with a dragon on their stoops.

I step over Niter's crossed front talons, ignoring his hackling crest and bared fangs, and push the door open. Inside, Granda sits across the table from Ixion. Ixion wears a flamesuit and armor; like me, he has been doing back-to-back patrols. Agga is pouring whiskey into two glasses from a bottle finer than any we own with shaking hands.

"Griff. Welcome," Ixion says. "I hope you don't mind my visiting your family during this busy time."

I scout the rest of the room quickly: Becca and Garet are crouched in the corner, quiet, but judging by the way they're fidgeting, they won't be for much longer.

"Lord Ixion was kind enough to come bearing gifts," Granda tells me.

"Becca, Garet, go out back."

"I'd like them to stay," says Ixion. He nods at the label of the bottle held in Agga's hands. "From Bassilea. The real kind. Another cup, for Griff."

Agga goes to the cupboard, retrieves a third cup, and fills it. She presses it into my hand, and though she doesn't risk looking up at me, I squeeze her fingers tightly as I take the bottle from her. She goes to stand beside the little ones, a little bit in front of them, as if not quite daring to make clear that she stands between them and Ixion.

Ixion lifts his glass, I lift mine, and Ixion toasts in softly accented Norish:

"To loyalty."

I tilt my glass back and feel the liquor burn its way down my throat.

Ixion sets down his glass. "Your grandfather and I," he says, "were just discussing an interesting bit of gossip that I seem to have missed while I was away in Bassilea. The fact that this entire rock can't stop talking about the Callipolans' peasant Firstrider. I was asking Grandfather how he thinks this happened, since no one on this rock *saw* the peasant Firstrider. Now, I know Griff claims he was the one sharing the story round, but we both know you're not that stupid, are you, Griff? Which leaves me to wonder who else might be to blame. Makes me wonder if it were not a case of childish indiscretion . . . or perhaps irresponsibility on the part of the mother?"

I hear the first rattle from Agga beside me: her lungs beginning to refuse air. Before I can say a word, she falls to her knees and places her palms on the floor. And then she begins to speak, and my stomach coils as I realize what she is saying.

Agga, in front of her own children, is reciting a Plea.

"Forgive me, my lord, for my indiscretions, which were not intended in faithlessness; grant that my punishment duly owed not be given to my family blameless—"

The Pleas are what you offer to the dragonborn when you have offended past explanation. When choosing your own words becomes a presumption, and you offer one of the formalities you were taught, as a child, to be ready with instead. The last time I heard someone recite a Plea, it was Mabalena, in the public square. They let her do it. And then they dropped her family anyway.

Becca and Garet have been learning the Pleas from Agga for the last year now.

But Agga's coughing ruptures the Plea midsentence, and as she coughs, Ixion smiles. He flicks his hand down to gesture to her, his eyes only on me. "This," he says, "is the kind of respect I like, Griff."

Garet has started to cry; Becca, who seems to understand that even that is not permitted in this moment, pulls him to her and shushes him. Granda has risen, and then frozen, in a half crouch from his chair, the lines of his face twisted.

Lazily, Ixion's gaze travels down to Agga's bent and shuddering head.

"Your Plea is accepted by your lord."

Agga lets out a sob of relief, her elbows folding under her weight.

"You may already know," Ixion goes on, "that the citadel is mobilizing for an expected attack from Callipolis. In reward for your piety, I would like to take your children into shelter somewhere safe until the threat has passed."

Agga braces on her wrists to twist up and look at me, searching my reaction with tear-bright eyes.

My reaction is that anything offered by Ixion is a threat.

"Thank you, my lord, but we would keep them here," I tell Ixion.

"I wasn't asking." Ixion lifts a hand to Becca and Garet, summoning them as he would a dragon or a dog. "Come."

Neither moves. Agga inhales, her shoulders setting, and then eases back onto her heels so she can turn to look at them.

"Go with your lord. You'll be safe with him."

Becca has started crying, too. "You'll come with us?"

Agga looks up at Ixion, who shakes his head. Agga's face ripples, and then stills again.

"I'll be waiting for you when you come back," she tells them.

She kisses them each on the forehead, as lightly as if she were sending them to market, and neither of them notices the discreet motion she makes with thumb and forefinger on their brows, tracing the sign of the Nag. Only after they have each taken a hand of Ixion's and the door has closed behind them does Agga lower her face to the earth and begin to sob.

For a half moment I am rooted where I stand. And in that moment Granda rises, goes to Agga, and pulls her stiffly into his wiry arms.

"The Nag will keep them, darling," he says. "Do not weep so soon."

But she can't stop.

A wild thought, so wild I don't dare look closely at it, has seized me.

I grip the handle of our door.

"Griff? Where are you going, son?"

"I'm going to find someone who can help."

I leave Agga in our grandfather's arms and take off, at a run, for the citadel.

Out of Clan Nag, across Conqueror's Mound and through the Humble Gate, up the winding stairs and down the Skyfish wing of the Provisional Palace, and then—

Delo emerges from a council room. Like Ixion, in a flamesuit. Ready for the alarm.

"Delo—Ixion took—my sister's kids—"

I'm panting from the run uphill. Only now that I'm facing him does it occur to me how mad it is to seek Delo's help in such a matter. That I've just assumed one dragonborn will take my side against another when he's got all the reason to be as bothered by rumors about Antigone as Ixion, and no reason to care the slightest about Agga's kids—

But Delo only looks alarmed. "Becca and Garet? Why?"

The sound of their names on his tongue makes my knees go weak. I lower my hands to them, gasping. "Said he was taking them somewhere safe."

Delo's brows draw together. "Maybe into the ha'Aurelian crypt with the citadel's women and children? That's where they're evacuating."

But that doesn't sound right. Why would two Norcian children be sheltered in the ha'Aurelian crypt? Especially not ones whose mother had just confessed to a transgression—

Delo, too, seems unsatisfied with this possibility from how he's frowning. As if he too understands that *safe*, from Ixion, means *danger*.

But before either of us can discuss it further, the alarm bells begin to toll.

And then there's nothing more to say. Not to Delo, anyway.

I take off for the Stormscourge armory at a run. Ixion isn't there; already in my flamesuit, I seize my pike and shield, scramble past the other riders, and take the spiral stairs two at a time.

Ixion is already in the lairs, saddling Niter himself. "Took you long enough—"

"*Where are they?*"

Ixion tightens the straps to Niter's flank guard with his forearm. "Who?"

I slam against him so hard his body hits the wall. As I hold him there, pinned, Ixion leans back against the wall to look at me. The chain of Sparker's key glints on his neck, within my reach—

Niter begins to growl. I can hear the murmuring of the Stormscourge Bastards and the ha'Aurelian riders farther down, all within a shout's distance should Ixion alert them. The nearest Norcian rider is Nolan, five nests away, and he and I would be outnumbered two to one—

On the other side of the stone wall, Sparker's growl answers Niter's, but Sparker is chained.

"What now, Gareson?" Ixion murmurs.

He looks almost bored.

Because he can work out, as well as I can, the ways this moment could unfold, every ill-fated grasp for control I could make—

And even in the versions that go the farthest, that result in the greatest triumph, Agga and Becca and Garet still pay the price. Because I am outnumbered here and would be in the air, and defiance would meet only one end.

We are face-to-face, so close that if I rammed my skull against his, I could break it. Ixion, unafraid, leans closer.

"You want those brats back? Get in the air and do what we've trained you to do."

16

THE BATTLE OF NEW PYTHOS

ANNIE

We skim within the coverage of the stratus clouds as the sun rises, hugging our dragons' backs for their warmth, but even a dragon's heat isn't enough in the biting cold to prevent ice forming on my visor. The karst forest of Sailor's Folly rises out of a sky turning a deep, rich blue. I can feel Aela's excitement coursing through me like a second pulse.

As we begin to weave through its pillars, silhouettes of wings, small in the distance like bats, peel from the karst and off into the fog.

Scouts. Heading back to New Pythos to alert them of our approach. Our skyfish set out after them and return empty-handed. I wave us on.

We outnumber them three to two, and none of our fleet is muzzled. Surprise or no, we'll face them.

At last, out of the blue mist, it rises: New Pythos.

The island fortress sits high and crooked on the waves like a storybook castle, the jagged pillars of karst black against the waves, tendrils of fog wisping and winding through the outcroppings of Sailor's Folly. At the base of the island lie the open arms of a natural harbor, and in it bob the shells of their fishing boats and mining barges and the Bassilean trade ships we've been ordered to burn.

From out of the citadel, from off the nearest karst, rises the aerial fleet like a flock of weighty birds. The rising sun flickers on tendrils of high cloud, on the aurelians glinting gold and the sky-fish silvery blue, and the stormscourges splotches of dark against the lightening sky.

Spreading out in formation to meet us.

Cor's group peels off toward the harbor and I call after him: "Remember, masts first—"

"Got it, Annie!" Cor shouts.

Power and I make for the island itself. My group splits to offer coverage for the stormscourge low passes, and as wingriders pair off, Duck comes to my side.

"At your wing."

The citadel rises to meet us, concentric rings of stone, the palace annex jutting from the highest keep across from the great hall. Our first targets, and between them, the Pythian aerial fleet arrayed across the cloudbanks like a wall.

Nothing we haven't drilled, although in drills our dragons' fire was doused.

"Barrel through," I tell Power, "and we'll engage."

In the lingering darkness, it's impossible to tell muzzled dragons from free.

We accelerate as we approach, the gravity of our descent to our advantage, and the first bursts of dragonfire light the still-dark sky.

GRIFF

Ixion waits until they are minutes, meters, from our wall of defense before raising his voice. The triarchal riders are in reserve at the center, followed by the Bastards, with the humble-riders on the front line, and Sparker, pride of the fleet, leads it. His great wingspan spreads on either side of me like a bulwark, looming all the larger in Niter's cast-off armor. Wing to wing, encircling the citadel in a loose cyclone, all the humble-riders are within range of Ixion's cry.

"Squires, your attention, please!"

A ripple through the riders holding the line. Helmeted heads of the humble-riders turning.

The line of Callipolans approaching, filling our horizon. *So many of them.*

And all of those Callipolans turned on the lords we hate with the sole mission of destroying them—

"Out of gratitude for your service," Ixion says, "your lords have taken it upon themselves to ensure the safety of your families. They have been offered refuge within the Greatlord's Hall, the Provisional Palace, and the ha'Aurelian manors. They will remain there until the fighting is finished."

On the triarchal row, meters behind mine, Delo lifts his visor to look at Ixion. And then his gaze travels past him, to me.

Garet and Becca aren't in the crypt. They're aboveground. In the most significant dragonborn strongholds on the island.

They're inside the targets.

Sparker lets out a growl low in his throat.

"We thank you," Ixion goes on, "for your full fervor in defending our great island and its lords."

Before any of us can answer, can even respond, the line of Callipolans is on us.

And then the world begins to burn.

ANNIE

I feel Aela's mind snap into connection with mine, the spillover initiated like a knot pulled tight. I'm riding low, pressed close to her, as we increase speed, covering the stormscourge charge with Duck on my wing.

Power sur Eater breaks through first, and as they hurtle down toward the citadel, we flip and roll into the sights of the skyfish they've swerved past. All around me, skyfish and aurelians are slamming into the Pythian line, engaging as our stormscourges break through it.

We'll hold them while the stormscourges turn their wretched citadel into a blazesite.

Aela and I break from the rider we're grappling with, momentum flinging us in opposite directions, and as we spin, I strain for sight of Duck.

He and Certa are locked in combat with a muzzled aurelian rider. She's forced a contact charge, and the two pairs are twisting and turning in midair like cats rolling in a fight as she strains to find an opening for her pike—

She fights with the desperation of a cornered animal. Duck can hardly gain the advantage. He fires. The rider screams but doesn't let go.

We charge, slamming into her from the far side, and when Duck fires once more, at last she disengages. Duck sur Certa is spinning, on the verge of freefall.

"You all right?"

"I'm fine." Even muffled through his helmet, I can hear his frustration. "She sure made it hard to go easy on her!"

Looking at the scrabbling pairs of dragons around us, I wonder how many more of my riders are making the same realization about the muzzled Pythians.

Showing mercy may not be in the cards if they're attacking like that.

"Stay at my wing."

Below us, fires have begun to sprout from the citadel. Its roofs, its stables, as our stormscourges begin to make their marks. And out over the harbor, the masts of the Bassilean trade ships begin to burn like so many lit matches.

And then I look again at the blazesite below and notice something else.

A skyfish rider, a Pythian, has landed in front of the great hall of the citadel. The roof is already smoking, its corner ablaze and spreading. The dragon has the doors of the hall in its jaws and is yanking.

Like it's trying to open them. Like they're bolted shut.

And that skyfish, I recognize him—

Delo Skyfish. The Alternus who was so cordial to me at the drop-off.

What is he doing on the ground during battle, yanking on doors?

And then a charge comes out of nowhere, into Aela's side, and I lose sight of the skyfish as we spin. We take in the black of a stormscourge belly, a wingspan the length of a warship, and I feel the flare of something like anticipation.

Gareson. Finally.

Griff's stormscourge charges with the momentum of a falling boulder. Aela and I swerve left, barely rolling under his wing to gain the advantage, but they roll with us, and I feel a thrill that has nothing to do with the battle and only to do with the fact that I haven't had an opponent to challenge me like this since *Lee*—

And then I hear something that cuts short all my joy of the fight. Gareson is sobbing.

It's muffled in his helmet, barely discernible above the wind and the roars of the dragons around us.

I hear myself say his name.

GRIFF

There are too many places they could be, too many fires below.

Too many Callipolan riders to hold off.

But Ixion and I do our best.

All my life we've flown together, vied against each other, loathed each other—but it seems today, that loathing has exploded into something else.

Something that moves across the skies over New Pythos like a storm as we take one after another of these Callipolan bastards down.

"You should be grateful," Ixion shouts. "Better they're safe in a proper fortification than in your bit of kindling—"

But if those fortifications catch fire?

They'll get out. They'll get to safety—

The words don't matter. All that matters is the hatred coursing between me and Sparker, molten. And I know that Ixion knows it, as I know it: This fury makes us powerful. It's in his interest to stoke it as it's in mine to feel it.

And in the few spare moments that we glimpse the earth, I see that he is wrong.

Antigone's doing just as Seanan and Bran hoped she would, and I scoffed at imagining.

Sparing the Norcian housing, targeting the ha'Aurelians and the exiles.

And somewhere below, in a home that isn't theirs, the little ones are huddling without even their mother to comfort them.

When we find her, Ixion and I veer like beings of one mind: me to occupy, him to descend from above. And in that instant I want to tear Antigone sur Aela apart.

For her mercy. For her discretion.

For being everything the fools of my village hoped she would be and it mattering not at all.

Ixion is rising up behind her, about to close the charge: We'll have her pinned.

And then she says my name.

ANNIE

"Griff?"

For a moment we both freeze. Our dragons are meters apart, preparing for another contact charge. I can make out his great stormscourge's fiery eyes beneath that iron muzzle.

The sound of Gareson's sobbing stops.

And then he growls, so low I hardly hear it:

"Above you."

We veer, a split second before a blast from above buffets us on its current. The heat of it explodes across Aela's left wing as we roll.

A second stormscourge bears down on us, and this one is almost as great as Gareson's in girth, its crest tipped silver and its armor bearing the sigil of Stormscourge House. The rider faces me as if the rest of the battle—the flames streaking across the sky, the smoke billowing from the ships below and merging with fog above, the screams of crossbowmen and the thuds of cannons unleashed—as if none of that exists. It's just the two of us, and our dragons.

And then Ixion charges.

GRIFF

She's got it in her. For a heartbeat that contains a lifetime of futile hopes, of fantasies that have clouded my vision between waking and dreams for as long as I've been Sparker's and he mine, I realize she'll be able to do it.

She'll best Ixion.

She's agile, precise, vicious.

And she doesn't have a damned muzzle on her dragon's jaw. She will end him.

I am frozen, the smoke and the fog and the burning island below for a moment lost to me as the future glares bright.

Ixion must feel the threat hanging, too, from how he begins to banter.

"Very good," he says, "concentrating your targets on dragon-born strongholds. Unfortunately, we decided we wanted to keep some of our peasants safe. Very safe. Inside our halls."

Antigone sur Aela freezes. I can see the understanding course through her, through her dragon.

I've never in my life felt such a clench of love for a stranger as I feel in this moment for this miracle of a girl.

Ixion presses his advantage.

"So your plan to spare them," he says, "that would be backfiring, wouldn't it?"

Her guard is open as she stalls. Ixion sees it and Niter tenses to spring—

—and a skyfish, coming out of nowhere, tackles them.

Antigone's wingrider, throwing himself between her and Ixion. The same one, I realize, from that scouting mission.

"*Duck*," Antigone shrieks.

The skyfish weighs so little, Ixion sur Niter could hurl it from his path. And for a moment I expect him to.

But then Ixion pauses, his helmet cocked at an angle I know from years of experience to witness with dread.

Ixion, noticing a weak link in his opponent's armor.

And instead of shoving the wingrider aside, he reorients Niter.

"Hold her off," he tells me, "while I take *Duck*."

I hear myself stammer, "My lord—"

"Do it," he says in Norish, "and then you can go find your brats."

ANNIE

Griff holds me like a brick wall. Heedless of the fire that Aela and I begin to hurl at him. As if he can't feel it. As if his stormscourge doesn't care that Aela's talons are piercing his wings and her fangs are slicing into his armor.

All we can think, the single thought filling our two minds as one: *Get to Duck. Get to Duck. Get to Duck*—

But Griff's momentum is too great, and with every beat of his stormscourge's wings he pushes us back.

Away from them. Away from the dragonfire whose heat I can feel blazing in bursts between Duck and Ixion.

But I can see them.

I see Ixion's stormscourge claw its way onto Certa's back like a mounting bear.

See Duck and Certa thrash beneath the weight.

See the stormscourge begin to gnaw at what I think, at first, is Certa's wing until I realize—

It's her saddle girth. The strap that holds Duck, in his saddle, to her back.

And then I begin to scream.

We are level with the lowest stratus, the fog mingling with tendrils of smoke, the citadel so far below that the screaming coming from its buildings and ramparts is muffled and distant.

Aela is sputtering, running out, but I can't stop her firing because her firing and my screaming are the same.

The girth is in shreds. It begins to slide sideways, and Duck slides with it.

The skirmishes of dragonfire, lighting the sky, seem to still around us. For all I've screamed, no one has heard us. No one has come.

I can hear Duck yelling, and then I hear him yelling my name.

So I begin to plead with the brick wall.

"Griff, *please*—"

Callish, then Dragontongue, then *Norish*, and at that point Griff lets out a noise like he's choking and I realize what he's choking, in his own language, back to me:

I'm sorry.

The girth tears. Duck begins to slide. Certa begins to shriek.

And we watch the fall.

GRIFF

There is a moment longer of struggling. While I hold her back, and Ixion keeps the dragon from diving after its rider.

I don't hear it, the moment of contact. We're too high, too far, for the sound to reach us.

Higher than the day Mabalena's family was dropped.

The skyfish feels it.

She lets out a shriek that sends pain straight to my bones even as the hair on my neck goes on end.

At the sound of the skyfish's widow-cry, Antigone's pleas fall silent. She goes limp in the saddle. Her struggling stops.

Ixion releases the little skyfish, and still shrieking, it dives headfirst for the ground.

Too late, too far, too silent.

And the rooftop of the Greatlord's Hall cracks, and the fires billow, and into those flames the skyfish dives.

Antigone sits frozen on her dragon like the sight has taken the air from her lungs.

Her opening is wide, but I don't fire.

Below us, the ships burn. Around us, dragons from my side and hers are sputtering as their dragonfire runs out. And from the island that is my home, smoke rises. My body is searing with burns from Antigone's aurelian; Sparker rasps from her scratches and bites.

Somewhere, among those blazesites, the little ones need me.

"Please," I tell Antigone sur Aela, my voice breaking. "Go."

17

—

LOSSES

LEE

I wait with Pallor at the head of the defensive team, scanning the horizon from the ramparts of Fort Aron. The edge of Sailor's Folly is barely visible, mere stubble against the horizon, as the sun rises; closer to shore I can make out Starved Rock, the site of the Pythians' first attack on Callipolis.

The first snow of winter begins midmorning. Dusting the ramparts, lowering the light, limiting the horizon to a gray blur. Which means, in the sky, rime ice.

I try to imagine what is happening over New Pythos and can't.

What remains real: Annie's face, pale beneath freckles, telling me to stay behind. Me, not arguing it. Because since the night of the Lyceum riot, I've been certain of only one thing about this regime: I'm done fighting for it.

And while that doesn't mean I want my family back, it doesn't mean I'm ready to take up dragonfire against them either. Julia was enough. Julia was—

—a *mistake*?

That's the terrible thing I keep wondering, the terrible spiraling fear as I stare out over the horizon waiting for my friends to return from a battle with my family.

Was all of this a mistake? Choosing Atreus over my father, Annie over Julia?

And with that wonder, the thought of the way forward presented in that moonlit half-dug bunker, when Megara smiled and offered her hand.

A city roiling with hunger.

You make a good speech.

There is only one war I still want to fight, and it's behind me in the city, waiting for my return.

Beside me, on the ramparts, Pallor growls and paws the snow, his snorts billowing steam. Full of a frustration for battle that I cannot, despite every reason I should, share.

With such poor visibility it's impossible to make a count of riders trickling in off the horizon. I'm going down the rows, identifying wingriders returning one by one, when Power sur Eater emerges from the whirling snow and skids across the ramparts. Power dismounts and makes his way toward me in a single motion as he tears off his helmet.

"Annie lost Duck."

For a moment I think he means literally, means she can't find him.

And then I realize that Power isn't smirking, isn't scowling, isn't looking at me with any of the hostility that has been shared between us for ten years. He looks frightened.

The hair on the back of my neck goes on end.

Annie lost Duck.

Power is saying something, talking about *Cor coming* and *find Annie*, but I don't hear him because I'm trying to understand—

"What—"

"He fell."

Power lifts an arm and drops it. And all my protesting questions come to a slamming halt at the illustration.

"From how high?"

Power shakes his head. "He fell into a blazesite. Certa followed him and didn't come out."

And I wasn't there to do anything.

I feel my spiraling doubts come to a halt like they've hit a brick wall.

Power looks past me, squinting into the snowstorm. His brows are frosted with ice. "There she is."

I'd know Antigone sur Aela by their silhouette alone, even in a world bleached of color. Power and I move as one toward them, to the rime-frosted figure sliding off the saddle. There are shouts in the storm, medics helping riders off saddles, dragons whimpering from cold while the snow blows. Annie's armor is blackened along the side, across the shoulder, and smells of burned leather, but she doesn't seem to notice. Her hair, when she removes her helmet, is frozen in spikes at her neck.

"I need to find Cor," she says.

Power catches her.

"Lee will take care of Cor. You need to get medical attention. Inside."

She pushes past him like she can't hear him. And then her brown eyes, which strain unseeing, find me. She tilts her head up, reporting to me like I remember her doing when we were children in the play yard. *Who hurt you? Tell me what happened.*

"Ixion did it. When he realized I was scared for Duck. He had his squire hold me off."

I feel a chill that has nothing to do with the cold. Power has frozen behind her, poised to take her by the shoulder. "I need to find Cor," she says again.

Annie and I first knew each other in states of grief. But I've never seen her like this. The fresh thing, the sleepwalking shock. I register this even as I realize it's happening to me, too, feel it taking over, turning my movements automatic.

Automatic and attuned to one goal: Protect Annie.

Behind her, Power is shaking his head violently, his eyes wide as they seek my own. I know Cor too well not to understand what he's getting at.

Annie shouldn't be let within twenty feet of Cor. Not right now.

"I'll handle Cor. You need to go with Power."

Power takes her shoulder. "Let's get inside," he says again, "and find the medic."

He turns back to me as she lets herself be steered away and adds in a low voice: "Behind you."

I turn to find Cor.

It's clear from his face that he already knows. His visor is up and his eyes strain past me, searching. For what or whom, I'm not sure.

"I saw it happen," he says. "I couldn't get there in time."

When he realizes I'm holding him, preparing to keep him back, he turns to face me. His face is black with ash, and his voice raw from smoke.

"She was supposed to keep him safe."

No, I want to tell him: I was. And I didn't.

I was here, doubting my choices with Julia. Staring at the horizon and imagining green scarves and protests at home, while

Duck was out there dying and Annie was watching it happen and I was here doing *nothing*.

This is what happens when I sit it out. This is what happens when I let Annie decide the flameshock is too crippling because I don't like how it feels to fire and remember Julia.

What happens is people I love pay the price.

GRIFF

Snow begins, the only mercy of this day, as we fly back to the citadel. Pumps used to empty the mines at high tide are being strung across the island, turning fires to wet smoke, and the falling snow sizzles and spits as it smothers what the pumps can't reach. There's so much smoke I can't begin to make out the damage. In the lairs, I unsaddle Sparker and Niter with fingers shaking in haste and am already turning to go when Ixion speaks.

"You're not done yet."

Numbly, I follow him up to the armory and help him disarm. Trying to block the memory of the Callipolan Firstrider's weeping as I fight panic.

Becca, Garet. I need to find Becca and Garet.

The room is full of subdued grunts of pain. Only two of the Stormscourge Bastards have returned so far. Nolan, visibly burned, is disarming them with sharp breaths. Hastening, as I am. We both have family to find. Once the Bastards leave, Nolan takes off at a limping run from the room. Ixion lets me continue unbuckling his armor until my words trip out in silence.

"My lord, please, do you know what building they were—"

My voice cracks. This time, Ixion doesn't pretend to wonder whom I mean. "I haven't the faintest idea."

With an air of disinterest, he reaches for a scroll lying on the table beside him.

"This might tell us. Manifests, of the shelters provided to the Norcians during the attack."

He passes the scroll to me without glancing at it. I look down, as if hoping that, in my desperation, the meaningless scribbles will turn into something I can make sense of. They don't.

Ixion is watching me, smiling.

The door bursts open and Phemi Skyfish comes in, covered in ash and looking distempered.

"Well, that was a disaster," she tells Ixion. Then she notices me, standing in front of him clutching a scroll, and makes a noise of impatience.

"For the love of the dragon, Ixion. Give it to me, Griff."

I pass her the scroll, and she unrolls it. "Who?" she asks me.

"Garet and Becca Eamonsdaughter."

Phemi nods, scans further, and then grimaces.

"They were in the Greatlord's Hall," she says.

The Greatlord's Hall: the blazesite into which that boy Duck fell, that swallowed his little dragon whole.

I don't wait for a dismissal. I run.

ANNIE

Down in the makeshift medical bay in the converted mess hall of Fort Aron, Power leads me to one of the cots stretched out among other riders already receiving attention. He helps the medic find and treat burns that I observe on my own body without feeling when we peel back my flamesuit and underlayers. Power's words are muffled, like he's shouting at me from a distance, and I respond slowly. I have trouble remembering the sentence that came before.

The surroundings come into focus gradually: Deirdre, on the cot next to mine, weeping. And then I realize what she's saying.

"I couldn't . . . I couldn't get to him in time. Some—awful peasant rider—tore him apart—"

She lost Max.

I've watched them spar together, daily, for as many years as I've sparred with Lee.

Deirdre's never held the difference of our backgrounds against me. She's always used the right language so carefully. But she lets the word *peasant* slip without even noticing, and utters it with a hatred that freezes my blood.

I look around the room for the first time, taking it in—my riders, my friends, gathered—some on cots, receiving treatment, others there at their sides, and all in grief.

And then there's Cor.

He's standing, two cots away, and his words cut through the haze like a knife.

"He could have stayed behind."

Lee's there, too, seizing Cor's arm.

"Cor, stop it—"

Cor wrenches free of Lee's grasp and takes a step toward me. "He should have stayed with Lee. *You were supposed to keep him safe*—"

"That's *enough*," Lee shouts.

He seizes Cor and slams him back against the cot. Cor responds to the wrestle like an embrace. He chokes, and Lee shifts, cradling him as the choking turns to something else. Lee wraps an arm around him, muffling the noise as Cor breaks down, and twists to look over his shoulder.

Not at me: at Power. Like he's cueing him.

I don't even realize, until I look down, that Power's arm is around me, too, and that I'm shaking.

"Let's go somewhere quieter," Power says, "and work on that report for Holmes."

Sitting next to a spitting fire in a darkened hall of Fort Aron, he, Rock, and I numbly go over the numbers. Corroborating *ships sunk* and *buildings bombarded* and *riders down and injured*. All the while I'm replaying the moment where I made the decision that Duck wouldn't go in Lee's group, because Certa had sparked.

Duck was underperforming. But I assumed my fears were disproportionate, my judgment clouded.

If I had just written his name on a different list—

"I should have put him in Lee's group."

"No, Annie," Rock murmurs, gripping my knee. "None of that."

Rock, who flew in Cor's group, provides an account of the maritime air strikes in lieu of Cor. He is quiet, unharmed himself, but on edge: His stormscourge, Bast, was clipped from a cannon to his wing, and Rock feels it. Since he learned of our casualties, he keeps rubbing at his eyes. I lapse into silence while he and Power finalize the report, the numbers washing over me, Cor's words replaying.

You were supposed to keep him safe.

In a dark council room, the winter storm winds whistling outside, Power, Rock, and I relay our report to General Holmes and the other members of the War Council present at Fort Aron to oversee the expedition.

We give them the numbers: a dozen ships burned; half the citadel and three manors afire; at least four Pythian riders down with status unknown.

Three of our riders lost. Orla, from enemy dragonfire. Max, who did not survive a mauling from a muzzled dragon. And—

The numbers.

Holmes describes them as an overall success.

It takes me a moment to understand what that means. I've pleased him. I've come home with three riders dead and more wounded and Cor unable to look at me and Duck *gone*, and Holmes is telling me I did a good job. Mission accomplished.

No. Not a good job. Not an *overall success*.

Suddenly I'm determined to convince Holmes it wasn't. "They had Norcians locked in the dragonborn strongholds," I tell him. "They couldn't get out."

This wasn't a part of the report Rock and Power prepped with me. Rock's pale face goes a shade whiter under the unscrubbed ash as he looks up from his notes. "How do you know that?"

"Ixion told me. Right before Aela ran out."

Rock is probably the only Guardian who could begin to share the depth of my horror. But that's little comfort. He lowers his head into his hands as his great shoulders begin to shake. "I bombarded those sites. I bombarded—"

If I were someone else, some better commander, I'd put my hand on his shoulder right now. But I sit frozen, inches from him, watching him break down. My lips offer numb comfort.

"You were following orders."

My orders.

Holmes's voice is curt. "Who was locked in the strongholds isn't strategically relevant. What's relevant is that we hobbled the Pythians before a long cold winter and will make them think twice before attacking us again."

Rock's fingers clutch the short spikes of his blond hair.

"I'll admit I am a little disappointed at our losses, however," Holmes adds. "They were greater than anticipated."

Losses. Deirdre, weeping for Max. Cor, his voice raw, telling me I was supposed to keep his brother safe. Duck, falling. *Losses.*

I answer the unasked question.

"We were . . . unprepared for significant aggression from the muzzled riders."

Lucian Orthos, the young chief of staff who once questioned my stomach to bombard Norcian peasants, has been watching our report quietly from Holmes's side. He speaks for the first time, his voice soft and insinuating.

"The muzzled riders whom you gave orders to show mercy to?"

I have no idea how he heard.

"Yes."

Holmes lifts a hand to hold off Lucian. "Did you issue a countermand to that order?" he asks quietly.

Countermand? In the air, with only bugles and horns to communicate? In the confusion of battle?

But the truth of the matter is that it didn't even occur to me.

My silence is its own answer.

Lucian Orthos is smirking like I've just proved all his prejudices right, and I find I can't summon up the energy to care.

"From now on," Holmes tells me, and his voice has gone deadly calm, "no more distinguishing. If it's got the Pythian sigil, you fire on it."

Through the numbness of my own horror I hear myself answer. "Understood, sir."

But he's not finished.

"I don't care if it's Norcian, muzzled, chained—if it's wearing Pythian armor, it's a target. You want to fraternize with peasants, you go find them in whatever village they rustled you out of and you fraternize with those. But the ones in New Pythos are our enemy. Just like their lords. And from now on, *that's* our policy."

Beside me, Power stirs, unnerved by Holmes's sudden vulgarity. Even Lucian Orthos looks too startled to be gratified. I have a brief, flashing memory of that moment when Griff Gareson raised his visor and said, *Above you.* But that's the last thing Holmes wants to hear.

And with Duck gone because Griff held me back—I don't want to think about it either.

GRIFF

I can't find them.

Not in the ruined hall, not in the smoking citadel, nowhere in the streets where I run calling their names.

I can't find them and that means only one thing.

I was the one who brought news of Eamon to Agga two years ago. I remember the walk. Preparing the words. The way her knees gave out when I said them.

The little ones were so little then.

I remember telling her she wouldn't be alone.

Now I won't even be able to say that. My poor sister who weeps quietly in the night when she thinks I can't hear, who always smiles for her children in the morning, how am I to tell her that they, too—

My steps grow more and more leaden at the approach. The thought that before I come home will be *before* and when I cross the threshold and she sees my face will be *after*—

A skyfish is curled in the alleyway outside our home, still in battle armor.

And then I realize that our door is open. Within, the house is so bright, every candle must be lit. And silhouetted in the door-frame is a single tall, skinny figure whose brown face and curly crop of hair I'd know from the other end of the earth.

I fall across the threshold.

Becca and Garet are in Agga's arms, unharmed. Agga is laughing and weeping as she holds them, and Granda is holding her. Garet is saying, *We got to fly a dragon, twice!*

And Delo is there, in his armor, covered in ash, explaining in his careful Norish that he would have come sooner except that he had to get the other Norcians down into the crypt—

Then he turns and sees me.

"Griff," he rasps.

Surrounded by my laughing, weeping family, in this glowing room, I suddenly feel that Delo and I are alone.

I drop to my knees and press my lips to the side of his boot.

Above me, Delo inhales a shuddering breath. And he sounds, for all the world, as though it causes him pain.

"Griff," he says weakly. "Griff, get up—"

But I don't rise. I croak out the answer I was trained as a child to say, the language of my people, not his, because it is in Norish that these professions belong.

"May my lord accept the gratitude of his servant, for mercy undeserving—"

Delo bends. He crouches to my height, so that we are both on our knees on the floor. And then he murmurs a single word against my ear.

"Enough."

His face is next to mine, forehead beside forehead. I don't dare lift my face for him to see it, wet, to see what it looks like to have lost dignity past even the desire for it.

He murmurs my name again, and then his hand finds mine on the hard-packed dirt floor. Something cool, metal, is pressed into my hand. Slowly, I uncurl my fingers and look at what he has given me.

Sparker's key.

"I had it . . . copied . . . before I gave it to Ixion," Delo murmurs. "But it wasn't until I saw what happened today that I . . ."

Our heads are still close, crouched together. Delo reaches trembling fingers up, touches me beneath my chin, and at the slight pressure I lift my face at last to look at him. We are inches apart. I can see every fleck of his irises, and his next words warm me with their breath.

Delo's voice shakes as if the words frighten him.

"Do what you need to do."

ANNIE

Night has fallen by the time the meeting with Holmes concludes. The corridors of the fort are dark, narrow, and drafty. I stop on the winding stair as the last of my energy drains from me, and Power stops, too.

"Where's Lee?"

I hear my own voice waver. I can feel it looming, the wave of grief that's about to crash, and the only thing I can think, as I feel it approaching, is that I need Lee.

I want a mother to hold me, a father to comfort me, but I don't have those. I have him.

Power blinks at the question. "He's . . . I think he's still with Cor."

You just sat there. You could have saved him.

Of course. I can't have Lee. Cor has Lee.

But I will not do this on a drafty stairwell of Fort Aron with Power holding my arm.

"Aela?" I manage.

"Okay," Power says.

He leads me back up to the ramparts. The storm has calmed, the snow collected in drifts. Where the dragons curl together, warmed wet stone radiates, snowless.

I find her among the aurelians, Pallor's wing tucked over her like a blanket. When she sees me, she rustles, opening her own wing, rumbling a purr. Inviting me into the crook under it.

Where I will be alone.

I turn to Power.

"I think I need—"

"Yeah, I get it."

He's already backing away.

"What are you going to do?"

Power rubs his face.

"Might take Eater out. Circle the harbor a few times. Try to . . . clear my head."

I don't remember, until after he's walked away, that I should have thanked him.

It's a tent of warmth under Aela's wing. The starless sky overhead is all I can see, the smooth scales of her side all I feel, the rise and fall of her breathing the only thing I hear.

But then my vision fills with dragonfire. Dragonfire on peasants my orders burned—

—Duck, smiling this morning when I kissed his cheek—

—Duck, slipping sideways as he cried my name—

I crawl out from beneath Aela's wings. She unfolds herself. And then she follows me as I climb. I half run up the stairs leading to the tower roof, the highest vantage point of Fort Aron, which looks out over the harbor, and the moonlit North Sea, and the jagged peaks of the highlands spreading west. We're alone. A small, dark silhouette of a single dragon crosses the night sky far overhead: Power sur Eater, seeking their escape in the vastness.

I inhale the cold air, so sharp it burns my lungs, wrap my arm around Aela's neck, and for the first time in a very long time, I imagine a different life.

If I hadn't been Chosen, hadn't been taken to the city, and lived as I would have, somewhere deep in the highlands, before I had ever known Aela, or the Guardians, or this weight.

I wish I could become nothing again.

GRIFF

We sleep together in the back room for warmth, but until tonight I've never thought of it as a luxury. Agga and I curl around the little ones, Granda lies on their other side, and as they tell the story of their adventure, Agga rises over and over again to kiss their hair until they complain and tell her to stop. They talk of

Ixion's dragon, and sheltering in the Greatlord's Hall with the other Norcian children, and the fire that began and the smoke that filled and the doors that wouldn't open.

They're so matter-of-fact about that point, hardly noticing how Agga's hand covers her mouth and she has to bury her face into the blanket for a moment to muffle a scream. I take her hand and her nails dig into mine.

And then, their story goes on: Delo came. Bursting open the bolted doors, helping the peasant children down into the crypt, and then calling Becca's and Garet's names specifically. They took particular satisfaction in this.

"And then we got to ride a dragon *again*," Garet thrills.

They transform from storytelling to a dead sleep mid-sentence. In the sudden silence of their lengthened breathing and Granda's gentle snores, Agga rolls onto her back.

"What did Delo say to you?"

I think of the way my skin thrummed when he touched my chin with the tips of his fingers, when we looked at each other. I've held a dragonborn's gaze like that before, but never—never once, with Julia—did I feel so strongly that we saw each other.

"He said—enough."

Enough.

I don't know if I mean it to stop her question or to answer it. I have the secret against my breast, the metal of Sparker's key warmed to the temperature of my body. And long after Agga falls asleep, long after the room is full of nothing but the sound of their breathing—the little ones, my sister, my grandfather—I lie awake, clutching it, the possibilities blinking like stars in the darkness before my eyes.

Do what you need to do.

Delo didn't define it for me. So I must. And after tonight, I don't have to think twice to know what it will be. We fight for lords who lock our children in burning strongholds while the enemy spares our thatched roofs.

I'm done playing for New Pythos. It's time I play for someone else.

Antigone.

Delo just gave me the only thing he could. Sparker. One dragon. Just one dragon.

Not enough to change the tide of the Callipolans' war. Not enough to do anything more than get my family killed. I might be skilled in the air, but what has that skill ever been except a mockery of my powerlessness on the ground, where I'm relegated to delivering letters and unlacing the Firstrider's boots, unable to so much as read my family's names—

When I finally see it, I rise in the darkness as if I've been summoned.

I make my way through the dark village with soft footsteps in the snow. At the gates of the citadel, I make the same excuse I made for years on trysts with Julia—*I've been summoned to Stormscourge quarters*—and the guards remember the excuse, and don't question it.

Then, inside the walls, I look up at the skeleton of the ruined Greatlord's Hall and remember my crimes.

The little Firstrider, who tried so hard to spare us.

And in return I held her back while Ixion took her friend.

Even if I want to turn, she'll never have me. Not after that.

I find my feet taking me into the hall. Rubble that was the roof before the blaze litters the ground, slick with ice and snow. At the back of the husk of a hall lies a crater of shattered rubble, and in the center of it, the snow-covered mound of the boy's fallen dragon.

I approach. Dust the snow from the dragon's closed eyes. She's long cold.

I search the snow around her until I find what I dread and desire in equal measure: the remains of a dragonrider's armor. A few tempered dragonscales from a bit of the cuirass that survived the blast.

All that remains.

And suddenly, holding these, a different purpose comes to me.

Let the Firstrider take me or not. She returned a body to us and I will return these remains, pitiful as they are, to her.

The only atonement I can offer for my crimes, the only thanks I can give for her mercy. Let me answer her honor with honor, where they think we have none.

The true gift of freedom is to act with this civility.

What's come over me, this bout of high-minded ideals?

I make my way down to the lairs.

Sparker rouses, seeing me. Tail flicking in the darkness. The lairs are deserted, the dragons sleeping for the night. The snow brings with it assurance of safety and a lowered guard: dragons unable to spark from the cold, no attacks from their side or from ours.

I reach up for his collar and slide the key in.

For the first time in my life, I free Sparker from his chain.

I've no flamesuit, but I don't need one. I've no saddle, no bridle, nothing.

It doesn't matter.

He emerges, and for a moment the thrill of it—him and me, together, without our lords—dances in my blood.

And then I clamber onto my dragon's bare back and kick off the ground.

New Pythos falls away, the night sky fills my vision, and—thighs burning against Sparker's scales, arms numbing with cold through my tunic and trousers—we head south, racing the clock of this madness. We give a wide berth to Turret and Thornrose, the karst pillars most often used by our sentries to keep watch, and we take to the cloud cover over Wayfarer's Arch just in case. Not another Pythian dragon in sight: The sky is ours. And yet, as the decision grows cold, as the karst pillars fade behind us but Callipolan shores have not yet grown on the horizon, I feel the first sharp spikes of doubt.

They'll find out. They'll drop them, one by one—

And after what you did today, the Callipolans will fire on you on sight.

Is this really worth the risk of everything, a bit of burnt armor in your pocket—

But I hold steady, clutch Sparker like my life depends on it, and eventually, the dark line of the great island arises.

Callipolis.

The winking lights of the town surrounding Fort Aron, a harbor beside it, and above them a single circling stormscourge.

I'd forgotten all thought of a parley flag until this moment; with fingers numb from cold I pull my own shirt over my head—in the moonlight it's close enough to white—and wave it as I approach.

The stormscourge has frozen in place where it coasts on the wind. As we level off, I see the other rider's only in a flamesuit. No armor, no helmet. And his face is familiar: the rider with the shaved head and Delo's brown complexion, who gave me Julia's body at the first meeting.

"You," he says.

I'm gripping Sparker's flanks so tightly with my knees, my skin sears where it's not numb. I raise both hands over my head and call across the wind.

"I need to speak to your Firstrider."

ANNIE

Aela notices before I do, the second rider approaching Power sur Eater from the north. Another stormscourge. Her tail lifts, her breath becomes a whining growl.

Even at a distance, I know which stormscourge it is.

But instead of facing off, the two pause only long enough for a short conversation before both turning back for Fort Aron.

What is going on?

Minutes later, Power sur Eater alights on the tower ramparts beside me, and in front of me a second stormscourge lands. From it descends Griff Gareson. No flamesuit, no armor. He is shivering, barely dressed, what seems to be his own shirt wadded in one fist. His dragon, its maw ever muzzled, crouches beside him with a wing half-mantling him.

Aela's hackles are raised in a growl, her breath rattling into an inhale as if attempting to fire despite the cold. Gareson's boots touch the ground and he lowers to his knees.

Kneeling, he holds something out to me, a lumpy, shiny thing.

"Forgive me."

It's a piece of Duck's cuirass.

GRIFF

For a moment, I think the Firstrider will have her dragon attack us anyway. And then, instead, she lowers her arm. The aurelian stands down, though her glare remains fixed on Sparker, her horns raised. Sparker glares back: They both have talon marks to show from their fight this morning. I give Sparker's ankle a kick, and the low hum of his growling stops.

Antigone reaches up to her neck, unfastens her mantle, and crosses the snow to put it over my shivering shoulders.

The boy's armor remains on my open palms in the snow.

Antigone turns to her friend. Callish sounds like Norish but *wrong*, and I recognize the sense of it. *Leave us.*

He looks unconvinced. "Annie—"

She repeats herself, with added emphasis. The rider gives a scowl worthy of Ixion, but he kicks his stormscourge into a launch all the same.

Alone on the tower, Antigone crouches before me and takes the remains of the armor into her own hands. She holds them, looking down at them, her face in shadow.

"I'm so sorry—"

Her fingers flick, discreetly, to her eyes. She speaks in her crisply accented Dragontongue. It's precise and slightly stilted, as if she's reading from a book. "Is your family safe?"

I nod. "They were locked in—but they got out before—"

I break off. What am I doing? I've no place telling her of loved ones who survived while she holds the remains of hers. But Antigone's mind seems to be shuttling in a different direction.

"My family was locked in once, too."

So that's why she wanted so much to spare peasants.

"It was good of you," I tell her. "Targeting so carefully, sparing Norcians—"

Antigone shudders as if I've reminded her of a horror. "It backfired. As Ixion pointed out. And in any case—after our losses—it won't be permitted again. I'm sorry, Griff."

She rises, holding Duck's armor lightly in her hands as if she were cradling a dead bird. "Thank you for bringing these remains back to me."

I realize that she means this as a farewell and lurch to my feet. "Let me help you."

Antigone, half turning away, goes still. She rotates on her heel. "What?"

I reach up, touch the chain of Sparker's key. And then I take a breath.

"I'm Ixion Stormscourge's squire. I'm with him all the time. I serve him at table, I attend him in his private quarters. I'm privy to his most privileged conversations and I have access to all of his correspondence. I can give you the information to help you bring them down. Only—"

I stop here, because this part is humiliating and mad, and most likely to make her give me up in scorn or disgust.

Antigone's eyes are fixed on my face, searching.

"Only?" she prompts.

"Only—it would help if I could read."

ANNIE

Griff's Dragontongue is fluid, easy, like Lee's the few times I've heard him speak his mothertongue. Barely accented. His voice is a growl, hoarse from a day of inhaling smoke. His square face, his balled fists, convey a determination that—if not exactly proud—is fierce.

I don't hate him, though I should. I see too much of myself in him to hate him. I know the taste of the kind of desperation that would drive me to do anything, commit any atrocity in the world, to save my family from the flames.

But work with him? Now, after what happened?

It was what I hoped for from the beginning. Now it seems foolhardy—and wrong.

He's the one who stood between me and Duck. He's the one I failed to get past, when my friend needed me. He's the reason I'll never see Duck again.

A hoarse apology and a bit of charred cuirass in my hands won't change that.

And that's all there is to it, until he says this.

Doesn't quite ask me, as if that's too shameful. But I hear it. *Teach me to read.*

Amid everything that has happened, dragonfire and families and friends facing death, Griff Gareson wishes he could *read*.

Of all the ways I've felt my heart be broken today, this was not one I expected.

They gave you a dragon, I think, *but they wouldn't give you this.*

When I fail, at first, to answer, Griff keeps talking.

"I can get out nights. We could meet, practice in secret. They wouldn't know I was gone."

He sounds desperate. Like bringing down New Pythos is something he wants but reading is something he *needs*, from deep inside his gut, and hasn't been allowed to have.

And of course he hasn't. Why would this have changed? When my father couldn't, my mother couldn't, no one in my village could—and surely in Griff's case, it would be especially convenient that he can't.

Because he is primed to bring New Pythos down.

But then I look at him, and think of Duck, and *can't*.

But perhaps Griff knows that. Because he doesn't make me say yes or no, tonight.

Instead, he places one arm on his hulking stormscourge's back and lifts the other to point down the coast, toward the blackness of the Callipolan lowlands. Then he names a place, a date, and a time.

Midnight on the Driftless Dunes, half a week from now.

"We'll be waiting for you," he says.

18

—

THE ISLAND OF THE DEAD

ANNIE

I wake to memories of a strange dream: a night where I met with Griff Gareson and watched Duck die.

And then I remember it wasn't a dream at all.

I think, for a moment, that my body won't move from the bed. I'm in the mess hall converted to a trauma ward, on a cot I must have stumbled into last night. Others are stirring. I can hear them. And I can feel it, a sudden unnatural weight, the Firstrider's medal still pinned to the uniform that I fell asleep in. A wave of self-hatred rolls over me, forcing me to my feet.

Then I do the things that need to be done, as if doing my duty today can undo yesterday. I force down porridge, confirm an agenda with Holmes—the riders and dragons fit enough for flight will return today to Callipolis, while those in critical care will stay here longer to convalesce—and prepare my things.

In contrast to last night, when the medical ward seemed to burst, to explode with noises of pain and grief, this morning it is deadly quiet. Rock, eating porridge at Lotus's cotside; Alexa, shaking Deirdre awake; Lee, on the far side of the room, packing with Cor.

And then there's Power, standing in front of me rubbing sleep from his eye with the palm of a hand.

"So what did you say to him?" he asks.

I tear my eyes from Lee and stuff down the ache of wanting him to look at me.

"Who?"

Power jerks a finger north.

Gareson. That part I might still have believed to be a dream.

"I'll . . . tell you later."

I organize a formation that we studied in textbooks, but never drilled, for the return flight: a funereal. Two by two, with the fallen riders borne by their closest comrades bringing up the rear, we pass over the snow-bleached countryside headed south. Orla is borne by Lotus sur Iustus; Max is borne by Deirdre sur Rhea. Their widowed dragons drift behind us, trailing their riders' remains.

Duck sur Certa's cuirass is tucked inside my uniform, warm against my skin, and though I know it deserves to be held by Cor, I don't know how to tell him how I got it.

So I don't give it to him.

Lee and I lead the cavalcade in silence.

This grief, I think, it's like a dirty house I abandoned that even years later I know how to crawl through blind.

Was there the same guilt then, that presses weight against my chest and makes it a conscious effort to breathe?

Another round of snow has begun, this one to accumulate by the feet rather than the inches. The dragons are sleepy, sluggish. They don't hibernate fully, but they slow in winter.

Which will mean, from now on, less drilling. Fewer patrols. And no air strikes. From our side, or from theirs. A seasonal, forced ceasefire with the dragons unable to spark for the cold. And during that ceasefire, life will go back to what it once was. We'll attend our classes, do our homework, go on rounds.

We'll do all the things we used to do, with people missing.

I wait for Lee to come to me. He doesn't.

I wonder if maybe he wasn't just holding Cor back when Cor said those things. Maybe he agreed with him.

I don't blame him.

LEE

The bodies lie in state, guarded by their widowed dragons, and the keepers tend their cuts and burns. I make a trip to the infirmary to tell Crissa what happened. She listens without interruption, weeping silently while I speak. Though I don't fill in the spaces of emotions, she guesses it. "You're all blaming yourselves. You, Annie, Cor."

I swallow, suddenly unable to answer, my imagination going one more time to what might have happened had I been fit for battle, *been there* to do something—

I see the three we lost everywhere. In empty seats at refectory tables, in empty beds in the dorm, in the silences in the solarium that they would have filled. Duck was never my closest friend, but he was always a part of things—at Annie's elbow, in Cor's shadow. Laughing, smiling, even when he was scared.

Duck lit up the room.

Crissa says, "It wasn't your fault, Lee."

I nod, words failing. And I wonder, for the hundredth time, why Annie hasn't come.

On the morning of the funeral, I'm sitting at my desk with legs propped on it, not so much as an open book to excuse my inertia, when Alexa comes to tell me that Annie has locked herself in the girls' washroom.

"Did she ask for me?"

"No," says Alexa.

"Then what do you expect me to do about it?"

Alexa gives me a hard look. "Don't act like this isn't your territory, Lee."

An Albans reference? An *orphaning* reference? In almost any other context, I wouldn't give the time of day to poorly fired assumptions about a past others have no business reminding me of. Today, it feels like the summons I've been waiting for.

Damn right this is my territory.

I vault to my feet and follow Alexa to the girls' dorm. Inside, Deirdre is half dressed in ceremonial armor, hammering on the washroom door and calling Annie's name. Orla's bed has been stripped, her uniform folded at the foot of her bed, to be returned to her parents at the ceremony. I move between Deirdre and the door.

"Can you use another washroom?"

"Our things are in there—"

"Yeah, well, Guardians aren't allowed possessions."

Deirdre glares at me; Alexa takes her arm. "Come on, Deirdre," she murmurs.

When they're gone, I rap twice on the door, a single knuckle.

"It's me."

She doesn't answer.

"Annie, if you don't say anything, I'm going to break the door."

Ear pressed against the door, I hear a single whimper.

I lower my shoulder, brace against the door, and shove. The bolt is old and rusted; it snaps open. I stumble over the threshold, imbalanced, to find Annie crouched in the center of a filled bath, curled in on herself, her face pressed against her knees like she's hoping, if she presses hard enough, she'll compress into nothing. The bumps of her spine, burn-smoothed, poke from her back. The bathwater is still steaming.

All at once the missing her, the needing her, becomes too much, and I don't care anymore why she hasn't come.

I close the door behind us, kick off my shoes, strip down to my underlayers, and climb into the bath beside her.

She doesn't even ask what I'm doing. Just unfolds, enough to crawl into my arms. She curls into me, the same way she always used to do. And even though we kissed little more than a month ago, I know that this is different. I keep my eyes on the top of her damp head and my arms around her waist and shins. Mindful, too, of burns.

"You're here," she says.

Like she wants me to be.

"I'm here."

She curls closer, and I think: Even if we were never to kiss again, even if it were never more than this, it would be enough just to hold you.

"I can't do this," she murmurs.

"The funeral?"

"The job."

I can feel a burning in my throat, moving up to my eyes. I tilt my head to stare at the ceiling, willing it to cool. "You're good at this job."

Annie shakes her head, like she's pushing away a thought, and then she breathes: "Good at choosing which of my friends die?"

My own guilt croaks out. "Better than sitting it out in cowardice."

The water lapping the sides of the tub, the droplets dripping from her hair, echo in the empty washroom. That night at the Lyceum, the morning on Fort Aron—both, I realize, were moments when I did nothing. And maybe I disagree with Annie about what *something* should have looked like. But I know, after Fort Aron, that nothing can't be the answer.

I can't sit on the bench anymore.

She presses her forehead against my chest, lowering her face to the water so that her hair spills like seaweed around her head, and speaks into the wet strands.

"Cor had asked me to let him stay in your group."

I've been bracing myself for mention of Duck since I slipped into the water beside her. Bracing for her blame, as I deserve. It's only now that I realize she's been too busy blaming herself.

Of course. That's why she hasn't come.

"My group was for unsparked riders."

"He was underperforming . . ."

"It's not your fault."

Annie lets out a dull moan. Like this is a line from a circle of reasoning she's trapped in. "Do you want to know the funny thing?" she murmurs. "The funny thing is, I think he thought he was protecting *me*."

She is laughing, and as it turns to tears, I pull her to me. "Well, that was pretty stupid of him."

Annie lets out a drunken-sounding snort that she smothers against my chest. "You can't say that about people who are—"

And then she starts crying, hard.

I hold her until the bath gets cold. Though there's no attempt at modesty under the water, we turn away from each other to dress. She's drying her hair when a knock sounds on the door and the person who lets himself in isn't Deirdre or Alexa, but Cor.

He doesn't question what I'm doing here, or even seem to notice me. Pale beneath hair that has been parted and combed, he stares at Annie's blotchy face and says, "I just keep thinking— Duck wouldn't want me to be an ass to you—at his—"

He can't say *funeral*.

Annie presses her palms under her eyes.

"Save it for afterward?" she suggests, her voice full of water.

Cor lets out a laugh like a sob.

***

The funerals for the fallen Guardians are held on the Island of the Dead, the burial site of the dragonborn before the Revolution. It's approached by a narrow footpath from the Outer Palace that winds to the far side of Pytho's Keep and connects, by a single footbridge, to the island in the center of the River Fer.

I realize, setting foot on it today, that I've never attended a funeral before.

What I remember of the island has changed: The sepulchers that contained the remains of my ancestors were defaced in the Revolution, and no graves were added for the dragonborn killed during it. I wonder, looking around the island, where they would have lain. My parents, my brother and sisters. There is no easy history of what happened to those killed on Palace Day, but I know enough to know they were not honored in death. Today, at least, a blanket of snow masks the old destruction.

We've made the walk on foot, the dragons processing above us, from the Palace to the island with the senior ministry officials and family members in attendance. When my boots crunch the unmarked snow of this ancestral island for the first time, I'm braced to feel the pain of Leo, Leon's son.

But when I see my friends gathered around the pyre, all other thoughts fade. Pallor, landing at my side, presses a nose against my hand, and his folding wings quiver.

The procession gathers. The biers are mounted. Riders with their dragons form a ring round the pyre; the widowed dragons have landed beside them. Their wings droop, their tails brush the snow, and when they lift their heads, their restless eyes find the horizon. They won't remain much longer.

Annie moves, with leaden feet, toward the Sutter family, gathered beside Cor. She bends into a bow and offers them Duck's folded uniform. When Mrs. Sutter reaches out to take it, Annie isn't able to let go.

Duck's mother stoops to take Annie's hand and pull her upright. "Annie, darling. Come here."

She folds her into an embrace. The rest of what she murmurs, as she presses her forehead against Annie's, I cannot make out.

Behind the pyres, a new plinth has been erected. On it, in Callish, reads:

THE FALLEN GUARDIANS.

Three names have been inscribed below. There is space for more.

Before the pyre is lit, Atreus delivers the funeral oration.

"Eight years ago, thirty-two young people from all over Callipolis stood before me and took vows that made history for our island. They vowed to ride for Callipolis, to defend her, to guide her to justice. They vowed themselves to this service until death released them."

I remember that day.

I remember saying those vows, wondering if I believed them. Feeling the chill of the words, and realizing I did. Realizing that I wanted to be a Guardian of Callipolis. To follow this man and to believe in his vision.

"We are all of us Revolutionaries," Atreus goes on. "Dreaming of a juster world for our children. Willing to sacrifice in the name of great ideals."

We are all of us Revolutionaries.

I suddenly feel that the words of Atreus Athanatos are more powerful than he is. Dragonfire that can't be contained. Because he is right, in more ways than he knows. I still believe those vows, even if I don't believe in the man.

Now, watching the pyres for my friends, more than ever.

"Today we recognize the first of you to complete their vows. We recognize their sacrifice. And we look to you, the Guardians who remain, to continue their work.

"Long live this Revolution."

Too cold to spark, torches are held before the widowed dragons's maws, and they breathe them into life. The pyres light and the dragons launch. Into the growing dark, into the empty sky. They bear no harness, no saddle; they never will again. They turn their course due north. Watching them move as if drawn on an invisible line, I feel the hair rise on my neck. I've heard the thing described before, but seeing it is eerie.

An exodus.

Lotus, standing beside me, has one hand lifted to shield his eyes as he watches the horizon, the other holding Rock's shoulder as his face streams. "Why north?" Lotus murmurs.

North of the Medean basin, the cold is too severe to be hospitable to dragons, much less the hot springs required for their hatchlings. New Pythos is already borderline.

"No one knows. The dragonborn assumed they go north to die."

Lotus looks startled, but before he can ask more, the singing begins.

Deirdre has taken Atreus's place before the pyre. Her voice is high and clear as she begins the Anthem of the Revolution, the arrangement minor, and she starts with the alternate verse.

We bleed, we die, for the glory of Callipolis . . .

She sings until the dragons have dwindled to nothing on the red horizon.

Afterward, in the growing dark, Pallor and I make our way through the seamless snow to the part of the island once dedicated to the graves of the Stormscourge family. Drakarchs and lesser dragonlords were buried on our estates in the highlands, but those who served as triarch were buried here. We wander through the sloping mounds until, at the base of the section, I find the youngest graves—the ones that belonged to my grandparents. I begin to wipe the snow away, steeling myself for what I'll find. Pallor breathes on the last of the ice and it melts to water.

The graves are cracked, the sculpted images of their faces shattered. I know that beneath the ground, their remains will be gone. Exhumed and dissolved in quicklime, as all the empty graves of this island were, when they were dug up during the Revolution.

It's family I renounced, when I came back from that duel with Julia, and Atreus renamed me under oath: *You are Lee, of no father and no house.*

But I will kneel at an ancestral gravesite and pay respect, even if I have forsaken living kin. Even if the dragon at my side is an aurelian, not a stormscourge.

It's grown so dark that I don't realize, until I hear her, that Annie has knelt beside us and is helping clear the snow. Aela nips at Pallor, who launches at her. They begin to gambol among the snowy stones, leaving a melting trail behind them.

"We could erect a memorial," Annie says.

I look up at her.

"To the fallen dragonborn. In the Revolution. I know it wouldn't be the same, but—"

Her cheeks are pink-flushed in the cold, her eyes ringed red, but in her Guardian mantle and ceremonial armor, she looks like a dragonborn lady out of our oldest legends.

I kiss her hand.

Antigone, who buries the dead.

A private wake at the Sutters' house is held after the funeral. Annie and I make our way back to the city on foot; the dragons return without us to the caves. In the silence of our pilgrimage along the narrow footpath that circles the foothills of Pytho's Keep back to the Fer, I think on Atreus's words.

And we look to you, the Guardians who remain, to continue their work.

The work that I have, that is waiting for me, lies ahead.

I don't know its shape exactly, until I see Megara Roper among the mourners waiting on the steps to the Sutter home.

ANNIE

When I accept Mrs. Sutter's invitation to the wake, and see how Cor's face changes, I know: This will be my last visit to Duck's family. I joked that Cor should save his anger for after the funeral, but now I know it was not a joke. Cor hasn't forgotten, and may never forgive me for sending Duck out when he could have stayed behind.

That's fine. I'll never forgive myself either.

So for this last visit to their home, I do what I do best. I sit quietly, soaking up the warmth of a home, a family close, the things I've lost. I add to them the fresher ache of Duck's absence like a hole in the heart of it all. Merina and Greg, playing in their funerary black and being told off; Ana, helping her mother prepare libation wine; Cor out back, with his father and the other guests, starting the wakefire.

I move through it all like a ghost. As if I'm already gone, and this world I walked in, borrowed from Duck, is already lost to me.

Until on the back steps, I hear voices that I know. Cor's, with Megara Roper's.

"We'll run it tomorrow," she says. "You like it?"

Cor says, "I think it sums it up."

"And Lee? Tomorrow night?"

"He'll come."

I back into the kitchen and stumble headfirst into Lee.

"Hey. You seen Cor?"

I could confront him here, could ask him now, but I'm too dizzy with wine and sorrow and suspicions I hope aren't true to say the thing I should. So instead of asking him outright about what it means that Megara Roper wants to meet with him, I jab a thumb. "Out back."

Lee notices something off in my face. "Are you all right?"

"I'm—yeah, I'm heading out."

His face fills with understanding.

"Of course," he says. "I'll find you later."

I stumble through the quiet streets of Highmarket alone, my mantle turned inside out lest an angry citizen take opportunity at the sight of a Guardian without her dragon, and that fear keeps at bay the thought that the last time I walked these streets, Duck was at my side.

I breathe freely only when I'm back inside the Palace gates.

I have the girls' dorm to myself; Crissa convalesces in the infirmary, Alexa has gone home with Deirdre for the night, and Orla's bed will never be filled again. I lie in mine, and close my eyes, and when sleep doesn't come, I think of how Duck once led me to this bed when I was high with insomnia, tucked me in, and told me a bedtime story. Not caring that I couldn't love him as he loved me, because he loved me more than that.

Annie, you need to sleep.

The tears come thick and fast. I press my palms against my wet eyes and strain to think of anything to escape this *pain*.

And all that comes to mind is Griff.

Soon, he'll be waiting on the Driftless Dunes for me.

And somewhere along the way, twined with the words of Atreus's eulogy, my mind made up. I'll go to him.

We recognize their sacrifice. We continue their work.

This will be my work.

I roll back out of bed, go to my desk palming my face dry, and light a lamp. It takes a bit of rummaging in my desk to find it: the Dragontongue primer we used in our first years as Guardians. The last time I looked at it, my handwriting was still a child's. It's like remembering an old friend, this girl who copied paradigms obsessively, who doodled tiny dragons in the margins during class and wrote *Antigone sur Aela* out in Dragontongue, to see how it looked. When my memories go to long evenings helping Duck with his homework, quizzing him on declensions while his face screwed up and his tongue stuck out, I let myself smile with the tears. He was always the one who convinced me we'd studied enough for the night.

As I remember, I begin annotating with an adult hand, for a different purpose.

Lee comes in much later to find me working. He and I are alone. He smells of the wakefire and libation wine; his hair has snow in it. I had thought to do two things: ask him about Megara, and tell him about Griff.

Instead all I want is to hold and be held by him.

"How was it?"

He shakes his head in answer and takes my hand. I get to my feet and follow him to my bed. We crawl into it together. Into each other's arms.

I fit into them perfectly.

"Duck once did this—"

His voice is soft. "I know."

Somehow his knowing makes it all right. That, and this. I snuff the lamp. Turn once, to kiss him, and taste the salt.

Tomorrow. I'll tell him about Griff tomorrow.

We fall asleep together.

The next day, normal life resumes.

Rations have been adjusted in the wake of the Passi's granary raid, but my appetite has been too little to feel the difference in a smaller helping of porridge. After breakfast, I make my way to Scholars Row, numb steps tracing snow-shoveled streets through the heart of the city, an unmarked mantle covering my uniform. Winter has taken the city full force and filled it with a strange hush. Except in the Lyceum courtyard, where students are building a snow dragon and laughing as they volley snowballs.

Snowballs. They're my age, but I've never felt less like them.

Inside, I follow the tide of students filing into the largest lecture hall. The only class I'm enrolled in besides Norish is History of the Revolution, a mandatory lecture that Lyceum students take in rotation. Lotus waves to me from beside an empty desk but I ignore him.

I sat with Duck for lectures.

So now I'll sit alone.

I'm making my way to an empty row when I catch sight of a handful of Gold students huddled around a single desk, their heads bent. One of them looks up, sees me, and jumps away from the desk as if it shocked him. Another elbows the girl in the center, whose head shoots up.

"Annie?" she says.

It's Hanna Lund, my patrician friend from Dragontongue class, the one I got to know while accidentally ignoring Megara Roper last term. A piece of raglike paper is suddenly folded in half, Hanna's hand atop it, but when she sees me looking, she stops short of shoving it out of sight.

"What's that?" I ask.

The professor hasn't arrived yet; I'm suddenly aware that I'm the only student in this class, apart from Lotus, who is wearing a uniform. Glances are darting between me and Hanna like sparks. She inhales and, with a frozen expression, holds the piece of paper out to me.

The Passi have covered our response to their granary raid.

The headline reads: Defending the Rich and Oppressing the Poor: Guardians Do What Dragonriders Have Always Done.

There are two poorly illustrated dragonriders firing on civilians underneath, in front of a crude rendition of the Lyceum.

The dragonriders are labeled Firstrider and Tertius of the Callipolan Fleet.

In other words, Power and I.

For all the ways I've reflected on the night of the Lyceum raid with guilt and shame, my first thought is that this printing is a gross oversimplification that will provoke unrest in the city. And that it will be my job to manage even as it undermines my legitimacy.

It's going to make my job harder, and then make it harder for me to do my job.

And it's a far cry from the coverage provided by the *People's Paper* and the *Gold Gazette*, which ran while we were in Fort Aron, highlighting the toll the raid took on ration allotments and praising the Guardians who defended the Lyceum as heroes.

I look up to see Lotus joining the group with alarm on his face. My classmates are staring at us, and I realize Hanna has said something. "We all know this is completely biased—"

We who? The Lyceans, who don't understand what it feels like to starve, who cannot fathom the kind of desperation that would drive class-irons to scale walls in search of grain?

I hear myself answer her like someone else is saying it. "You're not supposed to have this. It's illegal."

"Annie," Lotus murmurs, but it's like his voice is muffled.

Hanna's eyes are bright, and for a fleeting instant I think it's fear to be caught in possession of banned materials. But then the next thing she says doesn't fit.

"Are you all right?"

The last thing I need is a patrician's pity. I take Hanna's illegal leaflet, stuff it in my bag, and make my way to the nearest stretch of empty desks. And then I put my bag in the seat next to me, so no one will try to fill it.

On the far side of the hall, Megara Roper has taken a seat next to Cor, her long hair spilling down her shoulders.

The conversation overheard last night plays again in my head. *We'll run it tomorrow.*

Cor looked at that picture of me firing on civilians and approved it while I stood in his home.

And what am I to do now? I could report them; but even if I could convince myself Megara deserved it—does Cor? Whose sister goes hungry under this ration structure, whose brother I just led to his death?

Does anyone deserve to be reported for telling the truth?

Especially by me, the one guilty of everything they accuse.

My eyes are stinging, so badly that the chalkboard on which the professor is writing blurs. I blink them clear. Professor Lavinia has written a single word in block capitals: DRACHTHANASIA.

"Shall we get started?"

I listen to her lecture about the poison that killed the dragons during the Revolution with numb ears. *Dragons are immune to most toxins, and the creation of drachthanasia is a legendarily difficult art,* she begins, and I stare at the back of Cor's head, at Megara Roper's thick mane, unable to stop seeing that cartoon, seething as the professor's words wash over me, hearing nothing.

Why don't I remember Megara better from Dragontongue class?

But I know the answer to that: I was so focused on Lee and Tyndale circling each other, so starstruck by the patrician students like Hanna Lund offering friendship, that I had eyes for no one else in that room.

He'll come, Cor told Megara, when she asked about Lee.

Did Lee see this printing, too, last night? Did he approve it as well?

Professor Lavinia says: "Palace Day is the most famous day of the Red Month. But perhaps even more important to the success of the Revolution was a night earlier in the Red Month known as the Widowing, when revolutionaries took drachthanasia stolen from the dragonlords' own caches and used it to poison their fleet."

It's like her words wake me up. Suddenly I'm listening. Not just listening: alive. Alive with an excitement I'm not even sure it's decent to feel.

Drachthanasia. Dragon poison. Revolution.

It worked once. Which means it could work again.

"Drachthanasia is painless," Lavinia goes on, "designed to put dragons to sleep in old age, or out of their misery in cases of extreme pain. But the widowing itself is psychologically brutal for the rider. They suffer spells of sorrow sickness that lessen with time, but never entirely heal. This psychological blow to the triarchy, though often overlooked, played a huge part in the final stages of the Red Month. It was also the final, most intimate betrayal, because it was the moment when the dragonborn were betrayed by the servants they trusted most: their dragons' keepers."

Dragons' keepers.

Keepers like Griff.

This is how we could do it.

In the hour between Revolutionary history and Norish, I let myself into the Lyceum library to find Lee sitting at one of the corner tables, the Passi's latest leaflet spread in front of him. But he's not looking at it. He's staring into space.

I've spent the last eight years taking comfort in the dusty smell of old books, the solace of forced quiet in libraries, when dorm life meant this was the only kind of privacy that could be found. That blank look on his face as he waits for the grief to pass—I know it.

I take the seat beside him.

That dark hair, I ran my fingers through this morning; that face, I cupped in the dawn light; those lashes, I studied as I re-oriented myself from dreams where Duck was alive. I peel off my book bag and mantle and sit so our knees touch. There are students here and there around us, their work spread over tables, lamps glowing on their features, but the galleries of shelves stretching into the rafters have few windows, leaving the corner table in semidarkness.

He reaches gently across the distance to lay his hand on mine, and with the other, he folds the Passi's leaflet in half, hiding the printing. I realize, with a lump rising to my throat, that he thinks to spare me.

Of course he does. Because whatever disagreement there was the night of that raid, this is Lee. He has my back and I can trust him and now, most of all, I need that—

So I push away my suspicions.

"It's all right. I've already seen it."

Lee seems to work for words. Even for a whisper, they come out guttural. "How was class?"

I shrug. "It was about the Widowing. The night they . . ."

Lee's lips form a line. "I know what the Widowing is."

I noticed years ago that Lee avoids classes about the Red Month, but this is the first time I've ever heard him come close to admitting it.

The first time I've considered this fact with a spike of curiosity.

I don't know how to begin to find a dragonlord's cache of drachthanasia. But Lee might.

Asking him, on the other hand—that's hard to imagine. Lee's father's dragon wasn't killed in the Widowing; she was kept alive for later, to be executed in a spectacle Lee and I witnessed. But I'm sure whatever memories he has of the Red Month include the Widowing.

It must have been horrible.

"Deirdre and Alexa are back," Lee murmurs, which means no more sharing beds.

I nod, but don't remove my hand. The tips of his fingers trace my palm. It feels good enough to tighten my throat.

Tell him.

But maybe instead, I can start by showing him. "Lee, are you . . . free? Tonight?"

Lee's fingers arrest on my palm. "Why?"

"There's someone I want you to meet."

Lee avoids my eyes. "Can we do it another night? I've got . . . plans."

256

Megara's question to Cor returns to me and the date clicks into place for the first time. *Is Lee coming, tomorrow night?*

Plans indeed.

I release his hand.

"Did you know about it?" I ask.

I can suddenly hear my own pulse in my ears. In the quiet of the library, it feels loud.

Lee looks up, shoulders tensing. "What?"

I point to the paper folded between us. "Did you know about this?"

His eyes widen. He shakes his head.

But he doesn't tell me I'm mistaken to wonder. And I don't know whether to be grateful he has the grace not to deny it, or to feel even more betrayed.

"Seat taken?"

Lee and I both jump. Megara Roper's hand is on the back of the seat with Lee's bag in it, and she's smiling at him. Though we're in the middle of the library, her voice is barely lowered; nearby students have looked up from their work, startled by the sound.

"Oh," says Lee, fingers curling over the Passi's leaflet.

Megara reaches for Lee's bag and slides it to the floor. She takes the seat next to him, nods at the leaflet, and arches a brow at me. "Horrible what they print, isn't it?"

Lee's shoulders draw up and hunch forward, as if hoping to interpose himself between me and Megara.

But I don't want him to stand between us. I want him to tell her to go away.

He doesn't.

Doesn't look at me.

I feel the absence of his touch on my palm as if a cool draft had blown across it.

I get to my feet.

"Going somewhere?" Megara asks, with an air of disappointment.

I nod, because my heart is racing at such a speed I feel too dizzy to speak.

Lee finally looks at me, his face twisted. "Another night?" he proposes, desperation in his voice.

Like he realizes that I'm sliding away from him and wants to catch me before I do.

I stare back at him and imagine asking: Another night *what*?

Another night, I take Lee to Griff Gareson, the boy who kept me from saving Duck, and ask him to share his memories of the Red Month? Another night, Lee explains to me why he wants to share a table with Megara Roper, who disappeared the night of the Lyceum raid just before Southside's Daughter arrived?

It felt good, waking up in his arms this morning. So good.

Too good.

A single student watches me from the other end of the library tables, his arms folded over his chest, his shaved head cocked to one side. The wings of the Fourth Order glint on the shoulder of his uniform in the smoky lamplight.

With a surge of fury I think: Lee can keep his secrets. And I'll keep mine.

I hoist my bag onto my shoulder and cross the silent library to Power's table. He pulls the seat beside him out as I approach. I take it, swinging my book bag to the floor with a thunk that I don't bother to mask.

"The city guard really needs to get a move on finding this rogue press," Power says.

"Don't," I say, because the burning behind my eyes clogs anything more coherent.

"You know who probably could tell them where to find it?"

"*Stop.*"

Power makes a noise of exasperation. A student nearby clears his throat, glaring at us as if to dare us to keep talking. Power twists in his chair and glares back. It's the first-year from Norish. He recognizes us, flushes, and hunkers back down over his book with shoulders around his ears.

Power twitches back round and taps the book open before him with his index finger. It's his Norish primer.

"So do we go meet your new friend?"

LEE

I woke this morning muggy with desire. For a blissful few moments, Annie was the only thing in the world. I hadn't killed Julia, the fleet hadn't come back without Duck, and I'd never stood in the cold outside Cor's house as his family tended Duck's snow-smoked wakefire and poured libation wine.

There was only her. Auburn hair soft as down. A slender neck rippled with burn scars I knew by heart, freckles dusting pale cheeks that I kissed. Her eyes closed, her lips parting, her neck baring as she arched it back against the pillow and I thought, *Let this moment, let this sight, never end.*

I found the Passi leaflet at breakfast. Last night, when I spoke with Megara briefly in the street outside Cor's home, all that she said was that the Passi had something big planned for today. And even then, the half thought floated in my mind that perhaps it was not too late to convince Annie. To make the Passi something we did together.

Together, the way we lay tangled together this morning.

Surely, she would see the reason in it, the rightness. She told me once that New Pythos was the enemy, not Atreus, but surely together we could take on both—

I didn't realize, until I found that leaflet this morning, what Megara meant by *something big*. She meant a cartoon depicting Annie firing on civilians.

I looked down at that cartoon and agreed with all of it. We terrorized those we should have protected that night. We protected the rich and oppressed the poor as dragonriders have always done.

Not we. *She.*

But it felt like a fight from another life. From before Duck, from before the world shattered.

And all I could think, looking down at an illustration of exactly the thing Annie had done the night of the Lyceum raid that had so horrified me at the time, was that I didn't want her to see it. That today's reentry to normal life was going to be hard enough for her without this stupid piece of paper making it worse.

Now I watch her cross the library to take a seat beside Power. Her red-brown hair, in a stub of a braid that I watched her plait in bed this morning, bounces against the collar of her uniform as she slams down her bag.

Power's gaze forgets me as it finds her. Like his world has narrowed to a knifepoint.

"Classist prig," Megara mutters, eyes on Power. "Should have let Jester finish him when he had the chance."

I'd forgotten for a moment that she was here.

The leaflet rests on the table between us. I unfold it. Megara waits, twirling a long black strand of hair in her fingers, her smile calculating, her bright eyes as green as her scarf.

"So?" she asks. "You coming tonight?"

I look down at the illustration of dragonriders firing on cowering citizens.

Annie, who should be better than this, defending Atreus and his ilk from starving men.

Logs on a fire. Fires to burn the world down. A lifetime in the ashes of such a fire has taught me that it doesn't end there.

Anyone can start a fire. The problem is what happens after.

I refold the leaflet and hold it out to Megara. Then I get up, hoist my bag, and leave the library.

As I knew she would, Megara follows.

It's between bells: Outside, the corridor is deserted, classroom doors are closed, the stone walls bare except for bulletin boards advertising Lyceum student groups and posters of upcoming events. After I've closed the library door behind me, I round on her. My voice sounds loud raised from a whisper.

"Do the Passi have a positive vision of what they want? Or is it just more of this?"

I've had time to think on it, since the night of the Lyceum raid. To wonder about the stolen grain, to ruminate on the fact that the Passi set a granary on fire that they weren't able to empty. The cartoon this morning only solidifies my caution: Guardians make good scapegoats, but scapegoats make poor solutions.

The recklessness of fleeing with Southside's Daughter on the night of the riot was heady. But I don't intend to tie myself to a ship without a rudder.

Much less a ship making target practice out of my friends.

Megara's smile flickers. She tucks the leaflet into her bag without looking at it. The wall is at her back; there's barely a foot between us. She's tall, but even so has to tilt her head back just a little to meet my eyes. Her glance flits down to the Guardian emblem on the breast of my uniform before snapping back to my face.

She says, "Of course we have a positive vision. We want equality."

"That's too vague."

"How would you put it?"

"You want equal *rights*. Which means constitutional reforms. Abolition of the metals test, a reinstitution of the People's Assembly, protections for free speech."

Megara smiles. "As they did in Damos?"

"As they did in Damos."

It's like we're putting words to the thing I've been wanting since I returned from Pytho's Keep and Annie told me the truth. This is what I've been waiting for. This is what it's time to *do*.

Get the power out of the hands of the bastard who took it from my family and into the hands of those who deserve it.

"Well then," Megara says, green eyes dancing, "why don't you come tonight, and say that?"

19

—

NIGHTTIME WANDERINGS

GRIFF

The days after the Callipolan air strike pass in a haze. The feel of Sparker's key pressing into my palm at Delo's touch is like a dream, though the key is proof it wasn't. Memories of the moonlit meeting with the strange Callipolan Firstrider, the offer of another meeting in a few days' time—she'll come, I tell myself. She has to.

I saw her waver. I know her heart. And she's smart enough to know a good offer when she sees it.

The day I've planned to go and wait for Antigone, Ixion tells me I'll be serving at table for a council—an order I usually dread—and it's all I can do to keep from smiling.

The council turns out to be between Ixion, Rhadamanthus, and his son Rhode in apartments the ha'Aurelians have co-opted in the Provisional Palace since the Greatlord's Hall burned. The chamber looks out over the sea, down on the sloping backs of Thornrose and Knoll Karsts; the sigil of the Triarchy's three dragons circling the black clover of exile mounts the wall. This part of the citadel survived the air strikes well, though the windows buckled and stained in the heat. I'm preparing the steaming tea service at the side of the room when the door opens and a fourth guest arrives: Delo.

He stiffens at the sight of me. We haven't been in the same room, within speaking distance, since he brought back the little ones and gave me Sparker's key.

"You're dead," Rhode says.

Rhadamanthus gives his son a quelling look. "Delo, welcome. Come, sit."

Delo advances, sits, and Rhadamanthus offers a tight smile to the other two. "We have been informed that you were the one who let the peasants into the crypt with the dragonborn women and children. Is this true?"

Delo's words come stiffly. "It is, Uncle."

Uncle is an elder honorific within the Three Families; there is no relation.

"But this would mean that you not only violated our air strike protocol but abandoned the battle to do so."

There is a pause that I study from the corner where I'm checking the steeped tea: Rhadamanthus has the tips of his fingers drawn together, over which he studies Delo. I'm sure Delo can read the Greatlord's warning as well as I can: This is his last chance to explain himself before his father is involved. Nestor will be even less pleased.

Delo clenches his fingers on the arms of his chair. "The Norcians in the Greatlord's Hall were locked in."

This is, clearly, news to Rhadamanthus. And news to me that it's news to him.

Delo, seeing, rounds on Ixion and Rhode. I approach with tea.

"Rhode," Rhadamanthus says, "did you modify my directions to provide Norcian families with shelter?"

I pour tea into Rhadamanthus's cup first, Ixion's second, Rhode's third. My arm is steady. Rhode says, after a fraction of a hesitation, "A little, Father, yes."

Delo makes a noise of disgust. As I fill his cup, his eyes flick upward, lightning fast, to mine, then return to the conversation. I feel a pulse begin in my ears that has nothing to do with the subject they're discussing.

The last time we were so close, I was on my knees before him, and his trembling fingers touched my chin.

"Please explain your reasoning."

A slight edge in Rhadamanthus's voice makes Rhode and Ixion sit straighter. Ixion has paled even by the standards of his own pasty House. He looks at Rhode, then answers for him.

"It was only the logical conclusion of your plan," he says. "You wanted to disabuse the peasants of their infatuation with the Callipolan Firstrider. I thought that lesson would be better driven home if they were . . . not allowed to skip class. Especially for the humble-riders who might be considering fairer pastures."

For all my effort to control my hands, the teapot lands on the tray with a clank.

"And it was an effective lesson, was it not?"

I realize Rhode is speaking to me. The eyes of the other three rise to mine. Ixion's are sparkling with subdued mirth.

We haven't spoken of my family since that day. Ixion hasn't asked if the little ones survived, hasn't referenced any interference on the part of Delo, and from that I can only assume that he didn't care enough about the outcome to concern himself with it.

But the joke's on him, because I've found fairer pastures after all.

"Aye, my lord. We're all the fonder of our lords after they locked our children in burning buildings."

Delo snorts into his tea. Ixion scowls. But Rhadamanthus lifts a hand, nodding at me. "Griff makes the valid point. It's a delicate balance between too little fear and too much. You must tread carefully."

Rhode looks as though he is struggling not to roll his eyes.

"Has she replied to your latest?" Rhadamanthus asks Ixion.

She. Freyda?

"No. But she will. Especially when she hears news of what the Callipolans did to her ships."

I return with tea biscuits.

"Thank you, Griff," Rhadamanthus says. And then he adds, with a half glance up at me: "That was some spectacular flying during the attack. If only the rest of the fleet fought so bravely."

Delo sets down his cup. "Many of them could have fought more bravely if their dragons had been free to fire."

His voice is shaking. I stop dead, staring at him instead of returning the biscuits to the tea service. Ixion, Rhode, and Rhadamanthus glance, one by one, at me.

"We've been over the reasoning for this before," Rhadamanthus tells Delo.

Delo's fingers are curling on his knees. "The reasoning's absurd. We lost half the citadel because a third of our fleet was muzzled."

Rhadamanthus clears his throat and looks at me.

"Griff? Please excuse us."

I let myself out of the room with my heart racing. As soon as I close the door after myself, I hear the voices resume, raised, on the opposite side of it.

It's the first time I realize the decision to muzzle wasn't unanimous.

And that Delo opposed it.

"Is Papa in there?"

I look down. In the shadow of the corridor, I didn't even notice the child crouching by the door holding a doll.

"My little lordling Astyanax! Where's your nurse?"

"Don't like her," Astyanax says. He holds up his doll. It's a dragon sewn from black fabric, wings flapping loose. "His name is Sparker." Astyanax points to the snout. "He doesn't like it."

As much as I've always liked Astyanax, this takes me by surprise. I bend to look closer. The stuffed animal dragon has a little twine muzzle wrapped round his jaw. I feel a flutter in my chest like a caged bird. "No. He doesn't."

A figure appears at the end of the corridor and lets out an exclamation in Norish.

"Thank the shrines—I wasn't sure where he went—"

It's Shea, my sister's friend from Clan Thornrose, the one I never danced with.

"You're Astyanax's nurse?" I ask in surprise.

She takes Astyanax's hand, recognizes me, and fumbles to straighten her hair scarf with her free hand. "I am now. The attack—she was older, her lungs didn't take to the smoke."

Astyanax is testing dead weight on Shea's arm, oblivious to our Norish. "Can we go see the real Sparker sometime, Shea?" he asks in Dragontongue.

I crouch in front of Astyanax and answer in his language.

"Shea will bring you, but only if you listen well to her. She's my friend."

Astyanax gasps with full delight, Shea mouths *thank you* over his head, and I head out of the citadel with a spring in my step.

I've got Sparker's key waiting deep in a sack of grain, Becca and Garet home safe and sound, a secret trip to Callipolis all on my own tonight—and Rhadamanthus's youngest son is naming his doll after Sparker. Not Ryla, not Niter, but *Sparker*. My beautiful, wild, too-big Sparker.

Whose muzzle Astyanax's doll doesn't like and neither, it turns out, does Delo.

When I return home in the evening, the strangest end to this day is that Granda's out in the alleyway, touching up the signs of our clan-karst on the lintel. It's been a long time since I've seen him concern himself with more than his chair by the fire.

"Griff. Hold this, will you?"

He hands me a pot of woad, which he must have borrowed from a neighbor, because ours dried out years ago. I'm terrible at maintaining the clan signs.

"Granda, stop, I'll take care of it—"

"The fresh air's good for me."

Granda's just looking at the doorframe, like he's going to stare at it hard enough to take the warp out of it. "The boy's got new shoes," he tells me, as he traces each sign. Thumb and forefinger pinching together, then drawing apart, to form the Nag's bent head.

"Yeah."

"And your sister's got herbs, for her lungs."

"Yeah, they're from Delo. Lord Delo."

"Good of him."

I nod.

Granda finishes the last sign. He straightens, but instead of leading the way back inside, he turns to me. It's been so long since I've looked him eye to eye when he has a clear gaze that I'd forgotten what it feels like.

"When your da gets back," he says, "I want you to answer for this household without shame."

I feel a cold trickle into my gut.

Da's been gone for years, his charter never recovered. There was not an exact day where Agga and I went from hoping to mourning, but it wasn't a turn I came back from.

But it's always draining to talk about it with Granda, who's still waiting.

"Granda, he's not—"

Granda lifts a hand. "We're not talking about Gares. We're talking about Gareson. You've had to shoulder more than your share since he's been gone, but that doesn't mean you should be doing things for this family that don't—sit right."

I stare at him. To my surprise, his voice is rough with emotion.

"What are you talking about?"

"I'm talking about things these dragonlords might be asking of you that *you don't want to give*."

Slowly, like cold water seeping through the toes of my boots, I realize what he's talking about.

And even though I feel sick enough that I suddenly think I might vomit before my own granda, it comes with a feeling that something has finally been ripped open and shown to the light.

"I don't . . . anymore."

I hear myself say it, that one word *anymore*.

"Lord Delo?" Granda asks.

I feel light-headed as I shake my head. "He's never . . . asked . . . anything of me."

I'm glad it's getting dark. Glad he can't really see my face, nor I his.

"Good," he says. He places his hand on my shoulder, grips it, and releases. "I hope I live to see the day when Gares returns to find a son grown."

This time, I let the knife twist without arguing it.

He turns and leads the way inside.

We don't talk about it again for the rest of the evening. But the conversation doesn't stop turning in my head, circling like a puzzle I'm trying to solve. Until finally, after we've put out the lamp and the back room is dark, as the family falls asleep around me, I understand.

When I get up and head for the citadel, to make my meeting with Antigone, I take a single detour on the way to Sparker.

I know where Delo's chambers are, though I haven't visited them in years. Not since we were kids, and we got in trouble for his inviting me. I was beaten; he wasn't. We didn't try it again.

The hall is mostly dark, the nearest lit sconce around the corner. I knock, as softly as I can, and pray it's loud enough. For a moment, as I wait in the silence, the insanity of it tempts me to turn tail and walk away.

But then he opens the door.

"Griff?"

He sounds half asleep, and more than half confused. His curling hair is flattened to one side of his head, his tunic unbuttoned at the collar.

I step over the threshold, and then, because Delo seems too startled to move, I close the door myself. His chamber—the size of several homes from Clan Nag added together—is lit by a single candle by the bed, the shadows long on the high ceiling and floor-length drapes.

"You've never asked anything of me. You give, but you don't expect in return."

That's the realization that came from my conversation with Granda. Though can it really be called that, when words are put on the thing you've known all along, and suddenly you know why it matters?

"What? No, of course not—"

"You're not like Julia."

For the first time in my life, I've used Dragontongue's informal *you*. Delo's eyes focus on my face. And all at once, he seems wide-awake. "I try not to be."

We've turned, as I closed the door, so that now he stands against it, and I face him. We stand as close as we stood the last feast day, when I leaned toward him and he jerked closer. And his breathing has gone light again, telltale light, and I'm alive as if I'm riding Sparker—

"Griff, I don't . . . I never wanted it to be like that."

His eyes are so close, close as Julia's used to be. Except his are so dark they're almost black.

"It wouldn't," I tell him.

Our voices are soft, barely a whisper, as I lift my fingers to trace the back of his neck, to snag the curls at the nape.

"Why wouldn't it?" he asks.

"Because I want it."

Delo swallows—a beautiful, shuddering swallow—and I catch his mouth on mine.

When I leave, I don't tell him where I'm going.

By midnight, I'm flying with Sparker over the lowland marshes of the northern shore of Callipolis, familiar from the maps Nestor's shown us when he rants about the Long-Awaited Return. The Driftless Dunes, an uninhabited stretch halfway between Fort Aron and Basil's Cape, is a barren mix of dead seagrass and swelling dunes, and tonight it's a sea of darkness except for the single fire lit in a valley between two dunes a few hundred yards from the shore.

Easy to spot from the air, next to impossible to spot from the ground.

Antigone is there.

Waiting with her dragon and that other stormscourge rider, the one from last time.

"Knew you'd come," I tell her.

In the light of her driftwood fire, the corner of her mouth turns up.

The other dragonrider steps forward. "My name's Power," he says, "and this is Eater. We'll be doing patrols overhead while you two have . . . serf school. Or whatever this is supposed to be."

"Thanks, Power," says Antigone. "You can go now."

But Power seems to be puffing himself up for a good long threat. "Any funny business," he tells me, "and I will make you *wish* your lords—"

Antigone snaps at him in Callish and he rolls his eyes.

Once Power sur Eater has gone, Annie turns back to me. Her little aurelian is curled close to the fire, red in the light of the flames, and she's spread a woolen blanket over the sand next to her. "Are you hungry?"

"Oh yeah. Always."

She opens a satchel, pulls out books and bread, and settles on one side of the blanket. I tear into the bread with enthusiasm and only notice after about half of it's gone that Antigone has been watching me, not partaking herself. I swallow. "Thought you all had a food shortage."

A line appears between her eyebrows, accentuated in the warm glow of the fire. It occurs to me that I probably shouldn't be bringing up a food shortage caused by our air strikes on their trade fleet.

"It doesn't apply to people like me," she says.

"Lucky you."

Antigone rubs a thumb between her brows. "I've brought a Dragontongue primer," she says, rapping knuckles on one of the books spread on the blanket between us. "But before that, I want to ask you a few questions."

A *few questions* turns out to be an interrogation. Antigone opens a notepad and questions me about New Pythos for an hour. Numbers, names, family trees, maps she makes me label. And at the end, she asks some of the questions a second time. I think, at first, it's because failed to note my answers on the first go, but then I realize: She's double-checking me for inconsistencies. Making sure I didn't fabricate.

Thorough, this one.

"One more thing," I tell her. "Ixion's been making overtures to Freyda. The Bassilean princess. That was why she had those ships in port. The ones that you . . . burned."

Antigone cocks her head. "Freyda? Daughter of the God-King? What does he want with her?"

"She's of age to marry. I think he's hopeful that those burned ships might incentivize her to take a side."

Antigone exhales slowly, and a wisp of hair puffs away from her face.

"Well," she says grimly, "she'd be justified. As some of us argued at the time."

With a twitch of her shoulder, she reaches for the primer, opens it, and turns it so I can see the first page. She slides her lantern across the blanket to flood it with light.

"This is the Dragontongue alphabet," she says.

As we work, our dragons settle closer to us, and Sparker nudges his head against my side. Antigone's focus is unwavering and unsmiling, except for the one time she looks up and notices my spare hand absently working over Sparker's jaw, up under the muzzle where it's always a little sore.

"Is it locked on?"

"Welded."

"How long has he had it?"

"Since he sparked. They did all of us when he sparked."

"He sparked first?"

A little note of something I can't identify vibrates in Antigone's voice.

"Yeah. But it was bad timing. We'd sort of . . . attacked some-one. Someone dragonborn."

Antigone is staring at us, her brows contorted like she isn't sure whether to laugh or look horrified. I take a breath and admit my most terrible crime.

"We sort of attacked Ixion sur Niter."

It was, and remains, one of the sweetest moments of my life or Sparker's. And even knowing how it ended, a muzzle for every humble-dragon, I still have a hard time thinking I wouldn't do it all over again if I had the chance.

Ixion bawled like a child. I couldn't stop laughing, even during the punishment afterward.

"Oh," says Antigone.

"Had to live up to his name, didn't he?" I joke, patting Sparker's flank.

Antigone's lips part in surprise, a smile spreading that she doesn't explain.

I gave Sparker his name in jest. By the time they realized I had, he was already so used to it he wouldn't respond to anything else. But when he sparked, and his flames blanketed Ixion sur Niter until Delo and Julia pulled us off, it only made our sentence worse.

I was sure they were going to drop me after my time in the pen was up. When they gave the humble-dragons the muzzle instead, I almost wished they had.

After an hour, when Power sur Eater returns, my head's hurting from our study. Antigone presses the primer into my hands, along with an empty notepad and a pen for me to practice with, and we agree on another meeting in three nights' time. She's strapping her satchel to her dragon, and I'm smothering the fire, when I finally get the courage to ask her.

"So how do we do it? How do we bring them down?"

Antigone pauses, removing her boot from the damp fire.

"I've been thinking about that. The squires, you're in charge of dragonkeeping, aren't you? And that includes feeding?"

I nod.

Antigone snaps her satchel shut. "Then we should do it the way the Revolutionaries did in Callipolis. Poison their half of the fleet."

It seems too simple to be believed, and I should be thrilled at how simple it is.

Instead, I feel a little sick.

"Bung deal for the dragons."

I sound so soft, pointing that out. But I tend these animals daily. Cart their feed and dung and scrub them down. You can't help having a healthy respect for the beasts you count that many hours with.

Antigone nods. She seems to have thought about this, too. "I know. It would be . . . awful. For their riders, too. In our Revolution, it was called the Widowing."

I shiver at the word. Antigone rouses herself.

"War is awful. Giving dragons to terrible people is awful. There's no good answer, Griff."

I look into Sparker's doleful amber eye, blinking at me over that wretched muzzle, and ask: "Would it hurt?"

Antigone's face softens. "Not if we use drachthanasia. But I need to figure out how to get it."

Seeming to sense my lingering horror, she jabs a finger at our dragons. At wings and fangs and talons, and a tonnage of weight behind them. "I'm sure you've grown fond of them, Griff, but at the end of the day they're weapons. Attuned to the will of one lord who would not think twice before turning them on you."

She says it so forcefully, it's like she thinks she's the only one who knows it.

But she isn't. Maybe where she's from, but not on New Pythos. I yank my sleeve up.

"You think I don't know that?"

Antigone looks down at the scars where Niter's fangs left dents, and her eyes widen.

"I've been bitten and burned and gnawed on as many times as my lord gave the order. I've served as target practice in a pen, run in circles till I couldn't run more. I've seen my friends dropped. And then I had to scrub and feed and shovel the shit of the dragons that did it. *Don't tell me* what they can do."

Antigone's eyes are bright, her breath fast. Good. I yank my sleeve back down.

"I may have too big a heart for the monsters, but I'm no fool, nor a coward. Get me the poison and I'll do it."

Even as I see that I've satisfied her doubts, my own twinge.

There is one dragon in the fleet I know would never hurt me, whose lord would never order it, and for them I would very well be both a coward and a fool.

Already was a fool, tonight, a happy, lovestruck fool kissing him in the darkness.

How could I ever do such a thing to Gephyra, to Delo?

20

—

SECRETS KEPT

LEE

Megara gives me the pass phrase and the address of a pub on the border between Southside and Highmarket, managed by her uncle, for Cor's and my inaugural meeting with the Passi. The ministry's first official ruling on the group arrives earlier the same day. The decree, copied to the entire Inner Palace, will be printed in tomorrow's editions of the *Gold Gazette* and the *People's Paper*.

> THE SELF-PROCLAIMED PASSI ARE ENEMIES OF THE REVOLUTION. ASSOCIATION WITH THE PASSI IS PROHIBITED. ENEMIES OF THE REVOLUTION SHOULD BE REPORTED TO THE MINISTRY OF INFORMATION FOR QUESTIONING AND CORRECTIVE ACTION.

I stare at the memo and think: I need to talk to Annie.

The only thing I'm certain about the meeting I'm about to attend is that it will be illegal. And while I'm no longer committed to upholding the laws of this regime, violating them at this level of risk and behind Annie's back seems doubly foolhardy. I'm making my way down to the Firstrider's office when I hear voices from the armory.

Annie's, with Power's.

"I just think *maybe* we should tell Holmes," Power is saying.

"If we tell him, he'll forbid it. You heard him. *The Norcians are our enemy, just like their lords.* This stays between us."

I stand frozen outside the armory, picturing the conversation within. I've never heard Annie use that voice with anyone but me. Confiding and wry, the tone I associate with conversations we have alone.

"All right, all right," says Power.

It's also the first time I've ever heard Power *not* sound like an ass.

I can hear gear thunking as it's being removed from hooks, ground uniforms being unfastened and stripped to the floor. From the sounds alone I can picture it: I know what it's like, those moments alone in that armory with a patrol partner, undressing in front of them like neither of you is thinking about it, when you both *are* thinking about it.

Annie conspiring with Power, undressing in front of Power—

The funny thing about overhearing a betrayal is that it makes your own impulse to come clean evaporate. I turn on my heel and go find Cor.

He's in the dark, empty solarium, just staring at the decree.

"I'm still game if you are," I tell him.

His face breaks into a wolfish grin, the more startling for its absence from his face for the past days. An hour later, we head out to an illegal meeting with the Passi together.

Only as I'm making my way out of the Palace in the dead of night with Cor do I wonder: What are Annie and Power keeping secret from Holmes? Who was it she wanted me to meet, before Megara interrupted us? But as I wonder, and even as jealousy gnaws, I find I have no interest in discussing Annie's secret dealings with Cor.

The Roper family's pub is called the Misanthrope, and the Passi's meeting takes place in one of the upper rooms around a table where about a dozen young people are gathered, the shutters drawn and the candles in the center glowing on the faces in the darkness. When Megara takes a seat at the head of the table, she tells them: "Well, it's finally happened. We're officially illegal."

A cheer goes up, like she's made a toast. Megara grins. She produces a basket, unclasps her gold wristband, and drops it in.

We are all equally deserving, she murmurs.

It's a line from the most famous Damian philosopher. The one known in Damos as the father of philosophy.

One by one, as the basket goes round, every citizen surrenders their wristbands and repeats the phrase. There are no silver wristbands; most are iron or bronze, with Megara one of the only golds. But there are three silver-and-gold: mine, Cor's, and, taking one of the last chairs before the meeting begins—

Lotus.

"Dad's running late," he tells Megara. He nods at Cor and me, flicking back a coil of wiry hair as he scoots his chair in. "Welcome to the second revolution."

Cor grins back like the party's starting. "Poets for the Passi?" he says. "All right!"

Lotus lets out a bark of laughter. "Glad that decree didn't scare you off."

Was this how it felt, the thrill of potential, when Atreus did this ten years ago?

A red-bearded man seated opposite me folds his arms. It's the same one, I realize, who pressed a cleaver to Power's throat the night of the Lyceum raid. "This who I think it is?" the man asks.

Megara begins unrolling a scroll across the scarred table. "It is. Lee, meet Jester—director of popular engagement."

Lotus mutters, with a hand over his mouth, "And streetlord."

The door creaks open and the publican, Val Lazare, comes in alongside Lotus's father, Lo Teiran. The last time Teiran and I spoke, we were in the men's washroom, where he was attempting to interview me for an epic poetry commission about Palace Day.

And it turns out he's enmeshed in a radical protest group? Unexpected.

"Hello again, Leo," he says. "No talk of poetry today, I promise." There is a smile in his oddly flat voice.

"Lee's fine," I answer, hearing the edge in mine.

He and Megara's uncle take the final seats at the table, Teiran slim, brown, and groomed with precision, Val Lazare filling out the remaining space with his considerable girth strained over a stained tunic. Like Megara, like Cor, Lazare has the olive skin of Damian ancestry, and the rolling consonants of Southside. Despite his humble appearance, it's conspicuous from how the rest of the room attunes to him that Lazare is their leader.

"Well done, Megara," he says, looking me and Cor over like we're fat game brought in from the hunt. "This is quite the coup."

Megara smiles. She turns to me. "Lee? Tell us what you were saying earlier."

Many at the table are young enough to be Lyceum students. Megara's uncle and Lo Teiran are two of the oldest; Ana, Cor's class-iron sister, is among the women present. I clear my throat.

"The Inner Palace making decrees against you means that you've got their attention. Use it. Let me write for you. I can elevate the rhetoric, make the Passi's leaflets something the Golds take seriously."

Lazare's brow arches. Megara says, "Told you, Uncle."

Lo Teiran says, "We had a more direct path in mind for you, Lee."

It seems I'm the only one confused: Cor and his sister have exchanged a smirking glance and Lotus lifts his eyes with a sigh. "You're already on your way to being considered for Protector-designate, are you not?" Teiran prompts, like I'm a student slow on the uptake. "Possibly the Golds' favored candidate?"

Oh. That's why Megara was so eager to recruit me.

I feel a sudden twinge of unease.

"That's years from now. Atreus isn't planning to step down anytime soon."

Teiran's and Lazare's eyes meet. Lazare says, "No. He's not planning to, you're right. But it can't hurt to play the long game. Begin securing your standing for when the time comes."

"I wanted to push for constitutional reforms—"

"Good. You will be well placed to push for them as Atreus's successor."

"Any reforms will require strong leadership," Teiran adds. "A voice people will listen to."

That doesn't sound very democratic.

The first time I discussed succession, it was with Annie—the only person even less interested in a dragonlord's son regaining power than I am. But only now do I realize the difference that made. Megara, the Golds, this room of people—do they all just look at my face, see a Stormscourge, and *assume*? I spent a childhood unlearning the belief that to be dragonborn meant to deserve power, but now that my identity's in the open, it seems others are determined to assume it for me.

Even though, in principle, I see the reason in Lazare's and Teiran's arguments. The easiest way to ensure these reforms is to take the reins.

But I don't have Annie's steady gaze reassuring me, and her absence feels like a piece missing.

"I can—I can do that. But I'd like to write, too."

Lo Teiran's voice is dry and reedy. "That can be arranged, though you'll need to write under a pseudonym for now. In the meantime, you should begin attending events on the Janiculum and resume doing morale visits in the city. You'll want to develop a rapport on both sides of the river."

I hear myself ask, like a haggling trader seeking one last add-on: "What about the raiding?"

Megara sighs. Lazare, who has spread calloused hands on the table as if about to rise, pauses. "*What* about the raiding?"

It's surprisingly difficult to face this publican down. "It might be—counterproductive to your long game."

Lazare looks unamused, as if I'd made a joke in poor taste. Megara answers for him, quietly.

"There is no long game if people don't eat, Lee."

Jester the streetlord snorts, like he's pretty sure he's looking at someone who has never been hungry a day in their life. Which is wrong, but also enough to stop the retort I'm about to make.

Of course I agree, but it's not that simple.

Lazare glances at the window, drawn with blackout curtains. "Shall we save other plans for another night? The city is hungry, and we have bread to give them."

What happens over the next hour feels like a strange inversion of daily duties as a Guardian.

Sacks of bread baked from stolen flour wait in the cellar along with a hamper of green scarves. Lazare names streets, and members of the Passi claim them, taking a sack each and scarves to hide their faces. The shouting is cheerful, the Passi eager to set out into the night to leave gifts of bread on the steps of the unsuspecting poor. Unlike ration card distribution as a Guardian, this has the feeling of a noble effort, something the participants can feel proud to be part of, rather than guilty.

But the problems with the scene niggle the back of my mind: The bread is made from stolen grain; the luck of those who will receive it stems from their streets being within a walk of the Misanthrope, from living in the neighborhood of someone who dared rob a city granary. The metals stratification isn't fair, but neither is this haphazard redistribution—

After we watch the Passi vanish one by one into the night, Cor and I make our way back through the darkened streets to the Palace.

"Megara won't tell you this," Cor says, his voice low to keep from disturbing the sleeping city, "because she doesn't talk about it. But her mother was arrested by the Reeducation Committee when she was—eight? Nine? Spent about a year in the Vault. Megara was raised by Lazare. Even after, because rumor is her mum never really . . . recovered."

So I'm not the only one with personal grievances against Atreus's regime. The Vault is the headquarters of the Ministry of Information and the printing press of the *People's Paper*; it's also where the Reeducation Committee keeps political prisoners.

"What was her mother arrested for?"

Cor shakes his head. "That, I don't know."

The stars are bright overhead, the winter air fresh and crisp on our faces. "I think they really believe in what they're doing," Cor says.

I hear the desperation in his voice, to believe with them. I don't have the heart to point out that Atreus believes in what he's doing, too.

***

Dora's invitations to parties on the Janiculum have accumulated, mostly unread, in my mailbox since the Fête of the Fourth Order. I begin opening them, begin answering them, accepting every dinner party and salon invitation the Golds have to offer. I begin signing up for every morale visit the Ministry of Propaganda can throw at me. And I begin penning articles for the Passi's leaflets, to pass to Megara Roper between classes.

I tell myself that if I have the sort of face people follow, and the sort of voice they listen to, I should use them. I need not let my father's gifts go to waste. I will use them to uproot his kind of elitism where it grows like weeds from this new regime, and fight for the justice that my family, and now Atreus, has denied them.

I tell myself that I can use my father's gifts without becoming like him.

The day the first article runs, Annie finds me in the refectory at breakfast, takes a seat across from me, and places two hands on the table. It has been over a week since the funeral for the fallen Guardians. Over a week since we woke in the same bed and ended the day not speaking. I look past her at Power, watching us where he stands ladling four scoops of porridge—a Gold's full rations—into his bowl. Annie and I have each only taken an

Iron's worth. She and Power are both in flamesuits, as if they just got off a night patrol. Annie's eyes are ringed with dark circles.

The last few night shifts she's done have been with Power.

She places the Passi's latest leaflet on the table between us. It's the first time I've seen the piece printed, and the sight of it sends a thrill of triumph through me that I know Annie can see flicker in my face.

"There's a new voice from the Passi," Annie says, "styling himself as the Revolution's Son, advocating a reinstitution of the People's Assembly."

I take a bite of porridge. "And what do you think about it?"

Annie folds her arms. "I *think* association with the Passi is illegal. I think I have a war with New Pythos to prepare for. I don't have time for opinion pieces."

I open my mouth to argue with her—and something else comes out instead. "Then train with me." Train. Be ready for next time. As I wasn't for this time, when it all went to hell. If I'm going to take action, there's no reason I can't take action on both fronts. In the city and for the war.

Annie puffs out a breath, like this isn't what she expected and doesn't know where to blow her deflating frustration. "Fine."

As disinterested as both of us act about the proposition of sparring, the dragons out us. Pallor and Aela turn giddy when they realize what we're about. Wings twitching, snorting steam in the cold as we meet in the air over the Eyrie. Their excitement undermines, somewhat, the cold tone of Annie's follow-up question asked at coasting height.

"This assembly," she asks, "would putting it in place mean abolishing the metals system?"

So she did read it.

"Don't you think . . . maybe it should be abolished?"

I've become so convinced of this over the last few weeks that it surprises me when Annie frowns. "I don't know. People are born with different levels of intelligence and ability, aren't they?"

"Damocles said 'We're all equally deserving'—"

Annie's nose wrinkles. "Just because some old philosopher wrote it doesn't make it true. Anyway . . . what would happen to us? The metals test is how we got here."

She gestures around us, at the dragons we ride, the arena below, and the Palace complex surrounding it. Snow dusts them like an inverted frosted cake. It occurs to me with unexpected surprise how differently we must have experienced that test: I thought of it as a shortcut back to somewhere I belonged; but for Annie, it's been a ticket to something she never could have had otherwise.

"We'd still be Guardians. We'd still have dragons."

Annie's hand goes to Aela's side, which she rubs slowly.

"I'm not sure that's where this line of thinking leads," she says.

The Damians' philosophy led them to get rid of their dragons entirely. It's what they're known for, aside from their assemblies, equal voting rights, and advanced air defense technology.

I spread my hands. Pallor twitches beneath me on an unexpected gust, impatient to begin sparring. "You don't think something has to change? People are getting unequal shares of food."

"People have always gotten unequal shares of food." Annie drops the reins entirely to rub her face with both hands. Her cheeks are flushed from the cold, her breath steaming. "It's more that I'm not sure the Passi should be the ones in charge of changing things."

"Maybe they're getting on a better track."

"Maybe," Annie allows. "Or maybe they're just going to keep making my life harder."

She sounds so dismal, I don't know how to answer.

I'm still not approved for rationing supervision. We haven't discussed Annie's reasoning, though I find it transparent enough: She doesn't trust me to enforce, not after the Lyceum sacking. But that means the brunt of concerns about civil unrest fall on her.

"I'm going to work it from the inside," I say. "Talk to Dora, talk to the Gold Advisory Council—"

Even in my own ears it sounds desperately idealistic. Especially as I remember Megara's answer: *There is no long game if people don't eat.*

"Are you going to talk to Atreus?" Annie asks.

It hadn't even occurred to me. "I don't have anything to say to Atreus."

The silence stretches. Why would she think the man who ordered me dead, who authorized outlawing the Passi in their entirety, would be someone I'd try approaching with their agenda? Annie's bleak face is pinched, her eyes fixed on Aela's horned neck. For the first time, an unpleasant alternative occurs to me.

"Are *you* going to talk to Atreus?"

I'd assumed Annie's silence as a friend, but for the first time it occurs to me that if she really is opposed to what the Passi want, the ministry's exhortation to report *enemies of the Revolution* might be one she feels obliged to obey. Atreus would in all likelihood find what Annie has deduced about the Passi's membership very interesting, and the Ministry of Information even more so.

If she wanted, Annie could land me in a cell in the Vault for this article.

Annie's face ripples as though the thought itself hurts her. "I hope I don't have to."

I draw Pallor's reins up short at this answer, the wind buffeting my back, and he snorts in surprise. Annie lowers her visor. Her voice becomes muffled. "We should stop having this conversation. Let's train."

I think we're both relieved to be done talking.

It's too cold to spark, and we have to stay low over the arena to avoid the rime ice that claws at higher altitudes at this time of year, but neither dragon minds the added challenge. I haven't been in the air since the Pythian expedition and haven't sparred with anyone since before the duel with Julia. Despite my relief to be in the air again, I find myself gripping Pallor's flanks tightly with my knees.

You have to get over this. You're not going to sit on the sidelines the next time we face them.

It goes fine, better than expected, for the first few bouts. We've broken a good sweat, and the dragons are warmed up, eager for contact charges—when Pallor lands a hit and Annie grunts.

And it happens again. Like it did drilling with Crissa: The darkness of the ash seems to spread across my vision and all of a sudden I can hear *her*. The memory explodes into Pallor as a spillover that freezes us both.

Annie's voice snaps me back.

"Do you want to stop?"

I can feel a churning in my stomach, horror at the memory so great, self-loathing so acrid, it's manifesting as nausea. But I force myself to think of Max, of Orla, of Duck. Of Ixion making Annie watch.

"No."

We rein the dragons round, reset, and charge again. We only stop when the midmorning bells ring. We both have class within the hour.

"We'll do it again tomorrow," Annie decides, and I can't tell if she's suggesting it as a friend or ordering it as a commander, but at any rate it isn't a question, so I can't say no, and we do.

Day by day it gets easier.

What doesn't get easier is talking to Annie. Not when I'm handing articles to Megara Roper in the back of lecture halls to turn and find Annie's eyes on us. Not when I watch her on her way to class alongside Power, noticing how, night after night, her patrols pair with his.

Remembering that, not too long ago, I woke to a morning where I held her.

But I've had years of sparring with Annie when we had nothing to say to each other. Years of silence as we kept each other's secrets. This is no different.

She won't talk. She said she wouldn't—

But I know that's not quite right. She said she hoped she wouldn't have to.

Cor invites me home for Midwinter. He doesn't invite Annie. Half a year ago, Duck invited her home for Midsummer and she went. I walk in on her crying in an empty classroom and when I ask if she's all right, she tells me that it's nothing. When I visit Crissa in the infirmary and she asks for news from the city, I find myself unable to talk about the Passi, or Annie, at all.

I deliver speeches at morale visits, author democratic manifestos under a pseudonym, and spend evening after evening on the Janiculum Hill downing welcome wine and measuring the sentiment of the patricians like the temperature of water: *Not that I've read it myself, but I heard the Passi have run a few good pieces recently,* they tell each other. *Bit more intellectual rigor, I heard.*

When significant glances pass my way, at the moniker *Revolution's Son*, I nod and let them wonder. When I ask Dora Mithrides for an audience before the next meeting of the Gold Advisory Council, she tells me that she'll see what she can do. And when I stand on the streets of my city performing the morale visits I've been trained by this regime to give, I look upon these faces, these metal wristbands, and I think with a thrill of growing conviction: Enough is enough.

For now, I'll raise morale as this regime expects me to. But one day I will make a different kind of speech, and the people will be ready for it.

I just wish I didn't feel like I was working behind Annie's back to get there.

Three days before Midwinter break, Cor approaches me after class with a leaflet I didn't know the Passi had planned. It's a map of the city, headlined:

GRANARY LOCATIONS OF CALLIPOLIS.

"Did you give—?"

His face has drained of color. "Megara asked," he says, "but I had no idea this was what they were planning with the information—"

He knows as well as I that this, unlike the thinkpieces I've been running about ideal best forms of government, is a printing that forebodes action. Megara's and Jester's kind of action.

Raids, and riots, and violence.

A MESSAGE FROM SOUTHSIDE'S DAUGHTER, the leaflet reads. THE PEOPLE DESERVE TO KNOW.

ANNIE

I haven't had persistent nightmares since I was a child. Now the dream I cannot escape, that finds me every night I'm not on the dunes with Griff, could hardly be called a nightmare except that I wake from it every time feeling as if I've been cut open.

In the dream, I look over the group lists for attack, and I realize I wrote Duck's name down for Lee's group after all. And then I realize, silly me, Duck stayed behind. He's alive. Duck's right around the corner, right *there*—

I wake so full of hope that I'm drenched with sweat. And then, though I don't deserve it, though I am the last person who deserves it, I reach under the pillow and touch that bit of Duck's cuirass and wonder how many weeks and months and years it will take for me to forget his face as I've forgotten my mother's.

I learned years ago the ways to keep my nightmares from waking others. Bury the sounds you can't stop yourself making in your pillow till the lack of air makes you dizzy and your tears cool. The old trick feels like a forgotten friend. Grief feels like a forgotten friend. A friend that visits me and smothers me at night.

It is one of the times I'm doing the old trick when I hear sobbing that isn't my own coming from a few beds down the row.

Alexa is on a night patrol, Crissa still in the infirmary. The only other Guardian in the girls' dorm is Deirdre, and I'm not entirely sure, when I light the lamp and go to her, that she'll want me.

Me, the commander responsible for that mission. The reason Max showed mercy to a lowborn rider who tore him apart.

But when I wake her from her nightmare, she curls into my embrace and weeps.

"I'm sorry I woke you," she says.

It was what I used to say to them, before I'd mastered the tricks, and I feel a swell of compassion deeper than words as I hold her.

I'm strong enough to wipe my own tears and comfort someone else.

The day the Passi release the map of the city granaries, I'm stationed in Cheapside, supervising ration distribution alongside Power. We stand shoulder to shoulder, watching the queue wind round the square, trampling the latest snowfall into a brown mush. Our dragons huddle on the perch mounted in the center of the square, their wings tight against their bodies to preserve warmth.

I can't remember when it started seeming easier to pair with Power for patrols on the ground as well as on the nights I go to Griff. Only that, at some point, it became less exhausting than any other option. I'm waking daily from nightmares about Duck, racing from classes I'm barely on top of to drill sessions in stuck silence with Lee; after that, on rounds, I'm tracking reports of the northern coast for signs of movement from Bassilea and patrolling the city as unrest spikes, wave after predictable wave, in time with the Passi's publications. With so many other sources of pressure, it's become a relief to have a partner in on the secrets I'm keeping.

As to what Power gets out of it, I'm not sure, since he looks as exhausted as I feel but never complains. He's adapted to our new dynamic with unfailing irony.

"So," he says, as if we're on a stroll in the park rather than on the edge of a square being glared at by starving citizens, "what are your plans for Midwinter?"

My plans for Midwinter are to spend as little time as possible thinking about Duck. Or about his home, where I won't be. Or about Lee, who will be there, with Cor. My stomach growls: Rations keep being tightened, servings cut. I haven't eaten since last night.

"I'm going to that play, at the Janiculum Theater."

In recognition of the exigencies of this winter, the traditional Midwinter feast at the Palace has been replaced by a grand opening of the Revolutionary Players' winter season. All ministry officials and senior Lyceum students are invited. Drinks will be served, but no small foods. They learned from the Lyceum raid.

Power rolls his eyes. "Doesn't count, that's mandatory for Guardians."

I cede. "Library. I have to research the Widowing for Gareson."

"That is the most pathetic Midwinter plan I've ever heard, Antigone."

These days, Power can be relied upon to be civil about half the time. The other half, I don't have the energy to engage. This is old territory, anyway. Power's been making fun of my lack of family for as long as I can remember.

Above us, on the perch, Eater attempts to make more room for himself. There's a scuffle of wings and a squawk, and Aela kicks him off. Power scowls up at them; I realize I'm smiling. Just a little.

Good girl.

"It was stolen. I swear to you, it was stolen, please—"

At the other end of the queue, voices rise from the distribution booth. I feel the familiar jolt of dread mixed with adrenaline.

"I'm sorry, madam. If we've already marked your name off for the week—"

"I have children. *Please*—"

This sort of incident has become more and more common as the winter sets in; vocal outbursts of dissatisfaction have grown louder with each of the Passi's speeches and leaflets, with the slogans they paint on walls decrying injustice. The guard facing off with the woman in the booth looks queasy. His glance darts in my and Power's direction. The eyes of every single class-iron within earshot are on the woman, who is crying.

In these moments, it's my job to set sustainable precedent. Whether or not the woman is telling the truth isn't what matters. What matters is if a square full of people see someone get a second ration card on this argument.

I jerk my chin no at the guard, then murmur in an undertone to Power: "Follow her out of the square and give her a second card. Be discreet—"

"Saw you do that."

I look up. The woman, having been rebuffed by the guard, is making her way past us, empty-handed. For a moment I think she's talking about what I just said to Power, maybe even intends a thank-you, but then I see the fury in her expression. Her voice is full volume, almost shouting level, and she's glaring at me. "Saw you tell him no, you *bitch*."

One of the men standing in the queue nearby says, "That's all right, Sue, just keep walking, there's dragons overhead—"

The woman's eyes are like hard diamonds as spittle flies from her mouth. "What's it like to you people, watching us beg with your bellies full of Silver and Gold rations? *Everyone is equally deserving!*"

"She doesn't want any trouble," the man in the queue tells me. "Go, Susan."

The woman turns away from me spewing curses. Power glances at me, double-checking the order. I nod, and he follows her, reaching into his pocket for a spare ration card. Leaving me in the square, beneath the glares of Susan's friends in the queue, the stupid protest that I wanted to give her swirling in my head: My belly's full of Iron rations just like hers, thanks to Rock's signage in the refectory.

A scrap of paper, blowing across the muddy square, flutters against my boot. I flatten it with my heel and read the Passi's latest:

GRANARY LOCATIONS OF CALLIPOLIS.

My stomach, already lurching with hunger, rolls over.

When Power returns, his expression has none of its usual mockery.

"You all right?"

I nod unsteadily. Hold out the leaflet. Power looks down at it and swears.

"This is a national security hazard," he says. "All it would take is one triarchist-loving fool to ship one of these leaflets north—"

It's my thought, too.

"What are Lee and Cor up to today?" he asks loudly.

I fold my arms, feeling dizzy. "Don't."

"Lee doing another morale visit? Inspiring starving Callipolans with his soaring rhetoric?"

That is, in fact, exactly what Lee's doing, a few blocks from here. Since our return from the Pythian expedition he has agreed to do morale visits again. He talks about the war effort, he talks about tightening our belts for Callipolis, he talks about a brighter future.

He doesn't talk about the subjects he writes about, as the Revolution's Son. But the same voice, the same optimism and vision, shines through.

I told him I didn't have time for his opinion piece. But afterward, when I read it, I saw Lee in it. Not the furious one who came back from the duel: the one I've known from the beginning. Who loves so deeply, and thinks so clearly, and combines his love and thoughts into principles around which he orders his life. Who sees past all the petty details to something greater and nobler even when it requires sacrifice.

I knew his voice when I read it, and saw in his ideas about equality, and assembly, and democracy that old familiar beating heart, that love for someone he shouldn't love, the ability to recognize personhood in the most unlikely of places, where it had previously been denied.

This Lee, I loved. This Lee who was able to love me. Even after a childhood raised on the belief that I wasn't the kind of being worthy of it.

I read his piece and thought: Who am I, with all my mercenary considerations, to stand in the way of such beautiful *hope*?

I give Power the only answer I can think of that he might understand. "Maybe the people could use a little inspiration. Not much else to feel good about right now."

Power's lip is curling as he looks at me. "Do you *enjoy* playing the stick to his carrot?"

I lift my shoulders, hands deep in my uniform pockets.

No. I don't enjoy playing the stick. But I know I'm good at it.

And in my best moments, I don't resent Lee for standing on the other side when we once said we'd do it together. I don't blame him for being the inspiration that keeps his sight on the stars where mine is trained on the horizon and the ground. In my best moments I know that this Lee, who seems so bent on making my job harder, is the same Lee I've always found worthy and good.

Those are my best moments. Right now isn't one of them.

Power takes one last look at the leaflet, then crumples it.

Another blows past our boots.

"Annie, it's time we do something about this."

"What?" I ask hollowly, though of course I know.

They're everywhere, I realize, looking around us: leaflets blowing through the square, flopping wetly across sludge. None of the class-irons dares touch them with Guardians present, but they're glancing at the papers, curious, and I know that however thoroughly the city guard sweeps and confiscates, it won't be thorough enough.

Aren't the thinkpieces enough? I want to ask Lee. *Why must you make me choose—?*

But he's not here to answer that.

"Report them," Power says. "Report *her*, at least. They need to find this press and shut it down."

The city guard has been searching for the Passi's rogue printing press, to no avail, for weeks.

I look down at the leaflet. A MESSAGE FROM SOUTHSIDE'S DAUGHTER.

I think of the way my stomach curdled when Megara sat beside Lee and smiled at me.

I don't think I've ever despised a classmate as much as I did her in that moment. But jealousy and bitterness don't mean I want her interrogated or tortured, and that's what will happen if I turn her over to the ministry. "We don't know—"

"We know enough."

This is when I butt up against the limitations of Power as a confidant. Because where Lee's idealism is exhausting, Power's eager pragmatism alarms me. Like it's a glimpse of the road I'm going down and I don't like where it leads.

When this happens, the only thing I can think, to keep waters rising past breath, is that soon I'll have another meeting with Griff.

With Griff, I don't have to question myself for doing my job. I teach him to read and plot revolution and go home warm with the knowledge that in this one part of my life, I don't have to weigh evils to be sure I'm doing the right thing.

I just know.

The dragons know too. One night, we look up and find Aela taking Sparker's muzzle in her mouth. He's so much larger than her that she's had to lift up on her haunches to reach it. Gnawing on it gently, like she might a bone. Sparker sits quite still.

She's trying to remove it.

Griff has frozen, his face awash with such emotion that it's difficult to look at.

And then it occurs to me, looking at Aela: She could get it off.

"She could fire on it, heat the metal. If she heated it enough, she could break it."

Griff swallows. His pupils have dilated, a longing that isn't his flooding his features.

It's warm enough, this close to the shore and sheltered between dunes, that Aela can still spark. She inhales experimentally, her mouth filling with the light of a summoned flame.

But then Griff blinks and shakes his head. Rubs at his jaw like he's feeling a phantom.

"I can't. We'd—we'd get in trouble."

I can hear disappointment thick in his voice. I whistle to Aela, and she releases Sparker's muzzle. Sparker whimpers, frustrated. Griff murmurs his name, and Sparker comes to him, barreling against him with characteristic force.

"Not tonight, love."

He busies himself scratching Sparker's chin under the muzzle, half turned from me, like whatever he's feeling, he wants to keep private.

I watch his turned back, pondering. The plan for a Widowing waits on me and my research, but I realize now that there's another layer needed. "When I bring the drachthanasia, that's when Aela should break Sparker's muzzle. That way he could break the other squires' muzzles when you go back, and you could do it all at once. Widow theirs and free yours."

Griff's bent over Sparker, rubbing his belly while Sparker rolls in the sand. "Could be risky, if the dragonborn noticed Sparker didn't have his muzzle," he says. "Might be better if you and Aela came and did it. You speak a bit of Norish, don't you? My niece would be thrilled if you showed up. Most of the Norcians would be, to be honest."

"Me? Why?"

Griff snorts. "Are you kidding? We've had to forbid the kids from pretending to *be* you."

"But I—" I swallow, hitting on the thing that needs to be circled to even talk about. "There were Norcians in those strongholds that we attacked."

Griff's nose wrinkles. "Pretty clear whose fault that was for anyone with half a brain. Point is—you're a legend."

Coming off almost daily variations of getting spat on and insulted by Callipolans whose rations I'm charged with overseeing, I think at first he's joking.

When I realize he isn't, my eyes prickle.

Griff notices. "Sorry—I didn't realize that would upset you."

"No. It's not that. People don't really rally around me in Callipolis."

Griff's eyes go wide. "But you're everything the Revolution promised!"

His excitement is so great, so perfectly reminiscent of a press release from the Ministry of Propaganda, that I hear myself laugh. Then my thoughts go to a woman heckling me in a windswept square, to the Passi and their leaflets, to the map of our granaries displayed on ragged paper. A menu of potential violence, printed by my friends. Power, crumpling it in his fist. *We have to do something.*

"Maybe once. Now I'm the one in charge of the enforcing."

21

—

COMRADE-IN-ARMS

GRIFF

I should know better, I should know it won't last, but the problem is happiness brings on a fugue state. You can't remember what came before, and you can't imagine what will come after. Like a sunlit day between weeks of rain, you find it hard to believe, looking up at the sky, that it could ever not be filled with light.

I've grown up knowing winter as a time when hunger bites harder, the cold in your bones can't be got out, and every time a loved one coughs, you pray it won't turn to fever.

But this winter, everything seems to be going right.

Mornings serving Ixion, and rarely, training in the air, because the snow and the winds bite too fiercely on most days to spar the dragons. Staring at the papers he carelessly passes me and sends me to deliver, watching the symbols become letters I recognize, and the letters become sounds, and the sounds become words. Nowhere near fast enough. But soon. Soon I'll have information worthy of Antigone. He writes to the Bassilean princess often, and her replies come as swift as the trade ships on the passage from Vask will allow.

I try to find the words to tell the others. Agga and Granda and, most of all, the other humble-riders. But every time I try to tell them, the madness of it—Antigone in the dead of night and Sparker's key warm in my hand—sticks my tongue.

I don't know how to tell them. And always, when I imagine us turning on our lords, I imagine Delo.

To the point where every time Antigone arrives at the dunes and apologizes for not yet having drachthanasia, I feel relieved. Because everything—the nights with Antigone, the days harboring secrets in my chest—pale in comparison to the stolen hours between, when I've begun to go to him.

Parts of it are exactly as I remember it was with *her*: quiet walks through dark corridors, the pressure of our held breaths as I cross the threshold, the silence of it. A bed so deep and soft it's something to drown in, warm with a lover's body, blankets glimmering in the firelight.

But the rest of it is entirely different. The way, with Delo, I want it so badly that even in the moment I want more. The way, in so many small things, he gives where Julia only took. I feel as though, with every touch and kiss and breath, I am relearning something I've learned wrong.

The absurdity of it is that he thinks he's the one who doesn't know.

"I don't know—if this was how she—"

"She didn't."

There are so many things to talk about. Always whispering, as if the stone walls might hear us—memories to examine, worlds of things to say that we've been holding in for years. Training, and Ixion, and even Julia.

"Do you remember the day she beat Ixion for Firstrider?"

"I'll never forget it. The look on his face!"

I'm grinning just thinking about it, though in the dark, Delo can't see that.

"I miss her," he admits.

The memories shift around me: Julia the friend, Julia the lover, Julia the leader who feared nothing and listened to no one, unless she felt like it.

"I miss her, too."

When talk turns to that day, long awaited by the dragonborn, when Callipolis is regained, we talk about it as we always have. We talk about what we look forward to most.

"I'm looking forward to returning to the Skyfish Summer Palace," Delo decides. "It's beautiful. And never this cold, so far south. I'll take you there. What about you?"

It's so strange, to be able to switch between these forking visions so easily, the one Antigone and I discuss late at night, where the dragonborn of New Pythos are brought to their knees—and the one Delo and I have grown up being told about. I slide from the first into the second and answer automatically.

"My family being rewarded."

I don't think anything of saying it. But Delo swallows and is silent, for minutes, afterward.

Because the one thing we don't talk about, never talk about, is the night Delo rescued Garet and Becca and gave me Sparker's key. He never asks what I've been doing with it. And I never tell him.

Though sometimes, I wish I could tell him, not about the conspiracy or about Antigone, but about the simple wonder that I've begun to read. I had not known, until I began to spend time in his chambers, how much of Delo's time is spent in study. His desk overflows with books and old scrolls from Rhadamanthus's collection, and often I wake to find him working at it.

"What are you reading?" I ask.

"Oh—I didn't realize you were awake. It's just a bit of old poetry."

He says it carefully, with disinterest, and climbs back into bed with me. But a little later, when he goes to the washroom, I roll out of bed and look again at the open volume. It's still hard to read without sounding aloud, but slowly I decipher the section:

Let a single urn contain our ashes,
My comrade-in-arms, my friend, my beloved
So that not even our bones lie apart from one another
When you follow me from this world to the next.

As I understand, my throat constricts. Delo was reading this, privately, to himself. After being with me.

"It's from the *Aurelian Cycle*," Delo says, behind me. "About Uriel and his lover."

He's emerged from the washroom and is watching me as he towels his face dry.

"I didn't know he had one."

Delo nods. And then he drops the towel to the floor, picks up the book, and sits beside me on the bed. He begins to read aloud the section I was just so careful to read silently to myself. Listening to him, I feel a kind of pressure on my heart—as if suddenly, there is not space to contain it. His voice catches, uneven, on the word *beloved*.

"What happened to them?" I ask, hearing the roughness of my voice betray me. "Did they end—happily?"

Delo lifts a shoulder, turning away to set the book aside. He lays a ribbon down the page. "No. But they did get buried together."

"Fat lot of good that did either of them," I say without thinking.

Delo lets out a laugh of surprise. "It's just a poem, Griff," he says.

But there's something in his voice, private and restrained, that makes me know it will never be *just a poem* to him.

"Was he a peasant?"

I don't know why I have to ask that. And when Delo hesitates, I wish I hadn't. "No. He was another dragonlord. Back before the Aurelians had to flee Aureos. The two of them rode together, fought together. And loved."

And loved.

But they were dragonborn, both.

For all the ways I don't fit such a story, Delo's still looking at me. His voice still caught on the word *beloved*. He still read it in the middle of a night he's spent with me.

The words are on the tip of my tongue: *I can read the poems, too. I've been learning. Let me share everything with you, as these lovers did.*

But a lifetime of survival instincts taught me better. Delo defied his world to give me that key; it was a gesture made across a chasm; he reached across, because he didn't have it in him to leap. That reaching was enough to change everything. But I still know better than to ask for more.

Delo was ready to help me. But he isn't ready to look at what that would mean for his people or mine. And as much as I dream of sharing my own vision of the future with him, as much as I wonder, in my most peaceful moments, if maybe he would see not only the beauty, but the rightness of it—my people freed, his overthrown—I know these are the musings of a lovestruck fool.

So maybe I'm not ready, either.

And so, instead of telling him the truth, I pull him closer, and Delo sets the poem aside.

The next night, by our campfire, Antigone opens a new book.

"This is the *Revolutionary Manifesto* of Atreus Athanatos," she says. "I think you're ready to read it."

I'm sounding out the words, one painful syllable at a time, when a whole sentence comes out.

For too long have dragons oppressed our people.

A chill goes down my spine. At the words. At the fact that I read them. Antigone, seated beside me, seems to be holding her breath.

For too long have we slaved under the dragonlords' yoke. For too long has the triarchy feasted while its people starved.

A new order is needed. A new world is called for. And the old one must be destroyed.

I think of how Delo felt, warm in my arms, of the words he read to me with a shaking voice.

My comrade-in-arms, my friend, my beloved—

"Annie, tell me what happened in the Red Month."

She sounds surprised. "They didn't tell you?"

"I want to hear your version."

"The dragonlords were separated from their dragons. Their dragons were poisoned. And the Three Families were slaughtered down to the last man, woman, and child."

It's no different, her version and theirs. But when she says it, it's with the hush of awe rather than the choke of horror. For her, it was the beginning, not the end.

And it's a beginning she envisions for me.

I look down once more at the *Revolutionary Manifesto*, think of Delo, and feel the ground tilt.

I close the Usurper's book and hand it to her. "I should be heading back."

* * *

I ride through the night with her words stuck in my head like a refrain. *Down to the last man, woman, and child.* When I land in the citadel, I reattach Sparker's lead and go, not home to bed, but through the corridors that take me to the Skyfish apartments.

For the first time ever, I forget to press my ear against the door first.

And for the first time ever, when it opens, Delo isn't alone.

His brother and sister are with him, sitting around his desk with mugs of tea between them, gathered around what looks like some sort of map. Ethelo is laughing at something Phemi said. They fall silent at the sight of me in the doorway.

"Griff?" Delo says blankly.

Phemi's thick black hair, down from its usual braids, forms a cloud around her head. She taps a finger into it as her eyes narrow on me, then they turn to Ethelo with a roll. They're twins, miniature, lankier versions of Delo, three years younger than us.

"Told you," Phemi tells Ethelo.

Ethelo is a *passus*, forsaken by dragons, and it leaves him prone to joking—about himself, and about others. He wolf-whistles at Delo as he gets to his feet.

"We've been waiting on this one for years, brother." He lifts a mug of tea as if in toast and bows with a flourish. "Heartfelt congratulations to you both."

"Out," says Delo.

Phemi seizes Ethelo's arm. "Oh, we're leaving. We're leaving you *to it*—"

With a shriek of laughter, she pulls her twin from the room, and it echoes tinnily in their wake. For a moment we both stand frozen. Delo recovers first. "I should probably go after them. Ask them not to . . ."

Talk. But with Ethelo and Phemi, that's next to impossible. They're chatty with Roxana, and Roxana's chatty with everybody. "Yeah."

"I'll be right back—"

He leaves. I go to the desk, look down at the map. No: not a map. A plan of a city—of Callipolis. With certain buildings marked. The headline is in Callish script, but beneath it Delo has transcribed the Dragontongue translation of each word, and it's his hand that I study, deciphering.

Granary Locations of Callipolis.

I stare at it. The door behind me creaks open and I jump.

"They're a nightmare." Delo grimaces, then looks past me, at the blueprint I'm staring at.

"What is this?" I ask him.

"Information. About Callipolis. Father asked us to plan an air strike."

"On these places?"

Delo nods.

"What are they?"

He hesitates.

"Armories."

I stare at him. And then, instead of keeping my mouth shut like I ought to do, I open it.

"No, they're not."

Delo stares at me. I place a finger on the word *granary*. Delo looks from it to me and back again.

"I see," he says.

That's all. And then he begins to roll up the plan. Suddenly, he looks exhausted. He turns away before adding: "You're still in your flamesuit. The twins noticed."

* * *

The day after my conversation with Delo, Ixion asks me to serve at a private party he's having with the other dragonborn riders. It's in his apartments, which gets my alarm up, but it's not until I enter the room and realize no other squire is present that I understand the nature of the ordeal. Ixion is lounging on one of the sofas across from Roxana, Rhode, and a few of the lesser ha'Aurelians; Delo, Phemi, and Ethelo are by the fire with their Bastard Skyfish cousins; one of the citadel minstrels is working a violin by the edge of the room, his forehead shining with sweat.

A piece of paper is being passed among the dragonborn. The reason, I realize, for the celebration. A letter bearing the whale-fin seal of Bassilea.

I feel my attention focus on it like a beam of light.

This is information for Antigone. Here, floating around this room, from hand to hand that isn't holding a glass for me to fill.

"Gareson. Come here."

I slowly approach where Ixion lounges. When I bow, Ixion seizes a fistful of my hair and pulls down. Knees, rug. A palm flat on the weaving to balance myself. I'm breathing slowly through my mouth, my face a foot away from the floor.

My first thought is of Phemi and Ethelo, noticing the flame-suit. He's doing this because they realized. They reported. I'm on my way to being dropped.

"Julia used to say you were good at two things, Griff," Ixion says. "One of them was flying. Want to guess what the other was?"

Roxana lets out a shrill giggle.

Understanding creeps in. I'd be able to guess the answer, but don't need to: Julia used to tell me herself what two things she thought I was good at, though I hadn't realized she was also telling others.

And then I wish what the twins reported was the flamesuit, because sometimes, when you know you're about to be humiliated, you start wishing you could just be dropped instead.

How is it that even beyond the grave, Julia's able to shame me?

Miss her. I was a fool to ever miss her. A dog might as well miss its owner for all it meant to her.

And I've always known that. I don't need pillow talk divulged to Ixion as proof of it. I've always known what she was to me, and I to her.

When I don't answer, Ixion pushes harder. My forehead touches the ground.

"Ixion, for love of the dragon," Phemi says.

Which means Delo's too panicked to say anything.

"I asked you what she said, Griff."

I give him the answer, face against the rug, and then at Ixion's prompting I say it again in my own language. I hear the Norish how they hear it, crude and obscene. Rhode's snort cuts the air.

I hate how these people have trained me to hear my own language with shame.

"I would have thought," Ixion goes on, "that you'd mourn longer before finding another dragonborn's bed to warm, but apparently you just can't *get enough*."

I wait, counting breaths, for more, but after three, Ixion releases my hair.

"What are you waiting for?" he says. "Pour the wine."

* * *

I try, and fail, to read Freyda's letter as I pour. It exchanges hands too often; her scrawl is so unlike the handwriting I practice reading with Antigone that I barely know what to make of it.

And beyond that, I'm having trouble enough keeping my hands from shaking.

Delo sits like a frozen hare, eyes on his knees even when I pour him wine. When he rises among the first guests to retire, Roxana bids him good night loudly and drunkenly and he offers a rigid bow in return. When he's gone, her laughter turns to tears. She spills wine and tells me to clean it up.

It goes on for hours. Night is closer to morning and the gulls have begun their waking cries when Ixion and Rhode, the last of the guests to remain, at last slump unconscious from wine. Only then, as if pulled by an unseen force, do I trace numb steps to Delo's chambers. I've barely knocked when he opens it, murmuring my name, to pull me inside.

"Forgive us," he murmurs. "Forgive me."

I don't ask him for what. I don't tell him he should have said something, when Ixion pressed my face into the rug. But when I kiss him, I kiss him hard. Like I want him to feel pain.

Delo lets me. Lets me break it off first. And then holds me tighter.

"Griff," he murmurs, his cheek against mine, and I can feel the wetness on it. "Promise me . . . whatever you're planning, whatever happens to us in the end . . . don't let them hurt Phemi and Ethelo."

Whatever you're planning.

I could deny it. For a half breath, I think to.

But truth is so precious, so rare, I want to cradle it like he cradles me.

"I won't."

"And Gephyra—"

Gephyra. His skyfish. Sparker's sparring partner.

I kiss him, because I don't have a promise I can make, and he chokes down a sob.

He doesn't think to ask for mercy for himself.

* * *

The day after Ixion's party, I make my way to Bran's and find Fionna there as well, with him. Not just in his company but *with him*: His arm is around her where they sit by their small hearth, with his grandmother and mother and brothers. They rise when they see me, and Bran's arm again finds her waist, reaching down from his great height.

"I've got something to tell you."

"We've got something to tell you, too," Fionna says, smiling. "Let's do it outside."

Bran's family lives on the edge of Clan Turret, close to the breakers. We crunch through the snow, down to the cove where the lighthouse spears the longest peninsula, and stand among the puffins under the snow-draped cliffs looking out at Turret and Nag and, a little farther round the bend, sleepy Knoll. Our clan-karsts. As children, when we were only just beginning our training, we came here together and poached the lord's oysters and stopped caring that we came from different clans, because as squires we'd formed our own.

"What is it?" Fionna asks.

"You first."

Bran looks at Fionna, and she nods, and he looks back at me.

"Fionna's with child," he says.

I look at her and see a host of feelings cross her face at once as she smiles: fear, but also pride and joy and hope. And though I can think of a dozen reasons this is not just bad news, but the worst news, I feel a smile answer hers, as if the heart of the thing has a joy that fear can't stifle.

"Do they know?"

"No." Bran lets out a despairing laugh. "And even if we passed it off as another's, we don't know if . . ."

If they'd allow one of their riders to get with child.

"Congratulations," I tell Fionna.

She smiles at me, one hand on her waist, the other in Bran's.

That smile, I think, it could break a thousand hearts if the dragonlords could only *see* it.

For a moment *I* see it, the webs linking us like chains: Fionna to her child, Bran to Fionna, Bran and Fionna to their families and me to Agga and Agga to Becca and Garet, and our families to one another, bound across this island and weakened because we love.

But now that has to make us strong. Let the rivalries that they've used to drive our clans apart fall away before us: I from Clan Nag, Bran from Clan Turret, Fionna from Clan Knoll, and the rest of the squires from across the clans united by the fact that we are dragonriders and Norcian.

I tell them, "I've been meeting with the Callipolan Firstrider."

"You?" says Bran, in probably the most insulting tone of disbelief possible. "You sly bastard!"

My grin grows.

"How?" asks Fionna.

I reach into the neck of my shirt and pull out the chain of Sparker's key. Their eyes widen.

"Where did you get that?"

"Delo."

Fionna gives Bran a look not unlike the one Phemi gave Ethelo two nights ago.

"Griff and his dragonborn," she says.

Fresh off Ixion's party, I'm pretty well done with hearing remarks about my proclivities. "This is different."

Fionna touches my shoulder. Her teasing tone drops. "I know."

For a second I look out over the surf, feeling her hand on my shoulder and the memories it contains. The years of humiliation and burns and fear.

No more.

I cover her hand with my own. "The plan," I tell them, "is to poison the triarchal dragons and break the muzzles. But I understand—especially if you've got a child to worry about—if you don't want to risk that."

But Bran is grinning so wide it looks painful. "Are you joking? There's no risk more worth taking."

Fionna nods. "The squires are with you, Griff."

I find Antigone sur Aela that night with my words bursting. It's our last meeting before Midwinter, and the dunes are snow-dusted. As soon as I've slid from Sparker's back, he bounds toward Aela, freezing when she begins to sniff at him with her small smoking nostrils.

"I've got information for you. Your granaries. They know where they are. That's what they're planning to strike once the snows thaw."

Antigone inhales, slowly. "The Passi's leaflet," she says, like she's realizing something.

"The what?"

"Nothing. Thank you."

The dragons begin to circle each other, still sniffing noisily, a ritualized greeting that leaves rings of claw prints in the sand. Every time little Aela leaps at him, Sparker freezes. The perfect gentleman.

The perfect gentleman, who deserves to stretch his jaws at last. I blurt: "I told the other squires."

Antigone's eyes widen. Excitement makes my voice shake.

"We're ready. As soon as you can get us the poison. We'll do it."

Antigone swallows and nods.

"I'll get you some by our next meeting," she says.

22

THE JANICULUM THEATER

ANNIE

I've never seen any evidence that Megara's stolen grain found more deserving mouths than my daily rationing supervision does. But all the same, sometimes I wonder how it must have felt. Fleeing the Lyceum with those carts, high with the thrill of having stolen to feed the poor. Lee and Cor must feel it, wandering off into the night for their secret meetings, penning articles that bravely imagine a better world.

It must be satisfying the same way teaching Griff to read is, planning a rebellion to free his people. Like you know who the enemy is.

I can't blame the Passi for wanting it to be simple.

But when Griff bears news of the map of our granaries in the hands of New Pythos, I remember that it is simple. And not the way Megara Roper thinks it is.

This is what I'm thinking as Atreus Athanatos calls a meeting to address the joint summit of the Janiculum and Gold Advisory Councils, attended by a full assembly of the Inner Palace ministry, in the Palace Throne Room, on Midwinter's Eve.

He begins, "Damocles, called by some the father of philosophy, once wrote that everyone is equally deserving."

With his back to the Guardians arrayed on the dais, Atreus does not see how Lee and Cor stir. His voice is barely raised, the same mild tone he uses in a small seminar class, but it carries easily through the vaulted Throne Room. The audience, recognizing the Passi's slogan, sits completely frozen, except for Miranda Hane, the Minister of Propaganda. She sits in the front row, her gaze fixed unblinking on the Protector and her lips a minutely moving line, as if the words of this speech are ones she knows.

"A noble sentiment," Atreus admits. "But we must not forget the repercussions of this noble sentiment. Damocles's ideology threw the Damian peninsula into chaos. Without strong leadership or dragons to defend them, at the whim of an easily manipulated People's Assembly, they were vulnerable and divided in a time when they needed a unified front. The belief that *we are all equally deserving* nearly lost Damos the Second Bassilean War."

Lee's shoulders are drawn, ever so slightly, farther back than natural.

"The people in this audience are here for a reason," Atreus says. "They are here because they have been found, through a system open to each and every citizen, to be *more deserving*."

Lee's gaze wanders from Atreus to the room around us: the rain-spattered glass that has been paned over the three stone arches behind Atreus, which in the old regime opened out onto the Firemouth to welcome the dragons of the three Triarchs; the Revolutionary banners draped from the vaulted ceiling; the single chair for the First Protector replacing the Triple Throne that I've seen in tapestries and Lee has, in all likelihood, seen in person.

Lee remembers different constituents in this room, different banners from the ceiling, different speeches. Perhaps this is another reason why, as his gaze settles on Atreus, his lip twists.

"If the fact of your merit *rankles* compared to the egalitarian ideals of Damocles," Atreus says, and now his voice has hardness more fitting declarations of war, "I remind you that so long as you serve this government and this Revolution, it is the reality you live and the responsibility you bear."

He holds up the Passi's leaflet, the same one Griff Gareson described on the dunes at our last meeting. The one that leaks the location of our granaries.

"What began as a diverting intellectual exercise has become a national security crisis. I urge anyone with information regarding the Passi, or this leak, not to jeopardize their country any longer. Do your duty."

Across the dais, Lee's eyes meet mine.

I file the report immediately after Atreus's address adjourns.

Lee, Cor, Megara.

Three names. Three possibilities. One chance to choose. I stare down at the report template, stomach heaving, heart racing, and tell myself the choice I make is not motivated by personal bias but by my needs as commander of the Callipolan aerial fleet.

I submit the report to the Ministry of Information on my way to the Defense Wing.

The performance this evening at the Janiculum Theater will be the Guardians' last obligation before Midwinter, and leave has been permitted among the higher ranks and within city limits. As I have nowhere to pack for, I spend the afternoon convincing General Holmes that Guardians should take dragons with them on leave and that the city granaries should be relocated.

Holmes is reluctant at the latter request. "That's overtime work for the city guard when they'd rather be home with their families. We already doubled the guard—"

"Doubled guards won't protect the granaries from air strikes, sir. You heard the Protector's speech this morning. He's worried the Passi's map got into the hands of the Pythians."

Holmes's crisply trimmed beard makes it difficult to read his expression. I add, with a finger toward the window, looking out over the Firemouth, down which rainwater courses:

"It's raining. The snow is melting. If the warmth continues, we'll be exposed."

"Antigone . . . ," Holmes begins, and then hesitates. Since the attack on New Pythos, where he reamed me with birth-based slurs in front of my subordinates after acknowledging a mission well accomplished, he has started checking himself like this in front of me. He seems to change tack midsentence. "I'll see what I can do."

I leave Holmes's office with a moderate level of satisfaction.

I'm one of the last Guardians of the evening to arrive in the great reception hall of the Janiculum Theater. Decked in garlands and holly, lit by chandeliers shaped like bursts of dragonfire, its merriness has a way of catching—even when you're waiting, a pulse throbbing in your wrists, for the moment the Ministry of Information responds to your tip-off.

With a glass of mulled wine warm between my fingers, I observe the milling guests: Lee in the center of the floor, deep in conversation with Dora Mithrides and her cadre of patricians; Cor to the side of the room, laughing over his wine with Megara Roper, who wears a gown of muted green. Power, surrounded by his usual bevy of Gold girls. When he looks up at me, he doesn't look away for a long moment, and even after he does, I feel the touch of his eyes lingering as heat on my skin.

Members of the Protector's Guard stand at attention at every exit, their mantles crimson as the holly berries decking the wreathes.

"Hey, you."

Crissa takes my arm in hers. Discharged from the infirmary after a month of rehabilitation, she's propped on a crutch but leans on it with all the confidence of a scepter. Her dress is shining gold, bright as her hair. I'm relieved, and a little surprised, at her open smile. I'm the reason her leave request to Harbortown didn't get approved for Midwinter.

"I'm so sorry, Crissa. We're on high alert because of the warm spell—"

Crissa lifts a shoulder, her smile fixed. "It's all right. I'm sure we'll all have a good time at Cor's."

I don't quite manage to keep a smile up, and Crissa notices. "You're not going?"

"I wasn't invited."

Because it's my fault Duck is dead. Because Lee and Cor joined an illegal protest group that publishes cartoons villainizing me. Because I just filed a report that will destroy what is left of our friendship. What would she say if I explained all of it? A line goes between Crissa's eyes as she looks from me to the two boys on the other side of the hall, like she's weighing something. Then she smiles at me and nods at my dress. "This color suits you."

We're in gowns on loan from the Ministry of Propaganda. I chose red.

Revolutionary red.

I watch her limp on, joining Cor and Megara and Lee, who has broken from Dora with a frown. Megara turns to Crissa and Crissa smiles, her classic radiant smile, as introductions are made, and Megara responds to it like an opening flower. My stomach sinks.

Of course. Crissa's always been Cor's and Lee's friend first, mine second.

I wonder if I imagine the attention of the Protector's Guard on Megara.

"Will it be your first time seeing one of the ancient tragedies performed?"

Atreus, the First Protector, has joined me with one of his inscrutable smiles as the chimes begin to sound and the doors to the theater hall open. I push away the guilt I last felt at enjoying his attention: If I'm betraying Lee by speaking to the First Protector, I betrayed him more by filing that report to the Ministry of Information this afternoon.

Does Atreus know what I did?

"My first time seeing any play," I tell Atreus.

We move with the milling Golds who have begun to filter into the hall.

"About time, for a Dragontongue scholar as fine as yourself. You will find"—Atreus steps aside at the door, allowing me to enter the hall first—"much to appreciate about this play, I think."

At the aisle, he sets a hand on my shoulder, and his voice becomes a low murmur.

"Callipolis thanks you for your service."

LEE

"My dear boy," Dora Mithrides says, at the reception before the Midwinter's Eve performance, "I think we may have to delay your presentation before my friends with the Gold Advisory Council. Many of them did not *appreciate* the Passi's latest disclosure about the granaries. With the Protector's speech this morning, we're all feeling a little more . . . cautious."

Her voice is as hard as the gleaming beads of her necklace in the light of the chandeliers. When I start to say I had nothing to do with the Passi's printing, she only looks impatient.

"But you're friendly with those who do, are you not?"

Her throaty disapprobation leaves a dull thunk in my stomach that has been wound tight ever since Atreus's address this morning in the Throne Room.

The gall of him, to stand on the dais where my uncle once stood and lecture about who is *deserving*—

Dora gives me a pursed smile. "Be careful, darling," she tells me. She glides away. Megara takes her place.

"Of course," she says, watching Dora join a circle of conversation with Dean Orthos, and not sounding particularly sorry. "The Golds are losing interest."

I round on her. Megara's dress is one of the only ones in the room that's not full length, formal, or bespoke: But it is, of course, green. "How exactly am I supposed to win their favor if you're printing state secrets? Atreus is cracking down."

Megara knocks back her sparkling wine and discards her Palace-standard accent like a shed coat. "I wouldn't be so worried. There's more than one way for you to replace Atreus. It can be done with or without the Golds."

Constitutionally, it can't, but I have the sudden suspicion Megara doesn't feel so constrained. "That wasn't what Lazare and Teiran said originally."

Megara snorts.

"You may not have been listening closely enough. In case you haven't noticed, people in this city are starving. We will probably need to act soon. Preferably before your *girlfriend* catches up with us."

She nods at a figure draped in flaming red on the opposite side of the room that I realize, with a double take, is Annie. She looks like a vision of fire.

And she's in conversation with Atreus.

About to ask what Megara means by *act soon*, I hear myself say: "She's not my girlfriend."

Atreus has the look of a concerned professor, attentive and paternal, as he leans over to hear Annie's answer to his question. The kind of look I remember craving, when I didn't know he wanted me dead and lied about it.

Annie responds to his attention with the warmth I remember, her smile touched, her eyes bright. Just a little starstruck, her wine forgotten in a slack hand.

Are you going to talk to Atreus?

I hope I don't have to.

As I remember our conversation, I feel like kicking something.

Cor joins my side, looking like he's been stuffed in the ceremonial uniform against his will and his hair is protesting. Between its ill fit and the shadow of beard he neglected to shave, he looks rakish. The circle is completed by Crissa, glittering in a golden gown that I'm careful not to study and smiling at Megara with a question in her eyes. "I don't believe we've met."

Cor introduces them, half-stammering: "Megara Roper, Crissa sur Phaedra—Lee, a word."

He steers me by the shoulder away from the two girls. Behind us, Crissa lets out a perfectly charmed laugh at something Megara says. I have a half second to wonder why Crissa feels the need to put on a performance before Cor rounds on me. His voice is lowered to a severe whisper.

"I found something in Annie's saddle bag."

"You went through her *stuff*—?"

"Megara asked me to, after Atreus's address this morning. She wanted to find a way to keep Annie quiet. Lee, *look*."

The bells are chiming, guests beginning to filter into the hall, but Cor only pulls me deeper into a shadowy arcade. He holds out a battered composition notebook that is gritty with what seems to be sand.

It takes me a moment to understand what I'm looking at. The notebook is filled with Annie's handwriting in Dragontongue. For a moment I think it's grammar exercises from our earliest school days. Then I realize what she's been writing is names, and they're in her adult hand. Another, much less mature hand has copied after her.

Griff Gareson
Agga
Garet
Becca
Delo Skyfish

"She's been in touch with the Pythians," I realize.

That's what she's been doing, on those night patrols with Power.

"Not just any Pythian," Cor says, tapping the name *Griff Gareson*. "This is Ixion's squire. The one who held her off when Duck fell. She's been meeting with the person who helped kill Duck." Cor's voice trembles on his brother's name. "It seems fishy as hell and it makes me—sick. I know Megara would say we should use this information against her, as leverage if she tries to report us—"

But he sounds frightened, like the idea of blackmail, the idea of *needing* blackmail, is taking this somewhere over his head.

I'm starting to feel that way, too. I take the notebook from him. "Let me talk to Annie."

Ushers are waiting for stragglers to enter so they can close the doors. Annie and Atreus are already inside, Megara and Crissa making their way in while still deep in conversation, their laughter airy, their arms entwined. It occurs to me that the only thing I'm less in the mood for than interrogating Annie is sitting through an ancient Dragontongue tragedy that I distinctly remember boring me as a child.

"Citizens—I'm afraid there's some bad news."

Lotus has joined Cor's side, looking grave and pompous. "Just heard it from my father and Dean Orthos—apparently the Censorship Committee *modified* the play."

From his tone, I would have expected him to tell us someone died.

Cor pinches the bridge of his nose. "I don't believe this. Yeah, what a tragedy, Lotus."

"That's the thing," says Lotus. "It *isn't* anymore!"

ANNIE

The Dragontongue the players use is old, as old as in the *Aurelian Cycle*, but their acting is emphatic, enunciated clearly from behind their masks, so what I don't understand of the language I infer from their performance. My seat is next to Lee's, in the front row, among the Guardians of the Eighth Order and higher. The play is called *Flamefall at Aureos*, and toward the end of the first act, the Chorus turns to the female lead and sings:

You have a warm heart for such chilling deeds.

I touch my face and find it wet.

But after that—the story changes. It's one I've read before, in translation in junior literature classes, and in the original language later. I don't remember it perfectly, but I remember that it didn't end like this.

With a cheerful jingle, the neat triumph of good over evil, and a happy marriage between the two romantic leads. Even the Dragontongue shifts, becomes just a little more workmanlike— *Fair means each receives what they deserve!* the Chorus cheers.

That's when I realize; the play's been tampered with by the Censorship Committee.

It ends with the line: *Lucky are they whose lives know no taste of sorrow.*

The applause after the curtains go down is tepid, and then as if the audience remembers something, it turns emphatic and becomes a standing ovation. Lee and I glance at each other, once, before rising with the rest of the applauding hall. The players take their bows, masks lifted. As soon as they head offstage, Lee and I ease back into our seats to wait for the rows to clear.

"Well, that was not how I remembered it," Lee remarks. The botched ending seems to have shaken him out of his strange mood and left him in darkly good humor.

I'm straining to remember the play from studying it in class years ago. "Wasn't it supposed to be that the old king turned out to be corrupt, and killed her fiancé, so she killed him and then herself?"

"Yeah. I assume that was considered too destabilizing."

I can hear Mitt Hartley, Chairman of the Censorship Committee, bragging boomingly from a few rows back about the play's modifications as he queues to exit his row. *Much more what everyone's in the mood for, don't you think!* The voices joining his are loudly approving, but the muttering from other clumps of Golds are less enthusiastic. I spot Dean Orthos and Lo Teiran arguing heatedly in Dragontongue on the opposite aisle.

"The full line," Lee says, clearing his throat to make a rare switch into his mothertongue, "is—

Lucky are they whose lives know no taste of sorrow;
But for those whose house has been shaken by ruin,
So too will that sorrow be wreaked upon their children."

He hesitates on the word *children*, and as he does, my own memories twist like a knifepoint.

With a sudden rush of tenderness, I reach to take his hand.

That's how I find my notebook in it.

The notebook in which I've been practicing Dragontongue with Griff, that would have been in my bag this morning, among my other books, in my office.

Someone's been going through my things.

And though I should feel anger, all I feel is relief.

Now at last I can tell Lee everything.

LEE

Around us, the Golds have risen to leave the theater, but we remain sitting in the center of the front row, the notebook between us. The sour taste of that tacked-on ending is slowly fading from my mouth.

We're finally talking. And I didn't even have to ask.

"Gareson came to me, that night after—Duck. To ask my forgiveness"—Annie's voice thickens as she begins to explain—"and to offer to help. I've been teaching him to read, so he can pass me information."

"That's who you've been meeting, on your night patrols with Power?"

"Yes."

Talking feels good. Like exhaling after a breath held too long. Maybe, if we talk long enough, we can talk about everything that's been piling up since Duck's funeral. Including Megara, and the Passi. Maybe I can convince her once and for all not to report anything to Atreus—

Annie's eyes go up, to the gilded ceiling, for a moment. She grips the wooden armrest between us. Then she straightens and looks at me.

"The reason I've been meaning to talk to you about this is that Griff's not just passing me information. I'm helping him plan something there, too."

She seems stiff saying it, as if telling me makes her nervous. Even though, as far as I can tell, it would be the obvious strategy. "An uprising?"

Annie nods. She closes her eyes and presses her thumb between them. "We were thinking of using drachthanasia."

Suddenly I understand her reticence.

Annie's planning another Widowing.

The kind of uprising where you render your rulers helpless and then massacre them.

The obvious strategy.

And so typical of Annie, who is always ready to do what it takes. "Ah."

The relief I felt to be talking freely is fading fast. How can she speak of this to me? Surely living through one tragedy, no false happy ending to save it from horror, was enough. And now she speaks of another?

"The thing is," Annie says, with a furtive glance in my direction, then away again, at her fingers, "I can't figure out where they got the drachthanasia from. I know the dragonborn had to distill it for generations, and all the literature refers to family caches, but I don't know where they'd be now—"

"You were hoping I knew where to find some."

Annie nods. "Do you?"

She finally looks me in the face, and whatever she sees in my expression makes her blanch.

She opens her mouth—I have a split second to wonder, with a kind of fiery dispassion, if it will be in apology, because it turns out she's right to be reticent, I do have a problem with the idea of repeating atrocities like the Widowing on my own blood kin—when another voice shouts from the other end of the theater.

"Lee!"

Cor is elbowing through the exiting guests, forcing his way against traffic down to where we sit.

"Lee," he says, white-faced, "Megara's gone."

ANNIE

It feels good to remember I can trust Lee. To feel his hand in mine and tell him everything. It makes me wonder if even the report to the Ministry of Information will be something I can explain. Maybe it's not too late to reach an understanding, a full understanding, of everything.

And then I say the word *drachthanasia* and watch his face go to that place of fury so cold I can't reach him through the ice. The sounds around us, of Golds leaving the theater, grow muffled as my own voice, seeking his, strains.

And then Cor skids to a halt at the aisle beside us, gripping the seat on the end of the row, and I finally hear what he's yelling. *Megara's gone.*

I get to my feet. Dizziness takes me with such a force that I brace my arm on the chair for support, muffling others' voices and making mine loud in my own ears.

They did it during the performance.

"She was removed."

Lee gets to his feet as well. His wild grin has faded.

Cor's face twists. "What do you mean, *removed?*" he snarls.

It's a question that treads water, because we all know what *removed* means. We've all done rounds with the Ministry of Information, with the Reeducation Committee, at the Vault. We know how this works. I give the unnecessary answer.

"Removed by the Ministry of Information, for questioning."

We even know how it would have happened. Megara would have been tapped on the shoulder, during the performance. Led out into the foyer, quieted if she struggled, and led to a carriage that would take her to the Vault discreetly, with minimal attention.

Arrests of Golds are carried out most discreetly of all.

Cor isn't bothering to be discreet. Those exiting the theater have turned to watch the spectacle; I can see Crissa, gleaming in her golden dress, observing us from the far end of the aisle with her weight against her crutch. Power, slinking our way like a mountain cat through the edge of the crowd, his eyes on me.

"Questioned about *what?*" Cor demands.

"About the stolen grain. About the rogue printing press—"

"*On what charge?*" Cor shouts.

I'm gripping the back of my chair so tightly my knuckles have whitened. "Disturbing the peace under the name of Southside's Daughter. Sedition. Dissemination of state secrets."

"Then charge me, too!" Cor shouts.

Lee seems to snap to his senses. He has noticed, as I have, members of the Ministry of Information among those leaving, the Protector's Guard lining the exits. He seizes Cor and grips the side of his neck, a palm against his chin. "Enough," he growls.

"I can't charge you," I tell Cor, through the heat in my face. "Though I should. I need you both. I need you for when the Pythians come, because someone gave them that map of our granaries and they're coming for them."

Slack against Lee's grip, Cor's eyes widen.

"Yeah, that's right, Cor. *That's* what I've been doing with Griff Gareson. Getting information about the other side. Since you were kind enough to rifle through my bag and I'm sure you've been wondering. I've been helping my country win a war. Which is more than either of you can say for yourselves right now."

I hold my notebook up. Lee releases Cor and he sags, dragging a hand across his face.

A ministry messenger has broken from the crowd, approaching us looking harried, a memo in hand. Cor's staring at me, wide-eyed. Lee's no longer looking at me at all.

"Go home," I tell them, tasting the bitterness of my words, "and enjoy your Midwinter."

I watch their retreating backs with burning eyes. At the back of the hall, Crissa joins them. They leave the theater together.

Leaving me feeling suddenly, terribly, alone.

I have to read the memo pressed into my hand twice before I understand it.

Power joins my side to find me laughing.

I specified, on the report, that I would like to interrogate Megara myself. It was the only way I could conceive of sparing her the harsher methods she would be left to in the Vault.

"I'm approved to interrogate Megara," I tell him, as the laughter turns to something else. "Tomorrow."

Midwinter Day. Because the ministry noted that I didn't request leave. For some reason this, of all things, is what makes me feel like crumpling.

Power takes the memo from me with uncharacteristic gentleness.

"Before that," he says, "you're coming to my house for Midwinter."

23

—

THE SKY-WIDOWER

GRIFF

On Midwinter's Eve I seal and deliver a reply from Ixion to the last trade ship out of port before the feast day. His handwriting is easier to make out than that of the letter that made rounds at his party, and without the pressure of reading it through fury or shame, I'm able to decipher it in its entirety as I fold it:

> *My dearest Princess Freyda,*
>
> *I am overjoyed that you also see an alignment of our interests. We will offer pressure, and you, relief. But first, the catalyst. Shall we meet in person to discuss?*
>
>
>
> *Yours ever in amour and with ardor,*
> *Ixion sur Niter Stormscourge, son of Crethon*
> *Triarch-presumptive of Callipolis the West*
>
>

My next scheduled visit with Antigone is in a week's time, the day after New Year's. With all luck, she'll hear of this letter before it even reaches Vask.

Because I'm pretty sure she'll find it interesting.

I finish up the afternoon in the lairs. I'll be serving at the feast tonight, and with any luck I'll be able to bring home a few treats from the feast for the little ones, and then tomorrow we'll make the solstice pilgrimage across the water and up the winding stairs along the Nag's mane to her shrine. It's a pleasant-enough prospect that even shoveling Niter's dung is more tolerable than usual.

A clatter of stone in the corridor outside makes me straighten, sweat dripping down my back. The ha'Aurelians are paranoid after the drying up of the old line of dragons, so the lairs are kept a furnace in winter, to help the fleet through it. I'm expecting Ixion or maybe, if I'm very lucky, a Midwinter gift from the shrines, Delo—but it's Phemi, Delo's sister. Her hair is braided for the feast but she's not yet in a formal gown, and when she sees me, she grinds to a halt, clutching her side.

"Griff—thank the dragon—I was hoping you'd be down here—"

"Are you all right, my lady?"

"I'm fine, it's just—Father."

My stomach sinks. I've nothing against Phemi—even if I wish she and Ethelo hadn't gossiped to Roxana, she wasn't one of the ones who laughed at that party when Ixion shoved my face into the rug. She's tolerable. But Nestor's a different matter. He hates the humble-riders almost as much as Ixion, though his methods for making our lives difficult are of the subtler variety. The you-learn-or-you-burn variety. Which was pretty exciting while the squires were still shaky on our Dragontongue.

Why would I be needed for Nestor?

"I'm not yet done in the lairs, my lady."

"Griff, please. I don't want anyone else to see."

I drop the cart and follow her, wondering without much optimism whether *please* means she'll bother explaining to Scully where I went, whether I'll have to return to finish up in the lairs after the feast, whether my wages will be docked for my absence.

But Phemi's young, thoughtless but not malicious, and in any case—I'll admit I'm a little curious about Nestor.

"Your humble servant is honored to be so trusted by Lady Phemi," I announce as we make our way up the spiral stone stairs.

Phemi lifts her nose in the air. "I don't trust you. I trust my brother."

I'm surprised by how touched I am that she's insulting me by way of him.

She rounds on me at the top of the stairs and pokes a manicured finger into my chest. "And while we speak of it? I will burn you to a crisp if you ever hurt him."

Still more touched, I bow low. She gives me a look of disdain that could melt glass.

We enter the Skyfish armory and I finally understand.

The room stinks of alcohol; Nestor, badly drunk, is slouched in a corner glaring at us cross-eyed, a half-empty bottle of Bassilean whiskey and a battered suit of what I can only guess is his own pre-Revolutionary armor on the table beside him.

I've heard Delo mention, but never seen, his father suffering a sorrow spell.

"Where's Delo?" Nestor demands.

"I'm getting him, Father."

Nestor and Phemi are both speaking unnaturally loudly, as if to drown out something else.

She turns to me and lowers her voice. "Stay with him while I look—?"

"Shouldn't you stay with him—?"

"No," Nestor says, pointing at me. "He stays."

Grand.

Phemi mouths *thank you* and hurries from the room.

"Sit," Nestor says.

He sits at a worktable usually reserved for squires maintaining the dragonlords' armor. On the instinct, years in the making, against ever being caught idle in front of Nestor, I reach for the polish and a rag.

The old armor does need polishing. Looks like no one's done it properly since the Revolution. I slide his breastplate gingerly toward me and begin to work it.

"She didn't like boats," Nestor says.

My polishing freezes as I realize who this must be, because Delo's mentioned the boats before, too.

Delo's mother didn't like boats. This is why, when the Skyfish Summer Palace was overrun, and the minor dragonlord and his children missed the purge on a fishing trip in the Medean, she did not escape it with them.

"Fishing trip, come along, no, boats aren't to my taste, you know me. Who marries a Skyfish when you don't like boats? Elana loved Midwinter."

Nestor takes the bottle by its neck and gulps the contents like water. I consider whether my duties here include physically preventing him from consuming more alcohol. It doesn't seem worth the potential beating for laying a hand on a dragonborn. And even drunk, Nestor's dead weight would be considerable in a match of strength.

"I could feel it," he says, "when I lost her."

"Your wife?"

Tears spill down Nestor's cheeks. "My dragon."

The sweat trickling down my back feels suddenly cold.

"Just an—emptiness." Nestor gestures to the back of his head, as if he'd felt the emptiness in his skull. "And then I knew I'd lost Elana as well. Lost everything."

Panic is rising sweet and acrid as the resonances hit me. All that I'm planning with Antigone, all that I confessed to Bran and Fionna.

Delo. Sweet Delo, I can't do this to Delo—

I croak, "Not everything, my lord."

Nestor's vacant gaze fixes on me, sitting across from him, working over his rusted cuirass with unseeing fingers. Between who I am and what I'm doing and what I've said, he seems to recognize me for the first time.

"You," he rasps.

Because he's drunk, and we're alone in the room and I'm nearly certain he won't remember it, I look him in the eye.

"Me."

Nestor only blinks. Then he leans forward, blearily holding my gaze.

"You make him soft."

"I—what?"

But my hammering heart tells me what.

"Soft like his mother. Too soft a heart. Weak—"

"He's not weak."

Nestor stares at me. For a second I think: of all the stupid ways to earn a beating, contradicting a drunk dragonlord. Then, to my complete surprise, he grunts agreement.

"No. Not weak."

"Father?"

I jump, hard. Delo's entered the armory, Phemi behind him. He turns back to her and murmurs, "Go," with a hand on her shoulder gently steering her from the room as if to shield her from something indecent. Then turns back to us, and I realize he isn't able to look at me.

I jolt to my feet. This is an intrusion. A part of Delo's life he's kept private from me even after sharing his bed. It can't be an accident that for years I've hated Nestor but never been given reason to pity him.

Delo doesn't want his father exposed in this state of indignity.

"I'll just be—going—"

But Nestor seizes me by the arm, preventing my retreat. With the other, he fumbles for the window latch.

"Feel this breeze," he tells us.

Delo assists him in opening the window, his lips tight, his back turned to me.

"Balmy," Nestor says. "Sparking weather."

"Yes, Father."

"Tomorrow," Nestor tells Delo, still clutching my arm. "We do it tomorrow."

Delo turns to his father and, with resignation, braces an arm around him. He removes the bottle from the table.

"Tomorrow's Midwinter, Father."

Nestor tosses aside my arm to take Delo's face in both his hands, drawing it down to him. "Exactly," he whispers, like he's confiding a secret. "That is why it is the perfect time to strike."

His eyes gleam. Delo looks into them and sags. He lets out a cry of frustration.

"Father, do you not think we go too far—would it not be better just to *rest*—"

Nestor jabs a finger down at his old armor, shaking his head. "No. We're *so close*."

"It's a mad dream, Father—"

"It's the only thing we have left."

Nestor kisses Delo's forehead, and Delo closes his eyes, his face contorting and his shoulders shuddering. I think it's the first time I've ever seen Nestor show Delo affection.

I back away, bowing as I go though neither notices, while Delo turns from me to hold his father, and I don't breathe until I'm out the door and have closed it after me. Phemi stands in the hallway, her shoulders up around her ears, listening. She looks ready to cry, and for a moment, I consider laying a hand on her shoulder to comfort her.

Then she says, "I don't *want* to do an air strike on Midwinter."

It sounds like she's pouting about an ugly dress, not the prospect of bombarding unsuspecting souls on a family feast day. My pity for the lot of them evaporates.

"Callipolis will want it even less than you."

24

MEGARA ROPER

ANNIE

I wake on Midwinter morning in a room that isn't my own filled with blinding light. White sheets over a wide mattress, a white canopy overhead, sunlight streaming through white curtains. The only color comes from a sprig of Midwinter holly on the mantel and a painting that fills the wall opposite the bed, of a pair of skyfish crossing the open sea. GIFTED IN GRATITUDE TO THE HESPERIDES FAMILY BY THE TRIARCHY UNDER ARCTURUS, a small gold plate reads, in Dragontongue.

Slowly I remember how I got here: the play, Megara's arrest, and Lee and Cor and Crissa leaving for their holiday while I stood frozen. The fit of despair and loneliness that led me to say yes without a second thought to Power's invitation, to go home to the house of the boy who bullied me daily through my childhood.

I'm in *Power's house*, and Aela is with Eater in Power's garden.

And it's Midwinter Day, which means I'm scheduled to interrogate Megara Roper in the Vault this afternoon.

I reach for my ground uniform, which I left folded on the bedside table, and pull it on.

I run into Power on his way to the washroom, still in his under-layers, his face rumpled. I've grown up seeing the corps in stages of undress, fresh from sleep. There's no excuse for the scalding blush that spreads under the neck of my uniform at the encounter.

"How'd you sleep, Commander?" he asks, yawning.

I found my bedroom door bolted from the inside when I reached to open it this morning: Apparently, last night, I took precautions that I don't remember. But now, at his question, I realize the stranger fact. I slept well. For the first time in weeks, I didn't dream about Duck ending up on a different list. I didn't dream, as far as I can remember, about anything.

We find Power's parents downstairs in the sunroom, overlooking a bright garden, sipping coffee and exchanging newspapers in front of more food than I've seen on a single table in months. I can only imagine the number of ration cards it would have taken to provide it: bacon and eggs, biscuits and pastries, berries and clotted cream. Suddenly I can taste my own saliva.

"Hungry, dears?"

I'm preparing myself to do the thing I know I'll need to do, eat slowly, respectably, when Power begins to scarf. It's the first time I've ever noticed that he eats the way I do. Like he has trouble seeing anything but his plate.

So I start scarfing, too.

Neither of us speaks until our plates our clean. When I finally look up, I find Mr. Hesperides reading the *Gold Gazette* with great absorption; Mrs. Hesperides pats Power on the arm. "Good to have you back, Parry darling. And so nice to have you, too, Annie."

I smile back at her, and start to wonder, and can't stop.

What would it have been like, to end up here instead of in an orphanage? With rooms so full of luxury even your bare feet feel comforted by soft carpets, with food in abundance, and most of all with *love*? To wake from nightmares to someone like Mrs. Hesperides to comfort you?

It would have made all the difference in the world.

For the next two hours, I feel as though I'm living in a dream outside of time. Somewhere beyond this house, these great frosted windows and high ceilings, my life awaits me. My duties as a Guardian, as a Firstrider. To find Megara Roper in the Vault, and face Lee and Cor afterward. To move the granaries and prepare for attack.

But for now, I can wander through this other life trailing my fingers along it like the keys of an open piano.

Power shows me around the estate after breakfast, burping from satisfaction. We visit the dragons, wreaking havoc in the garden and frolicking in the fair weather while the Hesperides's gardener fumes on the edge of the lawn; we mount the grand staircase, and several narrower ones after that, to reach the suite of rooms Power claims as his own at the top of his house.

"My lair. Used chiefly, these days, for the seduction of women."

I fold my arms. Power rolls his eyes with a shrug and unlatches the door to his balcony. "Or not."

I leave a good three feet between us on the railing, unsettled by how I've reddened. We can see the whole city from his balcony. It's warm enough to stand comfortably in the breeze with only my ground uniform; Power shivers just a little in his undershirt. It's late morning, the sky gray with low stratus, obscuring the top of Pytho's Keep and leaving the Janiculum in shadow.

I summon up the courage to ask. "How old were you when . . ."

Power's gaze is locked on the horizon. "About three."

"And before it?"

"Don't remember."

A little too quick, a little too pat, like this is a wall not just for me but for himself. I know from an older conversation that his mother, a housekeeper for the Hesperides family, passed away in a poorhouse and he never knew his father. Whatever his situation was before this, he was hungry.

Still, when I think of a childhood waking up to Mrs. Hesperides piling food on your plate, I can only think of Power as lucky.

Below us, the city—smoking and steaming and gleaming from the evaporating rain—sits quiet and still for Midwinter. Power lifts a finger and points. Toward the far edge of the city, the great square rooftops of the Manufacturing District. Where the Vault, imprisoning Megara Roper, lies.

Soon it will be time to interrogate Southside's Daughter.

"So . . . did the ministry give you guidelines?" Power asks.

"They made clear what they wanted."

Power offers a feral grin. "At least you'll be doing it on a full stomach."

LEE

We're in the Palace courtyard, and Argus Aurelian, twelve years old, is doubled over, vomiting. He is asking for his father. He is asking for his dragon. He says, *I can't feel her.* My brother, Laertes, says, *Go get help.* The soldiers who are supposed to help laugh instead—

I wake Midwinter morning with a jolt. I'm in the boys' room of the Sutter house, under a patchwork quilt not quite long enough to cover my toes, on a top bunk level with a window overlooking city rooftops. I lie back, stare up at the cobwebs dangling from the ceiling, and remember what happened last night. The leftover nausea of the nightmare mixes with aftershocks of fury with Annie: At her plea for help with planning another Widowing, as if she wasn't asking for my help with an atrocity. At the way she calmly confessed to reporting Megara.

I feel guilt approaching horror that something the Passi printed is now a map in enemy hands. That wasn't what I joined sides with Megara for. But the fact is, air strikes have been a risk since the war began. A friend captured and facing torture at the hands of the government I work for is new.

Overhead, the roof creaks: a dragon shifting. We were ordered to take them with us on leave, because of the city's high alert. They're nesting on the Sutter roof.

Cor's asleep on the bed across from mine, his younger brother Greg curled beside him; his mother told us that Greg hasn't been able to sleep alone since the funeral. The room has three beds, but only two sons. I don't have to ask whose bed I've been sleeping in.

Crissa and I do the bulk of the talking at breakfast. Mrs. Sutter attributes her runny nose to the weather, but I don't think anyone is fooled. Eventually, even Crissa runs out of small talk, and it's a relief when Greg asks to be excused and the family trickles away from the table, leaving Cor, Crissa, and me together and alone to clear the dishes and finish up the breakfast tea.

It's the first time the three of us have been together in weeks, and it almost feels like a squadron meeting except today we're talking about the Passi and the rogue printing press and Megara and Annie, getting Crissa up to speed with all she missed.

Her frown deepens the more she learns. "What a mess."

"Right?" Cor fumes. "I can't believe she did this—"

Crissa makes a noncommittal noise. "Who," she asks, "Annie or Megara?"

Cor glares at her.

"You all right, Lee?" Crissa asks.

I nod, startled from my brooding. I explain the piece I haven't yet told them. "Annie wants to plan a Widowing, in New Pythos. She was asking me if I knew where she could find drachthanasia."

Cor whistles. "So that's what she was doing with Gareson?"

I nod.

"*Do* you know where she can find drachthanasia?" Crissa asks softly.

I lift a shoulder, wishing she'd stop looking at me. This isn't something I want to feel guilty about. It's the *Widowing*. I don't owe anyone, not even Annie, a damn thing when it comes to the Red Month.

"Have you ever seen someone lose their dragon, Crissa?"

Crissa eases backward in her chair, just a little, as her face pales. "No."

"We should check on them," Cor says, glancing upward.

Crissa leaves her crutch behind, gripping Cor's arm for support as she favors her injured leg up the stairs of the Sutter fire escape onto their roof. We find the three dragons curled on the slate shingles, lazing in the unexpected warmth like cats in the sun. The sky remains overcast, but the roofs have dried from yesterday's rainfall, our armor and flamesuits piled beside the dragons glaring in the light. Crissa kneels to inspect Phaedra's flank: Like Crissa, she's still on the mend.

A shrill noise comes from behind us, and I'm so little expecting it that at first, I don't recognize it. It's a child's giggle. Greg and Merina are peeking over the top of the fire escape, curious about the dragons. Cor turns in alarm. "I told you two to stay off the roof—"

Crissa places a hand on Cor's arm. "If you are very careful," she tells the children, "I can show you how to pet Phaedra."

The children tiptoe forward, and Phaedra perks her head.

Cor smiles a bit as he watches them scratch the skyfish under her chin. Then he looks out over the jagged rooftops of the city, toward the Manufacturing District, and speaks to me in an undertone. Crissa, cheerfully instructing the children, doesn't hear. "I talked to Val Lazare last night. He said we should storm the Vault. Three dragons, that'd be enough."

So that's what Megara meant by *act soon*.

Capturing the Vault would not only free Megara and the other political prisoners within it—it would also give us control of the *People's Paper*, the narrative artery of the city. It could serve as a base from which to take on the Inner Palace and the First Protector.

It would also be an act of open rebellion.

There's more than one way to replace Atreus.

With the city starving, the Golds disinterested, Southside's Daughter captured—is that what it's time to do?

ANNIE

A low pass over the city on the way to the Vault leaves me in no doubt of the anger in the streets: Word has spread of Megara's arrest, and graffiti the city guard scrubs from walls already reads FREE SOUTHSIDE'S DAUGHTER. Green scarves hang from lampposts and branches. Guards outside granaries stare down the citizens who have congregated in front of them in the wake of the Passi's printing with nothing else to occupy them on Midwinter Day. Some, but not all, of the granaries were able to be relocated in the night.

Callipolis feels combustible.

I stable Aela outside the towering, unmarked brick walls of the Vault. Inside, I thumb up my mantle to expose the Guardians' emblem of the gold and silver circlets entwined on my breast, the bugle of the Firstrider within them. I'm in full battle armor. Elias Wulf, the Minister of Information, comes down to greet me himself. A revolutionary from Atreus's generation, he sports an aggressively receding hairline, skin so pale it looks luminous, and a smile that does not reach his eyes. Though we know each other from rounds, this is the first time I've come to the Vault as an active official.

"Miranda Hane was the one who insisted you be allowed the first stab at this one," Wulf tells me as we make our way underground, to the level of the temporary holding cells shared by the Reeducation Committee. "Don't see why she thought it was necessary. My methods would have been perfectly effective."

I don't ask what methods he would have used.

Megara's cell is level with the city sewers. It smells accordingly. I lift my hand to cover my nose and mouth. She's little more than a silhouette in the darkness; a single torch lights the corridor, and it's far down the row.

"Antigone. Here to gloat?"

"I'd like to speak to her in a lit room with chairs and a table. Heated."

Ten minutes later, I'm sitting across from Megara in an interrogation room. A guard stands at the edge of the room, hand on the hilt of a saber. At the sight of him, I turn to Wulf.

"I'll speak to her alone."

"Pretend he's not here," Wulf says, with a dismissive wave at the guard. Wulf leaves the room; the guard remains.

So I'm to be watched on orders that outrank mine. From whom? Wulf? Miranda Hane, General Holmes? Atreus himself? Whether it's to assess my performance or my loyalty is unclear.

"Looks like you're on probation," Megara observes.

Her long hair has been cut close to her scalp, clipped in dark chunks like a poorly shorn sheep, for processing. The smell of the sewer lingers on her. Nevertheless, she seems cheerful.

I set my helmet on the table between us.

"I'm going to ask you a few questions. If you don't answer them, others will ask instead. And their methods of interrogation will be harsher—"

Megara lets out a laugh that cuts off my prepared delivery.

"You don't need to tell me what happens in here, Antigone."

My temper flares, my prepared words fall by the wayside. "Then you know that even if you don't talk, even if they don't kill you, they will keep you in here until this city forgets your name."

Megara smiles.

"Or maybe my arrest will be the spark that sets fire to dry kindling."

The confidence of her assertion fills me with a strange fury.

"Why are you so determined to make this city burn?"

Megara leans forward. "Why are you so determined to preserve it?" She spreads her open palms, her chafed wrists raw and exposed under the harsh lamplight. "I'm not the only one they're going to string up. Your turn is coming. Is this really what you want to be strung up *for*? Firing on commoners, interrogating imprisoned girls, telling widows they can't have a second ration card because of results from a test? Think about it."

The smell of her, of this prison, is all at once too sharp in my nostrils.

"I'd rather be strung up for preserving order than destroying it."

Megara's smile spreads like a crack across her face.

"Pity," she says. "My way's more fun."

Fun.

I try to imagine the last time I looked at my Guardian medal and felt proud of it.

My fists clench on the paper they grip beneath the table. "That's why you do it? Because it's fun?"

Megara's face twists. "No. *I do it* because this country deserves better. *I do it* because my father bled out in the street during the Southside Massacre. *I do it* because my mother was arrested for daring to speak the truth."

"This regime has never stopped anyone from speaking the truth about the triarchy's massacres," I snap.

Megara's answer spews spit. "The Southside Massacre wasn't pre-Revolutionary. It was post."

I stare at her. Behind her, the guard stands stiff and expressionless as a statue.

"I've never heard of it."

Megara lets out a wilting laugh. "Of course you haven't. It wasn't reported. It happened after Atreus disbanded the People's Assembly and instituted you lot. Pro-democratic factions rioted, the city guard was told to put an end to it, and they did. The old-fashioned way."

"That's not . . ."

I stop short of saying possible, because it is possible. The Ministry of Propaganda has enough control over information that they could have covered up the story completely, discredited accounts, arrested anyone who talked about it.

"My mother disappeared after she began to publicize what happened," Megara says. "She was let out a year later, a husk of herself. As I assume Richard Tyndale will be, when this place is done with him. Like my mother, like me, he disappeared without a trace or a trial because the Reeducation Committee works in unscrutinized secrecy."

Her eyes blaze, looking at me, like she knows that it's my fault he was taken, and I finally understand her point. Megara isn't concerned by Tyndale's guilt or lack thereof. She's concerned by the ease with which my report made him vanish.

It's all so possible as to be disquieting.

Megara's toothy sneer widens.

"This is what happens when you don't have freedom of the press, *Annie*."

Her use of my nickname, uninvited and dripping condescension, snaps me to my senses.

Whatever the truth of Megara's conspiracy theory, it doesn't change the fact that the Passi have leaked state secrets into the hands of our enemy, that the rogue printing press is a national security threat, and that if I don't get its location out of her, the Ministry of Information will find other ways to make her talk.

Get this over with, let her go, and then find answers.

Do what it takes.

"It would be a shame to make your family suffer even more."

I hold up a piece of paper and pass it across the table to her. She looks down at the list of names, blinks, and then whitens.

"You wouldn't."

"If this ministry is so happy to cover up its victims, why not add to the list? You said it yourself. I've been firing on civilians with abandon. Why should I make an exception here? Lex, Katarina, Val Lazare—"

"You *wouldn't*, you *can't*—"

She's right, I'm not legally able to make good on any of this, but I can tell from her face that I'm the only one who knows that for sure.

"Do you want to know what it felt like, *to watch?*"

Megara's eyes are so round as she stares at me, the whites are visible. I reach behind my head and grip my own hair. "I was held, like this. The first thing you hear is screaming, but it goes quiet as they begin to suffocate—"

Megara's launch from her seat is so sudden the chair rocks backward. The guard takes two strides and catches her across the chest as she throws herself across the table at me. "You're an animal. You're a foul, horrible, heartless *bitch*—"

"Yes. I am."

Megara is sobbing in fury. I wait, but when no further insults are produced, I proceed.

"Tell me where to find the stolen grain."

She sags against the arms of the guard holding her and lifts her head. Her eyes are shining, her teeth bared.

"In the bellies of the ones who needed it."

The moral superiority of her tone makes me want to smash something. "The printing press?"

"Foul," Megara breathes.

Yes. Foul. I feel it. Foul at my own sense of satisfaction as I wait because I know I have her.

And all I had to do was weaponize the memory of watching my family burn.

"The printing press," Megara inhales, "is run by Lo Teiran."

For a second, I think I've misheard her.

"Lo Teiran? The poet?"

The Callipolan poet laureate. Lotus's father. Whose estate on the Janiculum would be more than large enough to house, and hide, a printing press and be exempt from most searches conducted by the city guard.

Cor, Lee. And now *Lotus*?

"The very one," says Megara.

The floor vibrates.

Megara's guard speaks for the first time. "That's the alarm bells." His grip has slackened on Megara.

Too far underground to hear them, the bells' vibrations pound a rhythm beneath our feet. Hammering out the codes that every Callipolan knows to interpret.

Dragons. Attack. Take shelter.

The Pythians have arrived. Following the scent of those granary maps all the way to our front steps on Midwinter Day.

People are going to die because of this girl's idiocy.

As I reach for my helmet, Megara speaks. A serene smile is spreading across her face.

"Did you know," she says, "that there aren't enough bunkers for *everyone*?"

I yank the helmet over my head, barely hearing her. "What?"

Megara's blissful look has a wild edge to it. "They haven't finished building bunkers. There's a bunker *shortage*. I was doing a report on it for my *Gold Gazette* internship right before—"

But I don't have time for more of Megara's conspiracy theories. I push past her, spill out into the corridor, and take off for Aela at a run.

LEE

On the Sutter roof, the children have drawn close around Crissa's skyfish, trembling with excitement to pet a dragon and *oohing* at Phaedra's mother-of-pearl scales shimmering in the light. Mrs. Sutter and Ana have climbed to the top of the fire escape to watch. Ana wraps her arm around her mother, and a smile spreads over Mrs. Sutter's lined face.

"Mum, come pet her!"

"Oh, I don't—"

But Ana, laughing, pulls her mother forward. "Not every day we get three dragons on our roof."

That's the feeling I remember from this house, returning to me at last as Cor's family gathers around Crissa's skyfish. The ache of remembering, of missing, what this felt like. A family, and laughing, and *home*.

I'm remembering it, tasting it, as the distress beacons begin to toll out over the city.

Dragons. Take shelter. Attack.

And all at once the calloused calculations I made this morning feel ghastly. Weighing the likelihood that my own actions increased the risk of air strikes. If there is a fraction of a chance I've endangered my city, my friends, these children, by this mission of justice that is just as much a thinly disguised vendetta against Atreus—

Annie's right. The Vault, the Passi—none of that matters with a hostile fleet on the way.

The war that matters is the one in the air.

Mrs. Sutter's hands cover her mouth; Greg and Merina have started screaming, their voices shrill over the bells. The dragons lurch to their feet, while Ana straightens and looks at Cor in silent conference.

"The nearest bunker," he says.

Ana nods. She takes her mother's hand, ushers her younger siblings down the fire escape, and a moment later they're gone. Leaving us alone on the Sutter roof with three restlessly pacing dragons.

Crissa tosses me my flamesuit, Cor his, and we begin to suit up.

25

THE MIDWINTER ATTACK

ANNIE

Outside the Vault, Aela and I launch to a cacophony of alarm tolls. Low, ribbed stratus clouds spread out over the horizon like shredded sheets. Across the city, our fleet is spilling into the air: I spot Power sur Eater among the patrician riders ascending from the Janiculum; Lee, Cor, and Crissa are rising from the Sutters' house in Highmarket.

Our sky, filling with the Callipolan fleet.

My spiking fear calms as the world shrinks below Aela's amber wings. This is where I'm ready for anything: in the saddle. And because the Guardians were able to take their dragons with them on leave, the rest of the corps is ready, too. At the sight of Lotus sur Iustus shimmering on an updraft from the Janiculum, I don't let myself question what instinct is telling me to do.

"Lotus?"

"Yeah?" he calls.

"They know."

Iustus slows on the updraft. Lotus lifts a glove to his visor.

"Thanks," he says.

I return to the circling knot of riders, Crissa sur Phaedra, Cor sur Maurana, and Lee sur Pallor in the center, awaiting orders for their respective squadrons. I wonder for a fleeting moment about their Midwinter at the Sutters before forcing the thought from my head. It's easier to face the three of them with visors lowered.

"I want aurelians and skyfish forward, heading off over the Ferrish Plain. We'll keep them over farmland as long as we can. Stormscourge squadron in reserve over the city."

As Crissa and Cor peel off with their respective squadrons, Lee sur Pallor joins Aela's side.

"Do you need a wingrider?" he asks.

I lift my visor to look at him. The city below, the clouds above, the horizon a line my eyes are fixed on, and my heart pounding in time with Aela's: This is the place where everything else between me and Lee sur Pallor is put aside. If Lee's ready to fight, I'm ready to have him.

But I have terms. "I want Ixion."

Lee's visor is up; his lip lifts in something like a smile. "Then I'll take Griff."

I wonder if he's waiting for me to say *Go gentle on him*. Just like I did last time, when all my plans of mercy backfired.

I don't. Griff can take care of himself.

I lower my visor. Lee sur Pallor drifts to second wingrider position above and behind me, leaving me to lead.

One thing I didn't account for: The wind is in the Pythians' favor. It will take our fleet twice the strength to hold them against winds that blow south. The sun is low on the horizon, firing the edges of the clouds with gold, and as we flood the skies over the Ferrish Plain, I strain my gaze north. Aela's keen eyes spot them first. She tenses, and I feel her excitement like fire as I follow her gaze. The full Pythian fleet skims from cloud to cloud like skipping stones.

Still dwarfed on the horizon, but as they see us, they dive. Burrowing into the coils of stratus.

I sound the bugle to mount higher: We'll take the height advantage.

"Horns when they breach."

The order echoes as it relays down the skyfish and aurelian lines. We mount as high as the winter cold allows us. The rolling plains of the lowlands, barren in winter and scudded with drifts of snow, lie below us broken here and there by toy-size villages. Their tolling alarm bells echo distantly and pulse on the wind in my ears. I feel the cold of the higher altitude seeping through my flamesuit, biting my fingers, and breath begins to fog the edges of my visor—

And in the break between two great clouds the Pythians reemerge below us. Wings glowing in the low light, long skyfish tails trailing, great black stormscourge wings blotting out the ground below.

I motion with my fist, and the Callipolan fleet bears down on them, firing as they go.

It takes me only an instant to pick out the wingriders we look for: Ixion sur Niter, with Griff sur Sparker on his wing.

It feels like we're beating against the wall of the air itself to get to him, dodging through engaging pairs on either side of us, determined to engage him before he can come any closer to my city. We hurtle toward Ixion and ram him off course. Into a cloud bank, whiteness surrounding me.

And in my peripheral vision, Lee goes for Griff.

LEE

The thing I never understood, when our fleet returned from New Pythos, was how Annie could have been held off by anyone. I've spent a lifetime sparring with her, and I know that when Antigone sur Aela wants to get past you, she can. The fact that she was held off by a rider reported to be muzzled made it all the stranger.

But when Pallor and I come up against Griff Gareson and his stormscourge above the Ferrish Plain, I finally understand.

They're a brick wall. They ride fearless of dragonfire, of talons, of fangs—as if that muzzle makes their desperation deadlier. The stormscourge fights like a feral dog with the weight of a bear.

And the wind's in their favor.

Every time Pallor fires, they dodge. And every time they charge, we're rammed back.

South. Toward the city.

Fire is our first and best weapon, but while tussling with Griff and his stormscourge, it becomes about talon and fang as Pallor struggles, over and over again, to free himself.

An opening, over the stormscourge's wing. We fire.

Griff grunts in pain. His stormscourge howls.

An edge of blackness crowds my vision and I toss my head to clear it: *Not now.* Not the bloody flameshock now—

But I can't think.

And Pallor's wing is crushed to his side, and we are losing altitude.

Hurtling downward through clouds, I realize I no longer know where we are, what lies below, and the stratus glows a deep red in the setting sun—

—lost in clouds, the Sky Court of Pytho's Keep rises to meet us out of nowhere.

The two dragons slam against the flagstones. Pain explodes down the leg crushed under Pallor; he feels it and struggles to right himself, to alleviate the weight, and my sluggish fingers fumble to cut the bootstraps binding me to the stirrups—

The shadow of a great black stormscourge falls across us.

Now I'm exposed, pinned, about to be gnawed alive by Ixion's bulldog squire—

A knife is inserted into my bootstrap and slices. Pallor groans and shifts his weight while curling his wings inward, relieving the pain in my leg. The knife again, cutting.

An armored arm, thick and blackened with soot, hooks across my chest and heaves. Out of the saddle, onto the ground beside Pallor, and across the flagstones to the shelter of the nearest crumbling arch.

Griff Gareson has pulled me off my dragon. We are alone atop the karst of Pytho's Keep, shrouded in mist, under the eaves of a ruined column of the old Sky Court.

He's removed his helmet, revealing curling hair and shockingly blue eyes set in a tan face. His armor, Pythian white stained with ash, bears no House sigil. He glances out, squinting, at the sky around us. We are fully enveloped by the clouds and see only the occasional glow of dragonfire through the mist, accompanied by distant cries and horn blasts.

Gareson expels a breath through pursed lips and crouches in front of me.

Pallor's head swings round. He growls, hackles raising, wings rising and tail stiffening. A few yards away an answering growl, much deeper and louder, answers. Gareson's stormscourge, sensing a threat to its rider.

For the first time, I get a good look at its muzzle. The thing's even more ghastly up close. Crowding up around his horns, constricting his jaw—

"I'm not going to hurt him," Gareson tells Pallor. He adds over his shoulder: "And *you* calm down."

The stormscourge's growling subsides.

Gareson begins unfastening the armor on my crushed leg. Deftly, quickly, as if he's used to taking armor off other people.

"You're Leo. The one who killed Julia."

His Dragontongue is almost accentless. Like household staff who's been raised in service. His address, seemingly automatic, is that of a servant speaking to a lord.

His fingers pull free one plate, then another. Presses a thumb against my knee, searching for a reaction. When he finds it, he reaches for the arm guard punctured along my shoulder. His fingers come away wet and red. He pushes aside my fumbling fingers impatiently, peels back the neck of my flamesuit, and applies pressure.

I hear myself do the automatic thing in return, the informal *you*. "You knew her?"

His face darkens. "Aye. I knew her."

Griff uses a slightly different word for *knew* with an edge of fury that makes the hair on the back of my neck rise. He scrapes his fingers through dark curls and his whole face scrunches. He wipes carefully, applies pressure again. And then he murmurs, so quietly I wouldn't hear it were he not crouched by my ear:

"I'm glad you killed her."

There's no way Griff can know that this choice is the thing that has haunted me for months, that this was the reason my vision blackened and we fell. The fear that in making a horrible choice, I also made the wrong one.

He can't know the weight his words shift.

Of course he's glad she's dead.

Julia spoke about ideals she found absurd and serfs we owned. I had seen enough of where that got my father to balk, even if for Julia and me it remained a difference in principle.

It's more than a matter of principle for Griff Gareson.

Of course, of course, *of course*.

Gareson's voice remains low as it gains intensity. "I'm going to do the rest of them. Ixion, Rhode, all of them. With drachthanasia first, for the dragons. Antigone's getting me some."

Listening to Gareson, as he serves me so competently with the ease born of years of training to be useful to a lord, I feel my heart constrict: Though I backed away from Annie in horror at the mention of drachthanasia, I hear it differently now.

I hear Griff's words as the desperate hope of a people who have suffered for generation upon generation at the hands of the dragonborn.

And then the next thing he says makes sorrow bloom in my chest.

"I'm going to spare Delo sur Gephyra. He's—not like them. More like you."

He's refastening my flamesuit, his eyes fixed on it.

Delo I remember as unfailingly kind, unusually thoughtful, and reluctant in the face of violence. When the others teased Laertes for being passed over, he stopped them.

I straighten where I sit, fighting the round of dizziness that accompanies the sudden motion, the pain that redoubles in my shoulder. It's suddenly the most important thing in the world that Gareson understand what I'm about to say.

"Griff, you will be unleashing something you can't control. It may not be possible to *choose*. Even Atreus admits that Palace Day got out of hand. You need to be prepared for that."

Gareson shakes his head. His hands, red with my blood, turn to fists. He reaches behind him, fingers clicking to his great stormscourge, who comes to his side and crouches to mounting height.

"I'll control it."

There's an edge to his voice that brooks no arguing.

And is there a point in making him doubt himself, now? This is what he has to do.

Just as I had to kill Julia.

Gareson has one boot in the stirrup, about to hoist himself onto his dragon, when he turns back to me. "Does Antigone have the poison yet? Will she have it by our next meeting?"

Exhaustion hits me in a wave. A toll from blood loss, maybe. Or from the realization of what is needed. I slide to my feet, bracing my back against the brick. "When do you meet next?"

"At the end of the week. In the new year."

"I'll make sure she does."

ANNIE

Until I face Ixion today, I've never known what it is to hate someone with such a rage that I wish they could be wiped from the face of the earth. To wish they were incinerated.

This is the bastard who took Duck from me.

I'm not aware of the moment when my fury becomes Aela's; when we cease to be two and become one. I'm aware only of a desire, bigger than me, like a fire burning through my body, to consume this boy and let him burn. Ixion sur Niter's flight pattern is erratic, but not so much that we can't anticipate them, and for every attempt they make to shake us, we only follow tighter. Lost in a cloud's seamless white, there is nothing but Ixion and Niter and Aela and me.

Niter slams against Aela and doesn't let go. Aela struggles to free herself, but he's too big, his claws piercing deep and holding fast. She begins to bite instead. I know the name of Ixion's dragon through Griff, saw the scars of Niter's fangs along Griff's arms, and now Aela gnashes her own fangs against Niter with equal vengeance.

"What's the matter, Antigone, does your little peasant dragon have trouble sparking?"

We ignore him. We'll save our fire for when we need it. It's what we're good at.

And in the meantime we'll shred them with our teeth.

I cling to Aela's saddle in the whiteness, hardly knowing when we're sideways, upside down, sideways again as she struggles to free herself from Niter and we rise and fall with their erratically beating wings.

But then, as suddenly as it began, the cloud ends.

The world fills in around us. And I realize that in our mad tussle, we've allowed ourselves to be pushed south. We're no longer over the Ferrish Plain. The city spreads directly below us.

And so does the aerial battle. The other sparring riders have been blown back, just as I was. The cannons on Pytho's Keep are too shrouded in fog to provide coverage, but the ones on

And I realize that the one time I've ever seen Ixion sur Niter go in for the kill, it wasn't with fire at all. It was with fangs, biting through Duck's girth.

Aela isn't the one who has trouble sparking: Niter does.

How has Griff never mentioned this before?

Because Griff might not even have noticed. In training and in tournaments, sparked dragons spar doused.

Aela can smell Niter's fear. I can smell it.

And we can spark just fine.

Aela twists free, finally, of Niter's talons, launches from his grasp, and beats the air to right herself. She inhales—

Ixion lets out a rasping laugh.

"Look down."

I spare a glance and freeze.

Callipolis is on fire.

Fires are sprouting in the Manufacturing District. Southside. Scholars Row—

The Pythians broke our line. Even now their muzzled riders hold off mine, providing coverage while their stormscourges descend. Callipolan riders sound distress calls on their horns, tinnily muffled this high above, but the reserves are already engaged, with no more to come. Cannons are barraging from the Aurelian Walls, but for every Pythian they deter, another descends—

I held off Ixion, but that wasn't enough.

Not all of the granary sites they targeted still contain grain—much of it was moved in the night—but the fires are spreading. Catching on neighboring thatch and wooden frames, catching on homes.

Even if grain was saved, lives won't be.

And in my frozen moment of hesitation, I lose my opening. Griff sur Sparker fills our vision, wings fanning out on either side like great black sails. Protecting Ixion sur Niter from our blast.

They must have broken free of Lee.

"Where were you?" Ixion shouts.

Griff's voice comes out muffled. "Spending quality time with the traitor, my lord!"

Aela rams Sparker's side with a squawk of indignation: On the dunes, they're friendly. But Sparker doesn't budge. He forms a wall between us and Niter that Aela works against with rising frustration.

"You finish him?" Ixion asks.

"No, but I left him a little the uglier for you, sire!"

So Lee is decommissioned, *wounded*—?

Ixion barks a laugh. He lifts the bugle to his lips and sounds it. Below us, the Pythian fleet begins to disengage. Below them, the fires spread.

"You know why I'm calling my riders off, Antigone?" he calls. "When I make my return along the Triumphal Way, I want Callipolans to be alive to kneel for it."

My vision is blurring behind my visor, fogging as my eyes grow wet with fury.

"I'll kill you."

I've never said that before. Not when Leon Stormscourge torched my home with my family in it, not when bullies held me down, not when Aela rose to goads in the arena. I've never said it before, but this one time I say it, it's a vow.

Griff stiffens in the saddle, and Sparker's tentlike wings falter. Ixion only laughs.

"Looks like your peasants need you," he says. "Good luck feeding them."

He yanks on Niter's reins, then sounds his bugle again. His fleet is rising now, burrowing into the cloud cover one by one and vanishing. Ixion and Griff last of all.

"Until next time," Griff mutters.

He's gone before I realize he means it as a coded reminder.

Aela and I are left looking down over the blazesites spreading in my city like cancers.

Lee sur Pallor finds us moments later, emerging from the cloud cover with one shoulder hunched and Pallor rasping for breath. He shoves up his visor with a glance after the retreating Pythian fleet and then looks back at me. Streaks of sweat run down his soot-covered face, and his armor is stained on the shoulder with what might be blood, but he sits secure enough in the saddle.

I let out a hitching breath. Lee, at least, is fine. Or managing for now.

"Orders, Commander?" he calls.

I'm too shaken to dwell on the strangeness of Lee sur Pallor, Leon's son, asking me for orders. But the sound of my title brings me to my senses: *Commander*. As my wingrider, as my Alternus, he's offering to defend the city while I take a squadron into those clouds after Ixion, and so badly do I want it that for a moment Aela stirs beneath me at the thought of Ixion *dead*.

But I have a responsibility for more than my own vendetta. Souls are dying below. Pursuing the Pythians would take riders from a response team that the blazesites now need, and pursuing them into clouds like these would be a fool's errand. I look from the seamless stratus above, to the city burning below, and make the choice. Aela strains to pursue, but I tighten my grip on the reins, turning us back to earth.

Another day. Another day, we'll finish him.

"Form a perimeter," I tell Lee, and sound the summons to riders for extraction.

GRIFF

The burns left by Leo Stormscourge's dragon begin to wear me down as we make our way back to New Pythos. That little white aurelian might not look like much, but his fire packs a punch. As we descend into Sailor's Folly and pass the first clan-karsts, I have a moment of wondering if the pain has made me hallucinate: A dragon the size of a whale, with wings like sails, is perched on Thornrose Karst.

A goliathan. From Bassilea. Her wings, when they beat the air, create their own winds.

I've only ever seen them in tapestries.

Along the ramparts, alongside the banners of the Greatlord and the Triarchy, the crest of the Bassilean whale-fin flutters. Sparker lands heavily, clumsy with exhaustion, on the citadel balustrades, and I slice my bootstraps with fumbling fingers. It takes me a moment to notice the attendants flurrying around us. One of them tells Ixion: *She's here.*

And then trumpets begin to sound, and all around us, dragonborn whom I've never seen make obeisance in their life drop to their knees.

Stiffly, I lower to mine.

I hear her voice from the other side of Sparker's drooping wings. A guttural accent on her Dragontongue unlike any I've ever heard before.

"Welcome back, Lord Ixion."

Freyda.

"Your Highness. What a pleasant surprise. You . . . anticipated my invitation."

"I thought it might be time. And this—this must be one of these squires that I've heard so much about."

I keep my eyes trained on the ground, but in my peripheral vision, a floor-length fur mantle, snow white, flows across the stones and stops in front of me and Sparker. His tail trailing the ground, his chest heaving, Sparker aches for his lair so badly I can feel it.

"Look at me, serf."

I lift my head a fraction. Freyda has fair skin, delicate features, silken brown hair pulled into a long braid down her back. She is perhaps a year or two older than Ixion and I, and her round face conveys a compassion, her heavy-lashed eyes a curiosity, that's at odds with her cool tone.

Behind her, the goliathan's wings blot the horizon.

"In my country," she says, "slaves would never be allowed to ride a dragon."

26

—

FLAMEFALL

ANNIE

The one and only time our fleet ever performed extractions before today—Starved Rock, this fall—it was only a handful of villagers from a sparsely populated island. I was not authorized to go; Lee made the call that my history, the fact that the last time I saw a blazesite, I was a child being forced to watch, made me unfit to perform an extraction.

But today, I have no superior officer to exempt me from duty.

Blazesite response teams are already establishing a perimeter to contain the fires. Scholars Row's wide avenues and stonemasonry are the least damaged, the fires petering out; Highmarket already has hoses pumping water from the nearest banks of the Fer; but the Manufacturing District's fire has spread to Cheapside. And Cheapside, with its thatched roofs and narrow streets, is ablaze. Looking down on this city from above, I watch the pattern of the fires imitate the maps of poverty I've seen on rounds in the ministry for as long as I can remember. Poor neighborhoods, class-iron neighborhoods, in most vivid red.

As I circle closer, I realize that the feeling in my stomach, the heaving, is nausea.

I force the rising memories from my head. Around me, riders are pairing off to begin extractions. Lee joins Cor sur Maurana on the far side of Highmarket; Lotus and Rock are already taking turns diving in and out of the blaze in the Manufacturing District. Power sur Eater comes to my wing, the great breadth of his storm-scourge's wingspan blocking sight of the fires over Cheapside.

"You could sit this one out," he says.

At his suggestion, my flagging resolve hardens.

To hell with their pity.

"Spot for me."

Without another look at him, I dive.

Aela and I descend into a Cheapside two-story residential unit whose roof is lost to flames. We land on the shuddering second floor. The heat is all-engulfing and the flames fill my vision. For a moment a single thought overwhelms me as I cling to Aela's back and struggle to breathe: *This is how they died.*

No. I am not that child today. Today, I'm the one with the dragon. And I'll be using it to get the victims *out.*

I dismount and force a breath into my bugle, sounding through the smoke. All I can hear is crackling in answer—but then Aela cocks her head, her eyes focusing, and I follow her gaze—or perhaps it is with her vision that I see now, because the thoughts of my father and brothers and sisters have flooded into a spillover so strong, I am one with her.

I follow her gaze, stumbling through the fire, and find the huddled figures in the corner of the shaking floor. They're unconscious. I lift the child into my arms, hoist the woman's arm over my shoulder, and heave. Aela's silhouette bursts through the flames and she lowers onto her belly for me to drape the woman over her back. I clamber on, clutching the child and clinging lopsidedly to Aela's saddle, then hold us steady as she kicks, with full force, from the ground, her wings beating the air to lift her burden.

We land on the street outside the perimeter of the flames, where blazesite response teams wait with pumps and water and medics. I surrender the woman and child into the waiting arms of the medics and then kick back off into the air without waiting to hear if they are alive or dead.

I'll do this without looking back, or I won't be able to do it at all.

Back above the blazesite, Power shouts: "You all right?"

"I'm fine. Go."

I circle with Aela above the blazesite while he and Eater go in, and by the time it's my turn again, the heat of the fire has dried my tears. We continue, in and out of the burning buildings, as the sun and the fires go down.

"Annie," Power finally says, "let's take a break."

"We need to keep looking—"

"The fires are down, they're opening the bunkers. You need to hydrate."

We land on the riverbank, choked with ash. In this part of the city, downriver from the Manufacturing District, it's clogged with waste even on a good day, its muddy banks deserted. I pull off my helmet and splash soot-blackened water over my face. Behind us, the smoldering blazesite smokes into the dusk sky. I had planned, after this intermission, to get back into the air immediately, but now that I'm on the ground, I find my knees giving out beneath me. I sink to a seat in the mud, place my head between my knees, and begin to sob.

"Here."

Power has pressed his mostly empty canteen into my hand, and I drain it before thinking to protest. But I can't stop crying.

"Annie. Look at me."

His glove grips my shoulder, so tightly that I feel its weight.

"We just saved lives."

I drag my palms, one after another, across my face.

He's right. I wasn't the stick today. I wasn't firing on protesters or denying ration cards to those who wanted them. I was protecting my people.

Just like I believed, as a child when I took those vows, that I would.

The thought feels like a cool breeze, fresh as the sea, blowing through my heart and my head and my soul. And though perhaps it shouldn't, it helps prepare me for what comes next.

Rock, landing in front of us on his stormscourge, his visor lifted, his face ashen.

"Annie," he says. "The bunkers—"

And then his voice breaks.

LEE

We don't understand at first when we find it.

Such has been my singularity of purpose since parting with Griff on Pytho's Keep that even as Cor and I stand in the middle of the scene, looking around us at the evidence, I don't see it for what it is.

We're in the ruins of Highmarket, in the heart of its dying blazesite, in a clearing at the center of which is a sunken entrance to an underground compound that ventilates through slats in the cobblestones. A public bunker. And around us is a sea of motionless black ash that forms, here and there, shapes barely recognizable as—

Bodies.

Bodies everywhere.

Through the saturated filter of my visor I can smell charred flesh.

Cor has begun to shake so badly that his legs wobble. Maurana, perched with Pallor on a surviving main frame on the edge of the flare, begins to snort and kick at her perch. "Why aren't they . . . ?"

Why aren't they safe, alive, inside this bunker? I push past him and climb down the sloping entrance to the closed wrought-iron door.

I hammer on it, the metal ringing like a drum.

"Extraction, open up!"

There's silence on the other side. Behind me Cor lets out a hissing breath.

"Lee, they're class-irons."

I spin around. "What?"

"The dead—they all have iron wristbands."

The metal door creaks, a bolt turning inside, and I turn back to it as it opens. I find myself face-to-face with several members of the city guard. Behind them, civilians, faces hidden in shadow. Someone inside whispers, *That's Lee sur Pallor!* Instead of stepping aside to make way for their exit, I push between the guards and step into the darkness.

"Show me your wristbands. Everyone."

A glint of wrists raised, all glowing enough in the dim light for me to know: gold, bronze, and—in the case of the city guard—silver.

The bunker's not close to full.

"Get out," I tell the civilians.

They begin to trickle past. One of them brushes fingers on my armor, and I cast a brief glance at her before realizing that I know her: Mrs. Sutter, Cor's mother. I was in her house this morning. It's nearby, only a few blocks away; she must have sheltered here with her family, her husband and Greg on one side, Merina on the other. A Bronze family safe from the fire—

But then I realize Ana, who tested Iron, is not with them.

Mrs. Sutter's eyes are wild and bloodshot as her gaze flits from me to the guards. Mr. Sutter, beside her, is slack-jawed, his gaze unseeing as he holds Greg's hand.

"Bring us justice, Lee—" Mrs. Sutter whispers.

The Sutter family passes, and I look back at the Silvers whose job it was to oversee this bunker, members of the Highmarket garrison of the city guard, who have been standing at attention since I've arrived. Fists raised in the Revolutionary salute, hands on the hilts of their sabers.

It's good Pallor is outside, not with me, because if my fury were able to spill into him in this moment, these soldiers would be dead.

"Which of you is in charge?"

One of them steps forward, only a few years older than me, a spotty mustache unshaven. "Sir."

"Why didn't you let those Irons into this bunker?"

But before he can answer, howling cuts the air.

Through the open door, from the square outside. Once it begins, it doesn't stop. Low, anguished—and unmistakable.

Because I held that same person while he made that same noise, only weeks ago.

Cor, crying his sister's name like he wants the sky to crack open and answer him.

Ana.

The guard swallows, sweat beading on his pimply forehead. His fingers clutch the hilt of his saber.

"We were following orders."

ANNIE

On the choked riverbank, standing in the mud beside Power, Rock presses an iron wristband into my palm. Ash peels from it in flakes. He makes his report, weeping as his thick hands cover his face, pulling at fair hair.

Megara was right about the bunkers. Not enough had yet been completed to meet the needs of the city's population. The Callipolan ministry dealt with this shortage in its signature way: prioritizing certain lives over others, based on their worth to the state. In other words, based on their metals test.

The way this looked seems to have varied, depending on the neighborhood, the bunker, the particular garrison in charge of enforcing. In the more affluent neighborhoods like Scholars Row and the Janiculum Hill, servants were allowed into the bunkers last if they were allowed in at all. In middle-class neighborhoods like Highmarket and Southside, citizens were asked to form separate queues based on their wristband and admitted in order of priority. In the poorest neighborhoods, Cheapside and the Manufacturing District, the greatest problem was that there weren't enough bunkers in the first place.

The segregated queues in the middle neighborhoods were where things turned ugliest. Irons and even Bronzes were turned aside, forced to wait while Golds were let in as the fires began to rain down; and sometimes, if the soldiers panicked, they were not let in at all. In the most horrific cases, bunkers were found with room to spare and lower class-metals dead outside.

"The guard were asking to see wristbands," Rock says, his highland brogue returning as he loses control, "and they're all trained to show them, from rationing distribution, so of course they just . . ."

I stare down at the iron wristband in my palm.

"I don't know why I had to take it. I just kept thinking I wanted—evidence."

I hear what he isn't saying because I'm thinking it, too. *Evidence*, in case this regime tries to hide these atrocities. As we know it hides, and manipulates, information as a matter of course. We've known it for as long as we've done rounds with the Ministry of Propaganda, but only understood the full repercussions today: when Megara told me about a massacre I'd never heard of, committed by the regime I serve. And now this.

"Where are the others?"

Rock wipes his eyes, streaking his face with still more ash. "Lotus went with Cor, he said they were going to—take the Vault? They're working with the Passi, Annie. Lee, too, I think."

"I know."

But I no longer care.

I've been lost in details. Threads of merit versus fault, of whether the Passi are heroes or terrorists for stealing grain and leaking secrets. But none of that matters compared with this.

In the end, on the most fundamental point, the Passi are right. *This* is the crime that matters.

We are all equally deserving.

How is it only now, faced with this, that I understand?

LEE

Cor, his mother, his father, and his brother and sister are huddled together outside the bunker, gathered around a figure that Mr. Sutter leans over to embrace and Mrs. Sutter turns her younger children's faces from. Cor holds himself, rocking back and forward, as he weeps.

It feels obscene to approach them in this grief.

But when I touch Cor's shoulder, he rises to his feet. His blotched face contorts, the words coming out in gulps. "They separated them. Those bastards, they told her to wait—"

I seize his shoulders. There are two ways to survive this kind of anguish: with waiting or with action. And if I guess right, Cor and I both want the latter.

"The Vault, Cor."

Cor's bloodshot eyes widen.

"We take it, free Megara, take control of the *People's Paper.* And we tell the whole world what happened today."

Our dragons have landed on either side of us, and a dim part of me registers that we've both spilled over, that we're speaking through thick water, as if we were drunk. Pallor and Maurana are wild with our fury.

"Yes," Cor says. *"Yes."*

I reach for Pallor's reins, my breaths merged with his snorts of smoke.

"Find Lotus," I tell him. "I'll be there soon."

"Where are you—"

"There's something I have to do first."

Something I should have done months ago.

ANNIE

I leave Power and Rock on the riverbank, instructing them to meet me back at the Cloister as soon as they're finished with extractions and to tell the other Guardians they find.

The air above the city is thick and gray with smoke, and the mask inside my helmet so saturated that my coughing continues even with it lowered. When Aela and I reach the Inner Palace, we descend into the Firemouth and circle, peering through windows, until I spot the potted plants of Miranda Hane.

The windows of the Minister of Propaganda are golden archways of light. Aela and I land on the balcony that once was a lord's dragon perch and hammer on her door. When it isn't answered, Aela fires. I feel her fire like it is my own.

The glass of the door buckles. I slam a fist through, shattering it, and reach inside for the handle. I let myself into her office just as Miranda herself bursts in from the corridor.

"Antigone, what—"

"Close the door."

Miranda's wide eyes flick past me to the dragon silhouetted on the perch outside her office, and then reaches behind her to pull her office door shut. Dragonlords built these perches to summon with convenience from the Firemouth, a design that I'm exploiting today for the first time.

I'm standing on Hane's side of the desk, but I don't offer to change sides. Instead, I place the soot-covered iron wristband on it, between us. Miranda looks down at it, then back at me.

"Did you know the city guard was ordered to fill the bunkers based on class-metal?"

Miranda exhales slowly. Then eases herself forward, to the chair I've so often occupied myself, and lowers herself into it.

"I did not," she whispers.

"I don't believe you."

Miranda rubs her eyes, and I realize that they are reddening and wet. "I did not, though it does not surprise me. We were running behind on bunker construction, and the Golds were nervous. How many were turned away—"

"Too many."

She leans forward and places her head in her hands.

"What about the Southside Massacre?" I ask.

Miranda laughs softly into her lap.

"You're on quite the muckraking tear today, Antigone," she murmurs. "Yes. That is something I know about. The city guard was ordered to restore order and did so with excess fervor. By the time we called a ceasefire, it was too late."

"And then you helped cover it up?"

Miranda speaks like she has a head cold. "I'm the Minister of Propaganda. I . . . did what it took."

The First Protector's favorite expression. The job of Guardians.

Since getting to know her, I have thought of Miranda Hane as an uneasy ally, despite the department she leads. She has been someone whom I can trust as much as anyone, and more than many of the ministry officials working for Atreus.

She can have one chance to explain herself.

"Why?"

"Oh, Annie . . . You must understand."

Miranda lifts her head from her hands, her eyes bright. As if pierced by what she is remembering.

"In the beginning, it was glorious. I was their Megara."

Her voice flattens, deadens, and her eyes close.

"But keeping power is so much more difficult than gaining it. You have to make sacrifices. You keep sacrificing until you realize the thing you've sacrificed is yourself."

Miranda's face is bathed in gold from the setting sun, illuminating the lines that splinter from her eyes and mouth.

She looks so sad that I almost could pity her.

Except for the iron wristband of a citizen we failed, heavy in my hand. Except that this was the only thing that mattered, that we be better than *them*, and we weren't.

The metals test wasn't an answer to the dragonlord's dehumanization of us. It's just another form of it. And I've been in denial because it was a system that benefited *me*.

I'm done being complicit.

"Was it worth it?" I demand. "Sacrificing yourself? Doing what it takes?"

It feels so good to sneer those words. I can feel Aela on the balcony behind me, tensed with my tension, full of the desire to fire.

A sad smile curves Miranda's mouth, as if my fury makes her proud.

"For me," she says, "it was."

She reaches out a hand to touch the iron wristband between us. Ash comes away on her fingers. She lifts them to study in the golden light. Then her gaze passes to me.

"But you could be better."

My eyes prickle. Right now, that already feels too late.

"How?"

Miranda's mouth sets into a strange, sad smile. "Stop doing what it takes. Start asking yourself *what's needed*."

She points to the window, and I turn. A strip of sky is visible, blue in the wake of the sunset, with a single fresh column of smoke rising thick and fast from the other side of the Firemouth.

The First Protector's house has been set on fire.

"Starting with that," Hane says.

LEE

The Coach House is one of the few buildings in the Palace complex made of wood. It catches easily. I stand beside Pallor, watching the flames spread, smelling the sulfur of his fire, feeling the heat against my face and flamesuit. Watching glass buckle, paint peel, logs blacken.

Pallor lifts back his head and roars his flames into the smoke-filled sky.

I watch the front door, waiting for it to burst open. Waiting for him.

This has needed doing since I returned from killing Julia. Forget high ideals and lofty speeches, revenge delivered over toasts of sparkling wine. This man deserves the justice of a dragon's punishment.

"Come out, you bastard!"

A cool voice speaks behind me.

"It would be more like Leon if you locked the door."

Atreus Athanatos watches his house burn from the opposite side of his garden wall.

In two bounds, Pallor has seized him. His fangs hook on the neck of Atreus's tunic, dragging him over the wall and slamming him to the ground. Atreus lets out a huff as the air is knocked out of him. Pallor leans forward, letting out a long slow hiss that burns.

"My father is not the only one who has left burning peasants to their fates," I say.

Atreus doesn't move, matching the gaze of my dragon without flinching. But I can smell what Pallor smells: fear.

It smells good.

And then I start saying the words that have been pent up since Julia.

"My whole life, I told myself you were better. That this was better. That the rest of it didn't matter, not that you had them killed, not that I escaped, not even that you would have had me killed, too"—my voice shakes like it has hit an edge—"but in the end I *was* wasting my time because you are no better. This is no better. The rich still get fat and the poor still burn—the difference is you have the gall to say it's just!"

Atreus lets out a wheezing laugh, his chest bucking against Pallor's maw.

"Someone was always going to die needlessly. You begrudge me making an effort to choose the best to survive?"

Pallor hisses again, and Atreus inhales from pain. My answer is so loud it echoes in the courtyard, over the crackling flames. "The only people who deserved to die today were the men standing at the doors of our bunkers keeping others *out*."

Atreus reaches up, lays a bare hand on Pallor's snout. Pallor's nostrils flare.

"Oh, Lee," he says. "You have always had a too-great heart. It does your considerable intellect a disservice."

I can feel his hand on us. Its tenderness. Like a father's. A year ago, I would have wanted it.

Now, I'm repulsed.

The Protector's Guard is materializing on the edges of the courtyard, forming a line around the Coach House garden. Crossbows turned on me, on Pallor. Atreus lifts a hand, telling them to hold. And then he speaks to me in Dragontongue.

"Do you think this is the first time I've been flattened by a dragon, or had to explain myself to an enraged lord? Do it, Lee. Become what I feared you would from the moment I knew who you were."

For a moment the old fear stops me where I stand, even though I know he is deliberately stoking it.

In the light of the Coach House burning, a second dragon lands in the Protector's yard. Annie slides to the ground beside Aela, her tearstained face dried, her eyes only on me.

I look at her, and wait for her to stop me.

Her eyes are like stars in her face. She lifts her chin.

My choice.

And it's her eyes on me that give me the clarity to see this fear, which has haunted me for as long as I can remember, for what it is.

Bullshit.

I'm not like my father. I've never been like my father. And I won't become like this man either.

"Your vision of justice is a perversion," I tell Atreus, in Dragontongue. "The better future you promised this city is a lie. You have failed. You no longer deserve the seat you have usurped."

I close my fist, and Pallor lifts his head. Atreus's chest begins to heave.

"I will take this city from you," I tell the man on the dirt at my feet, "but not as a usurper nor as an avenging heir."

The sky is open, and though I still stand on the ground, I feel I'm already on a dragon's back.

"I will take it out from under you as you name me your successor from your knees because your people want it and your head. Then I will let death be a mercy to you, just as it was for my father."

The fire between us is reflected in Annie's eyes as she nods at me.

I am on Pallor's back by the time Athanatos has rolled onto all fours.

"We're taking the Vault," I tell Annie.

Annie says, "Good."

"Are you coming?"

Annie looks from me, to the Protector at our feet, to the city spread beyond us. And then she shakes her head.

"I think . . . I'm needed here," she says.

"Here?"

"Here," she repeats.

We're supposed to do this together, I nearly say.

But she looks so full of purpose, her shoulders squared, the wind in her auburn hair and the dragon at her side, as if she has found in this moment exactly what is necessary as I have.

Sadness pierces me like a cloud across a blinding sun.

But I am too ready for forward motion to question anyone lingering behind.

In the dusk's new darkness, Pallor and I make our way through the smoking sky, to the Manufacturing District, where the Vault rises from the center of a still-smoking blazesite.

From its roof, the green banner of the Passi already flies, and two dragons perch silhouetted in the dusk. Around it, a barricade is being built.

27

WHAT'S NEEDED

ANNIE

I have a moment, watching Lee sur Pallor's wings fade on the horizon, when I consider mounting Aela and following him. But for reasons I'm not able to articulate, I know that if Miranda is right, and my calling lies in doing not what it takes, but what's needed, then right now I am needed here. On this side of the Palace wall.

I go to Atreus. He is shaking, gasping, the terror of a dragon's punishment overwhelming him. It is unnerving to watch the Protector, who is usually so cool and composed, double over hyperventilating.

"Are you all right, sir?"

He seizes my shoulder for support and then looks up at me. Piercing eyes widen, as if he only now realizes what it means that I've just helped him to his feet.

"Antigone?"

I don't ask what he's surprised by. I steer him into the nearest entrance of the Inner Palace, where the captain of his guard sits the Protector down on a bench beside the stairwell. I hand the guard my spare canister of coolant.

"Good dragons above—"

General Holmes bursts through the doorway, purple in the face. "What the *hell* was that?"

"You missed the fun, Amos," Atreus murmurs as the captain begins to apply coolant to his shirtfront.

"There's fun happening all over this city." Holmes waves a piece of paper: a message from the city guard. "The Vault's been seized by the Passi. With the help of a few rogue Guardians. Cor sur Maurana and Lotus sur Iustus."

"Add Lee sur Pallor to that list," Atreus grunts.

Holmes swears. "I'll send Antigone out with the others to retake it, but really amid everything else going on—"

He doesn't hear me when I speak. I have to say it twice. Finally, he looks at me like he's remembering I'm there. "I'm sorry?"

"I'm not retaking the Vault."

Holmes just stares at me. Atreus, whose head is tilted back to the ceiling while his captain pats on coolant, lets out a single laugh.

"That's an order," Holmes says. "You can't *refuse* an order."

"I just did."

Holmes's purple face grows, if possible, purpler.

"Fine. You're demoted. We'll send whatever Guardian is up to your job after them—"

"That Guardian will have to go through me. On the barricade. Where I will join Lee and Cor if my services are no longer needed here."

Holmes stares at me. And then he explodes so loudly that the captain of the guard jumps.

"This is preposterous. First Lee sur Pallor, now you? Your job is to *follow orders*. I'll grant that's never been your strong suit—"

"My job is to *think*. My job is to guide this city to justice. Sir."

In the garden outside, Aela roars. Holmes is so startled by my equal outburst that his mouth, which was open, closes. A noise comes from Atreus, and as I turn to look at him, I realize that he's chuckling.

"Do not hold Antigone's impertinence against her. She is quoting me."

Atreus pauses, and our eyes meet.

"You've seen how the Passi report, Antigone. You would have them in control of the state's newspaper?"

I look between these men and wonder which of them conceived of the order to stage bunker admission by class-metal, and which of them approved it.

"If the *People's Paper* wanted to publicize the atrocities our soldiers committed today, would you let it?"

Holmes doesn't even balk at the word *atrocities*. "Of course not," he snaps. "That would be destabilizing."

I lift my chin, eyes not leaving Atreus's face, as Holmes's answer confirms mine.

"That's what I thought."

I leave that stairwell with the Firstrider's badge still on my chest.

My limbs are aching from tiredness as I make my way back to the Cloister in the early evening. Wondering whom I'll find. Who did not join Lee and Cor on the barricade. Who came back to receive my orders.

They all did.

The room is dark save for the fire on their faces, turned toward me. Everyone who returned from the air battle well enough for duty. Rock and his lowborn friends; Power and Darius with their usual patrician posse. Deirdre and Alexa, side by side.

And Crissa.

"You're here?" I ask, in surprise.

I had thought that Crissa would be with Cor and Lee and Lotus. She sits in a chair by the fire, an arm on each armrest, and flicks a curtain of gold hair as her lips purse.

"Vigilantism isn't really my style."

Rock, beside her grim-faced, nods. "Where you go, I go, Commander."

He says it easily, but I know it can't have been: Lotus isn't among us, and he was Rock's closest friend.

"So what's the plan?" Power asks.

A lump has risen in my throat.

There are so few of us, it doesn't make sense to go to the oration room. I can debrief them here. I remain standing, a last push of adrenaline flooding my tired legs with strength. There was a time, a few months ago, when I was skittish about delivering a speech to my peers. But right now, I can't even imagine that.

"Today there is blood on this regime's hands."

There are no looks of surprise, only grim-faced nods. My riders were at the blazesites. They saw and heard what happened.

"But the regime is about to be held responsible. *We're* about to be held responsible. The *People's Paper* and the Vault are now controlled by the Passi, aided by Lee sur Pallor and Cor. The paper they run tomorrow will call for change and lead to riots. The kind of riots that the city guard has a history of silencing with violence."

I lift one hand and make it into a fist.

"I don't want another Palace Day; I don't want the Palace overrun. But I want this regime to be forced to the negotiating table. I want it to answer for what it's done."

I place a flat palm against my fist like a shield.

"Until that happens, our job will be to keep Callipolan citizens safe."

LEE

The Passi base their operations out of the newsroom of the *People's Paper*, on the second floor of the Vault. The desks of its old employees have been cleared, their papers dumped unceremoniously on the floor; every single lamp around the room has been lit; and as the night wears on, the room fills. I find Megara, crouched on a bench to the side of the room with her arm around Cor, her shorn head bent over his, murmuring to him in Damian. She looks up at my approach.

"I reek," she warns me.

I take a seat beside them. "So do I. How was prison?"

She lets out a hollow laugh. Her fingers, black under the nails, rub small circles into Cor's neck, above the collar of his cuirass. His head hangs, downturned, like he has lost the will to lift it.

I'm still in armor, suddenly aching to remove it, but I reach for Cor's first. He barely responds when I touch him, unhooking the buckles binding his cuirass, loosening it bit by bit. Megara watches for a moment, then imitates with careful fingers on his other side. Plate by plate, we unfasten his armor and deposit it in a pile beside us while Cor stares down at his lap.

There is only one thing he can be thinking about. I hesitate, then offer the consolation that as a child I remember wishing I could tell myself.

"It would have been fast, Cor. She suffered very little pain."

His face collapses.

Megara takes him into her arms again, burying her face in his side.

I remove my own armor last. The energy that built inside me, facing down Atreus, is fading fast. Every plate weighs twice as much as it should. When I'm done, I grip Cor's shaking shoulder and lean my head back against the wall behind us. My eyes close.

When they open, I'm staring up at Richard Tyndale in a prison smock. He smells of sewer like Megara.

"My students," he says, smiling down at the three of us together.

I sit frozen: The last time I saw him, he was attempting to get me to contact my family in New Pythos. And then Annie had him arrested. All the ways he looks the worse for wear since I last saw him—gaunt, sallow, shaven nearly bald—are our fault.

But he isn't looking at me. "Megara. You did it."

Megara launches to her feet at the sight of her advisor. "Professor!"

She throws her arms around him. He grips her with one ema- ciated arm, then takes a step back and indicates her shorn head and his own. "We match."

Megara bursts into laughter, and it turns to tears.

We leave Cor sleeping on the bench when Val Lazare calls our first meeting. Inside the glass-walled office that previously belonged to the editor in chief of the *People's Paper*, he begins to review our position and our numbers along with Richard Tyndale and the Teirans, who arrived all together with Lotus carrying suitcases. Poetry professor and poet laureate reunite with the chumminess of old schoolmates, which, I suspect, they are. "Did they not feed you, the bastards?" Lo Teiran demands, squeezing Tyndale's scrawny arm, and Tyndale shouts back, "You should have been in there with me, you sly dog!"

When Lazare's meeting begins, I have it confirmed for the first time that Lotus, Cor, and I are the only Guardians who have joined the Passi operation.

"The others must have stayed with Annie."

"With Annie?" Lotus repeats, confused.

Haltingly, suddenly much less sure of the decision than I was when I stood in front of the burning Coach House making it, I describe my confrontation with Atreus for the first time, and my parting with Antigone sur Aela.

Val Lazare grunts. "Would have been easier to kill him, boy."

He's right, and the reasons I had not to do it seem stupider now that I'm several miles away in a stronghold fortified by three dragons and a lot of poorly armed members of the Passi. I'm surprised when Richard Tyndale comes to my defense.

"Not if we're after legitimacy," he says. "But Antigone staying could be a problem."

"Why?" I ask.

"Because it's a power grab," Lo Teiran says, nodding at Tyndale. "She'll be next in line for succession if we're attempting to force Athanatos's resignation."

"She didn't stay at the Palace as a *power grab*," I scoff.

The idea is so ludicrous I don't know how to begin explaining. Even if I didn't fully understand why she stayed with Atreus, I know as I breathe that it wasn't for any reason as crude as ambition.

Richard Tyndale and Lo Teiran exchange a glance; Lazare speaks first.

"The people need one person to turn to as they turn away from Atreus," he says. "There can't be a rival candidate for succession, not if we want to avoid a civil war. There needs to be only one beacon and it needs to shine clearly. Do you understand who we intend that beacon to be?"

Lazare doesn't know about the promises I made to Atreus when I bore down on him today. I look through the glass at Cor, slumped with his family on the bench in the main office, numb with grief. His sister lost because our city, its leadership, failed her.

"Yes. I understand."

The time for doubting my own fitness to lead is over. Now is the time to step forward and use every gift my father left me. Voice and face and words, whatever it takes to free this city from Atreus.

"But Annie isn't what we're up against," I add. "If anything, she's most likely to be a sympathetic ear. She's not our opposition."

Megara, who has been watching me with her chin resting on her hand, speaks for the first time.

"Did Antigone tell you she paid me a visit, while I was imprisoned here?"

Tyndale shifts to look at her, a question in his gaze. When I shake my head, her smile is full of teeth. "Then maybe there are some things you don't know about her."

Foreboding chills me like a draft of old air.

Lo Teiran glances at the slit of a window as the midnight bell tolls. "We have six hours until sunrise. It's time we begin preparing tomorrow's news and planning protest routes. If you don't mind, Val, I'd like to start making assignments."

Tomorrow's paper will be delivered, for the first time in its history, from dragonback. We write into the early morning. With some misgiving, I rouse Cor to ask him if he wants to pen the main article: the exposé about what happened today. Cor's face hardens.

"Help me?"

I sit beside him, working through it, line by line, like we did as children over rhetoric assignments. Neither of us acknowledges the pauses that Cor must make as his throat closes, as the words stop, as the sentences he gropes for and gets out through gritted teeth make him weep. His hand shakes too badly, his tears blot too much ink, for him to hold the pen. So I hold it for him.

After I help Cor with his, I write my own. My flamesuit is pulled down to the waist, my shoulder and leg throbbing, but I no longer feel tired.

I feel alive. Alive and furious. As if with pen to paper here, on the edge of a second revolution, the Vault in our hands and dragons on our roof, these words have the power to reshape the world.

It's early morning by the time our stories are finished, and it takes the next few hours to set them in the great printer in the next room. Lo Teiran directs proceedings with the help of Megara, experienced from her internship with the *Gold Gazette*. When the first papers are rolled off, steaming, a cheer goes up. The new masthead reads:

THE PEOPLE'S PAPER: HENCEFORTH THE FREE PAPER OF CALLIPOLIS.

We pound up the stairs with bundles in our arms, onto the roofs where the dragons wait. We clamber onto their backs without bothering with armor, cheered on by the Passi crowding the rooftops, and launch into the night.

The papers scatter over the moonlit squares and avenues like falling leaves.

After that, the tiredness hits me like a wave. When we return to the roof, I don't even make it as far as the stairs. I unsaddle Pallor and slide to the ground beside him. A watch is stationed at intervals between the green banners of the Passi, but this early in the morning, their voices are hushed.

"I know. A rooftop again. You'll be back in your nest soon, Pal."

Pallor snorts, as if he sincerely doubts this. He curls into a circle that encloses me, twitches his wing, and folds it over me. His scales are hot, and when his wing lowers, the warmth builds like a tent. I stretch out on my side, cradling my throbbing shoulder, and stare up at the sliver of night sky peeking between his wing and his crest. For a moment the stars spin as though I were still flying.

Tomorrow, the Revolution's Son will become Lee sur Pallor, for all Callipolis to hear.

As I slip into sleep, and Pallor's thoughts slip into mine, I find them full of Aela.

And then I'm out.

When I wake, a line of sunlight is pouring through the slit of his wing.

Pallor folds his wing into his side as I stir, and I sit up, blinking the light from my eyes. The sun has risen. It's quiet on the roof of the Vault, but I know that beyond it, the city must be exploding with noise. Sunlight means the papers have been found. Means the protests will soon be starting. Means that outside, the Vault is being scouted by the city guard, and the Passi within are preparing to defend the barricade.

I'm still in my flamesuit. My arm is stiff below the wound, my leg aching. I'm so hungry I feel my own stomach like a cavity. But I'm not sure when the next meal is, so I reach for a copy of the *People's Paper* instead.

That's when I see what Megara has written.

ANNIE

My plan is to wait the protests out. Keep the city as well in order as possible while they run their course, and at the end, I, as a representative of legitimate law enforcement, will help broker a deal with Lee in the Passi's name.

I assume my plan aligns very closely with the Passi's plan, until I read their first paper.

Copies were dropped into the Palace courtyards in the early morning, before dawn, from dragonback. The Guardians who've remained read them together in the refectory over meager servings of porridge. For all my hunger, as I begin to read, I lose my appetite.

There are two articles above the fold. One, by Lee sur Pallor, demands Atreus's immediate resignation, an end to the class-metal system, and a reinstitution of the People's Assembly. It is authored by LEE SUR PALLOR, THE REVOLUTION'S SON.

The second, by Cor sur Maurana, describes how his sister died.

I hear myself inhale as if the air has been punched from my lungs.

Cor's workmanlike style is familiar from a thousand assignments read aloud in class: *My sister, Ana Sutter, was asked to wait outside a bunker because of a band of metal on her wrist. She never did well in school.*

Ana, who always was so kind to me, so matter-of-fact about her place in the world and mine—

The poor Sutter family, losing Duck, now *this*—

"Annie, what—?"

Crissa's voice. The room, which has faded, returns like liquid glass. The Guardians who sit at my table have turned to look at me.

398

As Crissa takes the paper from me and sees the headline, her hand moves to cover her mouth.

"Oh, Cor," she breathes. "Oh no."

Next to Crissa, Power lets out an expletive and spits out his tea.

He's checked the article after Cor's. When I turn the paper over, he attempts to cover it with his palm. I shove his hand aside. Below the fold, an article penned by Megara Roper is titled: ANTIGONE SUR AELA: UNFIT FOR OFFICE?

It's a character assassination.

I read it with numb detachment, vision still blurred from Cor's article, like I'm reading a description of someone else. She begins by describing my interrogation of her in the Vault. My own words flash at me from the page: *Do you know what it was like, to watch?* From there she goes on to describe my notoriously strict enforcement of collections, of ration distribution, and my willingness to fire on civilians, some of whose only crime was stealing grain. Richard Tyndale, the professor whom I reported, is asked to comment: "It is unfortunately common that victims of violence later show a proclivity toward violence themselves. One cannot help but wonder if Antigone sur Aela, who suffered such unimaginable trauma as a child, is damaged in such a way."

But Megara doesn't stop there. She also explores my rumored romantic liaison with Lee sur Pallor, my dragonlord's son—obliquely evoking the sordid history of Stormscourge lords and their serfs. That Lee *is* a dragonlord's son is mentioned to highlight the fact that Lee proved his loyalty to the Revolution in a duel to the death with kin. The paragraph ends by pointing out that I was promoted to Firstrider on Lee's recommendation.

Megara ends by insinuating that I am unstable, vicious, and ambitious enough to seek to use the current political situation to rise even higher.

I've skimmed the article with so little emotion that I'm surprised when I look up from it to find Rock cracking his knuckles and Crissa wiping her tears as her mouth sets with fury. "This is vile."

"It's the truth," I hear myself say.

Reading my crimes listed in a row feels like looking at worms wriggling on brown grass with the stone overturned. I did these things, and they were terrible. Was I any better than those guards, who followed the orders that resulted in Ana Sutter outside that bunker, her family within, when I fired on civilians despite their screams and told myself it was necessary? Those guards and I were all *doing what it took*.

"It's not true. You're not sleeping your way to the top," says Crissa.

That's what she's appalled by? I nearly laugh aloud.

"I impersonated Leon Stormscourge to get a name out of her. If this article plays dirty, so did I."

Even Crissa doesn't seem to have an answer to that.

"*Did* you sleep with him?" Power asks.

I start to shake my head when Crissa lays a hand on my arm. "That's none of our business."

Only when I hear the slight tightness in Crissa's voice do I recall her history with Lee and realize she's setting it aside in order to stand by me. I squeeze her hand and she squeezes back.

Power rolls his eyes to the ceiling and mutters something that sounds like *typical*.

Rock cracks his knuckles. "Crissa's right. This is slander. The Passi should be ashamed." The others are nodding, and I could hug all of them for their solidarity except for the sudden thought that makes me feel worst of all.

"Do you think Lee authorized this?"

A line forms between Crissa's brows. "What understanding did you two leave with, at the Coach House?"

"I don't . . ."

I don't know. I didn't explain to Lee why I chose to stay with Atreus rather than follow him to the barricade because the reason seemed so obvious: He needed me to run interference from the inside. But in retrospect my choice to stay could easily have been mistaken for something more sinister, more calculating or ambitious—

And with Cor mourning his sister and Lee on the opposite side of the barricade, I have no way to explain otherwise.

My eyes are burning, and I think Crissa realizes from how she squeezes my hand and lifts her chin.

"They are hurting. This *city* is hurting. Hurt people hurt people. We must hold our heads above it."

The protests begin later that morning. Not just in the People's Square. In every square, in every neighborhood, except for the Janiculum and Scholars Row, where protesters are barred from entry. Even outside the Aurelian Walls, the Callipolans seeking entry protest, too. We can hear the shouting from the Palace.

I feel the familiar clenching in my stomach, the steeling to go out and do my job, as I begin to suit up with the other Guardians to meet the mob. That's when the memo is delivered by a messenger who enters the armory at a run, clutching his side.

"For the Firstrider."

In the current climate, the ministry thinks it best for Antigone sur Aela to remain inside the Palace.

It is unsigned, its department unspecified, leaving me to wonder who sent it. Miranda Hane? General Holmes? The First Protector himself? Do Holmes and Atreus feel vindicated, to see that the same freedom I advocated for the press has been used against me?

Looking at the tight faces around me in the armory, I remember civilians screaming, and Megara's words describing my actions, and what Miranda said.

Stop doing what it takes. Start asking yourself what's needed.

I look down at the memo in my hand and crumple it.

To hell with Holmes and Atreus. The spite of the citizens I'm protecting won't be new; I've been accustoming myself to it for months. I can handle a little bit more.

I have a city to keep safe.

"We're dousing from now on," I tell the Guardians around me. "No sparked fire on the protesters. We're keeping eyes on civilians and city guard both."

Glances are fired around the room, one rider to another, pale faces shining with sweat. Darius starts to speak and I add: "Anyone who has a problem with that can stay behind."

I reach for Aela's saddle and my helmet.

28

—

AGGA

GRIFF

I have two days' leave to recover from the air strike. When I return to duty, I learn that Princess Freyda's visit to New Pythos has been accompanied by a curious change in policies: Humble-riders are no longer training with the fleet.

Instead, the dragonborn have begun training with Freyda's goliathan.

I'm still expected to serve Ixion and to work in the lairs. The goliathan, which must also be fed, requires half again as many fish as the rest of the fleet put together, and her feed must be carted down the footpath to the cove below the citadel where she nests. She sleeps when she isn't flying, and hunts the nearby waters for catch to supplement our feeding, but even so, none of the squires want to linger in the company of a dragon whose eyes are the size of a human head.

The first time I report to Ixion's chambers after my bedrest, I find his rugs and desk littered by broadsheets covered in the Callish script. I can make nothing of them.

"What's all this, my lord?"

Ixion seems too distracted to tell me none of my business.

"They're newspapers from Callipolis."

I decide to push my luck, for Antigone's sake. After all, pushing luck is what I'm good at. "And how do we keep getting ahold of these newspapers, my lord?"

But this is too much even for Ixion. "Are you going to do your job or keep asking stupid questions?"

Well, it was worth a try. I leave him to his reading.

My next visit to Antigone is scheduled for the day after New Year's, in less than a week's time. I'm praying to the shrines that she and Leo Stormscourge will make good on their promise to get me drachthanasia. I feel the accumulated information I have for them weighing on me like a belly full of food: the grounded Norcian riders, the newspapers from Callipolis spread across Ixion's desk, Freyda here and her goliathan blotting our skies. I can't be imagining that these are winds of change and that whatever change it brings won't be good for my people, or the squires.

Freyda herself remains a mystery even as the island struggles to accommodate her. With so much of the citadel destroyed in the Callipolan attack, the New Year's feast would already be a strained affair to plan—it was going to be hosted in one of the minor ha'Aurelian manors that didn't burn, different from the one that hosted Midwinter—but Freyda's presence demands extravagance.

So Rhadamanthus invites the Norcian peasants to provide a New Year's gift for their visiting princess.

The tradition is that we tithe for our lords' tables at Midwinter, and they in turn offer to ours for New Year's. So *gift* is the nice way of putting that we're being double-taxed this year. Agga breaks this news to me as she sits sweating on the back step over a pail of shellfish that she spent the past few days collecting with the little ones off the shoals. They were to be our New Year's supper; now she's preparing them for our lords.

"Do you think we've enough?" she asks.

I take the seat beside her. "Enough for Freyda to feed oysters to Rhadamanthus's dogs, yeah. Every Norcian on the island's doing this."

I've served at enough of our lords' feasts to know how our offering will be spent.

It snowed last night, leaving drifts of maiden snow in the alley that the village children are in a battle to scuffle in. A screech goes up from among them; Agga looks up at once, recognizing the little ones' voices. They race toward us, shouting at each other as they go.

"Tell him," Becca says, getting to us first, teary with frustration, "that she *did*."

"She *didn't*," Garet insists.

Agga drops her shucking knife and pulls them both to her. "Who didn't?"

"They're saying," Becca tells us, pointing over her shoulder at a few boys a little older than her and Garet, "Antigone didn't care about Norcians. But that's not true. She was trying to *save* us—"

"Then how come she was firing on us?" Garet says.

Becca purples. "You don't know anything about—*anything*!"

She yanks free of her mother and takes off down the alleyway, ignoring Agga's call after her. Garet rolls his eyes. *"Girls,"* he tells me, lifting his arms in a gesture of exasperation better befitting a teenager than a six-year-old, and then stomps back over to the boys.

"Where'd he learn that thing with his arms from?" I ask Agga.

She reaches down for another oyster. "From you."

I consider this with some satisfaction.

"They're all still talking about Antigone?"

Agga nods. "Getting it from their parents, I think. I've given up trying to manage it."

And less need for her to do so, now that Ixion's ploy was effective enough to make half the Norcians draw the conclusion Garet just did.

"Agga, what if Becca's . . . right?"

Agga's knife stills, wedged between the lips of the oyster she holds. She looks up at me.

"Griff," she says, like whatever I'm about to say, she isn't sure she wants to hear.

But she has to hear. I've told the squires; I'm straining with every nerve of my being as I await the date, on the other side of New Year's, when I meet with Antigone again. I am done shucking oysters for another man's feast while my own go hungry.

Agga needs to know.

I take the oyster and the knife from Agga's hands.

"Agga, what if next year we didn't have to give our catch to our lord for their feasts?"

She lets out a frightened laugh. "What are you talking about?"

"What if we could keep it, keep it all? No lord, no tithes."

"Griff, what . . ."

I sound mad. I can tell I'm upsetting her but I can't stop myself. It's too beautiful a vision, and she has to see it. "What if we made it Norcia again, not New Pythos, put an end to the mines defiling our clan-karsts and tore down the conqueror's flag—"

"*Stop.*"

There's a clatter as she launches to her feet. The bucket of shellfish overturns, oysters and clams clattering across the step. Agga has her hands to her face, her eyes bright.

"Tell me what you're planning," she whispers.

After wanting to tell her for so long, dreaming of it and failing in resolve, I'm not prepared for it to go like this. Watching tears course down her cheeks even as I struggle to assure her. After I've told her everything—Sparker's key, and Antigone on the dunes, and the dragon poison on its way—she says:

"This is a fantasy that will get my children killed."

"Agga—"

I reach for her and she pushes me back, against the aging wood of our doorframe. It thunks on impact. "Did you not think of Garet and Becca? Did it mean nothing to you, after Eamon, when you said you'd take care of us?"

"I am taking care of you. I'm doing this *for them*. For you—"

Agga's eyes flash. "*Do not say* this is for me when you've never had to tell your children goodbye not knowing if it was for the last time!"

She staggers back from me and I slump. Because suddenly that memory, of Agga on her knees kissing the little ones before they followed Ixion away, is too much.

Maybe I've never had to do it. But I had to watch her.

Agga sinks down onto the step, lowering her head into her knees. Her voice comes out like a drunk, muffled murmur. "I can't bear it. Not again."

The world has blurred. I crouch beside her.

"That's why we have to do this. So you don't have to."

She rocks backward and forward on her heels, arms around her knees. "Could you not just—rely on Delo? He's been good to us. Kept us safe . . ."

The blurring increases. He has been good to us. So good to us. But it doesn't change a thing.

"That's not enough. You know it's not, Agga. Anyway . . . he was the one who gave me Sparker's key."

Agga exhales into her knees. "Then he's an even sorrier fool than we are."

"He isn't."

"He will be."

I don't know how to answer that.

"The other squires?" Agga asks.

"They know."

A tremble courses through her bony shoulders. I place a hand on one of them.

"And the dragon poison?"

"She's bringing it. At our next meeting."

I say this with all the confidence I can feel as I pray one more time to the shrines that Antigone will make good on her promise, that Leo Stormscourge will get her what she needs as he told me he would. That their help will come before our hour is up.

A shadow passes over us and I lift my head: The wings of Freyda's goliathan sail over us, circling the island, trailed by the Pythian dragons like so many small sparrows in the wake of a hawk.

And not a humble-rider among them.

Agga looks up too, her shoulders drawing together at the sight, and it strikes me how different it must be, to look up at the beasts above and know that you are nothing but a target on the ground.

Then she reaches out and touches my fingers. Tightens her arms around her knees as if to press the shaking from them. When she looks at me, her face is shining.

"Truth be told," she murmurs, dragging a frayed sleeve under her nose, "I've been waiting for this conversation for a long time."

I'm startled. "Since Delo came that night?"

Agga shakes her head, her smile tired, and gives me that look only she can give. Like she's remembering the boy who messed the bed and punched too often, and still sees him.

"I've been waiting for this day since they gave you a dragon."

29

—

THE BUNKER RIOTS

LEE

It's been hours since the first free printing of the *People's Paper* was delivered; half a day since the Pythians attacked our city and Ana Sutter died; and the Passi are due to march in protest against Atreus's regime within the hour. But before we join them, Cor, Megara, and I are standing in a holding cell on the first floor of the Passi-occupied Vault, shouting.

I've interrupted their morning, disregarded their undress, as I brandish the paper on which Megara's smear campaign of Annie is printed below the account that I helped Cor write last night in his sister's name. The cell they've repurposed has a single cot, a heap of ministry-issue blankets, and a slit of a window that streaks sunlight across the room.

This is not, I think, how either of them planned for me to find out about their union, but I'm too angry to be bothered by their discomfort.

"I didn't say anything that isn't true," Megara snarls.

She crouches on the cot, a ministry-issue blanket wrapped around her; Cor, in his underclothes, has gotten to his feet as if to stand between us. He looks furious, probably more at the fact that I've burst in on them than at what I'm saying, but I don't care. How Cor and Megara choose to find solace in their grief is not my concern.

"*None* of this is Annie. None of this is fair—"

"Take a close look," Cor shouts, "at your girlfriend, Lee, because she did all of this. And you know it. Reported Megara, reported Tyndale, fired on civilians, *threatened* to fire on Megara's whole family—"

The defeated, barely speaking Cor from last night has been replaced by someone manic.

The fact that he's right only makes me angrier. I hold the paper and rap a hand against the paragraph that makes me want to reach for a hot poker to burn it from the article. "*She's not some serf I rut with in the field!*"

Megara snorts. "Your wording. Not mine."

I want to seize her by that shorn head and shake her. I speak through gritted teeth. "Find a more fitting target. Annie was serving a regime led by *Atreus*. I understand that you're both angry—"

Cor explodes. "Don't tell me what I am, Lee. Don't act like you've got the monopoly on grief, just because shit happened to you when you were a kid"—he waves an arm, indicating torture and massacre—"because in case you haven't noticed, shit's been happening to my family, too!"

His voice cracks. Megara rounds on me. "If you hit him for that, I swear to the dragon—"

"I wasn't going to."

For a moment our heavy breathing echoes on the stone walls. Cor has the grace to look just a little abashed, like he's surprised at what just came out of his own mouth. Megara reaches for a strip of green fabric lost among the bedthings and begins to twist it round her shorn head. Girding herself up as Southside's Daughter once more.

"The best we can hope for," she says with her head turned, "is that she'll be too ashamed to show her face. One less problem for us to deal with."

But whatever else Megara might know about Annie that I don't, here I know she's misfired. A few insults in an article would never be enough to cow Antigone sur Aela.

Not by a mile.

This article hasn't made her one less problem. But it may have made her one less voice of reason within the Palace when it's time to negotiate.

ANNIE

I make clear to the captain of the city guard that lethal weapons on the protesters will not be tolerated: no sabers, no arrows, and no explosives. But I am able to issue no such orders to the protesters themselves. For all we attempt to stop it, pillaging on the edges of the protest sites begins, wreaking further damage upon a city already gutted by air strikes. Granaries spared from the flamefall by my tip-off are ransacked by citizens instead. The rioters tear cobblestones loose from the street to hurl at the city guard and forcibly remove the wristbands of citizens they find still wearing them. I don't wait for authorization from the First Protector before instructing the guard to cease enforcing wristband regulations.

I wear a mantle that hides my rank, but all the same, as one of only four female Guardians in the corps, I'm recognized. A name I've heard before—*bitch commander*—I hear again.

Also a new one.

The dragonlord's whore.

Aela and I do not spill over.

The Guardians separate skirmishes with ash, our dragons doused. The aurelians' small size and mild tempers make them naturally suited to urban patrol. They do the brunt of the work, with skyfish in support, and stormscourges, too, for as long as their tempers hold. Everyone has orders to get in the air if they spill over. I'm aware of Aela's spikes of fear and frustration like a second heartbeat. So long as I stay calm, she does, too.

The protesters don't. Their rage is such that I'm not merely worried about the granaries of the Janiculum and the Inner Palace—I'm worried about a bloodbath.

We block the bridges to the Upper Bank and prepare to cut them.

The shouting comes from across the river, from the bottlenecks of the bridges where the city guard and the Guardians face down protesters clamoring to cross from the Lower Bank. Green bandanas and scarves dot the crowd; some faces are covered, but many, by now, dare to show themselves. Of the fists shaken at us, not a wristband is in sight.

On the other side of the river, two dragons alight at the entrance to Highmarket Bridge: a white aurelian and pewter-gray stormscourge. Lee sur Pallor and Cor sur Maurana. Southside's Daughter is mounted behind Cor, the green scarf around her head visible even at a distance.

When they alight in the center of the protesters, the cheering begins.

Lee sur Pallor, his armor gleaming, takes off his helmet and lifts an arm. Phrases from his speech float across the river.

Everyone is equally deserving. Ana Sutter was equally deserving.

Then as the cheering swells, it transforms into a different phrase, chanted over and over, led by Southside's Daughter: *Lee sur Pallor, Revolution's Son.*

Mounted on dragonback, we are twice again as tall as those on foot, so when Lee turns and looks across the winter-gray Fer, I know the moment when he sees me. I sit frozen, wondering for the hundredth time if he approved Megara's article. If he believes that I'm unfit for office.

Lee turns away and continues with his speech. Cor and Megara don't look in my direction at all.

We hold the bank.

On the second day, the rioters begin breaking the wrists of people who are wearing wristbands.

They break the wrists of Golds.

And then they start to break the wrists of people they *think* are Golds.

Back in the Cloister, with my permission, Power begins going through my mail. He doesn't tell me the content of the letters he finds, mixed among the official communication, that he burns.

But I can guess.

LEE

At the end of the third day, I find Val Lazare, Lo Teiran, and Richard Tyndale in the glass-walled office off the newsroom that used to belong to the editor in chief of the *People's Paper.* The old title has been crossed out; in its place, hacked with a pocketknife, the title the leaders of the Passi have claimed for themselves: THE DIRECTORATE.

"When are we going to negotiate?" I ask.

I've felt the people's righteous anger as they strip their wrist-bands, their joy to shout the words *We are all equally deserving.* But I've also seen the broken wrists. Guards starting to reach for sabers rather than batons in their panic. Granaries on the Lower Bank pillaged where the city guard, which has retreated to the Upper Bank, wasn't there to stop them. And for all the stealing of grain, there is little bread to be found.

How much more can the city take before we broker talks with the Inner Palace?

They're poring over a map of the city, their backs turned. "In due time," Teiran says in his dry voice.

"Hankering for your moment?" Lazare jokes.

I turn away, too frustrated to answer, and Tyndale calls after me: "You've been doing well, Lee. I knew you had it in you."

He hasn't, since his release, referenced the conversations we had last term that ended in Annie's report accusing him of sedition, so this is the first time I hear something like an echo of the things he once said to me in an empty classroom. *I knew you had it in you.* A reference to my birth, to the blood determinism that I balked at, to the call of the triarchy?

I had thought Tyndale's ties to that old life would be cut now that he works with a group of radical democrats.

"This is different," I tell him.

Tyndale smiles and nods. I leave the office unnerved.

Outside, in the newsroom, Jester, the Cheapside streetlord, has arrived with a barrel of ale and a new sack of bread. "Donated by the good people of Callipolis," he announces to the room, and though I doubt *donated* is how those citizens would have described it, I'm too hungry to question the husk he presses into my hand.

The first proper meal of the day makes the room giddy. Toasts go up to Southside's Daughter, to the Revolution's Son. Someone says *bitch commander* and I turn. Cor sits at a cluster of desks along the wall, snorting into his ale and heaving with laughter at something Megara's said. Since Ana's death, he has fluctuated between moody silence and furious energy. He's saying, "You didn't print the worst of it. You wouldn't believe what else she's been up to. Meeting with—"

He's about to gossip about Annie's covert operation with Griff Gareson. In two strides I am at their desk, have my arm around Cor's neck from behind, and am bearing him down into the table.

"*Shut up.*"

"Dragons, Lee—" I release Cor and he sits up, massaging his neck.

"You're awfully wound up," Megara observes.

The revelry around the room has gone on unabated, but nevertheless I'm scanning it, heart racing, wondering who could have heard.

"How many days till New Year's?" I ask.

Three. Which means Griff Gareson will be meeting Annie in four days' time, hoping she'll have drachthanasia for him. And as far as I know, she still doesn't know where to find it.

And meanwhile this city is tearing itself apart and none of the Passi's leaders seem inclined to bring an end to it.

I need to talk to Annie.

When night falls, I go onto the roof where Pallor is nesting with the other two dragons and saddle him up. We're above the city in minutes, cloaked in the night sky; we descend into the Palace, to the Cloister courtyard, a quarter of an hour later.

In and out. No one need know.

I find Power in the Firstrider's office, going through Annie's mail. A roaring fire is lit in the hearth beside her desk. He looks up when I enter and pulls out his classic sneer. "Well, if it isn't everyone's favorite rebel leader."

I am in no mood to banter with Power.

"Why are you always breaking into this office?"

Power makes a show of stretching. "Seems like you're the one breaking in this time. I'm here on invitation. Sorting hate mail. That was a hell of a character assassination your friend pulled on her."

Though I've been feeling the same thing, his tone and the fact that it's Power makes me predisposed to argue. "Annie did a hell of a lot of things."

Power snorts. "You got a reason for being here? Other than defending Roper."

"I wanted to talk to Annie."

I need to tell her I had nothing to do with that article. And I need to find out if there's the remotest chance she's on my side enough to help quell a storm I'm beginning to fear is getting out of hand. But Power deserves none of that confession.

He lifts a letter up to his nose. "She's out. Taking Aela for a breather. Do you want to hear what they're writing? Here's a good one. *Go spread your legs for some other dragonlord, you peasant wh—*"

"Stop."

"Pretty sure she doesn't want to talk to you, Lee."

"I need to talk to her."

"About what? To *apologize*?"

Power's tone is scathing. I balk against admitting that he's right, and instead burst out with a different confession.

"I need to talk to her about drachthanasia."

He must be in on what they're planning, if he's been going with her on all those night patrols to meet Gareson.

Power pauses. "What?"

"Drachthanasia. *Griff.* I know where she can get it."

Power tosses the letter in the fire, where others are already curling into ash. "Don't know what you're talking about. But I'll tell her you stopped by."

I seize the doorknob. Power makes a flourishing Revolutionary salute. "See you on the barricade."

ANNIE

The protests go on for four days, and on the fifth, New Year's Eve, it snows. The city lies quiet and ruined beneath it. The *Gold Gazette*, which used to distribute only within Lyceum and Palace walls, is now the ministry's only means of mass communication with the greater city; copies of it litter the streets alongside the *People's Paper*, the ministry's propaganda vying with the Passi's. Snow accumulates on papers gathering at the edges of sooty ruins and in the growing shantytowns of displaced and hungry citizens. Between granaries burned by the Pythians and others pillaged by rioters, ration distribution on the Lower Bank has entirely ceased.

There is nothing left to distribute.

The Inner Palace sends its first communication to the Passi, and I await their response with an excitement I don't voice until Power finds their answer among the mail he sorts for me.

"Is it from Lee?"

I hope I hide how hopeful I sound. Power hesitates, then shakes his head.

"From the Directorate. Teiran and Lazare. They're willing to negotiate."

Why do I keep expecting to hear from Lee? The most humiliating thing is that I keep expecting an apology. Like a stupid schoolgirl waiting for an unfaithful lover to come back to her.

I resolve not to ask Power about him again.

The negotiation takes place in the center of Highmarket Bridge, connecting the Palace to the People's Square, an hour before dusk. Power and I stand guard on the Upper Bank; Lee sur Pallor and Cor sur Maurana guard the Lower.

I watch Lee, a silhouette on the opposite side of the river, and wonder what he's thinking as he looks at me. If he still thinks he's pursuing justice and that I'm opposing him.

It feels wrong, abominable, that it's been days since Ana Sutter died and I haven't been able to exchange a word of sympathy with Cor.

Atreus Athanatos and General Holmes meet in the center of the bridge with Val Lazare and Lo Teiran.

The conversation lasts fifteen minutes. At the end of it, Atreus and Holmes turn their backs on the leaders of the Passi and return across the bridge to us.

"Sir?"

Atreus shakes his head. Holmes growls, "Resignation, *pah!*—I warned them we have troops advancing up the Fer from the south. They weren't swayed. We'll rout them with cannon fire within the week. Even if your dragons don't join in."

I didn't realize it was going to be that kind of negotiation.

"What about their other demands?" I ask desperately. "The People's Assembly, the metals test—"

Atreus gestures to the city on the Lower Bank, steaming faintly in the fresh snow.

"Do these people deserve an *assembly*, Antigone?"

He points to the far wall of the river, where graffiti has been painted in red like shining blood:

HANG ATREUS AND BURN THE DRAGONLORD'S WHORE.

And then, a little farther down the wall: LONG LIVE THE REVOLUTION'S SON.

Atreus says, "The hypocrisy of it alone is proof they deserved the metals I gave them."

He turns away with a flick of his great black mantle, departing with Holmes and the Protector's Guard up through the Palace gardens. On the other side of the river, Lee sur Pallor and Cor sur Maurana turn their backs on the bridge and escort the leaders of the Passi into Highmarket.

I watch them go, and sway where I stand.

All of this for nothing. The insults, the violence, the hunger. I've stood between this city and its rulers waiting for the compromise, but it will come to a bloody end no matter what I do because of the hubris of a handful of men.

And all I've gotten for it is my people's hatred.

Black spots grow in my vision. I reach to Aela's lowered neck for support and she leans into me as I sway. Her smoking nostrils nuzzle my gloved palm; her crest flattens with pleasure as I lower my face into it. These days, she's as tired as I am, and in as much need of comfort.

At the end of every grueling day, as I scrub her down, I feel her missing Pallor.

"When's the last time you ate?" Power asks. He's dismounted and come to stand beside me.

I realize I can't remember. "The Cloister's out . . ."

Just like the city, with starvation on the horizon all over again.

Power rolls his eyes. "Only for the unprepared."

LEE

Cor and I escort Teiran and Lazare along the streets of Highmarket, piecing together what happened during the negotiation, on dragonback at the loping pace they keep when they travel by foot. The parts of Highmarket not burned to a husk are littered with the debris of days' worth of protests. I can't stop seeing that silhouette of Annie across the bank, her hair glowing red in the setting sun, her face in shadow—her thoughts a wall.

Teiran is unnerved by the threat of summoned troops, perspiring visibly as Lazare reassures him. Lazare, for his part, seems grimly amused. "An influx of troops will only make more mouths Atreus won't be able to feed," he says.

Cor and I ride in silence, but I wonder if he's realizing the same thing I am.

Forcing Atreus's resignation through protests has failed. When those troops arrive, it will stop being a negotiation. It will become a civil war. And we'll be committed to the side that has only three dragons, against cannons and the rest of the aerial fleet on the other.

Our party rounds a corner into Highmarket's main square and Cor reins Maurana to a sudden halt. It takes me a moment to understand why.

On the opposite side of the square is his family's bakery.

Or—*was*. The Sutters were lucky to lose only the roof of their upper floor in the flamefall; the shop below remained intact, and they've been living out of the lower floor since then.

Today, we find that lower floor sacked. The shopfront glass shattered, the furnishings of the bakery gone or strewn across the cobblestones, covered in flour like powdery snow.

Cor dismounts from Maurana like he's sleepwalking. And then, as he takes in the scene, he starts to hyperventilate like he's realizing the same possibility I am. How many family members can be killed in a month, in a week, in a *day*? I don't want Cor to learn the answer to that.

I slide off Pallor's back and onto my feet beside him.

"Stay here."

Cor looks from the hand I've planted on his chest to my face, and when I turn my back on him and walk across the square to the devastated bakery, he doesn't follow.

I make my way, room by room, through what remains of his house, not breathing. Finally I confirm: empty.

I return to Cor, who waits white-faced with the others, and shake my head. "Not here."

We find his family in the Vault. They're in the newsroom, being tended by Megara Roper. Greg is bleeding from the head, which was clipped with a hurled cobblestone; Mr. Sutter's wrist is broken.

Megara rises when she sees us, and her face is as white as Cor's.

"Cor," she says, her voice rising and breaking. "They're all right."

Cor hurls himself to his knees in front of his family and begins to murmur in his panicked mothertongue as his mother attempts to soothe him. Greg describes their attackers in Damian that I can just barely understand: I hear him say *green scarves.*

Cor looks up at me and his face says exactly the thing I've been thinking, so I say it aloud.

"This is too much."

Lo Teiran, who has been watching us from the edge of the newsroom, steps forward.

"Before anyone starts having second thoughts," he says quietly, "I will remind you that it's too late now to back out. The only thing that awaits you on the other side is a court-martial and a noose."

"And if Holmes makes good on his threat of cannon fire," Lazare adds, "we'll need to use those dragons to do more than guard soon enough."

Cor gets to his feet. His voice cracks as it rises. "Three dragons against the rest of the aerial fleet is suicide."

Lazare's expression is made of marble. "Did you not realize it could come to this?"

"Uncle," Megara pleads in Damian.

Lazare slams a fist into the table and changes language, too. "I am ready to die to bring down the regime that destroyed my sister, that killed your father, that left you parentless," he roars. "And you must be, too, Megara. We must all be *willing to die.*"

The last part is shouted in Callish, for the whole room to understand. Lazare's eyes are wild and manic. Megara looks away as if averting her eyes from something obscene.

I turn on my heel and leave the room reeling.

Suicide is not what I signed up for.

In the cell I've claimed as my own, I close the door. Suddenly, it feels like what it is: a prison cell. One I'm trapped in.

To hell with my high ideals. I should have killed Atreus when I had the chance. It would have spared greater bloodshed, greater stupidity, greater evil. The city is starving. Those seeking justice are now turning their violence on one another. The Inner Palace is unbending and so is the Passi. And those troops coming up the Fer will back us into a corner with no way out.

A knock sounds on the door, and when I look up, a young member of the Passi whom I don't recognize stands in the doorway, her golden hair bound in a green scarf. She puts her finger to her lips—and that's when I realize I know her.

"Crissa?"

"Keep your voice down," Crissa says, "and go get Cor."

ANNIE

I've reached the point, like a flipped switch, where the city and the protests and the Passi no longer matter and the only thing I can think about is food. After Atreus's failed negotiations with the Passi on Highmarket Bridge, Power and I head back to the Cloister together, and then he takes me to the boys' dorm. It's deserted, the beds made, the desks clear. I can't remember the last time Mistress Mortmane conducted an inspection but the habits die hard. Power leads me to his desk, sinks to his knees on the floor beside it, and opens the lowest drawer. A rancid smell emanates. I lift a sleeve to my nose.

A dozen-odd stolen refectory bowls are stacked inside the drawer, their contents spoiling.

For months I've judged Power's unwillingness to stint from anything but a Gold's share of rations at mealtime, but now I realize he has been stinting. He's been eating as little as I have.

And saving the rest here.

I sink down onto the floor beside him, like we're crouched at a fireside.

"It's not that bad if you scrape the mold off," Power mutters, not meeting my eyes.

He passes me a bowl of porridge spotty with bits of green and black and, in a bizarre gesture at civilized dining, a spoon. He has a second one for himself.

I look down at the bowl and have that teetering moment that I remember, like I'm leaning too far over a bank looking down at my reflection in black water. I remember the worm wriggling in my hand.

Then the world tilts, and I'm shoveling rotten porridge into my mouth. I'm so hungry it tastes good.

"Used to do this when I was a kid," Power explains between bites. "Until Mum found out and had a pantry installed in my room. Slow down, you'll get sick."

I come up for air, wiping my mouth on the back of my hand. "Lee and I used to hoard, too. It was for a trip to New Pythos, I was supposed to go as his maidservant—"

Power snorts. "That's kind of messed up."

Yeah. It was. Almost as messed up as getting called *the dragon-lord's whore* while people cheer for the Revolution's Son on the opposite side of the river.

We keep eating until everything but the furry bits are gone. Then we lean back, against the side of Power's bed, and gulp for air.

"Happy New Year," Power says, clinking his bowl of furry bits against mine like a toast.

New Year's. It's *New Year's*. I'd forgotten.

"I'm seventeen," I realize.

"You were born on New Year's?"

No. I'm just from the sort of family that couldn't read calendars, and marked age by the passage of feast days rather than the date of birth, but I'm not in the mood to expose this to Power's mockery, so I nod.

"Happy birthday," Power says, holding out a spoiled potato. I stare at it. And then I remember what else New Year's means. We're supposed to meet with Griff tomorrow night.

"I still don't know how to poison a dragon."

I lift my knees to my chest, the failure rising up over me. "The city's falling apart, and everyone's starving, and I'm going to have to tell Griff Gareson I can't help him—"

Power has stiffened beside me. He lays a hand on my shoulder, so lightly I'm not sure it's there until I look up at him.

"Annie, there's . . . something I should tell you."

LEE

Crissa waits in the cell while I go get Cor.

When he sees her, he folds into her embrace. It's the first time they've seen each other since the air strike, since Cor lost his sister. Crissa and Cor don't usually show physical affection, but the fondness born of years of running drills together has always come through. Squadron leaders together, when we were first learning how to lead.

"I'm so—tired," Cor says finally, shoulders slumping against her.
"I know."

The prison cot creaks when Crissa sinks into it, steering Cor to sit beside her. She's dressed in plainclothes, a full-length unmarked cloak around her shoulders. Paper crinkles beneath her feet; she looks down, sees Megara's article about Annie, and her nose wrinkles.

There's a creak from the doorframe, and we turn to see Megara herself standing in it. Her bloodshot eyes track from Crissa sitting beside Cor to her article under Crissa's boot, to me in silent question. But before I know how to answer, Crissa offers her a smile.

"Megara," she says, beckoning her through the door. "So good to see you again."

Megara eases inside, and as she takes a seat where Crissa pats the cot beside her, I close the door.

For a moment there's silence; Megara sits stiffly, her shoulders level with her chin. Then Crissa thumbs her curtain of blond hair over her shoulder and looks up at me.

"You need to negotiate with the Firstrider."

I've never heard Crissa refer to Annie by her title before. I'm leaning against the door, arms folded, to prevent intruders. The cell's so small our knees are all practically touching. "She won't have me. Annie's done nothing but fight the Passi from the start—"

Crissa's eyes lift to the ceiling.

"Let me explain a few things to the three of you." She bends down, takes the paper out from beneath her boot, and sets it on her lap. "The entire reason these printings happened at all is that Annie put her foot down with Atreus and Holmes the night of the seizure and refused to retake the Vault. She jeopardized her title and her office on that refusal. She's also been the one making sure the Passi protesters haven't been slaughtered by the city guard."

Of course.

And that means the Passi hasn't just been villainizing Annie. They've been villainizing Annie while she defended them.

No wonder she didn't want to speak to me.

I can hear Megara unstick her throat. "What did she say when she saw my article?"

Crissa's smile fades. "She said it was true."

Megara inhales a rattling breath, like Crissa just rolled a boulder off her lungs. I can't tell if it's relief or satisfaction. Crissa sets the paper lightly in Megara's lap and adds, "Awfully big of her, given how much of it wasn't. Do you know what they've been calling her, in the streets?"

Cor presses a thumb to the line between his brows. We've all heard it. We've seen it painted on city walls. Megara's fingers curl over the edge of the paper, then reach up to touch her shaved head: bare because she ended up in the Vault thanks to Annie's reporting.

"Maybe she deserves it."

A touch of impatience cools Crissa's voice. "Maybe. And maybe she's learned from her mistakes as you should learn from yours. Or perhaps you forget that the leak she reported you for was the one that provoked the Pythian attack."

Megara stiffens. "I was trying to do the right thing."

A look of distaste ripples in Crissa's face at Megara's defensive tone. "Yes," she says, "we all are." She turns to me. "I know that communication has never been your and Annie's strong suit, but this is absurd."

I extend my palms. "I tried. I went the other night—"

Cor has put his arm around Megara's shoulders, and at this news they both swing round to me in surprise. Crissa's head cocks sideways. "What? When?"

"Power said she didn't want to talk to me. I don't blame her—Crissa, I swear I didn't know we were going to run a piece like that—"

Crissa stares at me, her eyes wide. Then she leans forward and slaps her hand across my forehead.

"You are an idiot. You listened to Power? Why didn't you come to *me*!"

Again, now that she says it, it's obvious. I rub my forehead.

Cor looks between us, then lets out a shaking laugh, like he's remembering how.

"I've missed that," he says.

Crissa makes a noise of exasperation. "Get up," she tells me, "and get your mantle on. These riots have been going on long enough."

ANNIE

"Annie, there's something I should tell you," Power says.

We sit side by side against the end of his bed. Power is looking up at the ceiling as if whatever he's about to say would be easier said if I weren't here. "Lee came by. A few nights ago. He said he knew something about drachthanasia. I told him you didn't want to see him."

I lower the empty bowl to the floor as my heart begins to race. "Why would you do that?"

Power rubs his hands over his stubbly hair. "Because he's been an ass to you for *months*!"

This being absolutely true doesn't quell my anger. In three heartbeats I've gone from despairing to furious—and to something else. For the first time in days, I see light on the horizon. I feel like I'm about to purge something rotten.

I get to my feet. "That wasn't your call to make."

Power's voice is rising. "Yeah, okay, but I'm telling you now, aren't I?"

I let out a disgusted laugh. Does he want credit for being a repentant liar?

At the sound of my laugh, Power's face screws up. "Annie, don't you get it? You can be strong *without* him."

I see where this is going. "With your help?"

Power's fists ball. "Well, sometimes I do think you need the reminder!"

When we first began training together, Power would spill over at the sight of my spillover, exultant at the sight of my fury becoming Aela's. He's always found my wildness and my strength beautiful, and to his credit, it's true there were times when I needed it.

But I don't now. That's what I realize with a sudden rush of clarity as his words ring presumptuous and offensive in my ears.

I don't need Power's encouragement to be strong. I don't need anyone's encouragement to be strong. Strength isn't the problem. It's what you do with it.

I don't need Power to egg me on. Or Lee to rein me in.

But of the two, I know which impulse I'd rather have to balance my own.

"What have Lee and his stupid ideals ever done," Power is saying, "except undermine you? Printing lies about you in that newspaper—"

"Lee didn't approve that."

I knew that, as soon as Power admitted the missing piece of information. I knew it as sure as I've ever known anything in my life.

Because I know Lee.

Lee, who recused himself from office and named me his replacement because he believed in me. Lee, who held me after Duck's funeral and told me I was good at this job. Lee, who trained with me despite his flameshock, so determined was he to help me win this war.

Some things you don't have to see the proof of. Some things you just know.

Lee believes in my goodness as I believe in his.

Power just scoffs like he's listening to a lovestruck schoolgirl. "You don't *know* he didn't approve—"

But I'm done. Done doubting, done wading through the muck, done being dragged down and egged on. Allying with Power has had its uses. It has kept the loneliness at bay when I needed to keep my eyes on the ground and steel myself at the sight of my own dirty hands.

No more. I'm ready to look up, to set my sights on the stars, and I'm ready to do that with Lee.

"What I know," I tell Power, "is that you lied."

"For you!" he shouts, his voice cracking. "Because I care about *you*!"

He gets to his feet, too. Lifts an arm and waves it. "I wish you'd—look around at who's been here. I've been with you defying orders to meet with Pythians, I've been with you on the barricade facing the rioters, and I've been burning your hate mail while the Passi smear your name. Yeah, maybe I'm not good, I'm not noble, but I have your back and I've had it the whole bloody time!"

His chest is heaving with the effort of saying these things. He has dropped the habitual sarcasm, and without it his voice sounds strained and raw. It's enough for me to know that whatever reasoning I find like gaps of missing teeth in his words, this is Power's truth. That whether or not he's *good*, he has tried his best to be good to me.

His shoulders go down as he looks at me. "But you're still going back to him."

Fury subsides into exasperation. "It's not a zero-sum choice, Power, you or him—"

His face screws up. Eyes squinted almost shut, he says: "Maybe it is. For me."

And finally, I understand.

Oh, Power. He has a heart after all, and now that he's bared it, I'm breaking it.

"But it's not . . . for you," he realizes.

I shake my head, throat suddenly tight. "No."

Even if the earnestness in his voice made me wish, for a breath, that it was.

The room is suddenly quiet enough that I can hear, muffled through the glass, gulls bemoaning the cold. I can see motes of dust swirling over the empty bowls of spoiled porridge.

Then Power sneers.

"Fine. Run back to your lord like the good little *peasant* that you are."

At the sound of the old sarcasm returned to his voice, the guilt that filled me for a half instant is snuffed out. I inhale and then say everything I can think of to sum it up.

"You are a condescending, entitled, manipulative *bastard*."

Power's face twists, like I've just hit him exactly the way he was hoping I would, and he bows from the waist, a mockery of old-regime obeisance, like he used to do.

"My lady."

I slam the door to the boys' dorm on my way out.

Outside, in the corridor, I stand, fists clenched, chest heaving, so furious and wild that for a moment, I don't realize that half of what I'm feeling isn't mine.

It's Aela's.

She's full of joy, so overflowing, I can feel her all the way from the nests below.

Pallor's scent is on the air.

LEE

We've barely landed on the Eyrie when they find us. Annie, clattering out of the Cloister entrance to the arena and up the stairs to the platform; Aela bursting from the cave mouth with a delighted squawk. Crissa sur Phaedra and I dismount, separated from Annie and Aela by the expanse of snow-dusted stone, and for a moment Annie and I stand frozen, looking at each other. It's dusk, and the sun pierces the low stratus on the horizon, bathing the snowswept arena, and Annie's face, in golden light.

Pallor and Aela don't have our patience. They cross the distance with joyful leaps and then circle each other in small bounds, stirring snow up as they gambol. Pallor begins to nip on the horns around Aela's ears and she tosses against him playfully, purring with delight at the reunion.

Even if all the barriers in the world were between us, I would feel Pallor's contentment. And I can see Aela's written in Annie's face as she screws it up.

It's the face she wears when she's determined not to cry.

I put aside my own uncertainty, cross the flagstones of the Eyrie, and wrap my arms around her as her face ripples. I say the thing that's been pent up since Julia.

"I'm sorry."

Crissa busies herself unsaddling Phaedra on the other side of the Eyrie, her back turned, while I tighten my arms around Annie's shaking shoulders.

Snow has begun to fall like flecks of gold in the sunset. Fluttering on Annie's auburn hair, my arms, the dragons cavorting on the flagstones. As she notices it, Annie reaches out an open palm.

"Good," she murmurs.

She takes a step back from me, drags a hand across her eyes, and becomes businesslike as if a switch had been flipped. Snow dusts her eyelids, her nose, her lips, and all I want to do is kiss them—but I force myself to focus on her words instead. These words, these thoughts, this precise mind I've missed even more than I missed the sight of her.

"There's a compromise I'd like to implement, if you're up for negotiating," she says. "We'll have to be quick about it, to pull it off before reinforcements come up the Fer. It will involve a trip to Dora Mithrides's house and a meeting with the Passi after that."

"Would that be before or after I get you drachthanasia?"

There is nothing in the world as beautiful as Annie's smile.

30

—

THE SECOND REVOLUTION

GRIFF

I tend the lairs, cart fish down to the goliathan's cove, serve Ixion when Freyda dines with him in his apartments, and wait.

Bran and Fionna have told the other squires. The lairs were never a place of much conversation, but now they're silent. Every nip of fangs I jump to avoid, every burn that blisters from a lord's dragon, is a reminder of the tides about to turn. Every time Sparker aches at the binds of his muzzle, I console us with the thought that soon he'll stretch his jaws. And every time I slop fish into a feeding trough, I think: *This is how we'll beat them.*

It sickens me. But I think of Agga, I think of the little ones, and I harden my heart.

I enter Ixion's chambers in the evening with small foods and a bottle of wine to find him and Rhode lounging on opposite settees, Callipolan newspapers strewn across the table between them, arms tracing the air above their heads as they scheme tipsily.

"—but if they're clamoring for democracy—" Rhode is slurring.

Ixion holds up his goblet for me to refill. "That's nothing we can't use to our advantage."

"Good news for us, my lords?" I ask blithely as I pour wine. "Callipolans starving away?"

"Starving and rioting," Rhode confirms, with enthusiasm.

And poor Antigone having to handle it. I'll be seeing her in two days.

Ixion raises his goblet. "To my ingenious and ever-generous betrothed," he toasts.

I haven't seen Delo since the Midwinter air strike on Callipolis. Not alone. Briefly, I catch glimpses of him across courtyards or on the far end of halls. When I go to his chambers at night, they're locked, and he's gone.

I tell myself it's for the best. Tell myself I shouldn't see Delo now anyway.

This close to my meeting with Antigone, I'm afraid I'll lose resolve.

I'm telling myself this, I've nearly convinced myself, until the daybreak shift in the lairs when I glimpse a pale strip of wings against the gray sky descending in circles to land at the mouth of the Skyfish nests. Then the word *resolve* becomes nothing but a word, and I throw it aside.

I go to them.

Delo's stiffly unsaddling Gephyra, and the part of me that's trained so well to be a squire thinks he shouldn't be the one to do it, and notices how slow he is at it. He turns at the sound of my boots on the gravel. His face is chapped, as if he's spent the night on dragonback.

"Griff?"

"Where were you?"

Delo rubs his cheeks like he's willing warmth back into them. "On an errand for Ixion."

I see then what's poking out of his saddlebag. More newspapers in Callish.

"You've been doing runs to Callipolis?"

Delo nods. "Taking turns with a few of the others. We have a contact in the city who's been leaving them on the . . ."

He trails off.

I let out a slow, hitching breath.

They've got a contact, too. Which means I'm not just tiptoeing in the dark. I'm racing in the dark. Racing whoever they're in contact with and praying they know less than Antigone and I.

Pain enters Delo's face, then fades from it. Like he's just realized this is the kind of conversation it's unwise to have with me. He looks away.

Whatever you're planning, promise me . . .

"I can unsaddle her for you."

"It's fine. I'm better at it now."

I can hear in his voice that he only wants me to leave.

No. Not yet. We're not yet at the end. That end, the one we both see coming.

That's what I tell myself as I take a step closer. Reach past him, unhook her saddle one buckle at a time while Delo stands frozen, his back against her wing, between me and the dragon I used to serve.

One-handed, not looking, I'm still better at unsaddling Delo's dragon than he is.

When her saddle falls to the ground, Gephyra's crest goes up all the way down her back. I look from her to Delo's dark pupils, and I know.

I kiss him.

And I wonder if it's for the last time. The last time I'll kiss him. The last time I'll tend her.

Wonder if he's wondering it, too.

Part of me hopes he'll be the one who betrays first.

ANNIE

The snow puts an end to protesting for the time being, and in the meantime, negotiations are made.

Lee and I sit down, side by side, in an emergency meeting with the leading members of the Janiculum and Gold Advisory Councils around Dora Mithrides's dining room table. By now, Lee has spent enough evenings with all of the people in this room to know them by first name. The Janiculum granary does not have enough grain to begin to feed a city; but it might just have enough to feed its children, for a few weeks at least.

Who are the most deserving? Not the smartest, or the fittest, or the wealthiest: the youngest.

The future.

When we propose this, and the Golds balk, as we expect they will, Lee pulls out his most charming smile.

"Do you know what happens, when a starving city overruns the homes of those with food?"

When no one answers, Lee says, "I do."

He continues to smile as the faces around the room drain of color.

The chairman of the Janiculum Council turns to me. His name is Samander Eschros, and he probably does not remember that on our first meeting, at the Lycean Ball, he complimented my hygiene as a highlander. "You wouldn't allow that," he says.

Lee and I exchange a glance, and I nod. Lee leans forward. "Let us put it this way. Either the children of Callipolis will have that grain because you give it to them, or they will have it because their parents take it. Antigone and I will let you choose."

Dora says, "We'll starve."

"We will certainly be hungry," Lee agrees. "As most Callipolans already are. However, I am hopeful we will not be hungry for long. An envoy has been sent to Damos, requesting aid—"

"Already done, already denied," Samander grunts. "Months ago."

"The reply Damos gave was that they only give aid to fellow democracies."

Dora understands first. She lets out a bark of incredulous laughter.

"You go too far, Leo."

Lee and I alone of those at the table are in uniform. Flamesuits and armor, wings of the Fourth Order on our shoulders, the medal of the Firstrider on my breast. Our dragons wait out front in Dora's garden, and the guests at this table had to skirt them to enter Dora's home.

Lee does not have the look of someone who will be told how far he can go.

"The envoy," he tells the table, as if Dora has not spoken, "will inform Damos that Callipolis has reinstituted the People's Assembly. That each citizen will be given a vote of equal weight at that assembly. That our constitution will be amended with equal rights for all citizens. And that the metals test, and the wristband laws, have been suspended."

This provokes an uproar. Lee watches, supremely unruffled, until they have spent themselves. Finally, Dora says, "The metals test was instituted for the good of the people."

I speak for the first time. "Was it for the good of the people that they were left outside to burn during the flamefall?"

Several Golds blanch. Eschros waves a hand, grimacing. "A classic but unfortunate case of mismanagement—"

"Which the people in this room facilitated and benefited from."

Lee and I let that silence sit. The Golds around us shift in their chairs; faces either cloud with guilt or go very blank.

Even they are discomforted by the thought of what happened on Midwinter Day.

"I assure you, an assembly would cause more problems than it solves," Dora finally says.

For all her grudging tone, I hear what it is: the beginning of a concession.

"Perhaps," Lee allows, "and we will deal with those problems as they arise."

"Atreus would never allow it," mutters Samander.

I place a hand on Lee's. I notice how confident and clear my voice sounds. But why shouldn't it? These people don't frighten me.

"No. He won't. Nor has he shown any interest in resigning. Which is why we need to go around him and have the Assembly invoked by the Protector-designate."

"There is no Protector-designate," Samander snaps. "That's for the Gold Advisory Council to choose—"

He falls silent as he understands.

Around the room, Golds look at one another, and then their gazes flit from Lee to me in sudden measurement. I don't look at him, but I am aware of the pulse of Lee's still hand on the table under mine. Waiting. No one seems willing to speak first.

Dora, her lips pursing—whether with a frown or a smile I can't tell—turns to us.

"You're awfully young," she says. "I had been thinking a little later down the road—"

"I'm eighteen," says Lee, "Antigone seventeen. We're no younger than many triarchs were at their ascensions, and we are eager to learn."

Dora settles into her chair, necklaces clinking against her golden skin. "Which of you would be putting their name forward?"

Lee and I look at each other, and I smile at him.

"I would," Lee says.

Samander grunts. "We'd prefer the girl."

Lee blinks. I turn slowly to stare at the chairman of the Janiculum Council, who nods and waves a hand, as if he finds even bothering to explain himself tedious. "We've been reading the *Gold Gazette*'s coverage of the unrest. Rather have a firm hand at the helm. None of this . . . radicalism."

I nearly laugh aloud.

This entire city has been painting my sexual exploits on walls but I find that here, on the Janiculum, the bastion of bigotry itself, my hard line is appreciated and my low birth forgotten.

I'll take the compliment.

But no more than that. As Lee recused himself, it seems it's now time to return the favor.

Firstrider is a hard job. But it's my job, and I'm good at it.

"I'm flattered," I tell Samander Eschros, "but I think if I were named Protector-designate, there'd be rioting in the streets. My hands are full enough as Firstrider. Don't worry"—I flash another smile at Lee—"I'm quite willing to rein in Lee sur Pallor's *radicalism*."

Lee coughs a laugh into his hand. He has reddened.

The Golds stir around us, glances shooting between them anew.

"Would you give us a moment?" Dora asks.

Lee and I rise together and leave the room.

Outside, on Dora's grand stairwell, we stand facing each other, Lee leaning on the balustrade. The sounds of heated conversation, muffled, come through the door. Samander's booming voice rises as it clashes with Dora's.

I reach up to smooth Lee's hair, that Stormscourge black, where it's come up from his part, and straighten the collar of his uniform.

Moments like this, he looks so much like his father it chills my blood.

But right now, that's an asset.

"Are you ready?"

Lee nods.

"We do this together," he tells me.

"Together," I answer.

The door opens, and Dora stands in it.

"Leo? There are some terms we'd like to discuss."

LEE

The envoy, led by Crissa, will not be back from Damos within the week, and even if the Damians agree to provide aid, that aid will not arrive for a week after that. But in the wake of the destruction left from the riots and the air strikes, it remains our best option.

The Janiculum Council and the Gold Advisory Council agree in a joint summit to select a Protector-designate, to share their grain with the children of the city at large in a gesture of good-will, and to recognize a reinstated People's Assembly.

The Inner Palace, pressured by the joint summit, agrees to a sus-pension of the wristband laws pending an Assembly referendum.

The *People's Paper* is to remain independent, the Vault prisons to remain closed for the time being, the office of the Reeducation Committee indefinitely disbanded.

The Passi agree to cease their protests. The troops advancing up the Fer are sent orders to turn around.

All this takes place the evening Annie and I reunite. The following morning, the *People's Paper* announces that the Revolution's Son has been named Protector-designate, that he has invoked an assembly to be held tomorrow, and that today, in the afternoon, rations will be offered to the children of Callipolis on the banks of the Fer. Delegates from the millers' and bakers' guilds are invited onto the Upper Bank to prepare bread for the people, among them Cor's parents. Depots are set up along the bridges of the Fer, monitored by Guardians and their dragons, as families from across the neighborhoods of the Lower Bank form queues.

Annie and I walk together along the bank as Pallor and Aela follow us overhead.

The citizens we pass greet me warmly, congratulating me on my promotion. They don't seem to know how to address Annie, who smiles at them from my side. Nor do I, now that we have this time to catch our breath after all the meetings, and what feels like months to catch up on. We pass other Guardians as we walk along the riverbank: Rock and Lotus, reunited and bickering happily as they monitor the queues; Cor helping his family unload bundles of bread from their cart alongside Megara Roper. They wave, and I wave back, but at the sight of Megara, Annie hesitates.

"I'm going to run a piece correcting that article," I tell Annie as we walk on. "Or—parts of it."

Annie's smile turns pained. "Which parts?"

"You know which parts."

It's impossible to know if she's reddened under a flush from the cold. Her eyes fix on the river as she nods, pushing wisps of hair back from her forehead. "Thanks."

We pass city workers scrubbing graffiti from the river wall, but neither of us looks at it. On Highmarket Bridge, we pause at the summit looking out over the frozen Fer.

Children have begun to skate. Trickling down from the Upper Bank and Lower, skidding onto the ice, tracing loops across the surface. Laughter and shrieking echo on the frozen river and rise like the steam from our breath.

It's been days since the city has heard the sound of children playing, and it stills me to hear it. Annie, too, begins smiling at the sound.

The sound of a city peaceful enough for laughter.

"I'm going to see Griff tonight," she says.

She's turned to look at me, a question in her eyes.

ANNIE

I make my way back across Highmarket Bridge at dusk as the ration booths are closing. The Sutters are gathered together at their family's booth. Mrs. Sutter is calling Greg and Merina up off the ice, their mourning black in disarray, while Mr. Sutter confers with ministry officials on inventories and ration lists; Megara Roper, her green scarf tucked around her shorn head, is helping Cor saddle up Maurana. When they see me, Megara freezes. Cor's shoulders go up.

I find I have a hard time looking at Megara, so I go to Cor instead. In his hazel eyes and square jaw I see Duck, in the waves of his thick hair I see Ana. Close enough to touch, but still out of reach.

"There's something I should have given you a long time ago," I tell him.

I pull the cuirass out of the breast pocket of my uniform, where it feels warm and safe and a part of me. Where I trust it to be when it's not beneath my pillow.

But Duck isn't mine to keep.

"Griff Gareson returned this to me the night of the attack. It should be yours."

Cor looks down at the cuirass, and as he recognizes it, his face fills with that grief that, three months ago, I'd never seen in it. And now he knows too well.

"I'm sorry," I tell him. "About Duck. About Ana. I'm sorry about all of it."

He nods, his face downturned, as his breaths become gasps. I turn away.

In a half bound he catches my shoulder and kisses me on the cheek.

"I'm sorry, too."

I leave with eyes streaming. I don't immediately realize my name is being called until the one calling it lurches in front of me and blocks my path.

And then I realize that I'm looking at Megara Roper.

She looks beyond uncomfortable. Shifting on either foot, standing in the middle of Highmarket Bridge between me and the far bank. The Sutters are a few yards away, out of earshot. Her face is twisting like a flag in the wind.

"Annie, I need to talk to you."

My face streaming, Cor's apology a gift in my heart, I think: I can't do this. Whatever she wants to say to me or hear me say in return. After *Antigone sur Aela: Unfit for Duty*, after *bitch commander* and *dragonlord's whore*, I don't have it in me. I may be guilty of the things that earned Megara's hatred, but it turns out I can protect this city with or without its love, and maybe one day I'll be ready to make amends with this girl I wronged and who wronged me. But right now, I'm still too hurt.

"I have to go."

"Annie, I think *something's going on*—"

I shoulder past her.

Back inside the Outer Palace, I go to the Palace blacksmith and collect the order I placed last night: a muzzle made to fit an adolescent stormscourge of above-average size, with a hidden clasp under the jaw. A fake that Griff will be able to use once Sparker has been freed. Then I make my way to a forgotten wing of the Inner Palace to find the storage room that Lee described.

Or rather, reminded me of.

Do you remember that time, Lee asked me as we leaned on the rail of Highmarket Bridge watching children skate, *when we were exploring the Palace with Duck, and I fled?*

Lee was always the reluctant one on our exploits, but that time it was he who suggested we take the turn down one corridor, then another, to lead us to a door that turned out to be ajar.

But when Duck and I pushed the door open that day, he didn't follow. And when we turned back to him, he was gone.

"You fled because they were your old apartments?"

"Yes. And some of our things. I thought I wanted to see them but I—couldn't."

The door isn't ajar today. A plaque on it reads: THE PALACE REVOLUTIONARY COLLECTION. I fit the key borrowed from Palace maintenance into the lock and let myself inside.

The chamber I've returned to is cavernous and filled with spoiling riches. Chalices and candelabra laced with cobwebs, marble and brocade soft with dust, all glowing in the fractured light of fading stained glass. Forgotten, like that tapestry on the second floor of the Lyceum Club.

Lee's old apartments converted into a storage space.

Standing here again, knowing it for what it is, I remember Duck's voice from so long ago.

Look at this, Annie! Look at all this finery!

Without Duck, without Lee, I make my way through the finery of what was once Lee's winter home and search for a sealed amphora with the Stormscourge crest.

"They were bestowed," Lee explained today as he gripped my hand on the rail of the bridge, the words coming stiff and slow. "Amphoras of drachthanasia, when you had a Choosing. But my father's was never used at the Widowing, because Aletheia's execution was saved for the Palace Day spectacle."

The beheading that Lee and I watched together in the People's Square, when we were children, a year after Lee's family were killed. Lee's hand seized in mine at the memory, and I squeezed it tightly, remembering that day, how we wept for different reasons and learned why.

I find the amphora soft with dust and wipe my thumb across the embossed neck. When we were last here, I couldn't read Dragontongue; now I understand it without conscious thought.

DRACHTHANASIA FOR EXTREME UNCTION
PRESENTED TO LEON SUR ALETHEIA, STORMSCOURGE
UPON THEIR CHOOSING

Lee's father received this when he was a child. Younger than we are today.

The amphora is roughly the size and weight of a full vase, with curved handles on both sides. It is, as Lee predicted, still sealed.

Dust is thick in my mouth and in my nostrils. Stained light pours in from high windows, glowing on the forgotten grandeur around me. I remember wandering through these piles of old treasure, in awe and delight, with Duck's hand in mine. The whisper of the memory, of his smile as he led me on an adventure, leaves my palm tingling.

Isn't it beautiful, Annie?

I felt, giving that cuirass to Cor today, that I was giving up Duck. But standing here, remembering Duck's words, I realize otherwise. If my parents taught me to have courage, Duck taught me to *see*. To see beauty and to love it, to let myself smile. And in this small way, I will never lose him. Even if, as I did my mother's, I one day forget his face.

Duck's a part of me.

I think of the way Cor seemed to break apart when I gave him Duck's cuirass today, as if by giving him back a piece of his brother, I had handed him a key that unlocked him.

I too have felt that kind of opening, that kind of gift. My fingers rise to the rusted chain of my mother's necklace. I roll it between my fingers, remembering how it felt when we stood before the ruins of my home and Lee gave it to me.

As if this little bit of everything that had been taken from me was still mine.

But Lee has never had such a thing to hold.

I begin a second search. Rummaging through every compartment within a six-foot radius of the amphora until I find a worthy recompense.

A dragonlord's bootknife. Tucked into the bottom drawer of a writing desk, its hilt filigreed with Stormscourge heather and engraved with the initials L.S.

I hold it in my hands, feeling their trembling, as it occurs to me that possibly it was *this knife* that was holstered in Leon's boot as he knelt beside me that day—

And then I force my hands still.

The sun has set. Griff will be at the dunes in hours.

I take the amphora and knife back with me to the Cloister and prepare for our last meeting.

31

—

THE DRIFTLESS DUNES

GRIFF

The night I'm supposed to meet Antigone, I'm summoned to the chambers of Princess Freyda. She is being accommodated in a wing of the Provisional Palace that survived, undamaged, during the Callipolan air strike. The fire in her hearth is blazing, the room overwarm.

I make full obeisance, palms and knees to the floor, and she tells her servants to leave us.

I'm alone in a room with the God-King's daughter. The only sound I can hear is her breath and mine. The only thing I dare look at are my own grimy nails.

"Is it true," she asks in her gently accented Dragontongue, "that your dragon sparked first in the Pythian fleet?"

"Aye, Your Highness."

"How unnatural."

I study my hands, waiting. The sounds of a drink being poured, being sipped.

"And that you serve as Ixion's squire?"

"Aye, Your Highness."

"Would you say that Ixion makes a good master?"

Does she know I can read?

Is this some sort of tip-off, an unlikely offer of help from the Bassilean God-King's daughter to a serf?

Or is she even crueler than Ixion, to let me deliver my own arrest warrant?

Or is she perverse enough to *let me think* she doesn't know I can read—

But now's not the time to wonder.

As soon as I'm out of her chambers, I break into a run.

LEE

Annie and I go together to the Driftless Dunes to wait for Griff, a fake muzzle and Aletheia's amphora wrapped in a blanket and tucked in her saddlebag, along with kindling for a fire. When I ask if Power is coming, too, Annie's lips form a line. "No," she says, "I don't think so."

In the hollow between two dunes, on the windward side free of snow, we pile the logs and Aela lights the fire. It's warm enough, this sheltered and close to the sea, for her to spark. Annie throws a blanket beside it on which we sit to wait, Aela and Pallor curled beside us, and Annie reaches absently to scratch Aela behind her horns. Then she reaches into the saddlebag attached to Aela's back.

"I have something for you."

When she presses it into my hand, and I recognize it, I feel my throat closing.

"I found it in that room, by the amphora. I want you to have it. You gave me my mum's necklace and I wanted to—return the favor."

That she can even pretend those are commensurate actions makes me feel ashamed. Her necklace belonged to a mother my family left to starve; this is the knife of the man who took everything from them. And then add to that all the ways, in the past week and in the past months, that I've failed her. "Annie—"

She tilts my face up with the tips of her fingers.

"I know it's been hard for you, since the duel. Since—since the orphanage. You've been so busy at *not* being him, and you've been so beautiful at not being him, Lee—cutting off your roots every time it's been asked of you. I've watched you do it, and watched you hurt, and I think you've done it enough." Her voice hardens, her breath quickens. "When you look at this knife, I want you to remember it belonged to a father who loved you. And I want you to remember that I was the one who gave it to you."

She leans forward and removes the old knife from my boot. Her face is downturned, wisps of hair curtaining it. When my hands don't move, frozen holding the knife that was my father's, she replaces it herself.

I lean over, take her hands in my own, and hold them.

GRIFF

I land Sparker in the alley behind our home. The night is dark, but Sparker's darker, and when Agga steps out onto our back stoop and sees his towering silhouette, she lets out a shriek that I clamp a hand over.

"Agga, this is Sparker."

Agga shrinks, but I take her hand and Sparker lowers his muzzled snout to sniff her palm. She stretches trembling fingers up to trace the bridge of his nose as his great amber eyes focus on her. His tail perks up in interest and bangs against the roof overhang, dislodging thatch. Behind us, the door starts to open, Garet's shrill voice piping Sparker's name, but Agga yanks it shut again, keeping him inside.

"Why is Sparker *here*?"

"Because it's time."

Agga withdraws her hand from Sparker's snout and turns to me, sucking in her breath. Becca's and Garet's protests come muffled through the door as they hammer on it.

"I need you to tell the other squires: It's over. They're coming for us at dawn."

Agga puts her hand over her mouth. "But if they're going to arrest you, you should run," she whispers. "Get out—"

"I've got a better plan than that."

I'm smiling, and Agga's shoulders settle as she understands.

"Tell the squires I'll be back before sunrise with what we need. Tell them to wait for me. Also—there's one more thing I need from you."

At my description, she runs inside—the little ones' awed faces press briefly against the crack of the door—before reemerging and closing it on them again to muffled cries of disappointment. I stuff the bundle she gives me into Sparker's saddlebag and turn to embrace my sister. As we pull apart, I lay steepled fingers against her face to trace our clan-sign as we would paint it in battle woad. Agga inhales.

"Nag keep you."

Sparker and I are halfway across Sailor's Folly when I hear the bugle behind me. The sound carries muffled across miles on the sea below.

A search party. I've been missed.

LEE

Griff Gareson's massive stormscourge lands so hard in the sand, the ground shudders. He slides from its back already talking. "It's tonight, it has to happen tonight. Please by the dragon tell me you have it—"

Annie is on her feet. She holds out the amphora. "I have it."

"How much for each—"

Annie looks at me. I answer without hesitation: "It's powerful. It should be enough to divide doses among the fleet. Mix it in with their feed."

"Shrines bless you," Griff says, taking it. "Antigone, Lee, you should know—the Bassilean princess is there, in New Pythos. With her goliathan."

Annie frowns. "But goliathans are only claimed by male heirs—"

Griff just shakes his head, and Annie's eyes widen at the same time as we realize: Not anymore.

"We have to go," Griff says. "They're looking for me, we've got to go—"

Annie holds up the fake muzzle, her thumb flicking the latch. Her Dragontongue, I realize, is smoother than the last time I heard it, more comfortable from practice. Her accent is as I remember it from years of classes I spent listening to her learn my mother-tongue: utterly beautiful.

"Not before we spring Sparker."

Griff stares at the fake muzzle, stunned. Behind him, Sparker's wings flutter open and then fill the sky like great black sails, his horned tail lifting.

Griff turns back to him.

"You ready?"

Sparker growls in pleasure.

Aela ripples forward, nimbly mounts on her haunches, and takes the muzzle in her teeth. Fire glows and grows hotter, whiter, concentrated between her jaws. Sparker whimpers but holds still. Griff is breathing slowly through his mouth.

"Tell me if she's hurting him," Annie says. Her pupils have dilated as she rides the connection, her fists clenched in concentration.

Griff's face is scrunched up with pain. He clutches at his jaw and speaks through gritted teeth. "Just keep going."

The metal begins to glow red. Aela begins to gnaw on it, tugging as she applies heat.

Sweat is beading on Griff's brow.

He lets out a shout—

—and the muzzle breaks. Glowing metal thunks to the sand at their feet.

Aela sits back, her tail swishing in the sand.

Sparker flexes his jaw, just a little, testing it. And then he arches his back and yawns the slowest, widest yawn I've ever seen. His relief so apparent, I can practically feel it.

And Griff, who *can* feel it, starts to weep.

Sparker lifts back his horned head, throws open his jaws, and bellows flames into the night sky. They pour forth like a column of fire, and for a moment, as the entire valley between the two dunes is lit, I can't help thinking: *No wonder they muzzled this one.*

Annie, who must be thinking something similar, is laughing. Laughing as she wipes her eyes.

And then, from the periphery of darkness, comes a new voice. "That looked *very* satisfying."

On the crest of the dune, silhouetted in darkness, three dragons have landed. Two aurelians and a stormscourge. The voice that spoke was Ixion's.

GRIFF

For a moment Sparker and I are frozen, looking up at them. Ixion and Rhode and Roxana, here. Which means my time's up.

And then I remember what Sparker can do.

And Ixion is within my grasp.

I am on my dragon's back, we are charging up the dune, before there's room for a single second thought.

We ram against him. Sparker and Niter roll through the sand. Flames burst from Sparker's jaws with all the fury that's been years in the stifling.

I begin to slide, loose in the saddle without bootstraps. The ground rises up and slams against me. For a moment I lie winded. I've fallen from Sparker's back.

But Sparker continues his battle against Niter without my help.

Light and the sounds of skirmishes flare from the valley be-tween the dunes where we left Lee and Antigone, where Rhode and Roxana are bearing down on them.

Ixion's pale face looms over me. A fist slams into my gut. He's out of the saddle, too, come to finish me while Niter and Sparker scrabble in the sand like rabid dogs—

I can feel, every time Sparker fires, the rush of power. And it takes nothing, nothing at all, to flow it into my fist and land that fist in Ixion's face.

The last time we were firing like this, we had just sparked and Ixion was beneath us. But tonight no one is here to pull us off, and no muzzle will stop us.

I've got him on his back, I'm pummeling again and again with a sound coming out of my own mouth like a dragon's roar. Ixion twists, panting, and I realize that he's reaching for his bootknife—

I reach for *my* bootknife.

And then it's shining in my fist, and my hand is over his neck, squeezing, and his fingers are scrabbling at my hand like crabs.

Three yards away, Sparker has pinned Niter to the ground, where his wings beat weakly against the sand, and Sparker's fangs are on Niter's jugular.

I can taste Niter's blood in my own mouth. Taste its sweet-ness. Sparker looks up at me, awaiting my command.

Ixion's pupils are dilated and he blinks them, feeling his dragon's fear.

He begins panting names.

"Becca. Garet. Agga. Grandfather Grady—"

My grip on his neck loosens. My knife has frozen.

"They will drop every single one of them if we don't return with you to the citadel."

Ixion wrenches my slack hand from his neck and pushes me off him.

"Call them off," he pants, with a glance at Sparker and Niter and at the skirmishing aurelians below. "Come peacefully, and there won't be any need for that."

But Sparker is frozen, waiting, salivating on Niter's blood—

I force my head clear. No. Not a dragon's instinct, I have to *think*.

Sparker still wears his saddlebag, and its contents remain intact. Down in the valley, the amphora of drachthanasia and the fake muzzle lie untouched in the sand, forgotten during our fighting. And it's still hours until dawn.

Ixion knows I've been meeting Antigone. He knows we broke Sparker's muzzle. But he doesn't know the whole plan.

Or its alternatives.

My time might be up, but the game isn't.

I let the knife fall to the sand. Click to Sparker to heel. He growls and slowly, reluctantly, eases off Niter. I can taste his disappointment in the back of my throat.

"No more," I tell him.

Ixion lets out a snort of laughter.

"Like I said," he says, wiping blood from his nose and taking my bootknife up off the ground. "Piece of peasant shit."

He gets to his feet and lifts his voice. "Leo? Annie? Your friend's done fighting. I'd stop too if you want what's good for him."

Slowly, the muffled sounds of skirmishing falter. I risk a look down at the valley: Annie is staring up at me from Aela's back, her helmet yanked off, her eyes wide and frightened as Roxana struggles to right herself. Leo is disentangling from Rhode, his dragon kicking at molten sand.

"Griff," Antigone says, pain in her voice.

"Thanks for all your help," I call down to her. "Pity it didn't work out. Wish you could have met my sister—"

Ixion is mounting Niter with a snap of his mantle. "No one cares about your sister, Gareson. Just shut up and get on the dragon."

I shut up and get on the dragon. When my lords lift off, I follow them into the air.

And on the side where Ixion can't see, I unhitch the saddlebag containing the bundle and let it fall to the sand.

LEE

The Aurelian I tussle with holds nothing back and we don't either.

I don't know him. But I know who he is. Rhode ha'Aurelian, son of Rhadamanthus, heir apparent to New Pythos and Triarch-presumptive of the Triarchy-in-Exile.

Which in another world would have meant that he outranked me, but now only means we are on opposite sides of a war. This time, when Pallor's fire injures, blackness does not spread across my vision. No memories come unwanted. I only fire harder.

Until I hear Ixion's voice, echoing down the dunes, calling us off.

Pallor and I are half buried from scrabbling with Rhode and his aurelian, and blisters of melted sand, glowing as they turn to glass, radiate from our fight. Rhode is coughing, his arm to his helmet, as he pulls back.

"You blood traitor bastard."

Rage only makes me laugh at that.

But then my laughter stops, because Griff is climbing onto his dragon, and Annie's voice is choking as she says his name.

She says it like she's saying goodbye.

"He'll be dropped," Rhode tells me. "His family will watch, and if he's lucky, that's all they'll do. He'll be dropped and so will you and so will *she*."

His aurelian kicks off from the ground.

They're shadows above us, silhouetted against the stars—

And with a thunk, a saddlebag lands on the sand at Aela's feet.

As they dwindle against the northern horizon, Annie and I dismount. She kneels beside the bag and peels it open with shaking hands.

At first I don't understand what I see. Old fabrics, undyed, worn and patched and stained, that Annie holds in her hands uncomprehending until she lifts them and their shape becomes clear: a woman's fraying dress, a hair scarf. I stare at them in puzzlement.

"Those are—" I nearly say *peasant clothes* and catch myself. "Working clothes."

But I know by how Annie's shoulders vibrate that she heard the thing I didn't say.

I still don't understand what's happening until she says, "I haven't worn a dress like this in years."

ANNIE

It all comes together, the pieces clicking into place, as I hold Griff's sister's dress. The amphora at my feet, Aela at my side, a scarf to hide my hair. Griff didn't know I'd bring him a fake muzzle. He assumed I'd come back with him and break the muzzles of the squires' dragons myself, like he suggested so many weeks ago.

And I still can.

How many hours until dawn?

Lee's struggling to catch up. "You can't seriously be suggesting—"

"It was on the table. Griff and I discussed it."

"This is mad. We should go back, get backup—"

"There isn't time. And Holmes will hear the entire story of tonight as an ambush I walked into. The last thing he'll authorize is reinforcement."

My mind is racing to what else needs to happen for this to work. I reach up, to the Firstrider medal pinned on my uniform, the bugle encircled by silver and gold, and tear it free. I press it into Lee's hand.

"I should be back before this is necessary, but if not—Power sur Eater is acting fleet commander."

I have a fleeting thought to the fight with Power that sent me fuming out the door, but that doesn't matter now. What matters is I trust Power to do this job, and that if all goes well, he won't need to.

Lee pockets the medal without looking at it, nodding at the assignation as if he hardly hears it. His fingers are raking his hair. "But how would you even—find whoever you need over there—"

Wish you could have met my sister.

"I'll go to Clan Nag and ask for Agga Garesdaughter. Griff's sister. She'll be able to connect me with the squires."

"You don't speak Norish!" Lee shouts.

I start laughing then. This is how bad it's been, I realize. We've gone for weeks and months speaking so little to each other that Lee doesn't even know what classes I'm taking. And now, when we're finally talking, there's no time.

"I've been taking Norish at the Lyceum for months."

Lee's mouth has closed.

"I need to change," I say.

He stands rooted to the spot while I unclasp the neck of my flamesuit. The winter air bites my exposed skin and I inhale. Lee rouses himself. "It'll be warmer under Aela's wing."

He's right. She makes a cone of her wing under which the heat of her body and mine, trapped, makes it just warm enough that stripping is conceivable, though a draft stings my skin.

But when Lee steps into the space where draft comes through, I'm warm enough.

We've never undressed each other before. Apart from that surreal bath before the funeral, we have always kissed, touched, and held each other clothed. But tonight, when he reaches trembling fingers up to the clasps of my flamesuit and begins to undo them, I don't stop him.

I can hear, and see, and feel our breath as his fingers make their way down.

For a moment we face each other with the flamesuit at my feet.

Then he pulls the dress down over my shoulders. I turn my back to him so that he can tighten the laces behind. He holds the scarf out and I take it, wind it in my hands the way, years ago, my mother taught me. My fingers remember what my mind has forgotten. They twist the scarf over my hair and bind it at my nape in a single swift motion. I flip it over my head and look up at Lee.

He is frozen, looking down at me, his face in shadow in the darkness of Aela's wing.

"How do I look?"

"Like someone I was taught to ignore."

My breath skips.

"Good," I whisper.

He kisses me, so softly on the lips I barely feel it, only the shiver it leaves. His fingers reach up to tuck a stray strand of hair under the hem of my scarf.

"I could come with you," he murmurs.

There are so many reasons why he couldn't, starting with the fact that he doesn't know a word of Norish, and doesn't have anything to wear beside a Guardian's uniform, and most of all, that while my face might not be recognized by Lee's family under a peasant's scarf, Lee's would.

But I hear the fear behind it and understand: The only reason Lee wants to come is that he's scared out of his mind for me.

"I think," I tell him, "one of us should probably stick around to take care of Callipolis. There's an assembly tomorrow that you need to lead."

"With *you*—"

"No. That's not my path. This is my path."

It feels brilliant and blinding and free, the clarity that comes with this realization. We'll set our sights on the stars together. But they're different stars, and we'll stand back to back. I lift up on tiptoe to kiss Lee on the cheek. "Try not to make too much of a mess of things while I'm gone."

Lee lets out a puff of breath. "Come back before I do," he says.

I swallow, and nearly laugh, as my eyes prickle. There are days' worth of things to tell him. Weeks and months needed to make up for lost time and unhealed hurts. But they will have to wait.

"Before you know it," I answer.

Lee leans his forehead against mine, and though I could kiss him again, I don't. Forehead to forehead, I look into his face and memorize it.

Before I turn away, Lee's lips brush against my ear.

"Raze them to the ground."

32

—

THE PEOPLE'S ASSEMBLY

GRIFF

Ixion does not return with us to New Pythos. He peels off and doubles back, once we are out of sight of the Driftless Dunes, and soon more dragons dot the horizon, following him in the direction of Callipolis, streaking silently past us in the dark. I count them off and guess.

"What's Ixion doing with the Bastards?"

Rhode's laugh is swallowed by the night wind. "Wouldn't you like to know."

Back at the citadel, Sparker is muzzled again, then chained to the floor of his stall so tightly he can barely lift his head.

I can feel his fury all the way from the Glass Hall, where I'm hauled.

Delo is already there, seated in the center of the floor where, when I was questioned about Julia, he stood. The Callipolan attack blew out the Hall's great glass windows, and wind whistles between the slats boarding them. The sight of Antigone sur Aela's humbling of the Pythian throne room gives me courage for the half-moment I have to take it in.

Then the guard behind me shoves me to my knees.

Eyes on the ground, I glance at the boots of the dragonborn encircling us. Freyda and her long train are not present, but the Greatlord and the Triarchy-in-Exile are, with Rhode and Roxana present from the younger generation.

Delo's foot taps the ground nervously beside me.

I look at that tapping boot, and wonder: *Did you tell them?*

And then I wonder if I care.

"Griff has had quite the night," Rhode says.

Electra Stormscourge's throaty voice is full of alarm. "He didn't *thwart*—"

"Oh no," says Rhode warmly. "That's proceeding as we speak. Ixion rejoined Freyda and the Bastards on the way. And luckily it looks like this one didn't tell the usurpers anything useful."

An impending death sentence makes me punchy. "I told them loads of useful stuff, thank you very much."

Rhode's voice rises. "I'd stay silent, Griff, if you know what's good for you!"

Delo groans softly into his hands, and for his sake, I close my mouth. Rhode proceeds to recount the night I've had to the listening adults. I study my hands, listening to the sound of Delo's slow, even breathing beside me. Panic-giddy thoughts flash from Ixion and his mysterious plot proceeding as planned to this room my body is trapped in, the punishment I'm soon to be set. The pen, the drop, the flame? If they're feeling particularly vindictive, it will be all three.

Did Delo betray me?

I force myself to remember the bundle, dropping it, the way Antigone's eyes grew round as I told her goodbye.

She'll come.

When Rhode has finished his account, Rhadamanthus says:

"What I don't understand is how. How did Griff free his dragon? The humble-dragons should be chained."

Roxana gets to her feet, comes to my side, and slides a hand into the collar of my shirt. The chain of Sparker's key spills out.

"Probably, with the help of this."

The sound of metal clinks as the key is thrown on the floor.

"Ixion still has his," she says. "That's a copy."

"What on earth," Electra Stormscourge murmurs, like she is witnessing something obscene.

"Delo," says Rhode pleasantly, "would you like to explain any of this?"

I dare a glance upward. Delo's face is downturned, scrunched as he observes his knees.

"I gave Griff the key to his dragon."

"You authorized his visits with the Callipolan Firstrider?"

"No. No, of course not. I didn't ask what he was doing with it."

Electra's skepticism is shrill with surprise. "Why did you give it to him, then?"

Delo's voice is soft and shaking. "If you can't see why I did it," he says, "then I've no answer that will satisfy you."

I lift my head to look at him. He looks back at me. And that's when I know:

Delo didn't tell them anything. Delo stands by me. Even now.

I lower my head wondering if it's possible for a body to contain such triumph or such love.

Nestor gets to his feet, lifts an arm, and points it at his son.

"Everything you do, and have ever done, is a blight on your mother's memory and a shame to Skyfish House."

Delo's breathing is ragged beside me.

"Forgive me, Father," he answers.

Rhode yawns and uncrosses his legs. "Perhaps we can conclude this farce by confining cousin Delo to his chambers, and escorting Griff Gareson to the dungeon? Unless you'd rather we drop him now."

"Later," Rhadamanthus decides. "Better to make a lesson of it."

Next to me, Delo lowers his face into his palms and lets out a dry sob.

I listen to the sound and wish we were alone. Wish I could comfort him.

Wish I could tell him that Antigone is coming, bringing drachthanasia and a dragon to break the muzzles, and these fools don't even know it, but I'll keep Delo safe.

A mad smile, the smile of the damned, has overtaken my face.

"It's been an honor serving all of you," I tell them, as the guard pulls me to my feet, and I make the deepest bow I've ever made.

"Get him out of here," says Lady Electra in disgust.

The last thing I see of that room are Delo's shuddering shoulders.

ANNIE

Aela and I keep to the cloud cover, burrowing into the stratus as we cross the moonlit North Sea through the studded karst of Sailor's Folly.

It's early morning, the sky still black, when New Pythos looms before us.

Crissa's maps, labeled by Griff on our first meeting, inform my landing on the darkest tip of the shore, in a cove under the arm of rock that reaches the lighthouse. It's as I hoped: a deserted shoreline, where Aela can fold herself into the darkness of the jagged cliffs while I find the people I need.

"Don't be seen," I tell her.

Aela offers a disgruntled huff, then begins to track circles in a nesting spot with her tail curving behind her.

The amphora, stuffed into a bag over my back, makes me stoop with its weight as I set off. Heart pounding so hard in the silent night, I feel I can hear it. I make my way up the coastline toward the cluster of shacks that I hope I've correctly estimated to be Clan Nag. Bits of light peep through shutters here and there. I make my way down the outer streets of Griff's village, and stop a peasant I find warming himself at a hissing barrel fire. The Norish comes out stiffly, but the sounds of the language are close enough to Callish to disguise my accent.

"Where can I find Agga Garesdaughter?"

Ten minutes later, I'm standing in an alleyway in front of a lean-to the size of a woodshed. Smoke rises from the chimney; light filters through a crack in crooked shutters over the window.

I knock, and a young woman opens the door, a child on her hip who's half asleep.

The woman has Griff's round, stubborn face.

"Agga?" I whisper.

The woman's eyes widen. She brushes back the hair of the girl she's holding and whispers into her ear. "Becca, I have a surprise for you."

Becca twists to look at me.

"Is that Antigone?" she asks sleepily.

An unexpected lump rises in my throat as I nod.

"Hi, Antigone," Becca says. "I told Garet you would come."

It's only now, looking into the sleepy face of Griff's niece, that I finally believe it.

For this girl, I'm not the bitch commander.

I'm Antigone sur Aela, Firstrider of Callipolis. I'm everything the Revolution promised.

"You were right."

"Where's Griff?" Agga asks.

I swallow, shake my head, suddenly conscious of the presence of a child and the need to mask my words. A memory, an echo, of a childhood hearing coded phrases exchanged by adults who seemed so old and wise then, who I realize now must have been little older than Agga and I. Brewing desperate defiance of their lords to make a better life for children like Becca, like me.

And now it's our turn.

I tell Agga: "He's with his lords."

Agga inhales. Her fingers tighten on her daughter's nightshirt as a shudder goes through her. Then her expression stiffens.

"Come in," she says.

She leans against the door to widen it, and I step over the threshold into her home. She closes the door after me and tells the room, "She's here."

Six Norcians are crammed into her tiny front room, clustered around the candle stuck in the center of a table, and where there aren't chairs, they're seated on the floor. Between Griff's age and mine, men and women both, the same curly hair and olive skin and bright piercing eyes.

And all of them in flamesuits.

Their murmuring conversations fall silent as they all turn to look at me.

"Antigone," says Agga, "meet the squires."

"Have you got it?" one of them asks. Effortless Dragontongue, like Griff.

I rotate the bag from my back and peel it open.

"I've got it."

LEE

I'm back to the Cloister before sunrise. The Palace is still, quiet, waiting. Soon, the Assembly will bring citizens through the Outer Gates by the thousands, filing into the arena where we competed last summer in tournaments, here today for a different kind of ceremony.

And on the other side of the North Sea, Annie is about to gamble her life on an amphora and a semester's worth of Norish.

The Guardians gather in the refectory, helping themselves to warm ale that will be today's breakfast. I sit with the *People's Paper* spread in front of me along with notes for the Assembly address. Between the snow lowering the risk of attack, and the Assembly grounding many of the riders fit for duty, most of the corps are present at breakfast.

"Where is she?"

Power stands on the opposite side of my table with his usual glare. It's the first time since returning from the Dunes that I remember Annie's injunction to name him acting fleet commander in case of emergency, and for the first time, I hesitate at her choice.

But I'm done going against her behind her back. I pull the medal from my pocket and slide it across the scarred wood. "She'll be back soon. For now, we're saying she's on patrol. But if it comes to it, you're acting fleet commander."

Power's eyes widen and his voice lowers. He doesn't reach for the medal.

"You left her—?"

"She *went*. Her mission depends on speed and stealth. She didn't need my accompaniment."

Power scoffs. "Yeah, I bet she didn't. You don't know any Norish."

I'm not sure what his point is, and I resist the urge to point out that I am also needed here, for the Assembly that is about to take place and which I am required, as Protector-designate, to invoke. "Just take the badge."

Power reaches for it like he's snatching spilled change. He stuffs it in the pocket of his ceremonial uniform.

"Lee," calls Deirdre from the table where she's sitting with a few aurelian riders, "have you seen—"

Power and I answer together, "She's on patrol."

An hour later, I pull on my ceremonial uniform and make my way to the Inner Palace, to the Protector's office, where Atreus Athanatos waits for me to escort him to the People's Assembly.

The Protector's Guard open the doors to his office, crimson mantles rustling, and Atreus smiles at me from across his oak desk. A small, twisted smile. It's the first time we've met since the Gold Advisory Council named me Protector-designate, and before that since I burned down his house with him watching from the fence. His only company is General Holmes.

"There he is," says Holmes, lurching to his feet at the sight of me and emanating grim disapproval. "Shall we?"

The three of us leave the office together, and at a turn in the corridors, Holmes's chief of staff approaches.

"General? I need to borrow you for a moment."

Holmes follows Lucian Orthos away, leaving Atreus and me alone.

"That I lived to see the day Leon's son escorted me to a People's Assembly," Atreus says.

"I'm sure Leon would have been surprised, as well."

After what has happened, it should feel strange to talk about my father. To exchange these kinds of words, calm and not quite friendly, almost like banter. But it doesn't. It feels as if what has happened between us until this moment is the past, and this is the future.

"In a way," Atreus says, as we leave the Inner Palace together, making our way through the snow-covered Palace Gardens, the Protector's Guard filing in behind us, "and you will forgive me this observation, Lee, as it looks like observations are what I have left—this is the greatest proof of all that my system worked."

"We're about to completely dismantle the metals system," I point out.

Atreus smiles. "*You* are about to completely dismantle it," he corrects. "What greater proof could there be that my Guardians are the best of them all, than that they want to reform the very system that gave them power?"

I feel it briefly ruffling me like a warm breeze, that old pleasure at his approval, and today, because it doesn't matter, I let myself feel its warmth.

We walk together down the main path of the gardens that ends in the gate through the Outer Wall to the arena, and part at the stairs that will take Atreus up to the Palace Box, and me down to the stone platform of the Eyrie. The snow has been shoveled, the flagstones cleared. Overhead, the karst of Pytho's Keep towers in a gray sky.

The stands are filling.

As I prepare to mount the Eyrie where the Guardians will already be gathering, Miranda Hane, Minister of Information, touches my arm.

"Lee? I'd like a word."

I follow her into the nearest viewing box, used by our drill-master in poor weather to watch from shelter. She closes the door behind her, but even so, the rumbling of the growing crowd vibrates under our feet.

"Lee—something's going on."

I realize only now that Hane looks disheveled, as if she spent the night awake.

"Someone," she says, "has been collecting information for the Triarchy-in-Exile. Newspapers, communications. They've been using the Island of the Dead as the drop-off point, handing it off to Pythian dragonriders at night."

On the far side of Pytho's Keep, the Island of the Dead would be the closest site a dragon could land without easy sighting from the city. I struggle to grasp the significance of what she's saying. "So that's how they knew the location to our granaries—?"

"Probably, but that's not even my biggest concern right now. Lee, I was lucky the report of the sighting ended up on my desk. The path to that island is gated. The only Callipolans with keys to it are ministry officials; the only reason a drop-off was witnessed at all, ironically, is because of a construction order Antigone sur Aela put in for a memorial to the dragon-born killed on Palace Day." Hane seems to realize mid-grimace what connection I might have to such a project, and rearranges her expression. "The point is, this is happening from the inside, and I don't know who's doing it. Which means the Order of the Black Clover must be much more pervasive than we thought."

"The Order of the—?"

Hane snaps fingers impatiently. "It's a triarchist group. They've been more and less active in the years since the Revolution. My department . . . discourages discussion of them. Even internally. You won't have heard them mentioned on your rounds."

That explains who Richard Tyndale was working with last term, when he was trying to get me to take my family's side. But Tyndale isn't a ministry official. This Island of the Dead drop-off is being done by someone else.

A cheer goes up outside, the crier's voice coming muffled through the glass. The crowd is growing impatient. "Is there a reason why we need to get to the bottom of this—now?"

Hane nods, twisting a coil of her hair as she squints out the dusty window. "I'm wondering if we shouldn't have the Assembly."

After weeks of being pushed this way and that by adults who want a little more, or a little less, than I'm willing to give, this sets my teeth on edge.

This assembly is what the Callipolan people want. This is what we've fought in the streets for, this is what's been denied them for years. A chance to have their voices heard regardless of who they were born, or where they live, or how they performed on a test.

I weigh the odds, listening to the rumbling through the window.

"Is there any reason *this* assembly is a specific cause for concern?"

"No, not exactly, but—"

"Then I'm not calling it off. We can look into the Order of the Black Clover afterward."

I've compromised enough. For this, I won't.

Miranda lets out a puff of breath. "All right," she says.

We enter the arena to an explosion of noise. The ramparts are a shimmering display of Revolutionary uniform, the Protector's Guard interspersed under the fluttering red and black banners of the Revolutionary dragon breathing four circlets of fire. Miranda Hane leaves me at the stairs to mount the Palace Box, where Atreus and the High Council are seated as they were during our tournaments last year. I make my way up the ramp to the jutting stone platform of the Eyrie.

Only after I have stepped onto the Eyrie do I see what's missing.

The other Guardians aren't here.

They should be; it's well past time for their arrival. Their presence was planned to be on foot rather than dragonback, in a symbolic gesture that today, we all stand on the ground.

But I'm the only Guardian present. The Eyrie is empty.

They must be running late—

All of them?

And then I notice something else. Atop the arena ramparts bordering the Inner Palace, guards are disappearing down the stairs as if summoned by an alarm below. Whatever noise they might be making has been drowned out by that of the people in the stands.

The crowd, cheering my entrance with screams of *The Revolution's Son*, don't notice anything amiss. Nor does Atreus, who goes to the rail of the Palace Box and raises his voice. "I present Lee sur Pallor, Guardian of Callipolis and Protector-designate by choice of the Gold Advisory Council, whose right it is by Revolutionary law to call a People's Assembly."

And then he takes a step back. I suck in a breath, and tear my gaze from the ramparts and the empty benches of the Eyrie where the Guardians should be.

This is a moment I will live without distraction.

I walk to the edge of the Eyrie, listen to the cheering of the crowd, and let it build in my blood.

Yes. This is how it begins.

I fill my lungs, as Pallor does when he prepares to fire, and lift my voice.

"Men and women of Callipolis, we come together today with a new hope for our nation. To enter a new era, a second revolution, where every Callipolan—regardless of birth or test result—has equal voice in what happens to our great island. Where every Callipolan is equally deserving."

The cheers begin. I let them grow till they fill the arena.

There is nothing in the world so high as the thrill of this. After a lifetime of imagining triumph in the arena, I finally understand that *this* was the triumph we needed.

Not in the air. On the ground. I lift an arm for silence.

"Today, the first task of our reinstated People's Assembly will be to deliberate on the role of the metals test and the metals system"—boos begin to swell from the class-irons and class-bronzes present; I raise an arm again—"but before we begin that referendum, I would like to bring you our good news. Soon, as soon as can be hoped, aid will come from across the sea from allies who share our new purpose—"

Footsteps sound beside me on the empty stone. A hand clasps my shoulder. I turn.

Ixion sur Niter stands beside me on the Eyrie.

Like me, he is wearing ceremonial livery, his emblazoned with the black clover of the Triarchy-in-Exile. I have not stood so close to him since before the Revolution. His face is longer, smooth-shaven, an echo of Julia's and also our fathers'; his smile is full of an ice I do not remember from our childhoods.

He speaks in a murmur. "Dragons surround your Guardian barracks and all entrances to the Palace Box. The gates to your dragons' nests have been shut. You cannot summon."

While I stand frozen, slowly understanding—my friends, surrounded by enemy dragons, cut off from their own—Atreus and his entire government cornered in the Palace Box—and Ixion beside me, beaming—he adds, "Duck sends his greetings."

"Duck—?"

Ixion puts an arm around my shoulder, like brothers reuniting. "Cooperate, and none of them need to come to harm."

Duck's alive?

Hand still on my shoulder, Ixion turns his radiant smile toward the murmuring Callipolan audience.

"Your request for aid has been answered, Cousin," he proclaims, in lightly accented Callish.

Above us, the shadow of Pytho's Keep—*moves.*

Wings unfurl from behind it like sails.

A dragon unfolds from the karst and launches into the sky, casting a great shadow overhead. A dragon that has been lying in wait, on the far side of the karst, for this moment. A dragon the size of a warship.

A goliathan.

"I have come with an offer of generosity from our long-lost ally, Bassilea," Ixion proclaims. "Even now, ships are bound from the Bassilean coast, courtesy of the beneficent Princess Freyda, heir-presumptive to the Bassilean Empire, laden with grain for the starving Callipolan people. We have Lee sur Pallor, the Revolution's Son, to thank for brokering this deal."

His arm rises, gesturing upward, toward the shadow of the great dragon circling overhead and, on it, the dwarfed figure of a woman shining in her armor. "Princess Freyda brings the first installment today."

Strapped to the side of the goliathan is a bag the size of a horse. The armored princess looses the satchel, and it plummets to *thunk* and burst open on the Eyrie beside Ixion and me.

Bread spills from it.

Ixion bends down, picks up a loaf, and lobs it.

The bread arcs slowly through the air and into the stands, into the hands of a citizen raised to catch it. Slowly, the murmuring of the crowd transforms. Rumbling, low, and then rising as it sweeps the citizenry.

Cheering.

And all the while, with my cousin's arm on my shoulder, the thoughts pulse in rotation: Guardians surrounded in the Cloister. The Palace Box cut off. The gate to the nests closed. *Duck.*

Freezing my limbs in place, though my heart is pounding.

Ixion lets the chanting continue until the sound of the people's cheering echoes within the stone walls. And then he raises his arm, silence falls, and he speaks again, his eyes blazing and his smile widening.

"The full extent of Freyda's aid will arrive on Callipolan shores within the day," Ixion says. "The Bassileans' only price is the execution of the Usurper, the arrest of those who stand with him, punishment for the injustices the new regime has committed in the name of revolution—and a reinstatement of Callipolis's rightful rulers."

Silence falls.

Ixion sur Niter looks upon the Assembly and smiles.

"Shall we put it to a vote?"

33

—

PRISONERS AND THEIR GUARD

GRIFF

The citadel dungeon smells like piss and decay. My cell has no window, and the only light comes from the barred window in the door, looking out to the empty corridor. When food is brought to me, I'm surprised to see it's brought by a young woman, not one of the guards. Her hair is long, lank, unkempt, mostly shielding her face. But when for a fleeting moment the light reveals her profile, I recognize it.

"Mabalena?"

She pauses, her hand on the bowl of porridge, then pushes it the rest of the way through.

I haven't seen her since the day, years ago, when they dropped her family, and then her.

But before that, we were friends.

"Mabalena, please—tell me, have you heard anything—"

For a moment, she just looks at me. And then she sets a second bowl beside mine.

On the other side of my cell, a shadow I hadn't even noticed moves. The figure rises, takes the bread and water from her, and speaks in heavily accented Dragontongue. "Thank you, Lena."

My vision adjusting in the darkness, I squint at my cellmate. A badly burn-scarred face beneath a growth of wavy hair looks back at me.

And then I place that voice.

"Duck?"

The boy smiles like I've just issued a dare.

"Griff Gareson," he answers.

TO BE CONTINUED.

AUTHOR'S NOTE

The classics I nodded to in *Fireborne* were Plato's *Republic* and the *Aeneid*. For *Flamefall*, I will mention two more. Quotes attributed to the *Aurelian Cycle* in this book were adapted from lines of the last two books of Homer's *Iliad*, where Achilles and Patroclus have a final conversation and Hector's body is returned to his people. Those attributed to *Flamefall at Aureos* were adapted from Sophocles's eponymous tragedy about Antigone, who defies orders to bury the dead.

ACKNOWLEDGMENTS

My husband was my company for the writing of *Flamefall* through multiple reads, every high and low, and innumerable conversations about bunkers—many of which he couldn't escape, because we were in quarantine. Thank you for being the sane one during this insane year. Forsan et haec olim meminisse iuvabit.

My editor, Arianne Lewin, gave me the time and many turnarounds I needed, clarity in the final hour, and still more time. My agent, Danielle Burby, read more drafts than any agent should with persistent enthusiasm and insight. The teams at Putnam Books for Young Readers and Penguin Teen ushered this book the rest of the way into the world: Jennifer Klonsky, Alex Garber, Felicity Vallence, Laurel Robinson, Cindy Howle, the visionary Kristie Radwilowicz, and the indefatigable Elise LeMassena; Tessa Meischeid, with tireless enthusiasm and Crissa-themed powerpoints; and Anne Heausler, who caught both my timeline mistakes and my nerdy references. I'm grateful, too, to Kristin Nelson and the Nelson Literary Agency; Valparaiso Studios, particularly Jack Parker, who's as astute a reader as he is enthusiastic a fan;

"The Plug," Jeff Bishop; Alice Lawson at the Gersh Agency; Wayne Alexander at Alexander, Lawrence, Frumes & Labowitz, LLP; Jenny Meyer and Heidi Gall at the Jenny Meyer Literary Agency; and abroad, the publishing teams at Eksmo, Maxim Konyvkiado, Epsilon Yayinevi, and Arctis, with special thanks to Nadine Püschel for her incisive translation questions.

Flamefall took the village. Kristen Ciccarelli and Bridget Tyler inspected the foundations and straightened the walls; Joanna Hathaway, Erin McDonough, Eloise Andry, and Kaitlin Gladney helped patch the roof and put in windows; Katrina Hall, Phil Dershwitz, Paul Baker, Malayna Evans, Marcy Flanagan, Marie Nesfield, Grace Stone, and Lizzie Cooke advised the most important finishing touches. Michael Johnson, Reese Eschmann, Franny Billingsley, and the greater Chicago writing community offered every other kind of moral and creative support. The Facebook "hive mind," a collection of geniuses I'm lucky to count as friends, were my unofficial research advisors. I'm particularly indebted to the (multiple) kind souls who recommended *Coup d'État: A Practical Handbook* by Edward Luttwak.

My final thanks go to the readers who showed me—through your kind notes, posts, and comments, through class visits and book club invitations, through art and even poems—that this house we built was one you looked forward to visiting. You gave me reasons to smile and keep going. See you for the final act.